BLOCKADE RUNNER

JAMIE McFARLANE

Cover Artwork: Elias T. Stern

ACKNOWLEDGMENTS

To Diane Greenwood Muir for excellence in editing and fine word-smithery. My wife, Janet, for carefully and kindly pointing out my poor grammatical habits. I cannot imagine working through these projects without you both.

To my beta readers: Carol Greenwood, Matt Strbjak, Kelli Whyte, and Robert Long for wonderful and thoughtful suggestions. It is a joy to work with this intelligent and considerate group of people.

CONTENTS

PROLOGUE

A few prolific readers have kindly pointed out that - sometimes - between installments of Privateer Tales, they might forget the names of our heroes and their general physical characteristics. What follows isn't a full list, but it's certainly the starting crew of *Intrepid*. By no means should you take this as a guarantee of their safety. I'm quite willing to say, however, as of the first chapter, each of the following are just as we left them in *Give No Quarter*. I've also included a few additional definitions to help jog your memory.

I always enjoy interacting with my readers and sharing a little inside information about myself and the characters I create. When a new story is available or I'm otherwise inspired, I send out an email newsletter. If you are interested in joining my newsletter distribution, please visit fickledragon.com/keep-in-touch/ to sign up.

On with the list of characters.

Liam Hoffen – our hero. With straight black hair and blue eyes, Liam is a lanky one hundred seventy-five centimeters tall (which is a typical tall, thin spacer build). His parents are Silver and Pete Hoffen, who get their own short story in *Big Pete*. Our stories are mostly told from Liam's perspective and he, therefore, needs the least introduction.

Nick James – the quick-talking, always-thinking best friend who is usually five moves ahead of everyone and is the long-term planner of the team. At one hundred fifty-seven centimeters, Nick is the shortest human member of the crew. He, Tabby and Liam have been friends since they met in daycare on Colony-40 in Sol's main asteroid belt. The only time Nick has trouble forming complete sentences is around Marny Bertrand, who by his definition is the perfect woman. Nick's only remaining family is a brother, Jack, who now lives on Lèger Nuage. They lost their mother during a Red Houzi pirate attack that destroyed their home in the now infamous Battle for Colony-40.

Tabitha Masters – fierce warrior and loyal fiancé of our hero, Liam. Tabby lost most of her limbs when the battle cruiser on which she was training was attacked by the dreadnaught *Bakunawa*. She lives for the high adrenaline moments of life and engages those at one hundred percent. Tabby is a lithe, one-hundred sixty-eight-centimeter-tall bundle of impatience.

Marny Bertrand – former Marine from Earth who served in the Great Amazonian War and now serves as guardian of the crew. Liam and Nick recruited Marny from her civilian post on the Ceres orbital station in *Rookie Privateer*. Marny is one-hundred eighty centimeters tall, heavily muscled and the self-appointed fitness coordinator – slash torturer - on the ship. Her strategic vigilance has safeguarded the crew through some rather unconventional escapades. She's also extraordinarily fond of Nick.

Ada Chen – ever-optimistic adventurer and expert pilot. Ada was first introduced in *Parley* when Liam and crew rescued her from a lifeboat. Her mother, Adela, had ejected the pod from her tug, *Baux-201*, after it was attacked by pirates. She's a one-hundred sixty-three-centimeter-tall, ebony-skinned beauty and a certified bachelorette. Ada's first love is her crew and her second love is sailing into the deep dark.

Jonathan – a collective of fourteen-hundred, thirty-eight sentient beings. They - communicating as Jonathan - were initially introduced in *A Matter of Honor* when the crew bumped into Thomas Phillipe Anino. Jonathan is intensely curious about the human condition, specifically how this unlikely race has the capacity to combine skill, chance, and morality to achieve a greater result.

Jester Ripples – the newest member of *Intrepid's* crew. Very little is known about the Norigans, a semi-humanoid race. Jester Ripples' skin appears to be the consistency of a frog, but is composed of extremely fine hairs. Norigans are tri-fingered humanoids with a mouth that resembles a frog's and big black eyes mounted atop their skulls. Jester Ripples has brilliant red streaks embedded in yellow bands that start at his nostrils and flare out around his eye sockets.

Thomas Phillipe Anino – enigmatic inventor of Aninonium, the fuel that allows ships to enter fold-space. He helped Belirand send exploration vessels into other galaxies, which the company later abandoned. Looking to right that wrong, Anino sought out the crew of *Intrepid* to track down and rescue the abandoned colonies. He also has the capacity to transfer his consciousness from one body to the next; a secret he guards jealously. His last appearance was as a teen-aged youth.

Quantum Communication Crystals – Crystals that work outside of understood physics. The most important property of these crystals is that two halves of the same crystal will vibrate synchronously, even over galactic distances. Their most common use is in extraordinarily expensive communication devices.

Belirand – Earth-based corporation that implemented Anino's TransLoc gate systems between inhabitable human-settled solar systems. Belirand is also responsible for launching and abandoning a hundred missions to the far reaches of the universe utilizing Anino's technology. When you hear the saying about how absolute power corrupts absolutely, Belirand Corporation should come to mind.

Sol – the solar system where Earth and Mars reside. There are a few references to Sol governments, which I'll list here. Mars Protectorate is the sole government of the planet Mars and its moons. North America is the combined land of Canada, United States and Mexico and is a single government simply known as North America. The Peoples Democracy of China is essentially the same China we see today although with their own form of well-ordered democracy. I also commonly reference a group of nations NaGEK, which are the North Americans, Europeans and Koreans. Finally, there are many other un-mentioned earth governments.

GHOST FLEET

A body floated past *Intrepid's* bow, bumping silently along the pitched surface of the armored glass window until it finally ricocheted into space at an oblique angle.

"What in Jupiter's name?" I asked as external cameras displayed two more bodies being plowed from *Intrepid's* path.

"I'm picking up multiple near-space objects," Ada Chen, our pilot, announced with no more emphasis than if she were asking for an update on O-2 reserves. *Adjust delta-z to zero with debris field on my mark. Three, two, one, engage,* she instructed the ship's AI.

Unnecessarily, I gripped the arms of the captain's chair and braced for the wall of force that would hold us in place as inertial dampers attempted to overcome the force of *Intrepid's* four powerful aft-mounted engines.

Display debris field on primary holo. My face deformed momentarily as gravity and inertial systems adjusted. The ever-listening AI communicated my command to the ship and started enhancing video inputs from the sensor strips that ran the length of the hull.

"Belay that," Marny Bertrand ordered. "Lock on ship bearing twenty degrees to starboard, fifteen degrees declination at six hundred kilometers."

Intrepid had just dropped into a system we would later learn was named Mhina. We were ten thousand kilometers out from the origin of a long-lost quantum communication crystal signal. The crystal had been transmitting white noise for over a hundred and fifty stan-years, something our crew had agreed to investigate at the request of Thomas Phillippe Anino.

"All hands, prepare for combat maneuvers," Ada announced. As pilot, her announcement would shut down non-essential systems and ready our weapons. She was also warning the crew that she would do whatever was necessary to keep *Intrepid* intact, mainly keeping O2 on the inside and vacuum on the out.

We'd learned the hard way that in the vastness of space, evil lurked. What couldn't catch you was less likely to decide your fate.

"Hold on, Ada," I said.

"I don't like it, Liam." Ada had never taken to calling me Captain, which suited me just fine. I still remembered watching pirates murder her mother, Adela, when we were within a few frustrating minutes of being able to help. I'd promised Adela we'd look after her daughter, but the reverse was more often the case.

"Jonathan, are you picking up any power readings?"

"Negative, Captain," Jonathan announced. "Our mid-range sensors register forty-two derelict ships. Sending to secondary holo."

I nodded as Jonathan's data unpacked onto the holographic display to the left of the captain's chair. The closest ship, the one that had prompted Marny's concern, was eerily oriented, as if directly focused on *Intrepid*. Mesmerized, I watched as our sensor data started to tell the tale of an epic space battle, long since resolved.

"There are bodies everywhere," Tabby mused. Her workstation was on the starboard side of the bridge, giving her quick access to the hatch and the bumblebee fighters strapped beneath the ship.

I purposely ignored the smaller, humanoid blips as they resolved on the display. It was possible that a clever and well prepared individual could cause trouble for our one-hundred-twenty-meter frigate. That threat, however, was eclipsed by the damage potential of the six ships within a few thousand kilometers of our position, a group that included two battle-cruisers. They outweighed and, if active, outgunned us considerably. In all, Ada had good reason to be concerned.

"Nick, what do you make of this?" I asked.

"The Belirand mission's comm crystal is emanating from this ship." Nick illuminated the largest vessel, roughly in the center of the field of battle. The ship's design was similar to those of both North American and Mars Protectorate - a heavily armored, rounded rectangle with massive engines on one end and pointy looking weapons on the other.

"Jonathan, do you recognize the make of these ships?"

"Not directly," he replied. "Analysis of the corpses and ship designs indicate a single civilization. Captain, we've determined the events of this battle occurred one-hundred forty-two stan-years in the past."

"That's eighteen years after Belirand abandoned this mission," Nick added.

"They've just been sitting here like this for a century and a half?" Tabby asked, disbelief evident in her tone. "Who would leave their dead behind like this and why are they outside the ships?"

I had no answer for her. "Take us in slowly, Ada."

"This will be ugly." Ada adjusted course and accelerated toward the center of the long-ago decided battle and the location of the comm crystal. "There's no avoiding the bodies."

We watched in silence as Ada negotiated around the largest groups congregated near the derelict ships, only occasionally making contact. Even at relative speeds in the low thousands of meters per second, the impact was devastating to the frozen remains, causing them to break apart upon contact, often shattering into an icy mist.

"Marny, what's your analysis on what took this ship down?" I asked.

"Readings show kinetic strikes consistent with Kroerak technology," she replied. "The armor shows penetrations consistent with their lances. That mid-grade steel is a poor match for Kroerak technology."

The lance weapon Marny referred to was a devastatingly simple technology which the hostile alien species used to great advantage. The lances varied in size based on the type of ship that carried them, but the delivery mechanism was always the same - throw sharp, pointy sticks at the highest possible velocity and in great numbers. We referred to the attack simply as a wave, as the lances were often ejected in wide, difficult to dodge fusillades.

"Liam, we awoke something on the ship," Ada announced. "We're receiving a communication. It's definitely not Standard Galactic."

"Wrong galaxy," Tabby quipped as Ada put the comm on the bridge speakers.

"Weapon systems remain off-line." Marny answered the question I was about to ask.

Communication from the alien ship was clearly speech, but nothing I'd ever heard before. The syllables came quickly with exaggerated lisps, hissing, and what could best be described as yowling. Some of the phonemes, however, sounded human.

"Remarkable," Jonathan observed.

"Why is that remarkable?" I asked.

"As you know, the range of wave forms is infinite. Yet this species, just like most other species we've had incidental contact with, communicate in the narrow band between eighty-five and three hundred hertz," he said. "Couple that with similar linguistic structures and it is commonality where there should be none."

"Can you understand what's being said?" I asked.

"He's saying it's weird we can hear it at all," Tabby explained, to which I rolled my eyes. I'd already figured that out, but knew she was needling me all the same.

"While a direct translation isn't possible, we believe the message is a warning, demanding we keep our distance," he replied.

"What's our best way in, Marny?" I asked. While I found Jonathan's observations interesting, I doubted we'd run into any of the ship's original inhabitants and have direct need for translation.

"Cap, the main airlock is well armored and there's no reason to believe the ship holds atmo," Marny said. "Our best entry point is a breach just forward of the main engines. Something bigger than a Kroerak lance punched a hole in her there. It looks to be the disabling blow, probably took out her systems all at once."

"We'll mount a boarding party with Marny, Tabby, and me," I said. "Once we've secured the bridge, we'll bring Jester Ripples over to see about interfacing with their systems. I'd like to get Jonathan and his horde online. Our primary objective is to find that comm crystal and figure out what it's doing on an alien ship. Since there's a threat of Kroerak - and we know they can hibernate - we're going to make this quick."

Ada looked around the bridge. "Speaking of, where is Jester Ripples?"

"In our quarters," Tabby answered. "He's still having trouble with transition."

The small alien had bonded with Tabby and me. While we drew the line at letting him sleep with us, he was sneaky about joining us for naps, especially when our bridge shifts were split. His retreat to our cabin during transition made sense, especially considering how it affected his gastro-intestinal system. And just so we're clear, Norigans might be cute, but they're the last beings you want to share a room with when their system is upset.

"We'll load heavy." Marny stepped from her position at the gunnery station, ceding it to Nick.

With Belirand no longer on our tail, we'd scaled back our crew. I preferred traveling light to the hassles that came with managing a large group. With Jester Ripples' help, we'd upgraded the auto tracking software on the turrets. While computer targeting wasn't as flexible as a team of professional gunners, one person could mount an effective defense.

"I'll meet you in the armory," I said to Tabby and Marny as we made our way aft. "I'm going to check on Jester Ripples."

"Aye, Cap. We'll get your loadout ready," Marny replied.

I palmed open the door to my quarters and Filbert, the cat we'd recently recovered from Lèger Nuage, squirted out into the passage. I looked across at the pathetic blue-green alien lying on the bed. Large black eyes blinked slowly, acknowledging my presence, just as the sound of air escaping the internal confines of the small alien's digestive tract greeted me. I smiled wryly as I lifted my friend from the sheets, trying to ignore the bitter smell.

My eyes watered involuntarily. Whatever the fumes were, they would give butyric acid a run for its money.

"Feeling any better?" I asked.

"Considerably, Liam Hoffen." Jester Ripples wrapped an arm around my shoulder and grasped my vac suit with his warm, tri-digit hand, locking spindly legs around my waist.

I rubbed the fine yellow fur that looked deceptively like amphibian skin, encircling his large eye sockets. The gesture was something Jester had taught me was comforting to Norigans and he trilled his tongue in appreciation.

"You might want to head up to the bridge and see what's going on," I said. "Tabby, Marny, and I are going to visit an abandoned ship. Once it's clear, we'd like you to help Jonathan interface with the electronics."

"Jester Ripples should come with you," he replied. He didn't always refer to himself in the third person, saving it for moments when he was overly excited.

"I'll come back, Jester Ripples," I said. "This is important and it might not be safe."

"If it's not safe for Jester Ripples, then Liam Hoffen and Tabitha Masters should not be going."

I smiled at a conversation we'd had numerous times. Norigans were fiercely loyal and brave to a fault. The problem was, they were about as useless as sand in an air filter when it came to a fight.

"Check in with Nicholas and we'll be back as quickly as possible," I said.

Jester Ripples blinked in what I'd learned to recognize as mild annoyance, but climbed down. "I will place Liam Hoffen's bed sheets in the cleaner first."

***

'Going heavy' was Marny's term for bringing along the modified Colt 42816s we'd manufactured on planet Curie in the Tipperary system. Our version of the utility weapon included a back mounted, just-in-time ammunition manufacturing system. We'd stolen the idea from the mechanized Marine's exoskeletons used during our takeover of the Red Houzi dreadnaught, *Bakunawa*. The basic idea was the AI could create a perfect mix of projectile and explosive rounds on demand. When dealing with Kroerak, we loaded armor piercing, explosive ordnance as our default and ratcheted up from there. The biggest disadvantage to the system was the backpacks added between thirty and forty kilograms, restricting our movement.

"Do we have any of those grenade strips left?" I asked as Marny helped me into my 816's pack.

Tabby slapped an adhesive, ten-centimeter strip of grenade marbles across my abdomen. "Just don't be going all Divelbiss on me."

I smiled at the reference to a brave crewman who lost his hand when he stuffed it and a grenade into a Kroerak's beak.

"Marny, you have tactical," I said.

Tactical channel one, acknowledge Marny Bertrand team leader. My comment had been overheard by our AIs and a special comm channel had been established. As team leader, Marny would be given control over some of our suit's functions. She could also update our maps with primary and secondary kill targets.

"Acknowledged," I responded. I wasn't even remotely surprised to see that I'd been given the responsibility of third position. In a four-man team, I was better suited to the number two spot, but with our three-person team, taking up the rear was where I added most value. I'd spend most of my time walking backward and making sure nothing crept up on us.

Tabby mic'd in a second later and appeared on my HUD's tactical display as point. Finally, Marny showed up right in the middle, where she belonged. The choices for Marny and Tabby were straightforward; Tabby was by far the quickest thinking and most devastating fighter in the group. In the Battle for Colony-40, she'd lost both legs, an arm, and much of her spine and rib cage. When she'd been found, no one expected her to survive and even then, it would be as a multiple amputee. Through considerable luck and perseverance, we were able to get her high-tech replacements for her missing limbs. Thus, she was faster and stronger than either Marny or me by a significant margin.

"Jonathan, go ahead and deploy the remote," Marny said. "We're Oscar Mike."

"Remote surveillance launch in three seconds," Jonathan responded. From *Intrepid's* position next to the larger alien ship, none of our sensors had a good view into the breach forward of the main engines. The drone would give us a good look into the hole before we arrived.

"Liam, I want you to jump first and take position on the hull at this mark," Marny directed. She'd identified a location where I'd have a direct view into the breach. "Tabby, once Liam is in position, I want you at the mouth. I'll be two seconds behind. Make sure you stay beneath Liam's line of fire at two and a half meters. Stay low." As she spoke, a virtual cone from the position she'd assigned me indicated the space she wanted me to cover.

I nudged my chin forward and acknowledged her assignment. A green indicator lit up next to my name in the HUD's tactical display at the same time one lit next to Tabby. We weren't always this quiet, but preferred to keep the comms free of chatter in hostile territory.

"Drone is reporting the breach is clear," Marny announced as we entered *Intrepid's* cargo hold. We'd chosen *Intrepid's* hold as our launching point because it sported a pressure barrier when the main door was open. Looking through the translucent energy barrier, I took in both the enormity of the battle-cruiser class ship as well as the wholesale damage it had received along its flank. It didn't take much imagination to replay the ship's last moments as waves of Kroerak lances pierced its side. My eyes searched and found lances that hadn't completely passed through, most likely contacting the ship's internal skeleton where the ends shattered upon contact.

"Cap," Marny suddenly appeared in front of me, breaking my gaze. "I need you in the here and now. You got this?"

"Copy that, Marny. These guys never knew what hit them," I

said. "They were obliterated. Their armor shredded like it wasn't even there."

"Aye, Cap," Marny said. "Technology in war can be a terrible thing." She slapped the side of my helmet. "Now take your position, Soldier, or I'll make this an all-girl event."

"I'm in, Marny."

SENTINEL

I launched myself from *Intrepid's* hold almost perfectly in line with the AI's recommended path. Without adjustment, I'd land on the alien battle cruiser three meters from my mark. I slowly adjusted, preferring to make several minor modifications instead of one big change. The suits we'd obtained from Thomas Phillipe Anino utilized gravity waves instead of arc-jets. Here in the Mhina system, we were less than one and a half million kilometers from one of two gas giants, so there was plenty of whatever Anino's suits needed.

The ship had several hatches and my AI provided a few interesting statistics. The most important one being that the height and width of the doors were compatible with human forms. Whatever the species was, they were obviously no strangers to war. The ship fairly bristled with turrets, most of which had been damaged by their encounter with the Kroerak.

Upon arrival, I used my hands to slow my relative velocity and allowed my legs to absorb the residual energy. My first order of business was to lock down Tabby's landing zone. I pulled the stock of my 816 to my shoulder and used the rifle's auxiliary magnification to scan for trouble.

"Infiltration zone is clear," I announced, not finding anything beyond the expected jagged metal plating and torn decking. One can learn a lot about a species by looking at their ships and it was evident this one was behind humanity's technology curve, although not substantially. Numerous bundles of severed cables resembled a rat's nest and belied the presence of an integrated communications system.

"Copy that," Marny replied. "On your mark, Tabby."

"Go," Tabby replied.

I wanted to watch the two of them cross the three hundred meters that separated the ships, but I knew better. At a minimum, Marny would review my camera's view and reprimand my inattentiveness. The real reason, however, was that their lives might depend on my vigilance.

Instead, I continued to scan the breach, not allowing myself to become myopic, but broadening my sweep to different sections of the dead ship. It wouldn't do any good to miss an approaching threat because I was only staring into the hole in front of me. I caught Tabby's movement as she sailed into the breach. My AI showed her approach to be twenty-three meters per second and I winced as her legs absorbed the impact of a hard landing. Anyone else would have broken bones, but Tabby's legs were a titanium lattice and her muscles had been manufactured by the best scientists humanity had to offer. She didn't even grunt as she spun onto one knee and swept the deck I only had a partial view of. A moment later, and with considerably less velocity, Marny landed, struggling to gain equilibrium on the ship's uneven hull.

Just as Marny made contact, I pushed off and grabbed her heavily muscled arm, steadying her. Having grown up in the full gravity of Earth, Marny hadn't developed the same zero-gravity skills Tabby and I took for granted. Perhaps the hardest concept for her to overcome was that 'down' had no real meaning. For someone born and raised planet-side, the notions of up and down simply were too ingrained.

"Got it, Cap," Marny quipped. "Thanks." She was always embarrassed by what she saw as weakness and spent hours trying to train out her Earth-borne instincts.

"Passage is clear," Tabby announced. "Ten meters, hatch on portside. Passage is blocked at twelve meters. Looks like a standard descending atmo-containment bulkhead. Bulkhead did not fully deploy; looks like it was stopped by debris."

"Secure portside hatch," Marny answered.

Atmo-containment bulkheads were standard tools on ships and space stations. If a hull breach was detected, these bulkheads would drop and seal off the section exposed to space.

14

Unfortunately, for the inhabitants of this ship, something had prevented the bulkhead from sealing.

After a few meters of walking backward, hovering so I wouldn't stumble, my feet found solid purchase on the ship's deck. Technically, the motion was more sideways, sweeping back and forth, but I spent most of my time surveying the space behind us. The deck beneath our feet was coated in a soft, pliable material. It wasn't carpeting, but also not the grit-painted steel common on most human ships.

"In position," Tabby breathed.

My tactical orders were modified, requiring me to sweep and cover the other side of the open hatch. Since I expected the order, I smoothly transitioned from covering our backs to slipping past Tabby and Marny and sweeping across the open hatch. As I did, Marny and Tabby flowed into the room, first covering their zones, then sweeping the remainder of the room.

The room could have been cargo space on any Earth or Mars ship. It was unremarkable and mostly empty, save for a few crates. I was intensely curious as to their contents, but such was not our mission. We needed to make sure the area was safe first and keep moving.

I tabbed my chin into the soft padding of my helmet to indicate a clear status, noticing that Tabby and Marny had already updated their statuses.

"Secure the main passageway," Marny ordered, pulling a narrow jack from her pack and exiting the storage room.

Tabby and I followed. I resumed my backward orientation, slapping a surveillance puck onto the bulkhead next to me. The pucks were about the size of my thumb pad and a millimeter thick. Their entire job was to warn us of movement or sound.

Glancing back, I watched Marny place the thin jack beneath the failed bulkhead. The device was a simple but powerful machine that could exert enough newtons of force to split open two centimeters of steel plate. It would either lift the bulkhead or create enough of a dent in it that we'd be able to crawl beneath.

I joined Tabby, turning to face the unexplored hallway ahead as the jack lifted the bulkhead a meter and a half from the deck. The passageway was complete chaos compared to what we'd seen so far. Piles of long-undisturbed debris were everywhere and it made me shudder to realize corpses must be mixed in with the mess.

"Stabilize this hatch," Marny ordered. My HUD highlighted the object of her command.

The order was for me. I was the only one who carried a welding/cutting torch as part of my standard ship boarding kit.

I stepped up behind Tabby and pulled a strip of metal filler from my thigh pouch. One-handed, I slapped the strip beneath the door and against the wall. With my other hand, I brought out the small torch and melted the metal into the frame, bonding the sliding bulkhead to the wall. My AI reported a strong weld now joined the two permanently, making it impossible for the hatch to slide back down once the jack was removed.

"Fall in and move out," Marny snapped.

Tabby stepped forward, picking her way carefully through the debris. I scanned the passageway behind us one last time, ducked under the bulkhead, and followed Marny's retreating form.

"Hold," Tabby warned, pinging an open hatch where a body lay across the threshold. I knew better than to expect that Marny would let me get a good look at the ship's occupants until she was convinced of our general safety. "It's a Kroerak kill," Tabby said, focusing on the center of the humanoid form.

It was a scene we'd seen too many times. In this case, the body was anything but fresh, but hadn't been fed on, which was surprising.

I slapped another puck onto the wall and we pushed forward, stopping at a shaft that was open above and below. Tabby stuck her head in for a better view and reported a series of ledges on opposite sides of the shaft. Each set of ledges was spaced at around three meters.

"They must have gravity control in this shaft," Tabby said, adding to the list of technologies attributable to the species.

"Tight fit for Kroerak," Marny said. "I have an update from

Jonathan. The bridge should be seven decks up and another hundred meters forward. Up you go, Tabby."

"Cap, drop an A-P three meters down. We don't need uninvited guests following," Marny ordered.

I jumped into the shaft, dropped a few meters and slapped an anti-personnel mine against the wall. Our crew would be safe, but the mine would warn of intruders coming from below decks.

The three of us popped out of the shaft seven decks up into another passageway and to a now familiar scene of destruction. Long deceased inhabitants and debris were scattered everywhere.

"Cap," Marny stopped us. "Jonathan just informed me that their analysis shows evidence of Kroerak activity within the last several years. It's likely they left sleepers."

"Copy that. We're only a few meters from our target. Do you want to abort?"

Marny gave a quick shake of her head. "Negative, Cap. Not my call."

"We don't know what wakes sleepers up." Tabby spoke in almost a whisper, as if she were afraid of being the alarm that woke them. "Whatever we hope to learn better be worth it."

"Tens of thousands of aliens died to the Kroerak here and Belirand had some part in it," I replied. "If we ever hope to stop the bugs, we have to start learning what they're up to." I probably said my piece more passionately than was required, but Tabby and I'd had this conversation already.

"Move out, Tabby," Marny ordered, cutting short the conversation. The only reason Marny had asked the question was because the mission parameters had changed. Now that she knew what my decision was, she resumed tactical command.

"Copy," Tabby replied. It sounded like there was a little sulkiness in her voice, but I couldn't deal with now.

We continued down the passageway, clearing hatches and moving on.

"You guys seeing this?" I asked, highlighting the back-end of one of the corpses. A bright yellow blaze of color shown from a split in the corpse's suit.

"Cap," Marny warned.

I frowned, but took the reprimand and continued to cover our retreat, placing surveillance pucks every ten meters or so.

"Jonathan believes this to be the bridge," Marny announced, bringing us to a stop. The passageway had widened to double in size and a large bulkhead was closed in front of us. The passage split and continued around either side. All in all, it was reminiscent of the dreadnaught *Bakunawa*, with its heavily armored, centrally located bridge. "We need to secure the vicinity. I want mines on the forward, starboard and port passageways. Move out, Tabby."

We continued around the circular room and discovered hatches on the starboard and aft sides – or simply put, a four-way intersection with the rounded bridge at the center. Due to the width of the hallways, we dropped two mines into each passageway, except to the aft, which we identified as our preferred escape route.

"Look at that," Tabby exclaimed as we came around the final bend. A Kroerak lance had penetrated the ship's skin, avoiding all structure until embedding itself into the port-side exterior bulkhead of the bridge.

"Let's crack this hatch," Marny said, ignoring Tabby. She approached the aft door and swung her 816 to the side, taking up a defensive stance.

I inspected the door, attempting to discern its opening mechanism. Four scratches, ten centimeters long and two centimeters apart ran across a central raised panel. Upon further inspection, I realized it was a small hatch that slid to the side, revealing an inclined pad. The surface looked very much like a hand scanner, yet there were indentations for only three digits. I placed my hand on the pad anyway, but wasn't rewarded with any sign of acknowledgement.

Pulling out my welding torch, I switched it to cutting mode. "I'm going to burn it."

"Copy that," Marny agreed.

The amount of energy required to cut steel is considerable and

I monitored my secondary power system as I pulled a line of fire down the door. The metal slagged as I cut, but without gravity, it stayed put, requiring me to dredge it out with a hooked instrument. Fortunately, this was Mining-101. I'd spent my entire youth dealing with material that regularly bent or broke heavy machinery and I was a master with a cutting torch. I worked quickly and was soon rewarded with a clean line, deep enough to hook Marny's jack into.

For a few moments, the powerful jack spooled tension in its simple mechanism. All at once, the bulkhead shuddered, sending shockwaves along the deck and up through my armored boots. "Stand back," I said, stepping to the side, not sure what was about to happen.

Three thumb-sized security bolts tore out of the upper jamb, ripping through centimeter-thick steel. A whoosh of atmo blew into the hallway, momentarily fogging my faceplate as the door was once again still.

"That was exciting," I said as I released the tension on the jack and repositioned it. I'd only opened the exterior skin of the hatch by four centimeters and it would take more work to open it wide enough for entry.

I removed the jack and continued cutting away resistant portions of the structure. I then cut a new slot into the door and remounted the jack, repeating my previous attack. It took almost twenty minutes of cutting and prying, but the multi-layered door finally opened to about twenty centimeters. I pulled out a spray of what we simply referred to as fire-damp. One of the problems of working in vacuum was that it took forever for steel to dissipate heat. The problem was easily overcome with a readily available foam that would cover the hot spots and slowly leach the heat away, disintegrating when cooled to a hundred degrees.

Marny dropped a puck into the aft hallway and then nodded to Tabby who slid into the breach. Marny, thicker than both of us, had a more difficult time. As soon as she made it through, I followed and surveyed the alien bridge. While I couldn't imagine how any living being could survive for the hundred and fifty years this ship had been sitting here, I wasn't willing to chance it. We'd experienced enough surprises during our adventures that I was all for being careful.

"We're clear," Marny finally announced.

Unlike the rest of the ship, the bridge was free of chaos and debris. In the center was a single, elevated chair, atop which sat the desiccated form of a long dead alien. Dingy orange-red fur covered the narrow face of the sole officer who'd stayed behind. The material of its uniform was shredded, hanging in tatters. It was difficult to distinguish if the tatters were battle wounds or simply the result of time and decay. In the palm of the alien's hand, I found a single item - a decorative pin, a design I'd seen many times before. What a Belirand mission pin was doing in the alien's hand, I had no idea.

Pushing the pin into my pocket, I turned to catch the glitter of metal beside the officer's chair. Once highly polished, now tarnished, was the unmistakable hilt of a sword. The weapon was still in its scabbard, the end of which rested on the floor. A single narrow strip of aged leather kept the brittle sheath attached to a hook on the side of the chair. I surveyed the other chairs in the room and found they, too, bore similar hooks. I picked up the sword and laid it across the alien's lap. We wouldn't have time to recover the tens of thousands of bodies we'd seen, but I needed to make a gesture of respect, however small.

"Here," Tabby called from a workstation on the port side.

I turned. "What do you have?"

She pointed. "I found the crystal."

In and of itself, the crystal had little value. It was just a marker of a failed Belirand mission. In that we had the matching half now, it could be re-deployed. But more importantly, locating the crystal allowed us to place context around what Belirand's abandonment had done to this mission. There had been talk of excusing the Belirand Corporation from all liability related to their previous heinous acts in exchange for help with the Kroerak. The discovery of the alien race that clearly wished to harm humanity had people considering all sorts of idiotic ideas. Belirand finally decided to cooperate with Mars Protectorate, NaGEK and the Chinese by sharing intel they'd gathered over the last centuries. Apparently, fighting this new threat was more important than punishing what was being described as an overly eager and misguided corporation. The fact was, we were probably the only ones who cared about uncovering these abandoned missions and rescuing any who managed to survive. It also seemed like the only way to keep Belirand's feet to the fire for their immoral actions.

"What is this mission crystal doing on an alien ship in a system with two smaller moons that could possibly sustain life?" Tabby asked as I joined her at the workstation. "And what is this crap all over the crystal?" The crap she referred to was bubbling ooze that appeared to be dying in the vacuum to which it was now exposed.

"Jonathan, are you getting this?" I asked, directing the drone he controlled to inspect the goo that surrounded the crystal.

"We are," Jonathan replied. "The substance around the crystal appears to be a biological power source. We have also discovered that the ship is equipped with a regenerative power system. You should be able to restore power to the bridge."

"Is that wise?" I asked.

"A philosophical question that Schrodinger would appreciate," Jonathan replied. "The answer will not be known until after you've performed the action."

"What's the over-under?"

Jonathan and I talked at length about how his collective of sentients used what was, in effect, gambling to determine the odds of an event. Each sentient brought their own field of interest into the fray, often arguing for microseconds while the numbers shifted dramatically.

"Seventy-two percent believe powering the bridge will have negative consequences," he replied.

"Saturn's rings! Based on what?" I asked.

"History," Jonathan replied.

"What do I have to do?" I asked, resigned to my fate.

"Big gray lever on the workstation next to the crystal," Jonathan replied. "Push it forward."

"Then what?" I asked.

"Once power is restored, Jester Ripples will break through their systems so Jonathan may download the data," Jester Ripple's excited voice informed me.

"Just flip the switch?"

"That is correct, Captain," Jonathan replied.

"Marny? Tabby?" I asked.

"Frak it," Tabby said and pushed the rocker switch forward. For a moment, there was peace as pale blue lights illuminated the bridge. The wall-mounted, curved vid-screen at the front of the bridge scrolled text in an unrecognizable language.

Just as I started to release a breath, a blinking red light on my HUD's tactical display caught my attention.

"Frak!" I yelled. The surveillance pucks three levels below all reported activity. A second later, the AP mine I'd left in the shaft exploded.

"Captain, there's a Kroerak cruiser class spooling up. It must have been off-line when we arrived," Ada's voice cut in. "You have three minutes to exit that ship or we're going to be looking for a new interior decorator."

"Understood. Jonathan, get as much data as you can. Ada, don't let them have *Intrepid*. You copy?"

"I copy. Just get off that ship!"

I turned and for no reason I could put my finger on at the time, I picked up the officer's sword and slipped it between my ammo pack and my back.

"You have tactical, Marny."

MORE THAN ONE WAY

"Damn," Marny cursed quietly. Within a heartbeat, though, she snapped out orders. "Out the door, on the double. Tabby, forward, starboard side!"

Tabby jammed the communication crystal into a pocket, spun from the workstation, and flew toward the aft hatch.

"Negative," Marny exclaimed. "Port hatch. The bridge has power and *Intrepid* has given us crew access."

Tabby nodded over her shoulder, turned gracefully, pushed off the aft bulkhead and redirected to starboard.

"Deploying FBD," I announced, peeling a centimeter-wide flat disc from my chest and tossing it on the floor. The flash-bang-disc technology emitted extremely loud pulses of sound waves, while at the same time strobed blindingly bright flashes of light. The sound waves wouldn't do much in the near zero atmosphere, but the flashes of light would draw Kroerak attention. Our suits were sequenced with both the light flashes and the sounds, allowing us to operate normally. My next move was to deploy an anti-personnel mine next to the jimmied aft hatch and attempt to catch up with Marny and Tabby as they flowed through the now-operational starboard bridge hatch.

I hadn't moved two meters from the aft hatch when pointy claws poked through the narrow opening and started prying. While not surprised, I was dismayed. The Kroerak warrior was having little trouble widening the gap that had taken me a lot of effort.

"Let's go, Cap!" Marny roared.

From the corner of my eye, I caught a dark form race past the bug trying to come through the aft hatch. If things went according to plan, the bug would blow the mine we'd left in the passageway instead of finding Tabby and Marny.

"Tabby, you have incoming," I warned.

"Fall back." Tabby back-pedaled into the bridge and used the hatch for cover as she fired her 816.

Marny didn't hesitate and pushed forward next to Tabby, flipped her 816 to her left shoulder, and engaged just as I fired at the Kroerak warrior successfully forcing its way through the aft hatch.

"I have an explosive about to blow," I said. "We need to move out."

"Bogey down," Tabby announced and disappeared into the passageway. I disengaged combat with the wounded Kroerak at the aft hatch and sailed hard with my grav-suit, following the team.

"We have an escape solution," Marny said. "Go, go, go!"

I'd barely cleared the bridge when a gout of flame and a pressure wave threw me into the opposite bulkhead. I tumbled away from my team in the zero-g, dropping my 816 as I worked to arrest momentum. Through disoriented eyes, I watched in horrified fascination as a stream of Kroerak warriors squirted around the corner, cutting off any chance I might have of catching up with Marny and Tabby.

"Frak. I'm cut off," I said. "There are too many. Go on without me. I'll find another way out."

"No way, Cap," Marny said just as a mine in the starboard passageway exploded next to the leader of the Kroerak throng.

"Do it! I'm clear," I grunted as the mine's blast caught me and sent me tumbling backward again, further away from the team. I was amazed at just how well Anino's grav-suit absorbed the impact. I would no doubt have considerable bruising, but that was much better than the alternative. I'd been dangerously close to two explosions that would have shredded me in a normal suit.

"Damn you, Hoffen," Tabby exclaimed. I verified that she and Marny were headed away, even as I felt a smaller concussive blast. The forward hallway's mine had blown.

I twisted around and urged my suit away from the bedlam.

Tabby's invective simply confirmed she was respecting the play I was calling. Of course, she was also letting me know just how annoyed that made her.

"Captain, they're here," Ada warned. As she spoke, I heard *Intrepid's* weapon systems firing.

"Clear out, Ada. Nobody lives if they take *Intrepid*."

"Already moving, Liam. I'm sorry," she said more softly.

"Thank you for doing the right thing," I replied and then switched gears. "Jonathan," I said. "I'm going to need a new way off this ship; I've been separated from Tabby and Marny."

"Understood, Captain," Jonathan replied. His voice was even, although he spoke more quickly than usual. "There's a maintenance hatch aft, twenty meters down the next passage. The information we have is limited, but we believe this might give you access to a …"

"One thing at a time." I cut him off, bounding off a bulkhead angled at forty-five-degrees, my feet neatly grabbing the textured material. Whatever these aliens were, they were obviously comfortable in zero-g, as the bulkhead's angle made for an easy redirection.

My HUD illuminated Jonathan's hatch and I slowed, stopping on top of it. When I looked back in the direction I'd come, two of the tall, cockroach-looking aliens rounded the corner, careening against the walls of the passageway, fighting each other for position. The hatch had three thick indentions that appeared to work as some sort of latch. I stuck three fingers into the mechanism and attempted to pull, but it wouldn't budge.

The Kroerak hadn't slowed. While I was faster in zero-g, I was confused by their pell-mell race in my direction. It was almost as if they were fighting each other to catch me. Whatever the issue, I had precious few seconds to accomplish my task.

"Screw it." I pulled two grenade balls from my waist, set them for three seconds and flung them toward the approaching bugs. I then pulled the torch from where it hung on my waist and fired a heavy stream of plasma into the lock mechanism.

Only one of my pursuers made it past the grenades. The effect wasn't ideal, as the bug was launched down the hallway in my direction. One of the problems with the Kroerak was that their buggy exoskeletons were about as hard as crystalized nano-steel. If you could get an explosive inside the beast, they were done, but it took quite a lot to penetrate their shells.

I ducked as the warrior banged into the ceiling and ricocheted past my position. It dragged claws along the walls, scrabbling to gain position. My situation had gone from bad to worse. Now I had Kroerak on both sides. With precious little time, I pulled at the hatch and was momentarily relieved when it opened.

That relief gave way to pain that nearly caused me to black out. One moment I was considering the tween deck beneath me, and the next, I found myself smashed into the wall. I turned, desperately trying to get my bearings and found myself face to face with a bug. It had latched a thick pincer onto my arm and was pulling me to its snapping mandibles.

"Excessive pressure detected." My HUD showed an outline of my suit, the left arm blinking red. I was thrilled my suit had actually survived the initial contact, but knew if I didn't do something quickly, this bug would snip through my arm. Unlike Divelbiss, I hadn't thought enough in advance to grab a grenade to stuff in the Kroerak's maw. And since I was alone, I didn't think that maneuver would work as well for me as it had for him.

Thoughts of Divelbiss, however, got me to thinking about the plasma torch I did have in my hand. Without hesitation, I laid that torch into the bug's pincer where it joined the claw. A spurt of yellow goo sprayed onto my faceplate as the claw detached. I wasted no time and arched my back, pushed off with my legs, and dove down through the hatch.

"Captain, two meters portside there is a shaft that descends forty meters," Jonathan's voice announced.

I pushed against cables and pipes, almost becoming entangled as I twisted away from enemy pursuit. With dismay, I watched as big holes opened from the deck above. Several bugs were tearing the passageway apart, attempting to widen the entry so they could follow me below deck.

I dropped my torch and grasped the cables, working them out of my way, and dove into the narrow shaft Jonathan had identified. Free from utility lines, I rocketed downward.

"What's next?"

"Starboard hatch opens to a flight deck."

"Flight deck?"

"Yes. Are you available for additional information?"

I groaned inwardly. For all their combined brilliance, Jonathan had difficulty figuring out many of the subtleties in human situations.

"Yes," I said, pushing at the hatch. The same stubby, three-fingered clasp that stymied me before was preventing me from accessing the flight deck. This time, now that murderous bugs weren't right on my tail, I examined the panel more closely. I discovered narrow slots at the ends of the stubby finger-like holes. "Are you seeing this, Jonathan?"

"You'll need to cut the hatch," he said. "Your anatomy is not compatible with this configuration."

"Repeat that?"

A three-dimensional image of a furry, red, three-toed paw appeared on my HUD. From the ends of the toes, sharp, curved claws extended a centimeter and a half.

I pulled the torch from my waist, or rather I attempted to, and found just the narrow cable that joined it to its power source. The torch had been ripped off. I seemed to recall something pulling at me as I fled, but thought I'd just been caught on one of the ship's cables.

"More than one way … " I said to myself as I pulled the 816 rifle around and sprayed the hatch with more explosive rounds than were technically necessary to do the job.

"Captain? Are you okay?" Jonathan asked, conveying concern in his tone of voice.

"Improvising," I answered as I sailed through the open hatch and into a wide, open hangar bay. My heart skipped when I saw two ships still lashed to the deck. "Tell me you can get these ships going."

"Unknown, Captain," Jonathan replied. "We were able to see them on the ship's internal sensors, but there is no available communications link."

"Figures." I sailed across the deck to the first ship. Its sleek design allowed for two crew, which I suspected would be pilot and navigator / gunner. The fighter ship had swept-back wings and a tail section that meant it was designed for in-atmosphere duty. The view through the clear cockpit window made me think I was looking at an old museum-vid. The flight system was manual, including a central stick, several toggles, slides, and even buttons. I pulled at the single-piece canopy and was frustrated to find the same stubby fingered locking mechanism that had thwarted me on the hatches.

"Captain, the Kroerak are working their way toward you," Jonathan said.

"How about Tabby and Marny?" I asked.

"They've got us cornered," Marny replied, her voice accentuated by automatic gunfire. "We're holding them off for now, but we'll eventually run out of ammo. The narrow hallways are helpful."

"Can you get off the ship?" I asked.

"Maybe," Tabby replied. "But once we're off, we won't have any cover."

"Think about it," I said. "I've been trying to figure out why all those bodies were off the ships. It makes sense. The Kroerak don't have any propulsion in zero-g. You just need to get clear of the ship and hide in with the others."

The second ship in the hangar wasn't a fighter and hadn't been designed for atmospheric flight. To call it a ship was even generous. Best I could tell, it was a reaction-matter engine at the back of a steel box, all sitting on narrow skids, one of which was clamped to the deck.

"We're free from the ship, Cap," Marny replied. "You're right. Two Kroerak tried to follow us and now they're just sailing out into space."

"Take cover."

"Copy that, Cap," Marny replied.

"What are you still doing on the ship?" Tabby asked.

"I have an idea," I answered. "If it doesn't work out, I'll find you."

I felt a familiar tug on my ring finger. Tabby and I wore matching rings, each with a sliver of the same quantum communications crystal. The pieces were too small for ordinary communication, but if either one of us thumbed the crystal in just the right way, the other's ring throbbed in response.

"Love you, kid," I replied.

I pulled at the hatch to the second ship. Instead of the sophisticated, stubby, three-fingered lock, the ship boasted a simple hatch-wheel. While unsophisticated, the hatch-wheel was a tried and true mechanism. Spinning the wheel would pull pins away from the inside of the hatch and allow it to swing free. Whoever had last exited this ship, however, hadn't even made the effort to close the hatch.

I swung into the ship, hunching as I made my way forward to the cockpit. "Looks like a smaller species owned this craft," I mused as I wedged myself into the overly small seat and bent forward for a clear view of space.

"Agreed, Captain," Jonathan said. "We believe the device in front of you operates as a flight yoke."

I grabbed the rectangular grip in front of me.

"Any ideas on how to get it started?" I asked.

"We recommend the switches in front of you."

"Switches?"

My HUD illuminated tarnished silver looking, rounded pieces of metal sticking out of the forward bulkhead. "Seriously?"

"We recommend the following sequence," he replied.

I flipped the *switches* in the order indicated by a red blinking light. "Frak," I exclaimed as I unwound myself from the uncomfortable chair and raced down the narrow row of seats.

"Captain, the Kroerak have arrived," Jonathan warned.

As he did, my HUD alerted me to where the bugs had already entered the bay and were now racing toward me. I fired my 816 at the clamp that held the alien ship to the deck. I ended up doing more damage to the skid than I did to the clamp, but I wasn't feeling picky.

Jetting for an exit might have been the smart play. I was virtually guaranteed the bugs wouldn't keep up with me in open space. The problem was, Ada and *Intrepid* were being chased by a full-up Kroerak ship and might not make it back any time soon.

I flung myself back into the small vessel and spun the hatch-wheel, locking the door behind me. I considered myself something of an expert on steel and calculated just how long it might hold up to a Kroerak. The entire ship shook and I received my answer in the form of a dent the size of my fist appearing uncomfortably close to my head.

Backpedaling from the assault, I then raced forward, sliding back into the pilot's chair, repeating the sequence I'd started. A second impact shook the ship. The skids must have come detached from the friction clamps, as we started to roll across the deck.

I like to think of myself as patient with mechanical items. Rushing an engine that doesn't want to start almost always ensures that it won't. When the ship didn't fire up right away, I gave it a second, blew out a tense breath and tried not to freak out as a pincer tore into the side of the ship, opening the steel skin. Vibrations throughout the ship told me everything else I needed to know. I'd gained a crowd and things were about to go very poorly for me.

I tried one final time to start the reaction-matter engine and was probably just as surprised as the Kroerak when it did. With nothing to lose, I pushed the yoke-styled flight control forward. The small vessel twisted into a lazy, rolling spin. In that I was still inside the flight bay, I almost immediately hit the deck, although I didn't let off the controls. The push of the engine was considerably more than I'd expected and say what you want about skids, they can take a wallop. I pulled back and twisted in the opposite direction of the spin, overcorrecting. Another adjustment and things got better. This time I careened slightly off the bay's ceiling.

I'd like to say my plan was to shake the Kroerak loose from the ship by tactically slamming them into the docking bay. While technically that's what happened, I'll admit to being surprised at the realization I was both free of bugs and free from the ship.

"What's going on, Liam?" Tabby asked. I suspected she'd been watching through my HUD.

"Just working my way over to you," I said as nonchalantly as I could manage.

"That's an ugly ship," she said.

I let out a breath. "Most beautiful ship I've ever seen."

"Yeah, I suppose."

My HUD illuminated a group of bodies where Marny and Tabby had decided to hide.

"Liam, the Kroerak ship has broken off pursuit. What's going on over there?" Ada asked.

"I've picked up a shuttle," I said.

"I think they're coming to finish you off," she said.

I slowed the shuttle next to Marny and Tabby and slid back to open the severely dented hatch. The thick star field of the Dwingeloo galaxy shined through several of the new holes in the shuttle's skin.

"Welcome aboard," I said as Marny slid into the small passenger section. We removed our ordnance packs, as the space was too close for us otherwise.

Marny inspected the sword I'd taken from the battle-cruiser's bridge. "Where'd you pick this up?"

"I guess it was the captain's," I said and pointed to the hatch. "Close her up, Tabbs. We're not out of this yet." Sliding back into the pilot's chair, even with the ammo pack gone, I still felt like an adult in a child's seat.

Tabby slipped in next to me as I picked out my path through the debris. "I can't believe you found a working ship,"

"Ada, give me a nav-path that you can intercept," I said. "This old girl actually has some balls."

"Your idioms don't make sense," Ada complained, although a nav-path displayed on my HUD.

"Hold on, kids." I pushed on the stick. I felt a little bad for Marny, who was unable to do anything but lie uncomfortably across three seats. When I accelerated, she tumbled into the aft bulkhead.

"We're reading a substantial radiation leak in your ship's matter-reaction chamber," Jonathan warned.

"Can we take another hundred twenty seconds?" I asked. My AI had projected this as the amount of time required to reach velocity and rendezvous with *Intrepid*.

"You'll be okay, Liam," Nick said. "I need you to help Marny off the back wall, though. We'd like to have kids someday."

"I'm okay, little man," Marny replied, pulling herself forward over the backs of the tiny chairs.

Tabby reached behind my seat and wiggled a broken Kroerak pincer free from the roof, holding it up in front of me and waggled it. "Cutting it a little close, weren't you?"

Intrepid loomed over the top of us and I slipped into the cargo bay. "Hard to disagree with that."

INTRUDER

I know it makes me less of a person to find humor in someone else's discomfort, but I must admit that watching Marny attempt to extract herself from the narrow row of chairs in the ancient ship nearly had me in tears. Her problems were numerous. *Intrepid* was on hard-burn which put the cargo bay - and therefore our little ship - at 1.5g. To make matters worse, I'd sheared off one of the two skids and we were tipped thirty degrees to the side. If that wasn't bad enough, every movement anyone made caused the entire vehicle to rock.

"Marny. Hold still," Tabby ordered, sending me a dirty look.

Marny pushed against chair backs that weren't designed to hold her weight. "I'm about to blow a hole in the side of this thing." She was more annoyed than I'd heard her in months.

Tabby locked her feet into the base of a chair and offered a hand to Marny. Between the two of them, Marny ended up on her knees in the aisle. She was kind of wedged sideways, as the space was too narrow for her to slip through comfortably. When Marny finally got her feet underneath her, she had about half the head-room she needed to stand. The ensuing wiggle down the aisle reminded me just how much I enjoyed Marny's muscular form and how much I needed to avoid looking, lest I get busted for ogling by either her or Tabby.

"Ada, what's our status?" I asked when I finally exited the simple, mostly ruined craft. Now that we were back aboard, our comms had joined into the ship's primary channel.

"Kroerak vessel is still on our six," she replied. "Hold. Nope, they're breaking off pursuit."

"We have damage on our bow," Nick answered. "I'm headed forward to check it out."

"Through hull?" I asked.

"Roger that," Nick replied.

"Hold on, I'll join you," I said.

"Not necessary, there's only one," he said. "I just want to get it tied up."

"Jonathan, you might like to come to the hold and check out this relic we picked up. Not sure what you'll learn; it doesn't seem to have any sort of centralized AI."

"We're on our way," Jonathan replied.

I accepted my ammo pack from Tabby. Thirty kilograms of gear had grown to forty-five in the increased gravity, so I had to duck-walk it over to a grav-pallet. Marny joined me, dropping her own, heavier pack next to mine.

"I'll run the weapons back to the armory, Cap," Marny said. "There's some maintenance I'd like to see to."

"Thank you, Marny," I said. It was funny just how that simple phrase didn't seem adequate.

She pulled me in for an unexpected hug. "Appreciate the rescue, Cap."

"What do you want to do with this?" Tabby asked emerging from the alien craft holding the sword I'd brought back. She glanced up and gave us a wicked grin. "Oh. Do you guys want a minute?"

Marny let go and just smiled back. It was a long running joke. Tabby enjoyed needling me about my supposed unresolved feelings for Marny.

I accepted the sword, grabbing it just beneath its narrow guard. The sword was short, two-thirds the length of my arm. Its blade gently widened as it extended away from the guard and curved up to a point at the end. For a moment, I was mystified at how it might be extracted from its scabbard, since it was wider on one end. With a small amount of fiddling, I discovered the brittle leather sheath was slit along the edge and the sword was magnetically held in place.

"That'd be easy to clean up," Marny observed as the three of us worked our way through the airlock and into *Intrepid's* starboard passage on the main deck. The blade had been ornately inscribed, but showed significant tarnish and some pitting, the edge notched in several locations.

"I'd hate to lose any of this etching," I said.

"And I'd like to see the hand that would hold that comfortably," Tabby joined in.

I turned the sword over in my hand, inspecting what Tabby had seen and I hadn't. The hilt had wide grooves that looked as if they'd accept a small, three fingered hand. Similarly, the sword had small creases, centered at the end of each finger where a narrow claw could extend.

"It's not outrageously uncomfortable." I gripped the pommel. "Check it out," I said. "I think these aliens had retractable claws."

"You mean like cats?" Tabby asked.

"I think exactly like cats," I replied as Jonathan caught up with us, having come from the bridge.

"They refer to themselves as Felio," Jonathan offered. "That is, if you'll allow for our attempt at providing translation. The digits on the extremities of their limbs do indeed have retractable nails. With Jester Ripples' help, we found records for the entire crew within their computer systems."

A rendering of the Felio from the battle cruiser's bridge appeared on my HUD. The obviously female figure bore a striking resemblance to humans. Even so, significant differences were evident, the foremost of which was the short, red fur covering her entire body. The only markings in the red fur were two white blazes accentuating the cheeks of the Felio's face.

"She's beautiful," Tabby mused. "So strong. Look at those arms."

Tabby was right. Even through the fur, the muscles showed considerable definition.

"Was she the captain?" I asked.

"She appears to have been the equivalent of third-highest ranking officer. It was her duty to stay alive as long as possible, in the hope that help might arrive."

"But it never did," Tabby filled in.

"Ugh, that's a sad picture," I said. "I better catch up with Nick, he might need help."

"I'll check in with Ada," Tabby said as we came even with the bridge's primary entrance. "By the way, you're still wearing your slug-thrower."

I patted my chest and took off at a jog, which in 1.5g looked more like a funny, exaggerated walk. Sure enough, I'd forgotten to drop the heavy, slug-throwing pistol at the armory.

Locate Nick James.

"Nicholas James is on deck two, port-side," my suit's AI informed me.

Intrepid's forward two decks were unoccupied. In fact, if you didn't count the tween decks where the life-support systems were stored or the small corridor that allowed access to the four aft engines, the only place where a second deck was to be found was forward where the ship expanded to accommodate extra crew and visitors. For the last several runs, we'd been sailing with minimal crew, leaving the forward sections unoccupied and powered down.

I crossed in front of the crew's mess entrance and turned forward once again, heading down the far, port-side ramp to what we referred to as crew-country. I wasn't sure what it was that caught my attention first, but I instinctively grabbed the pistol strapped to my chest and spun around the corner.

"Frak, intruder!" I yelled. The lights around the top of the room immediately pulsed red and a warning klaxon sounded. In front of me stood a Kroerak warrior with deep scratches along its hard carapace. Beneath a fallen steel bunk, Nick's still form was crumpled in the corner. The bug was having trouble digging Nick out, not able to find a suitable angle. Each swipe with its claw caught the top-side of the cot, which sprang back when the bug's claw lost contact.

Without hesitation, I lined up on the warrior's head. The Kroerak have a centimeter-wide strip of flexible hide that allows the head to rotate. The spot is less armored than the rest of the nearly impenetrable exoskeleton. My first shot got its attention, although missing by a fraction the kill shot I'd hoped for. As it turns out, there aren't a lot of great places to shoot a charging bug, so I haphazardly plugged it a couple of times and turned, jumping into an adjoining hallway. Somewhere in the chaos, something hard hit my hand and the pistol spun wildly away.

"Tabbs, I've got real trouble," I said.

"Hold on, love," she replied. "Cavalry is ten seconds out."

I looked around crazily - as is common for me when faced with a homicidal beast of which I have little hope of defeating. As it turns out, this has been a pretty good strategy for me so far - and today was no exception. In my panic, I was unable to find the small pistol, which was no doubt my best chance at salvation. Instead, my eyes lit on the Felio sword I'd dropped only a meter from my position.

Kroerak warriors have pointy feet and claws which make a distinctive sound as they jab into the solid steel surfaces of a ship. If a person really had their wits about them, they could tell just how close the beast was based on the sound alone. For me, it was disturbing to hear the clacking and know a bug was closing in for a kill shot. I dove down the hallway, dropped my hand onto the pommel of the sword and rolled forward.

If you're thinking that standing head-to-head with one of these uglies with only a sword is a bad idea, you're basically right. The problem was that in my mind, the alternative was to cower in a room and wait for the creature to eat me. This was something I just couldn't do. When I went for the sword, I ended up hitting the deck harder than intended, not considering the extra gravity. Fortunately, Marny's continuous drills allowed me to instinctively adjust, rolling to my feet - face to face with the bug. I must have surprised the warrior because it stopped, possibly taking a moment to question my sanity.

Of course, it also could have been the distinctive sound of an 816 rifle drilling rounds into its back. To say I was insulted when it turned around like I wasn't any kind of threat would be an understatement. Sure, I didn't have a lot of fancy sword moves. And sure, if Tabby hadn't started firing, I would probably at that moment have been turned into bug food, but dang it, I was standing my ground and that should get a little respect!

"I'm short on ammo, Liam," Tabby said, her voice amplified by my suit's comm. "You need to take cover. Marny's on her way with a full mag."

I was about to do just that when my eye caught the smallest amount of yellow goo seeping over the top of the bug's armored shell near the spot on the neck I thought I'd missed. I've had a lot of bad ideas in the past, and I'm about fifty-fifty on how they turn out, but 'fortune favors the bold' is something I've thought of quite a lot, even though I've come to the realization that the saying has been repeated only by bold people who happened to live through whatever insane move they attempted. Bottom line is, I was drawn to that shiny spot like a moth to flame.

Cut full-burn. Captain's override, I said. I wasn't a hundred percent sure it would work, but the AI was all about translating and acting on commands.

There's a moment in shifting from full-burn back to normal when the gravity systems go a little wonky. It was the type of wonky that used to make Nick throw up back when we started sailing. I was counting on that moment, when everyone who was expecting it would freeze for a moment, allowing for the gravity system to kick back on. The unsuspecting who kept on moving usually ended up stumbling about. I, however, was in mid-air when this occurred and fully committed to my brazen plan.

I discovered that day that like the ancient Japanese, the Felio are excellent craftsmen with steel. The blade that had lain idle for a hundred-fifty stans cut neatly into the crease between the bug's head and shoulders, burying itself up to the hilt. In defense, the warrior attempted to tip its head back, and managed to snap a portion of the blade off, but the damage had been done. As if I'd flicked off a light switch, the bug stopped moving.

Restore normal gravity, I ordered. Gravity tugged at the beast and I rode it to the deck and extracted the broken blade. A four-centimeter section had been clipped off at the end and part of me was sad to have broken such a fine piece of craftsmanship.

"Shite, Liam! I could have shot you," Tabby exclaimed.

While possible, it was unlikely. Her AI had full access to the combat data-stream and wouldn't allow a bullet aimed directly at me to leave the barrel of her weapon. It's true the AI would have a hard time accounting for ricochets, so she had a point, but it wasn't like I was about to admit that.

"Nick is down," I said. "Bring a med kit."

***

"How are you doing, buddy?" I asked, noticing that Nick had started to stir. He'd spent the last twelve hours in the medical tank after we'd discovered the bug had punctured his abdomen, taken care of one of his kidneys, and done substantial internal damage.

"My gut hurts," he replied, groggily.

"You got new parts," I said. "They'll take some getting used to. Any idea how that bug got in the ship?"

"Must have squeezed through the hole I was repairing," he said. "Caught me in the tween deck. I tried to run, but it got me."

"The marks on its carapace were probably made when it came through," I said.

"Everyone all right?"

"Tabby's a little miffed. Apparently, I jumped into her line of fire."

"AI won't let her shoot you," he agreed weakly.

I slugged him in the shoulder lightly. "See! Now, that's what I said. But she's not buying it."

"Ouch," he complained.

"There's my little man," Marny's voice filled the room as she walked in, carrying a plate filled with steaming cinnamon rolls.

"I'll give you guys some privacy," I said, mussing Nick's hair. He hated that, so I reserved mussings for special occasions.

"Take a roll with you, Cap," Marny said. "You more than earned it - keeping my little man safe."

Nick grabbed my arm. "I knew you'd come, Liam. Even when I couldn't stay awake. I knew it."

His confidence caused the breath to catch in my throat and I found I couldn't talk. I smiled and patted his leg.

Marny placed her hand on my opposite shoulder, her forearm resting on my chest as she faced me. "You did good, Cap. Thank you."

I nodded and plucked a roll from the plate, attempting nonchalance and not necessarily succeeding. "Glad it worked out," I managed before exiting the medical bay. I shook my head as I walked up the starboard ramp toward the bridge, chastising myself for the lame 'glad it worked out' comment. I generally had better comebacks but not, apparently, when it came to accepting praise from people I cared about.

"Captain on the bridge," Ada said smartly as I walked through the hatch with a face full of cinnamon roll. I looked around. Jonathan, Ada, and even Jester Ripples stood at attention, saluting me as I entered. I pulled the roll as gracefully as I could from my mouth.

"As you were," I replied. I wasn't sure what was up because it was unusual behavior for any of them, especially Ada who rarely referred to me as Captain.

"We watched the vid of you taking on that Kroerak, Liam Hoffen," Jester Ripples said. "Ada Chen said that a salute would communicate our respect for your actions."

"Thank you, guys," I said. "It was either me or the bug. I guess I was afraid of what it would do to Nick and Tabby."

"The Kroerak do not respect life," Jonathan said. "It is unfortunate that they must be treated so, but we find no logical alternative. We too are grateful that you were willing to sacrifice yourself for your crew."

"We either stand together or we fall, apart," I said, rather proud of myself for coming up with something inspirational on short notice.

Ada smiled, rolling her eyes. "Indeed," she agreed.

"How far from the first moon are we?" I asked, accepting Jester Ripples' request to climb up onto me. The small Norigan preferred to maintain close physical contact with friends. So much so, that

I'd installed a second chair just above the arm of my own.

"I was about to call you up," Ada said. "As you can see, we're passing the gas planet J-F99214-D at six hundred thousand kilometers. The moon should be within view in a few minutes. According to Jonathan's research, the Felio had a colony there when the Belirand mission arrived."

"The Belirand mission clearly contacted the Felio," I said.

"The extent of which is unclear, Captain," Jonathan replied.

"I didn't show you this yet," I said, holding up the Belirand mission pin I'd recovered.

"Where did you get that, Captain?"

"The Felio officer was holding it," I said.

Ada peered at me and the pin. "Why would she have that?"

"I think the Felio and the people of the Belirand mission had more contact than we might have believed. I'd like to get a look at the habitable moons. I think we'll find that the Felio have a colony."

"It is unlikely a colony remains," Jonathan replied. "The Kroerak were quite aggressive with our approach. We believe they would treat any Felio colony similarly."

"Well, we won't know until we check it out," I said. "Are you ready for a ride in the Bumblebee, Jester Ripples?"

I referred to the Tison-4x fighters we'd procured from Mars Protectorate. The fighters were small, two-person crafts that had ridiculous acceleration and carried two missiles which were nearly as long as the fighter itself. In battle, the fighters did a great job of peeling off the annoying small craft and softening up larger targets. For us, however, they'd turned into excellent scouting tools. A Tison-4x could easily enter the atmosphere of a planet, locate a target, and make contact. The fact that they were filled with inertial gel reduced their value as a transport, but I didn't think we'd be staying long.

"Will Tabitha Masters also join us?" Jester Ripples asked.

"She will," I said. "Although Nick isn't in any shape to fly."

When we'd trained on the Bumblebees, we'd split up - Tabby and Nick in one fighter; Jester Ripples and me in the other. At the time, the choice to bring Jester Ripples along had been one born of necessity. As Norigans were pacifists, I'd worried that being in a fighter would go against his nature. As it turned out, if he was neither giving chase nor firing weapons, he had no qualms about accompanying me. I appreciated having someone take on navigation duties and target tracking which reduced the mental burden of flight considerably.

"Nicholas James is fortunate to be alive," Jester Ripples observed. "It is sensible that he would rest more. Who will accompany Tabitha Masters."

"I'll fly solo," Tabby said, entering the bridge.

"I was hoping you could link to her navigation computer," I said. "I'm not expecting combat."

Tabby smiled, lifting an eyebrow. "Yeah, right."

TALE OF TWO CITIES

"I look forward to exploring J-F99214-D-04," Jester Ripples said excitedly as I helped him into the Tison-4X fighter that had been dubbed *Sugar* after a boxer from ages past.

"You set, little buddy?" I asked, patting his shoulder amiably. Jester Ripples' seat was in front of my own and lower by twenty centimeters.

"I am very comfortable, Liam Hoffen."

I'd tried to convince Jester Ripples that he could short-cut my name and simply refer to me as Liam, but he would have nothing to do with it. For him, a name was not to be broken apart.

The layout of the Tison was configurable. I'd been chastised by a naval trainer about my predilection for forward flight. If I'd become a professional fighter pilot that preference would have already been trained out of me. As it was, I sat straight up in the seat directly behind Jester Ripples, which I argued gave me a view of both my virtual holo displays as well as his.

I swung into my seat and swiped at the prompt that asked if we were ready to close the fully armored canopy. The Tison had no armor glass. Instead, we were surrounded by ten centimeters of the strongest armor Mars Protectorate manufactured. Sophisticated technology provided a spherical view from within the closed pod. Perhaps one of the most interesting facets was that baked into the armor itself were millions of microscopic sensors. Even if you scraped away a section of the armor, you'd expose a new layer of sensors, ensuring the pilots were never left blind.

"Here we go." Waiting for the cockpit to fill with nav-gel from the reservoir now internally mounted within *Intrepid* was annoying but necessary. The gel would interact with the inertial systems and make quick acceleration possible without harming the crew.

"Ada, requesting permission for takeoff," I called.

"You're green, Liam," she answered. "Don't take any chances."

"Roger that, Mama-bear," I replied. "Ready to roll, *Rowdy*?" I asked, using Tabby's fighter's call-sign.

"Try to keep up, Flyboy," she replied and shot straight down from where the Tisons were mounted beneath *Intrepid's* belly.

While I couldn't hold a candle to Tabby in hand-to-hand combat, the same couldn't be said of our fighter skills. We were closely matched, but I still held an edge. Privately, I believed this was because she was uncompromisingly aggressive, where I was more of a finesse pilot. As it turned out, instead of competing, we used our differences to complement each other.

I punched the accelerator and squirted away from *Intrepid*. The first few seconds of flight always took my breath away as I adjusted to the massive power of the small machine. I caught up easily with *Rowdy*, flipped over and sailed across, canopy to canopy.

"Show off," Tabby giggled.

A second advantage of nav-gel was its use as a projection

medium for the holographic displays. From my vantage point, I could 'see' through my canopy as if it weren't there, my field of view only obscured by myself, Jester Ripples, and a ghost outline of the fighter's hull. I'd even configured my projectors to allow me to see through Tabby's armor when we were close in.

"Love you." I smiled as she spun away and I synchronized my flight with her own. Together we dropped into the atmosphere of the blue-green moon below us.

"Captain, we're transmitting coordinates for what appear to be five cities," Jonathan said over the comms.

"Cities?" I asked. "We're not reading any EM."

"That is correct, Captain," Jonathan answered. "We're just now resolving small electro-magnetic radiation signatures."

"A topographical rendering is available," Jester Ripples added.

With a micro-gesture, I pulled Jester Ripple's topographical map onto *Sugar's* holo. The cities were regularly spaced, forming points of a pentagon. To one side, a low mountain range elevated two of the cities and in the center of the pentagon was a deep, blue sea.

"I have a bad feeling about this," Tabby said.

"Wing formation, Tabbs," I said.

"Copy that," she replied and swung around, positioning herself forty meters aft and ten meters to my starboard. She would maintain that position to within a few centimeters until combat demanded otherwise. The wing-man position allowed her to focus less on navigation and more on potential threats.

"*Intrepid*, we're a hundred kilometers from first target. AI estimates a population center in excess of eighty thousand and we're picking up several small, rural settlements," I announced. "We're going to fly over an agricultural installation."

"Copy that, Liam," Ada replied. "We're tracking your data-streams in real time and pick up no enemy activity."

I nosed down and Tabby and I dropped quickly, leveling out at three hundred meters. The ground rushing up at us was anything but commonplace, as we spent most of our time sailing in space.

"Yeah-haw!" Tabby squealed in delight. "Now that's what I call flying!"

"Drop back five kilometers, Tabbs," I said. "Let's see if I draw any attention."

"Copy," she replied. "I'll warm up my rocks."

I chuckled. Technically, we were both carrying missiles and not rockets, but she'd taken to the terminology and now everything was a rock. "Let's try to save the rocks if we can. We're just here gathering information."

"No promises, pal," she replied. "If I see a bug, I'll be thinking squish."

Beneath us, the landscape was covered by spindly trees or wildly growing shrubs, reaching as high as fifty meters. I slowed as I approached a grouping of buildings and allowed the sensors a chance to improve the fidelity of the information being gathered.

"The buildings are constructed of a combination stone and ridged, fibrous plant material. Sensors detect an inactive, buried electrical grid and dormant agricultural machines within the taller buildings," Jester Ripples offered. "There is no evidence of sentient beings."

"How about bugs?" I asked.

"A biome as rich as J-F99214-D-04 will have a highly diverse insect and arachnoid population. Our sensors are filtering out this information. Would you like me to modify our search parameters?" Jester Ripples asked.

"No," I chuckled. "Tabbs, it looks like an abandoned farm. I'm heading on to the city."

"Copy that," Tabby replied. "And Jester Ripples, for the record, when any of us refer to bugs, we're talking about Kroerak."

Define 'for the record.' I heard Jester Ripples ask his AI.

I swung in a wide, slow arc around the farm, looking at it through the hull - or at least that's what the Tison's projectors had convinced my brain I was doing. It was surprising to find no sign of damage to the buildings. Everything had been neatly put away; the only disarray caused by nearly a century of encroaching flora. With a flick of my hand, I straightened our flight, orienting on underground cables that ran off in the direction of the city.

As we grew closer, the scene repeated itself time and time again. A homestead, neatly buttoned up, and overgrown by thick shrubs and trees that soared skyward in the lower gravity of the moon.

"Looks like they have gravity technology," Tabby observed, still several kilometers behind me.

Jester Ripples had been highlighting different technologies as the AI identified them and streaming the information on a low-priority channel. I wasn't surprised that Tabby was reviewing them.

"Don't you think it's weird that there's no sign of combat?" I asked. "Let's tighten up our formation. Something doesn't feel right about this."

"Farms aren't exactly strategic," Tabby answered.

I accelerated and closed on the city. "Jester Ripples, see if you can locate a facility that might be used for space-bound launches."

A moment later, a city outline displayed with an indicator on the northern edge where Jester was drawing my attention. We continued to fly in silence as we absorbed the unfolding landscape beneath us and the constant data-stream from the AI. The city, designed for under a hundred thousand inhabitants, was crumbling from lack of attention, just as the farmsteads had been. Empty wooden docks along the sea to the south were all but non-existent, most of the material having been torn from the piers. The sheer number of docks was testimony to prosperous times.

"They knew the Kroerak were coming," I said, the idea forming as I attempted to make sense of what we were seeing.

"Then why put your fleet in danger?" Tabby asked. She'd closed to twenty meters, responding to a command I'd sent.

"Not sure," I replied and accelerated toward the location Jester Ripples had marked as a probable launch site. The buildings grew in height as we approached the center of the obviously once busy metropolis.

The answer to Tabby's question became clear as the city's spaceport came into view. On the tarmac that now more closely resembled a grassy field, we came upon a sizeable wreck. The ship boasted heavy engines, all mounted aft. The only way the ship would be able to fly was to be set straight up in line with gravity. The ship appeared to have been knocked over in the process of launch, causing it to break open as it crashed.

"I'm picking up skeletal humanoid remains," Jester Ripples announced, highlighting hundreds of bright, white outlines, some still within the broken ship, others many meters away.

"Look here, Liam," Tabby said. A blue highlight illuminated several fist-sized holes in the ship's relatively thin skin. "I'll bet those were caused by Kroerak lances."

"Go in for a closer look." I swiveled to provide her with maximum defensive support.

Tabby didn't need prompting. She zipped forward, hovered, and then dipped down into the open hull of the ship, illuminating the darkened interior with bright beams.

"Shite!" Tabby exclaimed just as *Rowdy* leapt backward, out of the hull. Following closely was an arachnid, two meters across on its body. It scampered out, spraying a gooey, black mist on *Rowdy's* nose. "Frak, it inked me."

I laughed as the giant spider sprang upward, trying to capture its prey. If there was one thing Tabby didn't appreciate, it was spiders. I wasn't at all surprised when *Rowdy's* single turret spit out twenty rounds of high velocity slug-thrower ammo, exploding the spider into bits.

"Easy, girl," I said. "I doubt that thing could get through your armor."

"No sense in taking chances," Tabby replied, her face pinched. "Did we get a good view? If we didn't, you're going back in."

"Yes, Tabitha Masters," Jester Ripples replied. "There is evidence of damage from Kroerak lances. It is confirmed that this rocket-propelled ship was destroyed by Kroerak forces."

I turned *Sugar* to get a better view of the spaceport. "Jonathan, how would a ship like this launch and how many Felio would one of these ships hold?"

"Total Felio aboard each ship is five hundred, given a ten-percent margin for error," he replied. "The technology for launching these ships is rather clever for a society on the verge of fully exploiting gravitational waves. The ship is set into a vertical position with their engines embedded into the ground. A combination of gravity propulsion and thrust from external rockets allowed the vehicles to reach escape velocity."

I raised my hand, causing *Sugar* to gain elevation quickly. "Jester Ripples, configure our scanners to locate additional wrecks."

"Yes, Liam Hoffen."

As we rose, the AI discovered another. A thousand lives destroyed in two devastating wrecks.

"Liam?" Nick's voice came over the comm.

"Hey, buddy. Glad you're up," I answered, momentarily forgetting about the horrible scene in front of me.

"Why don't you execute a high-speed flyover of the remaining cities. I think we've gathered enough intel," Nick replied.

"I'm all right," I lied.

"All the same," he replied. "Jonathan has identified where the Felio's home planet is located. I think it's time to pay them a visit."

"What if the Kroerak wiped their home, too?" I asked.

"It's information we need," Nick replied. "Don't you think Admiral Alderson would like to know what the Kroerak are capable of?"

It was a conversation we'd hashed through many times. Mars Protectorate was currently embroiled in an international debate about the legality of Belirand's previous actions. They were having difficulty getting the other two space-borne, super powers - NaGEK and the Chinese - to pay serious attention to the Kroerak threat. Per Lieutenant Gregor Belcose, who we'd learned was Mars Protectorate Intelligence and worked directly with Admiral Alderson, it would take nothing short of an invasion to get any of humanity's governments to spend the necessary capital to mount a sufficient defense against an enemy like the Kroerak. The question was, if a full-scale invasion were to be mounted, were we already too late to start working on that defense? The bottom line was that discovering a new species that already had problems with the Kroerak was likely at the bottom of M-Pro's priorities.

"What about the other moon?" I asked. When we'd arrived in system, we'd discovered that both giant gas planets were well outfitted with sizable moons. Each planet boasted at least one moon capable of supporting life. We'd visited the most habitable first.

"We're four days burn," Nick said. "I think that's up to you."

"We'll get finished up," I answered. "Tabbs, ready?"

"On your six."

The other cities were in similar shape, although we found no more crashed vehicles. By the time we arrived back on *Intrepid*, we'd been gone for more than sixteen hours and I, for one, was exhausted.

***

"Heya, Liam," Ada offered sleepily.

"Heya, yourself," I said.

"All systems are nominal," Ada answered. "We're on course and six hours from the moon J-F00214-E-07." With a flick of her finger, she switched the bridge's primary display on the forward bulkhead to forty-five degrees off our portside. The view changed to that of the massive gas giant J-F00214-E and for a moment I felt like an insignificant spec of sand next to it.

"I relieve you," I continued in our tradition.

"I stand relieved," she finished. "Mind if I stick around for a while?"

"I'd have thought you would want to get some sleep before we arrive," I said. "It could be a long day for all of us."

"I just came on four hours ago," she replied. "I wanted to bring us in next to the planet just in case we ran into problems."

"Understood."

Ada took a breath. "I've been wondering something. Why do you suppose all those crew abandoned ship? And, why did the Kroerak leave the third officer on the bridge?"

"With the ships disabled, the Kroerak would have boarded," I

50

said. "Staying aboard would have been a death sentence."

"But the Kroerak ships could have shot the crew out in space like they were," Ada said.

"To what end? The Kroerak are, if anything, efficient," I said. "As long as those ships weren't going anywhere, the crew became insignificant."

"Except as food," Ada said, trying to make me understand why she was headed down this path. "But it's like they didn't care."

She had a point. The Kroerak used their enemies as food sources. It was a mystery as to why they left the Felio unmolested. "I suppose the same could have been true with the third-officer. If they didn't want her badly enough, they might have just left her alone."

She lifted her eyebrows. "Unless they left her there as bait."

"Like for us?"

Ada looked at me patiently. "I doubt even the Kroerak are patient enough to wait a hundred-fifty stans."

"Right, but they might have hoped she'd draw more of her own people out. I haven't read Jonathan's report yet. Did we figure out how Felio got out this far without TransLoc technology?" I asked.

"There's a wormhole only half a light-year away," Ada replied. "We think it's why Belirand chose this location."

"Because of a nearby wormhole?" I asked. "It's not like we have tech that would get us through that."

"No, but what if the Felio do?"

"Big if," I said.

"Agreed. Jonathan says the idea isn't a lot different than TransLoc gates, just more permanent," Ada said.

"That'd be something to see," I said. "Traveling in a wormhole."

As the morning progressed, the bridge slowly filled with our small crew. First Jonathan and then Marny and finally Jester Ripples, Nick and Tabby all at once.

"Sensors have located two settlements," Jonathan announced. "They appear to be larger in scope than the Felio cities, but with less technology. The moon's surface is colder and supports a less diverse array of life. We recommend approaching the settlement closest to the moon's equator as a substantial storm is approaching the other."

"What kind of storm?" I asked.

"The temperature is minus four degrees and frozen precipitation is emitting from the clouds. We estimate the storm will be intensifying for the next forty-two hours," he said.

"I'm coming this time," Nick said.

"Are you sure?" I asked. "Last time I saw you, you had a hole the size of a bug pincer sticking through your kidneys."

"If you run into trouble, Tabby will need me," Nick said. "If there isn't trouble, then I'll have a nice ride. Besides, the med-tank got me all knitted up."

I frowned. As usual his logic was infallible, but it didn't feel right.

"Marny?"

"Don't pull me into this," she said, holding up her hands. "Medical AI has cleared him for light duty. We've been arguing about what that means."

"Well, shite. Okay, let's do this," I said, turning the bridge back over to Ada.

***

Our view as we approached J-F00214-E-07 was much different than that of the previous moon. Instead of rich greens and blue hues, the moon was white and gray with narrow streaks of green.

"Looks cold," Tabby observed over the tactical channel that joined *Rowdy* and *Sugar*.

"It is, Tabitha Masters," Jester Ripples answered. "The mean temperature of J-F00214-E-07 is five point two degrees. The settlement we are approaching is currently reading one degree."

We dropped quickly through the thin atmosphere of the moon and leveled out at four thousand meters, still three-hundred kilometers from the first settlement. Unlike the first moon, the flora was not quite so verdant. Brush and trees grew closer to the ground and we found fewer open sources of water.

"Did you catch that?" Nick asked, highlighting an area on the ground as we flew over.

I slowed and allowed our sensors a moment to catch up. A group of small, brown furry animals raced across the ground beneath us. "How'd you catch that?" I asked.

"They were at the lake back there," Nick said. "I just happened to zoom in and saw them bathing."

"They're really moving," I said. The animals had large hind legs and were moving at seventeen meters per second, which was quite a lot faster than I could move unaided. My AI, sensing my interest, displayed several facts that I found interesting. On average, they massed thirty kilograms and there were twenty-eight of them.

"Have to be some predators around to have developed that speed," Nick said.

"I don't like predators," Jester Ripples said.

I smiled. In my opinion, he was traveling in the company of predators. It just turned out to be the case that we were no longer the biggest and baddest in the neighborhood.

"I'm picking up tunnels," Nick said when we were still twenty kilometers from the settlement. We still hadn't found any ordinary Felio dwellings and I wondered if the Kroerak had taken over the moon. The lack of an armed response to our presence seemed to be the best argument against that, however. As if reading my mind, Nick continued. "They're way too small for Kroerak. Could be local fauna."

"What about the species that would fit the little ship we brought back from the Felio Battle Cruiser?" I asked.

"Not sure," Nick said. "I guess I never got a chance to look at it."

"That follows, Captain," Jonathan cut in. I wasn't surprised that *Intrepid* was listening in on our tactical chatter. "The tunnels your sensors are picking up are consistent with a species that might propel itself in a horizontal position. We estimate the beings' mass to be an average of thirty kilograms and when vertical, reach one point two meters."

"Hands and knees?" I asked.

"A more likely explanation is flexible lower limbs," Jonathan replied. "Such a species might find it possible to propel itself in a prone position and achieve a vertical orientation for other tasks."

"Yeah. Geez. Alien one-oh-one, Liam," Tabby chided.

"I'd like to see that," I said as we arrived at the outskirts of what Jonathan had referred to as a settlement.

I'll be the first to admit that judging a species' construction technology based on how it has fared after a hundred and fifty stans is probably not fair. That said, very few recognizable structures remained standing. White building foundations poked up through drifts of dirt and debris and a few skeletal steel structures, never reaching higher than two stories, stood as bleak markers of the city's complete failure.

"I think the reason it looks so trashed up here is because this isn't where they lived," Nick observed. "The tunnel system beneath the ground is quite extensive, intricate even."

"How deep do they go?" I asked.

"Our sensors are only able to penetrate to a depth of ten meters and the tunnels extend well beyond that," he answered.

"How about a spaceport?" I asked.

"I have it marked on your map," Jester Ripples replied just as a vaporous, blue contrail extended from *Sugar* across the city. We zipped across the ruined city and as we did, the AI outlined five dilapidated landing pads.

"What is all of the white debris?" I asked. The field below us was covered with what looked like thousands of white sticks.

"Those are bones, Liam," Nick answered grimly. "It doesn't look like any of these inhabitants escaped. There are other signs of Kroerak predation. My AI estimates thirty thousand dead, which lines up with the estimates for the city's population."

"That's horrible," Tabby replied.

"It   was   a   massacre,"   he   said.

INVASION

"Where do you think the Belirand mission ship ended up?" I asked as I lifted Jester Ripples out from the cockpit of *Sugar*.

"In reviewing the Felio computing machinery, I see evidence of algorithms unique to humanity," Jester Ripples said. "It is logical to assume that the Felio people had contact with the Belirand crew."

"What sort of algorithms?" Nick asked as we pushed through the airlock from the cargo bay and into the aft hallway.

"Jonathan sent them to me for analysis while we were returning from J-F00214-E-07," he replied. "The algorithms are related to travel through wormholes."

"That doesn't make sense," I said, pushing through the door to the bridge. "Humans don't know how to travel through wormholes."

"This is true, Liam Hoffen," Jonathan interjected. "The algorithms were modified to fit with the Felio engines, but were unmistakably the design of Thomas Phillipe Anino. We estimate these algorithms made wormhole travel more efficient. Jester Ripples has also verified these findings."

"How about we have Anino take a look?" I asked.

"I have tried, but he has been unavailable," Jonathan replied.

"What do you mean unavailable? When did you try?" I asked. It wasn't like Anino to ignore us when we were out on a mission. Our introduction to broken Belirand missions had been his pet project since the first time we met.

"We have been transmitting constantly since our initial contact with the Felio fleet," he replied. "We have been out of contact for twenty hours."

Nick and I exchanged worried glances and we sprinted to our

stations – mine, the captain's chair and his, just to starboard. "Raise Mars Protectorate," I said.

"On it," Nick replied.

"Mars Protectorate, this is *Intrepid*, come in, please."

"Mars Protectorate, this is *Intrepid*, come in. Over."

We waited in silence for what seemed like forever.

"Mars Protectorate, this is *Intrepid*, come in," Nick repeated.

"*Intrepid*, this is Lieutenant Commander Qiu Loo. Go ahead," a woman's voice answered.

I recognized the MINT (Military Intelligence) officer's voice, but it was a blast from the past. The last time we'd talked to Qiu was when we rescued her from Harry Flark on Jeratorn station.

"Qiu Loo?" I asked. Her first name was pronounced 'tso' where the t was almost silent. "It's good to hear your voice, but where's Gregor?"

"Commander Belcose is unavailable," she replied. "Is there something I may assist with? And, it is indeed nice to know that you are well."

I exchanged a look with Nick. For Qiu, her response bordered on gushing. I hoped it wasn't a portent of things to come.

"We've run into something and we're trying to raise Anino, but he's not answering. We were hoping you might be able to run him down for us," I said.

"Thomas Anino's status is unknown," she replied too quickly for her to have checked.

"What's going on, Loo?" I asked.

"At 0627, 501.04.21, the Tipperary and Sol systems were invaded by separate Kroerak fleets," she replied.

The date was just yesterday.

"Frak. How many ships?" I asked in disbelief.

"I'm unable to share that information over an unsecured channel," she replied. "The North American and People's Democratic fleets have joined and are actively engaging the enemy."

"What about Mars Protectorate?"

"Sorry, Liam. I can't give that kind of information," she replied.

"What about Tipperary?" I asked. "Are they headed to Grünholz?"

"Curie," she replied. "We believe Thomas Anino was their target. The reports we're receiving say Curie was lost. "

"They've taken the planet?" I asked, horrified. "What about the planetary defense weapons?"

"There's little information available."

"How is this happening? Kroerak don't have fold-space technology," I said, although in the back of my mind, the wormhole conversation we'd just had gave me a bad feeling.

"They arrived via the TransLoc gates in the two systems," Loo replied. "We believe they gained access to the gates and established a connection from their home planets."

"I didn't know that was possible," I said. "Are they still coming through the gates?"

"No," she replied. "At 0632 on 501.04.21, Thomas Anino disabled the TransLoc gates, as well as all Aninonium."

"We're stranded?" Nick observed.

"What do you mean disabled? How do you disable fuel?" I asked. "Jonathan, is this possible?

"It would be consistent with the nature of the fuel," he replied.

"I'm sorry, Liam," Loo replied. "We were unaware of this possibility, but it appears Anino had a fail-safe that was automatically initiated. Because of his foresight, Belirand was able to strand a second wave, consisting of more than eight hundred Kroerak ships, in the deep dark."

"Eight hundred? Loo, how many ships are on their way to Earth?"

"I can't say, but the second wave was smaller than the first," she replied. "Liam, I'm sure you have many questions, but I have urgent duties demanding my attention. Leave this channel open and I'll set an audible news source next to it. I will return as duties permit. I wish I could do more."

"Stay safe, Qiu," I replied. "Hoffen out."

The tension on the bridge had risen steadily at Qui's news and Ada spoke first. "A Kroerak invasion. We have to get back!"

It was one of the often-discussed fears that our crew shared. The Kroerak had made it clear they intended to find their way to humanity, but none of us believed it would happen so soon.

"I'm not sure we can," Nick replied. "You heard Qiu Loo."

"We have to find a way," she replied. "All of my family … all of humanity."

"I agree, Ada," I said, my mind raging with plans and ideas. I needed to stop and think. "If we can get back, we will."

"North America, China and Mars probably only have twelve hundred ships between them," Tabby said. "And I doubt more than three hundred of those could stand up to what we saw back on the Cradle. If that first wave was bigger…" She was referring to the attack Mars Protectorate had made on a planet where the Kroerak forces held thousands of humans as livestock.

"Nick, contact Celina on Lèger Nuage. I'll raise Mom. Jonathan, please monitor the news-feed Qiu set up," I said. "Ada, let's get out of orbit and stand off half a million kilometers. I don't want those Kroerak sneaking up on us. We'll reconvene in an hour."

"Cap?" Marny asked, stopping me in mid-stride.

"What's up?"

"Crew needs food and rest," she said.

I felt a surge of anger and bit off my first response. Who gave a shite about sleep when humanity stood on the verge of a war that threatened our very existence? "Frak, Marny. What would you have us do?"

"Not get lost in the big picture," she said, returning my hard stare. "Look, my family is on Earth and I'm worried about them. I have cousins on warships, likely headed into battle. But we can't do anyone any good if we run ourselves into the ground."

"Fine," I replied, still annoyed. "Let's reconvene in an hour in the officer's mess. Ada, will you work up a watch schedule? If Qiu is right about TransLoc, we won't be going anywhere soon anyway." I pushed my way through the bridge door and walked aft toward Tabby and my quarters.

"Hey," Tabby called, catching up with me in the mess where I'd stopped to grab a cup of coffee.

"What?" I asked, instantly irritated that my voice sounded so hostile.

"You need to take it down a notch," she replied. "Marny's right. We can't run ourselves ragged and expect to operate at full capacity."

"What if the Kroerak invasion is my fault?" I asked.

"What?" Tabby said. "Why would you even say that?"

"We'd never heard of them, but I just had to rescue those people," I said. "I should have left them alone."

"That's stupid," she answered. "Belirand was already there."

"But, they didn't show up in Sol until after we rescued those women."

"Check your facts. They sent a ship more than ten years before that. Remember Buhari? We were all there and I know for a fact we had no other choice," Tabby replied, slamming a quantum comm crystal on the mess table. "Stop being such a self-absorbed little pissant. You have a crew that depends on you and if you hadn't noticed, we're stranded in a system overrun by Kroerak."

Tabby turned and walked away, muttering to herself.

"Where are you going?" I asked.

"I'm going to go work out," she said waving a hand over her head, but not turning back. "Get your head out of your ass, Hoffen."

I picked up the comm crystal and palmed my way into our quarters.

Jester Ripples was already in the room. "Tabitha Masters is angry with you," he said. "Her idiom referencing your head was not very complimentary."

"What do you think, Jester Ripples? Did our visit to Cradle cause the Kroerak to attack humanity?" I asked.

"I do not believe Liam Hoffen is being sufficiently specific," Jester Ripples answered. "I am certain you already know that the Kroerak has been aware of humanity for a significant amount of time before your arrival. It can only be a question of timing with the Kroerak."

I blew out an annoyed sigh. Jester Ripples wouldn't answer the question because I hadn't asked it to his liking. I knew it wasn't his fault, but at that moment I was not in the best frame of mind. "Fine. Do *you* think our attack on the Cradle caused the Kroerak to attack earlier?"

"It is possible," he answered. "It is more likely that the timing of the attack is related to the Kroerak overcoming the technical challenge of interfacing with a TransLoc gate. I do not believe Liam Hoffen participated or has sufficient knowledge to share that information."

I swallowed hard. His logic was reasonable, but I couldn't escape the feeling I'd betrayed the entire human race. Defeated, I sat in the chair at my desk and slid the quantum crystal into its receptacle.

"Petersburg, this is *Intrepid*, come in. Petersburg, this is *Intrepid*. Come in, please. Over." I stared at the crystal; willing someone to answer.

"Greetings, *Intrepid*. Merrie here. Is this Liam?" Merrie's voice was upbeat as usual.

"Copy that, Merrie," I answered. "Is Mom around?"

"You're calling pretty late. Should I wake her?" Merrie asked. I checked the time, it was 0100 on Ophir's new and thriving city of Libertas. Petersburg station had moved their geosynchronous orbit to rest directly above the city and thus, had synchronized clocks to make commerce easier.

"You should wake her," I said.

"Stand by," Merrie replied.

Ten minutes later I heard shuffling in the background. "Liam? Is everyone okay?" Mom asked.

"How soon will Ophir's TransLoc gate be online?" I asked. Ordinarily, a TransLoc gate took over a year to build, but it could be brought up more quickly if you were willing to rough it. Mars had been dropping massive quantities of Sol-based steel into the Ophir system and I knew the gate was close to coming online.

"Within the next ten-day," she replied. "Is that why you called? Where are you? I thought you were chasing another Belirand crystal."

"Mom, who's in the room with you?"

"Just me. Merrie said you sounded stressed."

"Yesterday two Kroerak fleets invaded Sol and Tipperary. They used the TransLoc gates to do it," I said. "You can't let that gate come online."

"How is it that Greg doesn't know about that?" she asked.

"Munay? As in Commander Munay of the *George Ellory Hale*?" I asked. "I thought he would have returned to Sol by now." *Intrepid* hadn't been back to Petersburg station for several months, but last I remembered, Munay and his ship were due to set sail.

"You know the Navy," she replied. "Hurry up and wait. Apparently, Mars Protectorate wanted to leave a capable crew in system to protect their investment."

At face value, it was a reasonable idea. Mars Protectorate was expending extraordinary capital to expand its newly claimed territory, Ophir. It was reasonable they would leave some force behind that had teeth. Something in how she referred so informally to Commander Munay caught my attention, but I let it go for the time being.

"Anino shut down all of fold-space, including the gates," I said. "Munay's ship isn't going anywhere for now. If the Kroerak figure out how to get things turned back on, that gate will bring them right to your door."

"If Anino shut down fold-space, then where are you?" Mom asked, picking up on the concept very quickly.

"Dwingeloo galaxy, system J-F99214," I said. "Two habitable moons, but we have a local bug problem."

"How big of a problem?"

"Single cruiser class ship," I said. "I think they've been here for the better part of a century and a half. They're not a huge problem, unless we're stranded here for an excessive period of time."

"That's a lot of weight for *Intrepid*," she replied.

"Copy that, but it's slower by half than we are," I said. "We just need to stay clear of it."

"You said Tipperary, too? What about Jack, Celina and Jake?" she asked.

"Nick's reaching out to them right now," I said.

"Copy that," she replied. "I'll contact Munay. I just talked to him this evening. I can't imagine he didn't know, but I suspect he's not cleared to talk about it. Are you doing okay otherwise?"

"I suppose," I said. "Can't help but think I had a hand in the Kroerak's timing. Tabby says I have my head awkwardly placed, biologically speaking. Jester Ripple's words, not hers."

Mom laughed, a sound I found comforting. "Listen to her, Liam. You tend to wallow and it's not productive. Your priority is the safety of your crew. After that, you can work on saving the galaxy. The most common failure for an officer isn't incompetence, it's being paralyzed by indecision. It's okay to question yourself, but now is not the time."

I felt as if a weight had rolled from my shoulders. She was right. I had to live in the moment and let everything else work itself out.

"Be safe, Mom," I said. "And for the record, Munay's a pretty good guy. I think Dad would have liked him."

"Liam."

"Love you, Mom. *Intrepid* out."

"What will we do now?" Jester Ripples asked.

"We shall make dinner," I said, picking up the small blue alien and exiting into the hallway. I found Marny already at work in the galley.

"Heya, Cap." She smiled at me cheerfully, searching my face for the reproach I'd shown her earlier on the bridge.

"Sorry I bit your head off," I said, setting Jester Ripples on a stainless-steel stool magnetically clamped to the floor.

"Get things worked out?" she asked. It was one of the things I liked most about Marny. She wasn't even remotely complex, emotionally. If she had a problem, she'd say something and she wasn't easily offended.

"I've decided to stay in the moment," I said, repeating a phrase Marny often used on me. "That is, after some input from Tabby and Mom."

Marny guffawed. "Pointed input, I take it?"

"Tabitha Masters suggested he had struck an anatomically impossible relationship between his cranium and his rectum," Jester Ripples offered.

"Is that so?"

"Jester Ripples and I came out to help with dinner," I said, hoping to change the conversation.

"Perfect timing, in that case," Marny replied. "We need cookies." She pinched a recipe from her HUD and flung it at me. It was a recipe I'd made before, so I joined her in the narrow galley and pulled out the ingredients.

Forty minutes later, the three of us had place settings for the entire crew set out. Marny had gone all out, preparing one of our favorite dishes of noodles with a red sauce and fresh, hot bread.

I felt hands wrap around my waist from behind. "Sorry I pushed on you," Tabby's voice whispered in my ear.

I leaned back into her, accepting her comfort. "I had it coming," I said. "And, for the record, you'll have to ask Jester Ripples for his interpretation on what you said."

She laughed softly, her breath brushing my cheek. "Maybe we shouldn't fight in front of the kids."

"Fighting is fine," I said, turning into her. "Otherwise, how would we make up?" I leaned in and kissed her, not minding how sweaty she was.

"Hey guys, maybe you could make up after dinner?" Ada said.

"Food's hot," Marny said. "Everyone sit. Cap, you have anything you want to say before we dig in?"

"I do." I placed a bucket laden with ice and beer on the table and passed out drinks. When I got to Ada, I pulled a half-liter of white wine out and handed it to her. Jonathan was fine with beer, but I handed Jester Ripples a pouch of a red fruit juice he particularly appreciated.

After taking a long drink, I sat at the table, rubbing Tabby's arm affectionately. "The situation is pretty clear. For the foreseeable future, we're stuck in this solar system with a Kroerak cruiser and a Felio ghost fleet. Our *first* order of business is equilibrium. And by that, I mean I want to take out that cruiser."

"We wouldn't stand a chance," Tabby retorted, picking up her beer.

I smiled. "Au contraire, ma cherie." I waggled my eyebrows suggestively. "Jonathan, how many Kroerak ships were in the initial assault on the Felio fleet?"

"Fifty-two ships."

"Any reason to believe there is more than a single ship remaining?" I asked.

"Cap, you're just my kind of crazy." Marny tipped her beer in my direction and we bumped the pouches together.

HONOR IN SACRIFICE

"Ohh," I complained and rolled over, my leg flopping onto Tabby's naked back.

"Shh." Tabby pushed her head into a pillow.

I rolled back the other way and reached into the night stand for two hangover med-patches. I gingerly placed one on my forehead. Relief was almost instantaneous as the nanites quickly replicated and streamed through my body, undoing whatever damage our night of drinking had done.

While the nanites worked, I installed my earwig and checked the time. It was 1000. We'd gotten to bed at somewhere after 0100 and I vaguely recalled Jonathan offering to take an extended bridge watch.

Establish comm, Jonathan.

"Good morning, Captain," he replied. "I trust your rest cycle was satisfactory?"

"Very much so," I answered. "Everything still quiet?"

"Smooth sailing, Captain," he answered. "There are no incidents to report."

"Copy that. Hoffen out."

"Could you talk *louder*?" Tabby complained, pulling a second pillow over her head. I considered her, trying to find the break in her skin just below the top of her pelvis, where human tissue turned to synthetic. I was soon distracted, as my eyes traced over her bottom and down her long legs. I still couldn't imagine what she saw in me. I stood, turned and then launched myself onto the bed, landing on Tabby's back. I ignored her groans of pain and playfully slapped the med-patch onto her butt, then ran my hands down the side of her chest, allowing my fingers to search for the reward I knew she had pressed against the covers.

"The patch doesn't work as well down there," Tabby said with a laugh as she lifted and pushed me onto my back, rolling us both over. I accepted her movement and successfully snagged the payload I'd been searching for. "And, don't be starting something you can't finish."

***

"Your jab is really improving," Tabby said as we walked back from the gym.

"Appreciate you slowing it down," I said. "It's fun landing a combo occasionally."

"That's awesome, right?" Tabby replied cheerily. "Marny found a resistance program for our suits. It simulates different gravities. She likes it because she can train in earth's gravity."

"You weighed yourself down? I hate to ask, what were you running?" I said.

"Two point five," she replied.

I'd long ago accepted Tabby's physical dominance. Per her doctor, Tabby's body was having an unusual, although not unprecedented, response to the artificial muscles. Where most people with similar catastrophic injuries peaked rather quickly at ten to twenty percent improvement in strength, Tabby continued to grow stronger and stronger, although her rate of growth had slowed with time.

I palmed the security panel that controlled entry into the bridge, having already showered in the gym's head.

"Captain on the bridge," Marny announced as Tabby and I entered. Instinctively, I glanced at the vid-screen that occupied the entire forward bulkhead. The star field ahead of us was foreign but no danger lurked as far as I could tell.

"Okay, now that we're all rested up, what's our first step?" I asked, clapping my hands together. Getting a good night's sleep and spending time with Tabby had done amazing things for my attitude.

"I might have something," Nick said. "Remember the

algorithms Jester Ripples discovered?"

"Sure. And you said something about how the fleet traveled through a wormhole to get here. Is it as easy as reprogramming our engines?" I asked.

"No. We need to replace *Intrepid's* TransLoc engines with Felio jump drives, but we have to leave our TransLoc drives behind. Our cargo bay is too small. Worse, *Intrepid* needs to be physically adjacent to whichever ship we scavenge the jump drives from," he replied.

"And that requires us to go back to the fleet and take out that Kroerak sentinel?" I turned to face him. "Are we really willing to leave our TransLoc drives behind?"

"We have the intellectual property to manufacture them," Nick said. "The critical component for TransLoc remains the Aninonium."

"Cap, something's been bothering me," Marny interjected. "The Kroerak warriors have been in system for a hundred-fifty stans, give or take. Why haven't they eaten the bodies of the Felio?"

"We believe the system likely supported two species: Felio and Musi," Jonathan replied. "The Musi are physically smaller than Felio. The more significant question is why have we found no Musi? Their absence is conspicuous. We have found smaller corpses but they bear similar suit designations and orientation to other nearby Felio. Our conclusion is that the smaller Felio are juveniles."

"Orientation?" Tabby asked.

Jonathan tossed an image forward from his HUD to the primary vid-screen. For a moment, I was stunned as we considered the two figures, floating in space in an embrace. The darkened helmet of the smaller of the two was turned sideways and lay on the chest of the larger. A sense of melancholy settled over me as I imagined the pair's final moments together as they ran out of breathable atmosphere.

"That's sad," Ada said, breaking the spell Jonathan had innocently cast.

"Aside from the obvious tragedy, why is it significant?" I asked.

"A hundred and fifty years is a long time to go without a food source," Marny replied. "Even as inelegant as the warriors are in EVA, they would certainly have figured out how to retrieve those bodies. And maybe it's just me, but the Kroerak that chased us seemed off - different."

"Frantic." I finished the sentence for her. She was right, the Kroerak were aggressive on a good day, but the memory of the bugs crawling over each other trying to get at me was still fresh in my mind. "It's an interesting point, but I'm not sure how it helps us take out that cruiser."

"Agreed, Cap. It's just been bothering me."

"It looks like there weren't any Kroerak casualties," Tabby said. "Were the Felio overwhelmed?"

"The Felio crew held out for thirty minutes before the Kroerak critically damaged the cruiser *Cold Mountain Stream*," Jonathan said.

"What was that name?" I asked.

Nick picked up on my confusion. "Felio ships are all named for natural objects and *Cold Mountain Stream* was the cruiser where you found the quantum comm crystal."

"We have reconstructed the battle if you would like to see it," Jonathan said. "We had to manufacture some of the ship positions, but believe it to be eighty-five percent accurate."

"You and your percentages," I said. "Put it on the main holo." The projector I referred to would set up a holographic field in the center of the bridge, just in front of the captain's chair. It was positioned so that every bridge station had a good view.

The scene opened with the Felio fleet closing on the green-blue moon we called 'Dorf,' given its designation of D-04. The ships, which we'd seen battered and broken, were replaced with brightly painted originals sailing in proud formation.

"What are they doing?" Tabby asked, impatiently.

Before anyone could answer, three long ships sailed into view. They were smooth and narrow except for large, slowly rotating wheels connected by spokes to the hulls. On the inside edge of the rotating wheels, gleaming glass windows reflected the bright light of the system's only star. It was with a sense of majesty the three ships entered orbit behind the proud fleet.

"Are those transport ships, Jonathan?" Nick asked.

"Yes. The circular devices at mid-point are rotating at a speed that generates .85g. This gives us insight as to conditions on their home planet. We believe each ship capable of transporting forty thousand personnel," Jonathan continued.

"Forty thousand?" Ada asked. "How long are those ships?"

"Three thousand eight hundred meters," Jonathan answered. "The diameter of each of the living spaces is nine hundred meters."

"That's gigantic," Ada replied.

"Look there." Tabby stabbed her finger into the middle of the projection as a new cylindrical ship broke through the cloud cover of the small moon. Seconds later, five more ships emerged.

"They're abandoning the planet," Nick said. "They had plenty of time for preparation. Otherwise, how would they have known to build the transports?"

"Which is what we saw planet-side," I said. "Everything on Dorf was neatly packed away. The only chaos was at the spaceport where there were wrecks of ships, which, if I'm not mistaken are identical to those breaking through the atmosphere."

"That is correct, Captain," Jonathan replied as the ships from the moon split off, each docking at the ends of the much larger, long-range vessels.

"Didn't you say those ships lifting off from the planet held five-hundred souls?" I asked.

"An interesting phrase, Captain," Jonathan said. "Aside from the interesting philosophical question of what constitutes a soul, your recollection is correct."

"Six ships would hold three thousand," Tabby said. "That's more than thirty trips. Do they have enough fuel? How long will that take?"

"This evacuation continued for seventy hours." Jonathan accelerated the timeline and we watched as the cylindrical ships returned to the moon only to reappear, dock with the transports, unload, undock and repeat the entire process once again. "If I could draw your attention." At the edge of the holo-field the bow of a Kroerak ship appeared and was soon joined by the remainder of the fleet Jonathan had previously described.

"The Felio are too late, those transports will never get away," Tabby observed, her voice more panicked than I'd have expected.

"The Felio are a heroic species," Jonathan said as we watched the warships roll across the field of battle, prepared to meet the superior Kroerak head on. "We find this difficult to review, but wish to honor the bravery that is exhibited."

Immediately, two transports spooled up their engines, turning away from the battle as they did. The third transport, which we'd observed having a slower turnaround with the surface ships, sat steady, obviously unwilling to leave behind the approaching personnel transfer ships. Mystifyingly, the two cylindrical ships turned back toward the moon.

"What are they doing?" Tabby asked, her voice rising. I got up from my chair and stood next to her, wrapping an arm around her waist.

"This happened a hundred-fifty-stans ago, Tabbs," I soothed.

She took in a deep breath and blew it out. "I know."

"Look. The third long-range transport is leaving," Nick said. "The transfer ships are sacrificing themselves."

I felt a lump in my throat, blinked back tears, and turned my attention to the battle. Unexpectedly, the Felio ships were doing very well. What they gave up in armor, they gained in focus and the first ship to be destroyed was a Kroerak destroyer-class ship.

The battlefield changed as the Kroerak fleet became aware of the long-range transports making an attempt at escape. Instead of taking on the Felio fleet directly, the Kroerak changed their tactics and worked to intercept the transports.

"The long-range ships aren't accelerating fast enough," Ada observed. "They'll never make it."

As the Kroerak engaged the Felio, they lost two more mid-sized ships. I wanted to cheer, but I knew why the Kroerak were sacrificing their ships, as did the Felio fleet commander. A few minutes later, one of the largest battle cruisers broke through the Felio line. We watched it labor to run down the trailing long-range transport ship. The battle cruiser's armor took a beating as the Felio gave chase, but the Felio weaponry was mostly ineffective against it. Just as the Kroerak entered weapons range, three light Felio frigates streaked from the otherwise disciplined formation and sacrificed themselves into the aft of the enemy battle cruiser.

For a moment, it looked like the sacrifice had been successful. The huge ship shuddered under the impact and explosion causes by the smaller ships. From my observation, there was no chance the battle cruiser would survive the collisions.

"Once the transports reach this point," Jonathan indicated a location a considerable distance from the fray, "the Kroerak will have no capacity to overtake the fleeing transports before they reach what we believe to be the entrance to a naturally occurring wormhole."

"They can make it," Ada offered hopefully.

"No," Tabby replied, defeat in her voice. "The Kroerak ship fired a fusillade." Tabby turned away and rested her face on my shoulder. I stroked her hair and held her, knowing she was reliving her last moments aboard the *Theodore Dunham*.

The Kroerak had released a well-aimed sheet of the lance-shaped kinetic weapons. At the last moment, the long-range transport seemed to recognize its peril and attempted to execute a turn, but it was too late. The wave of destruction crashed first across the aft of the long ship and stitched destruction along the hull until contacting the habitation wheel. At the same time, the Kroerak battle cruiser and the Felio long-range transport exploded brilliantly.

"Forty-thousand souls," I lamented quietly.

"I can't watch, Jonathan," Ada said, her voice husky with emotion. I didn't have to see her face to know she'd been crying.

"We apologize for distressing you. Perhaps this was ill-considered," Jonathan replied.

"No," Marny said. "Keep going, we owe it to them."

"She's right. Keep going, Jonathan," Ada answered.

We turned back to the virtual battlefield and watched as, even in the face of critical failure, the Felio fleet moved quickly and repositioned themselves between the escaping transports and the rest of the Kroerak. The Felio fleet moved as a unit, but instead of rigidly sailing in strict formation, the individual ships moved fluidly through the battle space. For almost twenty minutes, it appeared the battle might go either way, which I found remarkable given just how much the Felio gave up in armor and weaponry. In many cases, it was simply a matter of confusing one Kroerak ship into firing its deadly maelstrom into the path of another by sacrificing themselves. Each minute of battle, paid for by the blood of the courageous Felio Navy, allowed the transport ships to separate further from the battle.

"They can make it," Tabby whispered. I breathed a sigh of relief when the two remaining transports, carrying an estimated eighty thousand souls, crossed the imaginary point of safety.

Apparently, Jonathan's calculations were the same as the Felio were using. The battle shifted at that moment. The Felio fleet broke from combat and accelerated away from the battlefield. With my AI's help, I checked their heading. It would put them right where we'd found the floating wreckage.

"Why are they running?" Ada asked.

"Civilians on the planet's surface," Marny replied. "They're leading them away."

"They're noble," Ada said, stepping up next to Tabby and sliding an arm around her waist from the other side.

"They'll lose their entire fleet," Tabby said. "They already know that."

Jonathan sped up the sequence as the Kroerak gave chase. As we already knew, the battle ended on the fourth day, when the Felio turned and made a final stand. Unlike the previous battle, this engagement ended quickly. The Felio crew, seemingly accepting their fate, were cut down within twenty minutes of starting the engagement.

"Why didn't they just jump back with the transports?" Ada asked. It was a question I'd been wrestling with. In our estimation, there were perhaps a few thousand civilians left behind on Dorf and the value of the fleet was considerable if the goal had been to defend them. The quiet on the bridge suggested that no one had an answer to this question.

"Jonathan, turn it off, please. We can all watch the remaining sequences on our own time if we want." I released Tabby and stepped onto the small platform where the captain's chair sat. "That was hard to watch, but we learned valuable things about the Kroerak and the people we've come to know as the Felio. Now we need to use that information so we don't give the Kroerak another victory. It's not unusual for us to be the underdog in a fight. I'd say most of us don't even consider it a fight unless that's our starting point. The Kroerak aren't brilliant tacticians. They're thugs. Bullies. Every problem for them is a steel rivet and every solution an impact-hammer. The warriors left behind are starving. We caused them to expend resources in chasing us and that's going to make them more frantic. We will press that advantage."

"What about the fact that we're stuck here?" Tabby asked.

"We're going to leave the problems of tomorrow for tomorrow," I said, softening my tone. "Think about it. The worst case is we're stuck on Dorf with the responsibility of rebuilding the human population."

Tabby quirked her head to the side, not sure she'd heard me quite right. She turned to Ada whose eyebrows shot up in surprise. They shared a shocked look as understanding dawned.

"You're a sick man, Liam Hoffen," Tabby said, shaking her head.

IN THE MOMENT

"I still don't like this idea, Hoffen," Tabby said.

"I trust you," I said, exiting *Sugar* and stepping onto *Cold Mountain Stream's* flight deck. Tabby, Nick, Jester Ripples, and I had left *Intrepid* twenty thousand kilometers away from the ghost fleet's final resting place and flown *Sugar* and *Rowdy* carefully through the graveyard so as not to wake up our ultimate prey, the Kroerak cruiser. Our fighter ships had significant firepower but were no reasonable match for the heavy ship. That said, the cruiser couldn't easily lay a finger on us, either. It was an uninteresting stalemate and best to avoid the complications that might arise.

It was no easy matter to exit *Sugar* as we had to bring an external bladder to off-load *Sugar's* nav-gel. In an emergency, we could exhaust the material, but with the bladder system Nick rigged up, we could recover the gel and exit the fighter without losing tactical capability. That said, *Sugar* looked ridiculous with a big bag of goo floating off its bow.

"I'm out, Jester Ripples. Time to shove off." I grasped the little alien's shoulder and smiled at him through my armored helmet.

"I'd prefer to stay, Liam Hoffen," Jester Ripples argued a final time.

"I know, buddy. I'll be safer if I'm not worrying about you getting hurt," I said. "And Nick needs control of *Sugar's* gun, but it can't be from the deck.

I smiled as Jester Ripples pursed his blue-green lips, an expression he'd learned from Tabby. Fortunately, he acquiesced and lowered the fighter's canopy, allowing the nav-gel bladder to refill the cockpit.

Bait it is, I said to myself and turned toward the passageway that led into the ship. Jonathan had given me a device to deploy once I was aboard. He and Nick had manufactured what amounted to a camera painting device; a fist sized, autonomous vehicle that sprayed a material containing tiny sensors on surrounding surfaces. The sensors recorded and transmitted both video and infrared.

"You're clear, Liam," Nick said as I stared down the long, dark passageway. I sighed and leaned forward causing myself to move. The notion of hunting for Kroerak had sounded easier while still aboard *Intrepid*.

I'd chosen to travel light, only carrying a dozen grenade marbles, a plasma cutter, and my favorite Ruger pistol. Speed would be my best asset and the ammo packs for the 816s were too cumbersome. And really, what could go wrong?

Cruising down the hallway of a ship that had been dead for a hundred-fifty stans was just plain creepy. Even though I trusted the video devices being laid out in front of me, I couldn't help but feel I was being followed. At first, I sluffed off the feeling as natural paranoia. I was in a bad place, after all.

"Nick, I think I'm being followed," I finally admitted. "Could there be something in the tween decks?" The ship had a common design; the actual decks were separated by smaller spaces, called tween decks, where mechanicals were run.

"It's possible," he replied. "We don't have eyes in there. Are you seeing something?" Getting a visual was the only way I'd logically be able to pick up on our quarry. Atmosphere had been vented long ago and vibrations wouldn't transmit through a vacuum.

"No." I pushed forward with an increasing feeling of unease.

A cruiser is a big ship. So much so that even with open hatches, it would take at least thirty minutes to traverse the main corridors on each deck. Unfortunately, the hatches weren't all open and I finally pulled up on the third of seven decks. For whatever reason, I was okay with moving forward, but getting trapped at the end of a passageway bothered me a lot.

Something Marny drilled into me was not to ignore gut feelings. The sense of dread I felt grew as I approached the hatch.

"What's going on, Liam?" Tabby asked. "Your blood pressure is elevated."

"I don't like it," I said.

"We have as much time as you need," she said. "Don't get pinned in."

I nodded, but didn't answer. My HUD showed the hatch ahead, free of obstruction. All I needed to do was release the latch.

"Back off your bot, Jonathan," I instructed and reeled out a strip of explosive fire-wire from my waist pouch. Technically, it wasn't explosive as much as it was something that got hot - really fast - and easily burned through most things. That's not to say there weren't explosions. You applied the wire by trapping it against the surface to be burned with an epoxy that set up hard and momentarily resisted the heat. Whatever got burned created enough gas that an explosion was the most common side-effect.

Having traced a line around the entire hatch, I drew an 'X' through the center and backed off to a stubby hallway I'd passed only a few meters back. Once I had cover, I ignited the fire-wire. A wave of gas and metal shrapnel blew past.

"Liam, go!" Nick's excited voice filled my ears. I didn't need any encouragement. I ducked out of the short hallway and rocketed back down the passageway, retracing my steps away from the blown door.

"Coming out of the deck, five meters around the next corner," Nick warned.

I reached for two grenade balls and hurled them toward the forty-five-degree bumper at the end of the hallway, programming them to explode in three seconds. Never would I have expected my pod-ball training to be so valuable. It was an easy shot, although I doubted the Kroerak would appreciate it. I smiled grimly as I rolled over in mid-flight and bounded off the same bumper the grenades had left only a moment before. The Kroerak warriors, still emerging from the hatch in the deck below, never knew what hit them as the grenades exploded less than a meter from their position. The force wasn't enough to kill them, but they were thrown violently to the sides as I screamed past.

"Nice move. Now don't get cocky, you have five warriors on your tail," Tabby cut in. Strictly speaking, she shouldn't be talking on the tactical channel unless she had something of critical importance. It made me wonder if she thought I got cocky too often. Of course, this was usually the point where Marny's voice reminded me to stay in the moment. At least, she would have if she'd been in my head at that moment.

By the time I made it to *Cold Mountain Stream's* flight deck, Nick reported twenty-three Kroerak warriors had joined the chase. Instead of following me back, the sensor painting bot had continued forward and was left unmolested by the frantic Kroerak.

Instead of retreating and jumping to the relative safety of the deep dark, I hovered just off the flight-deck, five meters out into space. What the Kroerak didn't know was that *Rowdy* and *Sugar* sat below sight line.

"Don't shoot right away," I said. "I want the whole lot of 'em."

"Copy," Tabby said.

The first Kroerak ignored all wisdom and launched itself straight at me. With no mechanism for adjusting flight, the desperate bug was easily dodged. The next few ran up to the edge of the flight deck and were soon joined by a boiling mass of angry bugs.

"That's all of them," Nick announced as *Sugar* and *Rowdy* rose up, gaining a clear view of the flight deck.

The Kroerak warrior's armor is heavy, almost impenetrable to any weapon a person can carry. The same cannot be said for the weapons mounted on the Tison 4-Xs. I'd never been outside the craft when the sleek fighters' turrets were fired. I was struck by just how ridiculously powerful the tiny ships were as their guns tore through the bugs as if their armor was made of soap bubbles.

"That's for trying to take my fiancé out for lunch," Tabby said, as she turned *Rowdy* and blasted the warrior that had inadvertently escaped destruction by launching itself into space.

So went the clearing of *Cold Mountain Stream, Morning Sun on Snow* and *Peat Claws*. In all, it took three days of switching between Tabby and me playing bait, but we cleared the big cruiser and two smaller destroyer class ships. We attracted the attention of the Kroerak cruiser more than once, but found it had little interest in chasing our fighters for more than twenty or thirty minutes and even refused to fire on us after the second time.

"Don't take their complacence as an invitation to get sloppy," Marny warned as we rejoined the rest of the crew aboard *Intrepid* at the end of the third day.

"I don't think it's complacence," Jonathan said. "We've had an opportunity to inspect the Kroerak corpse Captain Hoffen dispatched aboard *Intrepid*. The assessment that the Kroerak are starving appears to be well founded. Their bodies are extraordinarily efficient at storing energy. Couple this with an ability to enter a low-energy hibernation and their roles as sentinels is easily understood. They do, however, have limits. We believe their lack of interest in chasing *Intrepid* or even *Rowdy* and *Sugar* is more related to energy conservation than complacence."

"Have you finished manufacturing the equipment we need?" I asked, changing the subject. Marny's warning was reasonable and Jonathan was right. I wasn't interested in getting bogged down in the minutiae however.

"Yes. It will require a close pass by *Intrepid* as we've discussed," Jonathan answered. "It is reasonable to believe the Kroerak will respond to our presence."

"I'm up for it," Ada replied. "It's easier now that I know where they'll be coming from."

"I want everyone to get a full sleep cycle," I said.

***

Ten hours later, Tabby, Nick and I were positioned in *Intrepid's* cargo hold. I had the gravity dialed down to 0.1g and as soon as Ada dropped from hard-burn, the supplies we'd replicated would unweigh. Nearly two metric tonnes, currently wrapped in loose packaging, would be more manageable to move with the stevedore bots we had aboard.

"We're coming in warm, Liam," Ada informed over the tactical channel about the same time we started getting a view of the familiar Felio fleet. 'Coming in warm,' was a new term Ada had invented. The Kroerak were aware of our actions, but were not moving from their position to chase us down.

"What do you think they think we're doing?" I asked. "Have they no curiosity?"

"Don't you remember teasing Filbert with a string?" Tabby asked. "After a while, if he wasn't allowed to catch the string, he'd just give up."

"We're a go, Liam," Ada announced as we pulled alongside *Cold Mountain Stream*.

Nick negotiated the stevedore bots as Tabby and I transferred smaller, more sensitive components between the two ships. We repeated the process with *Peat Claws* and *Morning Sun on Snow*.

"Good luck, kids," Ada called as Nick, Marny, Tabby, Jester Ripples and I stayed behind on *Morning Sun on Snow*.

Our big plan was straightforward. Fortunately, Felio technology was like an earlier evolution of human spaceship engine design. While the engines were horribly inefficient with their fuel, and fragile by our current standards, they were also simple. What the Felio had that I was unfamiliar with was their regenerative energy cells for powering the ships' many systems. Like *Cold Mountain Stream*, the power on *Morning Sun on Snow* was shut down and simply waiting to be turned back on. We wouldn't do that right away, as it would draw too much attention.

Upon entry, we split up, sending Tabby and Jester Ripples to the bridge to work on control systems. Tabby was outfitted with an 816 and a full pack of ammo. Jester Ripples had a toolbox containing tools he'd designed and manufactured himself. Marny, outfitted similarly to Tabby, accompanied Nick and me as we headed straight for the disabled engines.

We'd started with *Morning Sun on Snow* because it was the least damaged ship and still retained much of its original firepower. Like other ships in the fleet, the Kroerak had targeted its engines. Once disabled, the weapons systems had become uninteresting.

"This doesn't seem crazy to you?" Nick asked as we positioned sheets of steel onto the starboard engine.

"You'll have to be more specific," I said. "Is it that we're in a system unknown to most of humanity or that we're repairing an alien ship to help us defeat an entirely different alien species which is trying to wipe out humanity?"

"I guess I was thinking we should be applying the patch to the interior wall," he replied. "Less pressure on the welds. But sure, if you put it that way, that stuff's pretty crazy too."

"You dork!" I exclaimed and followed him around into the dark cavern of the huge engine.

As it turned out, simple design was a relative term and we spent several hours shaping and applying patches to the engine, only to discover we were missing a few parts. It wasn't that we couldn't manufacture them, but I wanted the work to be done. Stress about the upcoming battle was starting to wear on me. There was no getting around the fact that we'd be taking on a Kroerak cruiser with ships that had been sitting idle and unmaintained for a century and a half.

"How much progress would you say you've made?" Ada asked as we joined her back aboard *Intrepid* and dug into the food Jonathan had prepared.

I shrugged and looked at Nick. "Ten percent?"

"That's probably right," he agreed. "We're getting better at it, but there's a lot of damage and *Cold Mountain Stream* got hit harder than the other two."

"We'll take the Tisons over after we get some rack-time and get going again," I said.

***

As much as I wanted to be patient and meet each day without expectation, I found myself growing more and more annoyed as the days stretched on. I'd given the crew an impossible task - to repair three ship's engines all while under the watchful eye of the enemy.

"This next part could get dicey," Nick said on the twentieth day. We'd only been run off three different times by what amounted to Kroerak saber rattling. They would fire up their engines, move in our direction and when we scrambled away, settle back into position.

"What's that?" I asked.

"Engine test," Nick said. "There's nothing more we can do without trying to fire them up."

"Meh, I got this," I said.

"How?" Nick asked.

"I'm not just a pretty face," I answered. "We've talked about this. You and Tabby need to get your butts back to *Intrepid*."

"Even if you get underway, they're not going to just let you go."

"*Sugar* will keep me safe," I said.

"Not against those lances. Remember, you won't have agility on your side anymore," Nick worried.

"See you on the other side, buddy."

"I am not sure I understand the human idiom 'other side,' Liam Hoffen," Jester Ripples said as we climbed into *Sugar* and filled it with nav-gel from the exterior bladder.

"Other side? It's abstract. I'm explaining that I'll see him when we're done with this mission," I said.

I squirted us out from the hangar bay of *Cold Mountain Stream*. Our plan was to first test the destroyer, *Peat Claws*. After having worked on it, we believed its systems to have been most effectively repaired. Part of our work had included extending each ship's controls to a cavity we'd hewn out from the underside of each ship. The cavity was just large enough for us to dock a single Tison fighter within.

"I have withheld my questions, but I don't understand what you hope to gain from this configuration," Jester Ripples said as we connected to *Peat Claws*.

"You've hung in there for this long, give me ten more minutes and if it isn't clear by then, I'll explain everything," I said.

"Very well, Liam Hoffen."

Hail Intrepid.

"Ada, we're ready for your close pass," I said.

"Copy that, Captain. Close pass in four minutes," she answered. The plan was to test the engines and if successful, separate *Peat Claws* from the rest of the fleet. Its engines were bigger than we needed, but could be transferred to *Intrepid*.

"Contact in twenty seconds," Ada updated us on her progress.

"Good enough for me. Jester Ripples," I said. "Try starting up those engines, if you would."

"They are started, Liam Hoffen," he replied almost immediately.

"Seriously? We've been struggling to repair these engines for twenty days and they just start on the first try?"

"That is right. They are not complex machines."

I wasn't about to argue and pushed forward on *Sugar's* stick, to which *Peat Claws'* control systems had been slaved. Satisfyingly, the ship lurched forward.

"They're on us, Liam," Ada answered. "Marny hit them with two missiles and we appear to have their full attention."

I pulled back on the stick and halted our progress as an idea quickly took root. I made quick gestures and rapidly worked up a navigation plan.

"What are you doing, Liam Hoffen?" Jester Ripples asked.

"Transmit this to Ada," I said.

"Ada, I need you to hit that plan at emergency burn," I said.

"That's awfully close, Liam, are you sure?"

"We have the advantage; they just don't know it. We have to use this," I said. "Jester Ripples, put *Intrepid* and the Kroerak on holo." Instantly, the interior holo field showed *Intrepid* taking a tight curve, swinging around to orient on *Peat Claws* as the Kroerak ship gave chase.

"I'm on your line, Liam. I hope you aren't about to do what I think you're about to do," she said.

"I probably am." I hastily instructed the AI to give me a countdown to *Intrepid* and the Kroerak cruiser's positions. "Marny, don't lose its interest, fire on it if you must."

"Copy that, Cap," Marny replied. "Weapons are free." *Intrepid's* rear facing turrets lit up and while it was an impressive display of fireworks, I knew better than to think it was having any real effect.

"Jester Ripples, when I give the word, I want you to detach us from *Peat Claws*," I said.

The navigation path I'd given Ada would bring her right over the top of us. At the speed she was moving, our timing needed to be perfect.

"Almost there, Jester Ripples," I said and engaged the engines, pulling us up into *Intrepid's* path.

Apparently, I'm only good enough to time a single event. I successfully missed the aft end of *Intrepid* by a small margin. The problem was, I'd placed us into the path of the Kroerak cruiser that was moving just as fast as *Intrepid* and was only moments behind.

Release, I demanded and pushed forward on the stick, causing us to shoot forward as only a Tison can. Unfortunately, the Kroerak captain - or whatever it might be called – decided pulling up was its best evasive maneuver as well. Success came when the Kroerak cruiser struck *Peat Claws'* bow at about dead center, basically, a perfect hit. The minorly unsuccessful part for Jester Ripples and me was when *Sugar* was hit hard and we spun out of control in a random direction.

***

"Liam Hoffen, are you well?" Jester Ripples asked as *Sugar's* automated, secondary systems worked to bring us back to level.

"How long was I out?" I asked.

"It has been thirty-five minutes," Jester Ripples said. "Tabitha Masters is hailing. She requires that you respond."

"Go ahead, Tabby."

"Are you frakking out of your mind? That wasn't the plan!" Her red face appeared on my forward holo display. "You could have died, that ship missed you by ... Gah! That ship *didn't* miss you."

"We're both up, Tabbs." I pinched at the display in front of me. We'd tumbled quite a distance, but Tabby, in *Rowdy*, had accompanied us all the way out. "Yeah, it felt like a good plan at the moment. Did it work?"

"I don't want to tell you, because you'll start to think it was a good idea," she said.

"So, it did work? The Kroerak are gone?" I asked.

"Obliterated," she said, grinning wryly at me. "I don't know if I should kill you or what."

"Let's go with 'or what.'"

"Fine. It was a good move and I know you're really good, but I thought you'd killed yourself, like those Felio did to save their transports."

"I'm nowhere near that heroic," I said.

"Not sure that's true," she said. "Let's get back to *Intrepid*. I'm sure *Sugar* needs some tender-loving care after what you put her through."

"What about me? Don't I need that?"

"We'll see."

THE BLOCKADE

"What's the latest on the invasion?" I asked.

So far, the news reports audibly transmitted from Qiu Loo painted a grim picture. Humanity's hastily assembled fleets had met the Kroerak at five hundred thousand kilometers from Earth and only just repelled the initial assault. The battle finally broke off when the ravaged fleets fell back to Earth's moon. The losses among the combined fleets were reported to exceed sixty thousand sailors and forty percent of the ships.

As for the Tipperary system, Curie fared even worse. As of a few days ago, the resort planet was under Kroerak control. With the TransLoc gates inoperable, there was no hope of a rescue in sight. Unlike Earth, the small planet had few planetary defense weapons and couldn't hope to rebuff a sizable fleet. While we hadn't heard any official confirmation, we believed the attack on Curie was for the single purpose of locating and capturing Thomas Phillipe Anino, the only sentient alive who knew the formula for creating Aninonium.

"I heard from Jack and Celina," Nick said. "Nuage is on alert, but there are no signs of Kroerak. They have an emergency plan to go to the surface in case war comes their way. They signed an emergency peace deal with Oberrhein if it comes to that."

I sighed at the mention of the beautiful cloud state of Nuage. At one time, I'd considered making it my home. The people were friendly and there were opportunities for trading all over the area. Belirand had put an end to that when they'd leveraged the small nation into attempting to detain us. Oberrhein, however, was another thing entirely and they couldn't have represented a starker contrast to Nuage. Set up as an authoritarian state, Oberrhein was a nation that needed a good shakeup.

"I talked to Mom last night. Commander Munay is taking being cut off from the fleet pretty hard," I said. "The last orders he received from Mars Protectorate were to fortify his position, which is difficult with the limited manufacturing on Ophir. I guess he's taken command of the TransLoc gate and Mom hasn't seen much of him since then."

"At least we won't have to worry about that gate coming online while he's there," Nick said.

"Unless he tries to use it to get back to Sol," Tabby said.

"Won't happen unless they get Anino to turn it back on," Nick argued.

"So, what about the wormholes?" I asked. "Can't we just find one that gets us home?"

"According to the information we've pulled from the Felio cruiser, there is only one wormhole in this system. A hundred fifty years ago, it led to the Felio home world," Nick said. "Just to be clear; the phenomena we've been calling wormholes are naturally occurring."

"How did the Kroerak get here?" I asked. "Did they come from the Felio system?"

"They did not," Jonathan replied. "We believe the Kroerak, using their capability to endure long trips over extraordinary periods of time, simply sailed here. It would explain why the Felio had enough time to construct long-range transport ships and execute an orderly withdrawal from the moon."

"Why here? It's a pud-winkle system," I said. "Barely habitable. What would be the point?"

"The wormhole was the Kroerak's target. It bridges a considerable distance between this system and the Felio's home," Jonathan replied. "It's not the moons that are interesting. The Felio belong to a massive, multi-system government called the Confederation of Planets. This wormhole is a gateway to the Aeratroas region of the Dwingeloo galaxy which is ruled by the confederation. This is a strategic point of entry for the Kroerak."

"How can you be sure the Felio have access to the other planets in the Confederation?"

"We aren't. There is absolutely no information in any of the ships that reference Aeratroas, the Confederation of Planets, or even information about the wormhole entrance in this system," Nick said.

"You love this," I said, shaking my head. "You know I'm going to say that doesn't make sense. What you're really saying is that it's the lack of information about Aeratroas and the Confederation that makes you suspicious."

Nick raised his eyebrow and smiled. "It would be impossible for the Felio not to be aware of their numerous neighbors. They would have had ample opportunity to communicate even without the wormhole capability. You're right. The information is conspicuous in its absence."

"I helped Jonathan find that the Felio computer systems had been purged," Jester Ripples said. "The only information on the ship's systems was related to ship functions, current personnel, inhabitants of J-F99214-D-04 and significant stores of information related to this system."

"Okay. I give. I'll accept that this system is interesting because of the wormhole and its access to Felio," I said.

"It's valuable information," Nick said. "This system's location is huge. It gives us some idea where to find the Kroerak. If they were close to Felio, they'd have just sailed there. As it was they chose to come here first."

"Doesn't it seem possible the Kroerak took the wormhole and did to the Felio what they're planning to do to humanity?" I asked. "What if this was their last stop; not their first?

"Doesn't work," Nick said. "Why send the transports through the wormhole if that's the case? No, our choices are simple. We stay here, wait out the war, and hope Anino is still alive and can turn TransLoc back on."

"Or we take a blind leap and jump through the wormhole." Tabby finished his sentence for him and looked at me.

"We'll have to do something," Marny said. "We're about halfway through our consumables. What are you thinking, Cap?"

"I don't think it's up to me," I replied, looking around the wardroom. "I'd like everyone to weigh in. The way I see it is just as Tabby described. We jump into the wormhole blindly and deal with whatever we run into or we wait it out here. Ada, you've been quiet, what do you think we should do?"

"If there is a chance we could help the war at home, we must take it," she replied.

"Marny?"

"Aye, Cap. We're not the type to sit out a fight and I don't see that changing now," she replied.

"Nick?"

"I'm in."

"Jester Ripples?"

"I would very happily construct a dwelling on J-F99214-D-04, but I would not be happy to see my friends leave. I will follow the crew of *Intrepid*," he replied.

"Jonathan?"

"For many human standard decades, it has been our objective to reach Aeratroas," Jonathan answered. "We find the risk acceptable."

"Tabby, what's your answer?"

"Much as I love you, I don't think you'd live long if you tried to force me into settling down, planet-side," she replied. "I'd like to keep moving forward."

"Sounds like we're in agreement. Ada, set in a course. I'd like to start moving those engines right away," I said.

Nick lifted a hand. "We're actually ready to go. All we need to do is raft-up with *Soft Bark* and we'll be in business within a week. Mounting plates are already being manufactured."

***

"She's all yours, Ada," I said.

Nick's estimate for swapping out the engines had been soft by a factor of two, but the miracle, in my mind, was that we made it work at all. The Felio jump drives had been installed and, with a leap of faith, we watched the TransLoc engines float free.

Ada took a deep breath and lifted us away from the Felio destroyer we'd scavenged. "Moment of truth."

"Feels right," I said. *Intrepid* didn't feel any different with the new engine configuration. "How's acceleration?"

Ada punched the stick forward, landing just shy of hard-burn. As far as I could tell, nothing had changed. Nick thought we wouldn't even know modifications had been made, but I wasn't exactly the trusting type when it came to my ship's operation.

"Perfect," Ada agreed.

"That's not the real test," Nick said.

"Oh?"

"Yeah. Just like fold-space, if we get dropped out in the wrong place, we'll be stranded."

"Excellent pep-talk there, Nick. I'll be sure not to think about that while we're inside the wormhole," I said.

"You won't know," Nick replied.

"What do you mean?"

"The wormhole is like a single fold in fold-space. The jump will happen immediately. We'll either get to our destination or we'll be dropped into the deep dark."

"Probably be worth not saying that ever again," I said.

***

Three days later, we arrived at the entrance to the wormhole. I hadn't been sure what to expect. If I was honest, I'd admit that I expected the area to look like all other normal space. As it turned out, that couldn't have been further from the truth.

"It looks like a thunderstorm from home," Marny said. "Only more purple."

Earth storms weren't something I had any experience with, but on Mars we'd seen clouds and rain a few times. It was about as apt a description as I could come up with. Dark purple clouds played across a seven kilometer stretch of space. Bolts of electricity arced irregularly through the clouds and from my perspective, it was far from inviting.

"What crazy person would have run into this and decided to sail their ship through it?" I asked.

"We know little of Dwingeloo wormholes," Jonathan replied. "We are picking up magnetic fluctuations and energy spikes that are quite significant. It is reasonable to expect that a connection of two points in space, so far from each other, would cause local disturbances at that point of connection."

"You really have no idea, do you?" I said.

"We agree with your assessment," Jonathan replied.

"Ada, fire up the wormhole-drive and send us through. Everyone else, strap in. If the Kroerak are on the other side, we won't have more than a few minutes before they're on us."

"Heading in, Liam," Ada replied.

I pulled my shoulder harness over my head and locked it into position as we approached the swirling mass of purple clouds and lightning. *Intrepid* shook and lights briefly flickered as the first strike of lightning hit the armored hull. It was followed by a second hit and then a third. I briefly considered telling Ada to back out, when suddenly we were through.

"Emergency burn. Evasive!" Ada hollered as she pulled on the stick, rolling us hard to starboard, then immediately port, and finally sweeping *Intrepid's* tail downward with our docking thrusters. An explosion rocked the ship and a familiar warning chime sounded. We'd been holed and were leaking atmo.

"I'm on it," Nick said excitedly.

I searched the holo-projection and discovered myriad small devices filling the entirety of local-space in every direction surrounding the ship.

"It's a minefield, Cap," Marny warned.

"All stop!" I ordered.

A second explosion followed as Ada abruptly slowed us. Just as I thought we were in the clear, a third explosion rocked the bow.

"Nick, damage?" I asked. "Marny, hostiles?"

"Affirmative, Cap," Marny replied immediately. As she did, my view zoomed out. Just beyond the mine-field sat a massive, armored space station out of which a veritable armada of ships poured.

"Damage to bow only," Nick replied. "We've sealed all compartments and are maintaining hull integrity. That said, we took some big hits."

"Frak, now what do we do?" Tabby asked.

"Stay put and try not to look threatening," I said. "Nick, do we have any room to maneuver?"

"Not even remotely," he replied and flicked a close-up view of *Intrepid* onto the central holo projector. Somehow, Ada had wedged us into an impossibly small space with mines located only meters from the hull in multiple locations.

"How in Jupiter did we only hit three? Nice flying, Ada."

"We're receiving a hail," Ada announced, her voice shaky with adrenaline.

"Can you translate, Jonathan?"

"It would appear unnecessary," he replied. "The broadcast is multilingual and includes human standard as one of its options."

Accept hail.

"Unidentified vessel, this is Abasi *Coals Between Pads*. You've entered a restricted area and are in violation of Confederation Treaty 7A2093-12. Prepare to heave-to and submit to inspection." The voice was clearly machine generated.

"Any insight, Jonathan?" I asked.

"It is the best possible answer," he explained. "You should indicate that we are requesting safe harbor and would like to register the crew as alien guests of the Confederation of Planets."

"Copy your request, *Coals Between Pads*," I replied. "This is Captain Liam Hoffen of *Intrepid*. I request safe harbor for my ship, *Intrepid*, and am formally requesting Confederation of Planets' alien guest status for my crew."

For a moment, all that was transmitted was a yowling sound and then a more understandable voice could be heard. "Captain Liam Hoffen, you are currently illegally located in restricted space. As such, we are unable to grant your request for safe harbor. You will be treated as a violator of laws until a tribunal can rule on the matter. Your request for *Pherani* is granted and your crew will be conferred all rights and privileges accordingly. You are instructed to deactivate your weapons and sail forward on the heading we are transmitting."

"I've got it, Liam," Ada answered, flicking the translated navigation path onto the primary vid-screen. The path led us straight through the mine-field.

"Copy that, *Coals Between Pads*. Currently, we're pinned down by your mine-field and have received damage. We cannot comply with your order, as it would destroy our ship," I answered.

"The explosive defenses along the provided route have been deactivated," the still unidentified speaker replied. "Your ship's armor appears resilient enough to absorb the impact of the now inert devices."

"*Coals Between Pads* has terminated communication," Ada announced.

"Ahead slow on provided path," I said. "Let's not give them a reason to shoot at us."

As we'd been communicating, the collection of ships amassing just past the edge of the provided navigation path had grown significantly. While recognizable Felio ships made up most of those present, there were other ships with designs that varied significantly from the white, long, round-edged boxes the Felio seemed to prefer. Probably the most radical-looking was a big, armored sphere.

"Ahead slow," Ada repeated, nudging *Intrepid* onto the path provided. "Brace yourselves. If this is going south, it'll happen now." The forward vid-screen showed a close-up of an explosive mine just off the bow of *Intrepid*. The mine was a ball, two meters in diameter, bristling with conical whiskers that poked out in all directions. I suspected the whiskers were made of something hard that when propelled were designed to do maximum damage. When the device contacted *Intrepid*, it bounced off, just as Newtonian physics would demand. I hadn't realized I'd been holding my breath. I exhaled in relief as a second, then a third mine bounced off and Ada slowly gained speed.

"Nick, can we take a hundred meters per second?" I asked.

"I'd rather fifty," he replied. "No reason to damage the armor."

"Fifty it is," I replied. At that speed, it would take us over an hour to exit the mine field. There was no value in damaging the ship further, however.

As we sailed along, several of the mines we set in motion ended up contacting live mines only a few hundred meters from our position. Idly, I wondered if the Abasi had opened the entire lane for us or were deactivating individual mines as we approached them. I hoped we wouldn't find mines with inoperable comms.

"The fleet is shrinking," Marny observed.

Originally, our reception committee numbered a hundred twenty ships, including two I believed rivaled the biggest battleships we'd seen in Mars Protectorate. By the time we reached the edge of the mine field, only a single battleship with a vanguard of twenty-five smaller ships remained. Although, to use 'small' as a descriptor was flawed. *Intrepid* was only larger than six of the ships we approached.

"We've received a turret lock-down request," Nick announced.

"At least they're asking," I said. "I don't think we're in any position to argue. Please comply."

"We're being hailed again," Ada announced.

Accept hail.

"Greetings Captain Liam Hoffen, this is Mshindi Prime, First of the Abasi commission *Thunder Awakes*." The voice was very much what I had imagined to be Felio. "We are gratified to observe your safe passage from Confederation of Planets' mine field. Your strict observance to orders has eliminated unnecessary loss. I further require that you bring your ship into zero relative acceleration with our fleet or risk being fired upon."

I nodded to Ada who was awaiting approval and she immediately zeroed our delta-v with the battleship, *Thunder Awakes*.

"Greetings, Mshindi Prime," I answered. "It is our objective to comply with all reasonable requests and to clear up any notion that we pose a threat to the Felio people or Confederation of Planets."

"Will you comply with an inspection of your vessel?" Mshindi Prime asked.

I was about to answer when Jonathan interjected. "Captain, you have the right, under Confederation of Planets treaties, to request assignment of an advocate."

"Mshindi Prime, I formally request assignment of an advocate," I said. "We are unfamiliar with your laws."

"So assigned. A craft will be dispatched within forty-six point eight minutes. Do not fire on this vessel as it will contain your advocate, Keenjaho, along with our inspection team. To destroy this vessel would be taken as an expression of war to which we would respond most directly. Mshindi Prime desists." Mshindi Prime closed the channel, apparently not interested in a response.

INSPECTION

We watched as a blocky shuttle broke free from the slew of fleet tender vessels zipping between the larger ships.

"Well, let's go greet them, shall we?" I suggested.

"Ada and I should stay behind, Cap," Marny said. "We're not exactly on a first name basis with the Felio or the Confederation."

"She's right, Liam," Ada agreed. "We'll keep things warm here, just in case."

"Probably no good reason for optimism on my part," I said. "We're not exactly shooting fifties with guests."

Tabby raised an eyebrow at my pod-ball reference. Fifty percent from the field was generally accepted as the measure of a good scoring team.

"I bet they won't have heard of pod-ball, either," she said, grinning.

"Cap, you and Tabby need to wear sidearms," Marny said.

"Copy that, Marny," I agreed.

"Are you sure you need weapons, Liam Hoffen?" Jester Ripples asked.

"I hope not, Jester Ripples," I said. "Marny's right, though. If we appear weak, it is possible we won't be respected. We've already allowed for an inspection of our ship."

"Carrying weapons of war could also suggest that you are interested in a combative relationship," Jester Ripples pushed. "Norigans see weapons as threatening and we would hesitate to interact with a visitor who brought them along."

"Good information, Jester Ripples," I said, exiting the bridge and heading aft to the armory. "When we visit your home, we will be careful not to carry weapons to our meetings. The Confederation fleet, however, has already advertised that they're not opposed to a show of force."

"We might be loading too light with just sidearms," Tabby continued as I pulled the lighter, but faster shooting flechette she preferred from the armory's rack. "They might think we're pushovers. Hand me a clip of blunts. I don't want to be killing anyone."

I exchanged the clip she handed me with a clip of blunts. Flechettes weren't ordinarily lethal and were used to deter would-be attackers. The choice of blunts lowered the potential damage, although they hurt more when they connected.

"I'd say if it comes to force, we have new trouble," I said. "That battleship might not have our advanced armor, but it wouldn't have any issues putting us down."

"All about perception," Tabby said as we turned forward and rejoined Nick and Jonathan in the starboard passageway leading to the primary visitor's airlock, which was about a third of the way back from the bow.

"Liam, the Confederation shuttle is alongside and the universal airlock clamps are engaged. I'll let you open up when you're ready," Ada informed me.

"Copy that, Ada," I said as we turned the corner into the rectangular reception area adjoining the airlock. "Here's the way we'll do this. Tabby and I will open the airlock and bring them back here for introductions. Otherwise, we'll get bottlenecked."

"Yup," Nick agreed, grabbing Jester Ripple's hand and stepping to the side of the sparsely appointed room. The small alien looked up to Nick and I could read that he wanted to climb onto my friend for comfort. Nick, however, wasn't extra cuddly and shook his head to say no.

"Ideally, we'll bring them back to the civilian conference room, but we agreed to an inspection, so we'll need to be flexible," I said.

The panel next to the airlock hatch cycled from red to green as Tabby and I approached. I avoided leaning down and looking through the armor-glass. Instead, I placed the palm of my hand on the security panel. A vaporous cloud formed and just as quickly dissipated as the shuttle's atmo combined with *Intrepid's*. Through the cloud stepped a single, lithe, feminine form. I'd been working to construct a mental image of the Felio, but the figure I was confronted with quickly dispelled that image. As a youth, I'd always expected alien people to show tremendous variety. I'd assumed that the human form was generally unique and other sentient life forms would take on their own, radically different shapes. The Felio, like Jester Ripples, was bipedal, which I already knew from the multitude of corpses we'd encountered. However, judging a species from long dead corpses doesn't prepare you for the reality of a live encounter. This Felio had bright intelligent, yellow eyes that resembled Filbert's. A short layer of red-orange fur covered every visible patch of skin, which wasn't much given the slightly puffy looking vac-suit she wore.

The female Felio stepped forward, placing herself in front of Tabby and began speaking. It took a moment for the AI to translate, but I soon recognized the pressure of a noise cancellation wave and the Felio's stream of speech flowed into my ear. The AI did a great job of matching inflection, tone and pitch with the translation. The Felio's face was foreign enough to me that I couldn't even tell that her generous lips, split just beneath a broad, flat nose, weren't in sequence with the human-standard speech in my ears.

"On behalf of the Abasi people and the Confederation of Planets, it is I, Mshindi Tertiary who greet you." As she spoke, she placed her fist at about her solar plexus and bowed until her head was at chest level with Tabby, who was roughly the same height. Behind Mshindi Tertiary stood eight more figures who all bowed, just as she did.

Tabby, caught off guard by the Felio's gesture, looked at me with raised eyebrows. Mshindi Tertiary had clearly assumed that Tabby was our leader and now she had no idea how to respond. I suppressed a chuckle at Tabby's discomfort.

"Welcome aboard *Intrepid*, Mshindi Tertiary," I answered, extending my hand. Unlike Tabby, I'd talked with Jonathan about different ways to interact with alien species. Just as Mshindi Tertiary had greeted us in her custom, I would greet her in my custom. That way I could avoid any potential for offense by improperly using gestures I was unfamiliar with. "I am Liam Hoffen, captain of this ship and am pleased to introduce to you to Tabitha Masters, Nicholas James, Jonathan, and Jester Ripples."

For an uncomfortable moment, I held my hand out to the female Felio as she slowly rose and panned her view from Tabby back to me. An unmistakable look of surprise flitted momentarily over her angular, fur-covered face as she realized her faux pas.

"I apologize most profusely for my error in understanding." Mshindi Tertiary turned and repeated her initial bow.

"Your assumption is most understandable, Mshindi Tertiary," I said. "Tabitha Masters is a formidable presence. I offer my handshake as a symbol of the peaceful intent of my ship and the people within." I was repeating a phrase I'd worked out with Jonathan.

The Felio's face was quite expressive and I read confusion as she worked through the translation she'd received. Hesitantly, she raised her gloved hand toward me, but in seeing that my hand was uncovered, she pulled it back and removed her glove. As with her face, her hand, complete with stubby fingers, was covered with a lighter, similarly-hued fur.

I slowly reached forward and gently wrapped my fingers around her outstretched paw and gave it a single pump. The warmth of her paw and softness of the fur was offset by a moment when the tips of sharp claws extended, contacting my palm.

"It is my duty, Captain Liam Hoffen," Mshindi Tertiary straightened up fully and looked me directly in the eyes; the challenge obvious, "to inspect your ship and verify that you harbor no enemies of the Abasi or the Confederation of Planets. You have requested an advocate. Mshindi Prime has assigned this duty to Keenjaho. Keenjaho, step forward and be recognized."

"Yes, Mshindi." A male figure, similarly lithe in shape but with slightly broader shoulders and hips stepped forward. The fur beneath his helmet and around his neck was considerably longer than Mshindi Tertiary's and was a much darker brown. His facial fur was short and tan colored. "I respectfully request a short time span with our guests, that I might provide to them excellent counsel."

"This is allowable," Mshindi Tertiary agreed.

"Mshindi Tertiary, if I might modify this proposal. Nicholas James is best suited to the fine details of protocol and if Keenjaho would accompany him as we walk, we might, as my people say, kill two birds with one stone," I said, stepping into the room so that more of the Felio could step onto *Intrepid*.

"A most provocative statement, Captain Liam Hoffen. I presume your intent is not to treat us as birds," Mshindi Tertiary replied.

I suppressed a chuckle. "It is my turn to apologize, Mshindi Tertiary. This human saying simply suggests that we might accomplish two goals at once. There will be no killing or combat of any kind involved."

"Then we should proceed," she replied. While I couldn't entirely read her face, she seemed somewhat disappointed. "Keenjaho, you will accompany Nicholas James. Tabara Second, your first squad will accompany us and your second squad will remain in this location."

"Yes, Mshindi," replied another female Felio, who had just emerged from the Abasi shuttle. "Your weapon, Mshindi." The Felio identified as Tabara Second, handed a sword to Mshindi in a formal gesture. The sword was nearly identical to the one I'd taken from the dead Felio aboard *Cold Mountain Stream*. It hadn't escaped me that the Felio who commanded the battleship *Thunder Awakes* and the lead Felio on the boarding party all shared the same first name, Mshindi. I stored the fact away for future consideration.

"Perhaps Tabara Second would accompany Tabitha Masters so that questions could be answered as they come up," I offered.

"This will not be necessary," Keenjaho replied. "Only Mshindi can ask questions during this inspection."

Mshindi flashed a dark glance back at Keenjaho. "Tabara Second, you will accompany Tabitha Masters."

"Yes, Mshindi," Tabara replied quickly.

"If you'd come this way," I said, ignoring the tension. Fortunately, Mshindi was amenable and accompanied me as I led the unusual group through the passageway that joined with the primary bow-to-stern starboard passageway.

"Humanity is a civilization that has spread to five solar systems in a galaxy different than your own," I started. "The planet our civilization started upon we call Earth and it is this planet where *Intrepid* was constructed. *Intrepid* is in the classification of ships we refer to as frigates and is designed for two roles, first as a fleet support ship and second as a scout. While *Intrepid* has impressive armaments, it is mostly designed for speed and has traded armor density for this purpose. *Intrepid* has the capacity for sixty crew, although we're currently under sail with a crew of seven."

"Why are you sailing with so few?" Mshindi asked. "Is the Earth government impoverished?"

"You need not answer this question, Captain Liam Hoffen," Keenjaho prompted from behind me. "It is beyond Mshindi Tertiary's scope of inquiry."

"Thank you, Keenjaho," I said. "But it is information we don't mind sharing. The simple answer is no, Earth's primary governments are all very prosperous. To answer your unasked question, we are not associated with any of Earth's governments and have a complicated relationship with the government of Mars, which is positioned as the fourth planet from the same star as Earth, which occupies the third position."

I'd stopped outside the crew's mess in the forward passageway joining the starboard and port ship length passageways.

"*Intrepid* is homed in a system named Ophir after its single inhabitable planet, Ophir. This is the fifth and newest system colonized by humankind. We are short of manpower because we have no intent to engage in combat," I said.

"Doesn't this place you at a significant disadvantage?" Mshindi Tertiary asked.

"We have not found many ships capable of outrunning *Intrepid*," I said. "And those that can catch us, have neither the armor nor the weaponry to threaten us."

"Why did you allow yourselves to become ensnared, then?"

"Mshindi Tertiary, you forget your place," Keenjaho prompted. "Captain Liam Hoffen, I must insist. There are legal consequences to your answers."

Mshindi turned. A low growl emanated from her throat as her lip curled upward, displaying a sharp fang. "It is you, Keenjaho, who forgets his place. I will not be called to task by Gunjway."

"I have said what I must," Keenjaho answered, but stood still as he did.

"If not for *humans,* I would discipline you now."

I looked from Mshindi to Keenjaho and then to Nick. It was an uncomfortable few moments until Mshindi Tertiary finally spoke again.

"My apologies, Captain Liam Hoffen," Mshindi Tertiary said. "Perhaps you would resume."

"This way," I said and pushed into the crew mess. "When fully crewed, this mess hall is where non-officers eat meals. It doesn't currently get much use. And through this hatch is the forward observation lounge that we use for relaxation."

"How are you able to see through the hull?" Mshindi asked.

"Transparent armor," I said. "We call it armored glass, but its composition resembles steel more than it does glass." I kept walking and pushed through into the gymnasium. "One of the priorities for long journeys is exercise, which we're able to do in here."

"Captain Liam Hoffen," Mshindi interrupted. "What is the purpose of the roped off square that is elevated?"

"It is acceptable to call me Captain or informally, Liam," I answered. "We call that a boxing ring. It is where we spar with each other in physical combat."

"To the death?" Mshindi asked.

"Definitely not," I said. "Although, I'll admit it sometimes feels that way."

"Who is your champion? Is it Tabitha Masters?" she asked.

"Damn straight," Tabby replied.

"It is as I suspected. She walks as a warrior. I would very much enjoy a test of combat with you, Tabitha Masters," Mshindi said.

"Anytime, anyplace," Tabby replied.

"Mshindi, this is not allowed," Keenjaho interjected.

"Be quiet, Gunjway," Mshindi said. "Please continue, Captain."

"Below this deck is where the crew sleeps," I said. "Currently, it is abandoned."

"We would see it as part of our inspection," Mshindi said.

"Very well," I agreed. We exited the gym and took a U-turn to the ramp leading down to Deck-2. No sooner had we crossed into crew territory than Mshindi drew her sword and took an offensive posture, stepping in front of me.

"What is the meaning of this?" Mshindi asked. Tabara and three other female Felio rushed forward, taking positions near Mshindi Tertiary. Significant, however, was that Keenjaho didn't move – he wasn't carrying a weapon.

"I'm afraid you have me at a disadvantage," I said, unholstering my heavy flechette. "What are you referring to?"

"The scent. It is old, Mshindi," Tabara said.

"There is much, though," Mshindi said.

"You speak truth," Tabara agreed.

"Where does this passage lead?" Mshindi asked.

"Only a few more meters," I said. "This is my ship. If there is danger, I will face it." I pushed around the guard that had formed near Mshindi and received strange looks that I interpreted as confusion.

"I think they're smelling the Kroerak," Tabby offered.

Mshindi abruptly turned on her heel and looked at Tabby. "You have Kroerak aboard?"

"Not one that's living," I answered.

"Explain yourself, Captain Liam Hoffen," she replied.

"Nothing too difficult to understand," I said. "A Kroerak entered our ship in the tween deck just forward of here. We killed it."

"Show me."

"Mshindi, these are our guests," Keenjaho said. "You must be careful with your tone."

"Silence, Keenjaho. We are on the hunt."

I stepped around Mshindi, not caring to deal with her and Keenjaho. I pushed open the final hatch and made my way over to the panel where the Kroerak had entered the ship.

"It boarded our ship while we were in combat," I said. "We didn't become aware of it until we set about repairs."

"How did you slay the Kroerak?" Mshindi asked.

"The Kroerak's cortex was severed by the insertion of a sharp weapon between the skull plate and the thorax," Jonathan replied, overly quick. So far, he'd been quiet. His answer was meant as a warning, as well as an accurate answer to the question.

"You did this, Tabitha Masters?" Mshindi asked.

"Oh, no," she replied. "That was all Liam. Don't misjudge him. He's not just a pretty face. He's got some real fight in him."

Mshindi placed her hands on her hips and threw her head back in a loud yowl that I eventually understood to be a laugh. "So he is. What a fine mate he would make, then."

"You have no idea," Tabby replied.

I cut my eyes between the two of them in confusion. Tabby had picked up on a cue and made some sort of connection with Mshindi that I couldn't fathom.

"What did you do with this Kroerak?" Mshindi asked.

"The corpse is in a medical bay," I replied.

"Would you show this to us?" Mshindi asked, looking askance at Keenjaho.

"Certainly," I said. "It's easy enough to go that way." I led them around to the starboard side, a deck beneath where they'd entered through the airlock.

"These rooms are all vacant," Mshindi said. "Do you not require rest?"

"Our quarters are located closer to the bridge," I said. "As is common for officers."

"I understand."

"Here we are," I said. "I'll warn you, it does not smell great in there. Even with our technology, rotting bugs smell rotten."

"Tabara, accompany me," Mshindi Tertiary ordered. Tabara

nodded, and stepped forward as I palmed my way into the medical bay where the Kroerak still lay across two tables we'd pulled together. Most of the inspection had been done by Jonathan, but I knew Nick had spent time helping as well. I covered my nose and led the two Felio inside.

"I struck here," I said, showing where I'd delivered the killing blow.

"Tabitha Masters is right. You are a brave little one," she said and there was no mistaking her patronizing tone. "I have heard that Felio and human are quite compatible."

"You know of other humans?" I asked. It was something I was hoping to discover and didn't believe I'd learn about it so quickly.

She quirked her head at me, but didn't answer otherwise. "I've seen enough. By my calculations, we've successfully inspected only half of *Intrepid*. Please continue."

I led them from the room and up the starboard ramp, heading aft toward the bridge. I noticed that Marny stood in the passage, in front of the bridge. She'd donned an armored vac-suit, held a blaster rifle, and stood at attention.

"Captain." She saluted as we approached.

I played along, I wasn't sure what was going on, but I was more than willing to run the play called. "As you were, Master Chief."

"Impressive," Mshindi observed. It was a fair statement and something I'd often thought.

"We've arrived at the bridge, which is the control room for our ship. We'll allow a single Abasi representative to inspect," I said, reading a prompt from my HUD as I received it. "Your technology scanner must remain in the passageway."

Mshindi Tertiary raised her eyebrows at mention of the scanner. "Very well. Tabara, please inspect this bridge."

"You'll need to surrender your scanning device." Marny placed her hand up in warning. Tabara looked from Marny to Mshindi who nodded agreement. After surrendering the device, Tabara followed Marny onto the bridge and reemerged a few minutes later.

"All that remains is our cargo bay and the engine rooms," Nick said. "We'll have similar issues with technology scanners inside the engine room."

Just then Filbert chose to poke his head around the corner.

"What is this?" Mshindi asked as Filbert stalked forward as if he owned the place.

"That is Filbert," I answered. "He is a non-sentient cat from our home world. Be careful, his claws can be sharp if he is startled."

"I am sure you are correct. Come here, tiny Gunjway." Mshindi Tertiary knelt and scooped up Filbert who seemed quite enthralled with the graceful alien. "I see someone has removed your Gunjway seeds, yet you are still so handsome."

"Gunjway means male?" I asked.

"Captain Hoffen," Keenjaho replied. "It is a derogatory term used to reference a male Felio who has neither testicles nor honor. It is not used in formal settings."

"It is an apt term for those that forget their position," Mshindi Tertiary replied.

I continued walking, not interested in getting pulled into Mshindi Tertiary's argument. "Here is our cargo bay." I palmed open the interior hatch. The cargo bay was stacked high with steel sheets and fuel we'd confiscated from the Felio ships. The fuel, while not as efficient as our own, would work in a pinch; we'd loaded up on it before jumping through the wormhole.

"What are you doing with a Musi runabout?" Mshindi asked, although her eyes rested on *Sugar* and *Rowdy*.

"It was captured in the system on the other side of the wormhole," I said. "Truthfully, it saved our lives."

"You really were there," Mshindi said. "You were in Mhina?"

"Mshindi is referring to the system J-F99214," Jonathan replied. "The system of the ghost fleet."

"The Abasi fleet still sails?" Mshindi asked.

"Mshindi, I really must insist," Keenjaho interrupted. It was, apparently, all that Mshindi could take. She leapt from her position, pinned the larger male to the floor and drew her sword in a single, fluid motion.

"You must really remain quiet, Keenjaho," Mshindi said, pressing her blade to Keenjaho's neck.

"If Mhina is on the other-side of the wormhole, then yes, we were there," I said. I wasn't about to watch her cut off Keenjaho's head. "We found a fleet of Felio ships that had been disabled for many stans."

"It is legend that humans would come through the Mhina gate someday," Mshindi looked up at me from her position atop Keenjaho. "And that you would come as friends, but would be our enemies instead. Tell me, Captain Liam Hoffen, do you come as our friend?"

MSHINDI'S PRIDE

"You did not need to protect me from Mshindi Tertiary," Keenjaho said as we watched the armored shuttle pull away from the airlock.

I turned to him. "She was going to remove your head. The fact is, I didn't tell her anything that wasn't going to come out one way or another."

"Confederation law has little flexibility," Keenjaho said. "It is best not to provide information voluntarily."

"What laws are we accused of violating?" Nick asked.

"Destruction of Confederation property," Keenjaho answered. "When you entered the Mhina gate, your ship encountered explosive mines. The destruction of these mines is a primary charge. You will also face charges from the Confederation of Planets for violating the space around the Mhina gate. As visitors, you were not bound by this treaty. By requesting guest status, an argument will be made that you became bound at that moment."

"What is the punishment for destruction of property?" Nick asked.

"If it is assessed that the property destruction was incidental and without criminal intent, a simple restoration of that property is all that will be required," Keenjaho answered. "If criminal intent is determined, punitive fines, seizure of property, incarceration and physical punishment are all possibilities."

"Welcome to the Confederation. Here's your bill for visiting," I quipped. "Not exactly throwing out the red carpet."

Keenjaho tipped his head in my direction. "My translation unit senses a human idiom, but is unable to sufficiently translate. Indeed, the Abasi welcome *Intrepid's* crew to our home worlds."

Tabby was having none of it. "If Ada weren't such an amazing pilot, we'd have been destroyed. It doesn't seem like any sort of welcome." she sneered.

"What's next?" I asked.

"Your presence will be requested for tribunal," Keenjaho answered. "It is there the Strix will bring the charge of property destruction against the crew of *Intrepid*. Ordinarily, this matter would not rise to the level of such a high court, given the low value of damage caused by your arrival. It is your status as alien guests that caused this matter to be turned over to the Confederation of Planets for adjudication."

"Who are the Strix?" Nick asked.

"They are legal arbiters of this region of the Confederation of Planets. It is most unfortunate that they have a claim against you, Captain Hoffen. The Strix are often successful at defending Confederation property."

"We have no basis for understanding value, but what are the reparations being requested?" I asked.

"One point four billion Confederation credits," Keenjaho said.

"Captain, we've been allowed access to public Confederation data streams," Jonathan interjected. "Using iron ingots, steel sheet, oxygen crystals and several hundred other data points, we've established a currency conversion. Ten Confederation credits are equivalent to four Mars credits."

"They're charging us six-hundred million credits?" I asked, quickly doing the math. "What were those mines made from, gold?"

"The bill is exhaustive," Keenjaho said. "It includes replacing destroyed mines, restoring to order the mines that were displaced, plus fuel and salaries for moving the fleet into a protective position. It is not within my authority to provide opinion beyond these facts."

Ada's voice cut through on my comm. "Liam, we're receiving a hail from *Thunder Awakes*."

"Send it through," I answered. "This is *Intrepid*."

"Captain Liam Hoffen, it is I, Mshindi Prime, first aboard *Thunder Awakes*. My progeny, Mshindi Tertiary has reported a satisfactory inspection. I invite you and your crew to join us aboard *Thunder Awakes* for a traditional Abasi welcoming ceremony."

My mind was still reeling with the fact that we were facing a lawsuit and I was tempted to throw the invitation back at her. If I were dealing with humans, I would have, but I held my tongue.

"Your invitation is most kind, Mshindi Prime," I said. "We accept it in the spirit in which it is offered."

"Details will be transmitted. Mshindi Prime desists." Mshindi Prime closed comm.

"Not extra chatty, is she?" I asked, turning away from the airlock and heading back into the ship.

"It is high honor that the House of Mshindi would make such an invitation," Keenjaho said. "Much more so that it comes from Mshindi Prime."

"Explain to me the names," I said. "I currently know of three different Felio named Mshindi; Prime, Tertiary and a Mshindi we discovered on the derelict ship *Cold Mountain Stream* and she was dead a hundred fifty stans. That Mshindi didn't seem to have a numeric position."

"Abasi families who are of the ruling caste share a familial name. Only the female Abasi may be granted the family name upon their birth. If you found a Mshindi in the Mhina system, it could only be Mshindi Prime's ancestor. I am unfamiliar with House Mshindi family lore, but I am certain Mshindi Prime would be interested in whatever information you have ," Keenjaho answered.

"So Mshindi Tertiary is Prime's second or would it be third daughter?" I asked.

"Mshindi Tertiary is the second daughter upon which Mshindi Prime bestowed the familial name," Keenjaho explained. "I know of several other daughters."

"Who were what? Kicked out of the family?" Tabby asked, scandalized.

"No," he said. "The daughters lead productive lives and are allowed use of the secondary name which is Neema. It is Mshindi

Prime's sister's daughters that have tenuous familial rights."

"Let me guess, Mshindi would find use of the Neema name offensive," I said.

"The name is not offensive," Keenjaho said. "Mshindi is more of a title where Neema is an informal name, but accurate all the same. The Neema family are well-respected business people and politicians."

"That's not going to get confusing," I said.

I palmed open the bridge. "Marny, any concern for Keenjaho being on the bridge?"

"Negative, Cap," Marny replied.

"What's the verdict," Ada asked. "Did we pass inspection?"

"I think so," I answered. "Only the Confederation of Planets is suing us for busting up their mine field."

"That can't be good. What's that going to cost?" Ada asked.

"They've put the price at six hundred million," I answered.

Ada whistled. "You're joking. Where would we come up with that amount of money?"

"Keenjaho, has the Confederation of Planets seized ships to pay debt?" Nick asked.

Keenjaho stared at the floor uncomfortably. "I am not at liberty to say."

"The value of the destroyed mines is suspiciously close to the value of this ship," Nick replied.

"You're saying the Felio are trying to steal our ship through legal channels?" Ada asked. Her voice rising as she spoke.

"This is a matter you might consider taking up with Mshindi Prime," Keenjaho answered. "If you are given the opportunity."

"When would a property seizure occur? Could it happen if we lost a legal fight?" Nick asked.

"I apologize. I am not able to provide this information," Keenjaho answered.

"Are you obligated to report conversations you observe to either the Abasi or Confederation of Planets' governments?" Jonathan asked.

"Yes. Thank you for asking," Keenjaho's pointy ears drooped.

His facial expressions were mostly unreadable, but I sensed relief on his part.

"Tabby, would you escort our friend Keenjaho to an open bunk where he will be comfortable?" I asked.

"Yeah. I've got him," she answered.

I gave her a wry smile. "Be nice, Tabbs. I think Keenjaho is in an awkward position here."

As soon as Keenjaho exited the bridge, I turned to Nick. "What of our technology? We can't just turn over our tech to an alien government."

"The only species we're aware of with sufficient technology to penetrate our system's security are the Norigans," Nick replied. "Jester Ripples, is it possible to limit access to any technology that might be stored on our systems?"

"These safeguards already exist," Jester Ripples said. "It is part of every piece of intellectual property with a sufficient security rating."

"If this ship is taken, they'll try to break in," I said. "They might even have Norigans working with them."

"It would be exciting to visit with my family again," Jester Ripples said. "There is no doubt much can be learned by observing the technological advances your people have gained."

"Liam, I've received a navigation path from *Thunder Awakes*. They must have put a welcoming party together quickly, because they've given us permission to come alongside immediately," Ada replied.

"Let's table this conversation," I said. "Perhaps we will learn more from Mshindi Prime. I'd like everyone to be in attendance."

"Everyone, Cap?" Marny asked.

"We'll be sitting next to a battleship. If they intend to do us harm, we'll have nothing to say about it," I said. "Let's be ready in sixty minutes."

"Weapons, Cap?"

"Nothing provocative," I answered, knowing full well Marny would bring a weapon one way or another. "I'll be in my quarters."

When I entered the captain's quarters, I found Tabby lying on the bed with her knees up and her eyes closed. I flopped onto the bed next to her.

"What's shaking?" I asked.

"They're going to take our ship, Liam," she replied. "I want to kill someone."

"Jury's still out on that," I said. "Besides, if they really wanted our ship, they could have just tried to kill us like all the other pirates we've taken on. Only these guys could have really done a number on us."

"How can you be so calm?" she asked. "It's infuriating. And, it's going to happen without a fight."

"I haven't given up," I said. "Besides, our options forty hours ago were to settle on a planet we knew the Kroerak had already conquered or come here. Everyone is alive, Tabbs, and they don't have our ship yet. I was just going to give Mom a call, want to listen in?" I pushed up from the bed and sat at the desk where the quantum communication device sat.

"Petersburg, come in, this is *Intrepid*," I called, waited thirty seconds and then repeated.

After my third try, Mom's voice replied. "Can't you ever call during waking hours?"

"Who would know when that is?" I asked. "Any news on the Kroerak?"

"Yes. It's bad," she replied. "They are making a push for the moon. They've taken out most of the orbital defenses and pushed back the combined fleet. So far, ground troops are holding on, but Greg says it's only a matter of time before the Kroerak seize control."

The news was bad enough that I wasn't interested in giving her a hard time about her first-name basis with Commander Munay. "We can't drive them off? How is that possible?"

"Our fleets have been cut in half," Mom said. "And we've inflicted even more than that to the Kroerak. For some reason, though, they're pushing hard for the moon. Apparently, some higher-ups are considering peace talks."

"With the Kroerak? That's insanity," I said. "They think of us as food!"

"I know. But people are scared, Liam. If the fleet can't stop them at the moon, we could lose Earth. And if Earth falls, humanity will fall with it," she said.

"Not if TransLoc isn't restored," I said. "We still haven't heard from Anino."

"No one has," she said. "The rumor is that the Kroerak have taken Curie. You must have called for some reason, Liam," Mom replied. "What's going on?"

"We made it out of the system called Mhina," I said. "We're now in the Felio's home system in the Aeratroas region of the Dwingeloo galaxy. Apparently, we've landed in legal trouble by entering through a restricted gate."

"What kind of legal trouble?" she asked.

"Aeratroas is governed by a body called the Confederation of Planets," I explained. "They've set up a blockade to keep the Kroerak from using that restricted gate. Long story short, we made a mess when we entered and they're suing us."

"They have lawyers? That's awful," she replied. "They're aliens?"

"The Felio look close to human," I said. "That's the second species we've seen that does. Kind of makes you wonder if there's a reason for it. Look, we might be unavailable for a while. I just wanted to let you know we're relatively safe, aside from the pending lawsuit."

"It sounds horrible," she said.

"That's what I said, Mrs. H.," Tabby said, leaning over my shoulder. "Makes me feel like we never left home."

"We have to get going, Mom. I love you," I said.

"Love you, too, Liam," she replied. "Remember, you're stronger as a group. Stay together."

"Copy that. Hoffen out." I closed the comm channel.

"They took Curie." Tabby looked at me, bewildered.

"And, they're going to take the moon," I said. "Our universe is changing and we aren't even there to help. I feel useless."

"One day at a time, Liam," Tabby repeated. "If the fleets stop the Kroerak from landing on Earth, there's still hope."

"Over a billion people live on the moon," I said.

She reached out to take my hand and spoke softly. "There's nothing we can do for them right now."

I felt like a fraud as I pulled on the dress clothing we'd procured back in Léger Nuage. The clothing was so bright and cheerful that it didn't accurately depict how I felt about myself or our predicament. I yearned for the simpler time when just upgrading our clothing was a new adventure. The weight of the universe settled on my shoulders once again.

"Do you like it?" Tabby twirled in her Nuagian clothing. She looked spectacular, but I had a hard time feeling it through my funk. Tabby's eyes caught my own and I knew she'd caught me. "Knock it off, Liam. You solve nothing by getting moody. You're always the one we can turn to when our backs are against the wall. Now, we're about to go meet an alien commander, on her vessel, at a party in our honor, somewhere in the Dwingeloo Galaxy. If you can't see the fun in that, you're an idiot."

I chuckled despite myself. She had a point. We'd come so far, there was no reason to focus on the negative. "Want to help me put together a gift for Mshindi Prime?" I asked.

She nodded. "Of course."

***

"Airlock is green," Nick announced as we stood together, ready to cross through the companionway that joined *Intrepid* to *Thunder Awakes*. The companionway was L0 space, which meant it was too dangerous to enter without a vac-suit. We'd all switched to ordinary vac-suits, which were less bulky than Anino's grav-suits. They also fit beneath our dress clothes.

"Lead on, my friend," I said, placing my hand in the small of Tabby's back as we followed Nick and Marny.

After we cycled through *Thunder Awakes'* airlock, Keenjaho escorted us aft. On our approach, I could make out the murmuring sounds of a moderately-sized group of people. The din continued to grow as we walked down the passageway. We ended up at the entrance to a wide-open bay that looked out over the unfamiliar star field.

Three chirps that I would have mistaken for a bird, sounded in quick succession as we entered. Thirty Felio turned to get a glimpse of their new visitors. For a moment, the feeling was surreal, almost like we'd shown up late to some sort of bizarre costume party. I didn't have much time to process it, as five Felio broke away from the group and approached. Keenjaho's body language, which stiffened at their approach, queued me to their relative ranks.

A dark brown furred Felio, with subtle, ochre spots stepped forward. Her ears were adorned with a significant number of earrings, like those in the ears of the Felio behind her, but more numerous. I suspected they were rank designations or bestowed honors.

She raised her clenched paw to her chest, a gesture mimicked by all the Felio in the room. "To the crew of *Intrepid*, House Mshindi and the Abasi people welcome you." My AI's translation halted momentarily as she delivered the greeting in human standard speech. Upon finishing her welcome, she bowed deeply, straightened and held her hand out to me, just as the AI translation popped back on. "I understand humans prefer to shake hands in greeting, Captain Hoffen."

"On behalf of the crew of *Intrepid*, thank you for such a warm welcome, Mshindi Prime. You honor us with your presence," I replied, focusing on her mouth. I was heeding the advice of Keenjaho to avoid staring directly into the eyes of ranking Felio as they would take it as a show of disrespect. I also appreciated that he'd warned me that Mshindi Prime would be first to welcome us. "May I introduce Tabitha Masters, Nicholas James, Marny Bertrand, Jonathan, and our Norigan friend, Jester Ripples." I paused between each introduction so she had a moment to exchange handshakes.

Mshindi Prime stepped aside and gestured for the other -

apparently senior members - to also greet us. Initially, I hadn't had the cognizance to study the Felio in the room, only picking up peripherally on what I thought were a wide variety of uniforms. As it turned out, the Felio uniforms were little more than short skirts with missing panels on the outsides of the legs and hips. There was also a narrow front panel that covered the important parts of their chests, but little else. The fact that they had fur covering their entire body seemed to make up for the lack of traditional clothing, but it challenged me on a number of levels. Beyond the earrings and uniforms, they each wore a sword at their side just as varied as the colors and patterns of their pelts.

With introductions complete, Keenjaho invited us to join the remainder of the assembled Felio leadership.

"Captain Liam Hoffen." Mshindi Prime had appeared at my side so quietly that I startled. "My apologies. It has been some time since I have been in the presence of humans."

"No harm done," I replied. "You know of other humans?"

"Would you walk with me?" she asked. "I have duties that require my presence."

"Of course, Mshindi Prime," I replied, and caught Tabby's eye so she would know I was leaving.

"Captain Liam Hoffen, do you mind if I am direct in conversation?" she asked once we were in the hallway.

"I prefer it, Mshindi Prime," I answered, nodding my head. "Please, call me Liam, at least while we're in private."

"That is acceptable," she replied. "Liam, what did you find in the system of Mhina and why did you travel there?"

"The why is the shorter of the two questions. Mhina was the destination of a mission by a corporation from earth called Belirand," I said. "We were sent to Mhina to determine what the outcome of that mission was and to render aid to whatever survivors might remain."

"We know of Belirand," Mshindi Prime said. "Seven hundred thirty-eight humans arrived in the Mhina system, one hundred sixty years previous. The Felio people rendered aid and helped relocate the human survivors to a nearby system."

"Are they still alive?" I asked.

"They are," she replied. "You are welcome to visit with them. Please, Liam, what did you find in Mhina?"

"The final resting place of a large Felio fleet," I said, pulling the Belirand mission pin from my pocket and handing it to her.

Her face communicated surprise as much as any human's would. "And you found this?"

"Mshindi Prime, we found *Cold Mountain Stream* while looking for an artifact they carried," I said. "The ship had a sole occupant at the helm. We believe this occupant was your ancestor, as she was also named Mshindi."

"She stood the last watch?"

I pulled out the sword I'd broken while killing the Kroerak that had boarded *Intrepid*. I'd hidden it in the folds of my Nuagian dress clothes. "I must apologize. This came to damage while in my possession."

She accepted the sheathed sword I'd brought along and wrapped her paw around the grip. Claws from the end of her thick fingers extended and found position in the narrow grooves. "Mshindi Safiri. This was her sword. Tell me how you came to damage it?"

"It was rather inadvertent," I said and explained how the sword was in my possession while being attacked by the Kroerak aboard *Intrepid*.

She held the sword out to me. "You have honored Mshindi Safiri and my family, Captain Liam Hoffen. To slay a Kroerak is a duty of the Abasi people. I find myself in your debt."

I blocked the return of the sword. "I would have you keep the sword, Mshindi Prime. It is an artifact that belongs to your family."

"What happened to the rest of the fleet?" she asked.

"They didn't stand a chance," I said. "We viewed the data-streams and a large Kroerak fleet destroyed them after they successfully escorted transport ships through the wormhole. If you haven't had access to these data-streams, we'd be more than happy to share them with you."

"Your cooperation in this matter will be most valuable to us and makes the matter I must now discuss with you more difficult," she said.

"We agreed to be direct, Mshindi Prime," I prompted.

She clucked her tongue and looked at my chest. It gave me the impression that she was embarrassed. "The Confederation of Planets is a series of treaties that bind how we, the Abasi, interact with other governments. Our role and responsibility is to defend one of three entry points into Confederation space that the Kroerak have previously advantaged. You are now adjacent to the blockade for which I bear responsibility."

"It seems you have this well under control," I said.

"The legal matters of the Confederation of Planets, in this and many systems, are directed by - or as some might say, ruled by - a race called the Strix," she continued. "The lawsuit that has been leveled against Captain Liam Hoffen and *Intrepid* will be successful. Such is the nature of dealing with the Strix. You will be led to believe that there is some chance your petition will be fairly heard. In the end, however, your ship will be forfeit to the Confederation."

My heart sank. "How?" I asked. "Why would they do that?"

"The technology of your ship is great," she replied.

"That is not honorable," I said, using something I knew we both valued.

"It is not," she agreed. "There are those who will privately argue it is for the good of the Confederation. I believe it makes us little better than Kroerak. But I do not make the laws and have sworn my life to uphold them."

"Why are you telling me this?" I asked.

"It is not yet illegal for me to disagree with the judgements of this rotting republic," she said. "You must know this, Captain Liam Hoffen. The Strix *will* take your ship. There is nothing that can be done about this."

"Do you believe you have a ship in this fleet that can catch us?" I asked.

"Even now, Abasi engineers have installed explosive charges

on your ship that will be ignited if you divert from approved flight paths," she replied.

"If we attempt to remove them?" I asked.

"You will be destroyed."

I frowned in my confusion. "You wanted to tell this to me face-to-face? Why?"

"It is unwise to focus on things that you cannot control. It is energy lost." she said. "With forewarning, you are able to make plans. There is one thing that works in your favor. The Strix are not able to assess a fine greater than what you own. They may not detain you or your crew nor levee a debt upon you."

"You have to know how bad this sounds," I said. "You are thieves, bandits, stealing from me."

"Focus, Captain Liam Hoffen," Mshindi said. "If you attempt to flee, it will be I that hunt you down. There is no system where you may hide that we will not find you. I do not tell you this to frighten you. I have known many humans from York, the human settlement of Belirand. It is their friendship that I honor by telling you this."

"You have given me much to think about, Mshindi Prime," I said.

"Please do not become my quarry. I would find no pleasure in hunting you."

CLEANSING FIRE

"She said that?" Tabby asked when we were safely back on the bridge.

"Which part?" I asked.

"All of it," Nick said. "I can't believe we let our guard down."

"It wouldn't have mattered," I said. "With the fleet ahead and the minefield behind, what were our choices?"

"We're not letting them take the ship," Ada said. "We need to get out of here."

"Mshindi Prime was very direct," I said. "Nick, can you verify the charges placed on the engines?"

He sighed and nodded. "I have."

"You can't seriously be considering letting them do this," Tabby said. "They're thugs. We can't stand for this."

"Nick, any ideas?" I said.

"We stand no chance against this fleet."

"Gah!" I said.

"You're completely dismissing fighting our way out of here?" Tabby asked. "What kind of rat-shite is that?"

"Plan it out, Tabbs." I turned to her. "If I could see a way out of this that I felt gave us more than fifties on survival, I'd do it. Ever since we've arrived in this system, we've either been surrounded by live mines or within striking distance of an entire fleet."

"We can't just roll over," she said.

"But we can know we're substantially out-matched," I said. "I'll trade everything I own for the wellbeing of anyone here. That's what we're faced with. We can't protect this ship at the expense of our lives. I'm all about taking risks, but there must be an objective. Every time we've put it on the line, it's been because we've had no other choice. We have a choice here."

120

"Mshindi Prime's prediction of your failure in the Confederation of Planet's legal system is not binding," Jonathan said. "We have already filed a protest on your behalf in contradiction to the charges as filed by the Strix. We have been contacted by a Cetacar organization that wishes to argue in your defense."

"Cetacar?" I asked.

"Per the public information available, the Cetacar species are highly intelligent and pacifistic. According to the public information feed, Cetacarians have historically been active in social justice issues. Perhaps the most relevant being their defense of the Belirand mission. It was determined that rescuing the Belirand colony ship cost substantially more than the ship's worth. The crew were to be interned until the difference could be repaid. The Cetacar proposed a change in Confederation law and successfully lobbied the member planets so that the fines could not exceed the value of the property seized," Jonathan replied.

"And this same organization wants to represent us?" I asked. "Do they have a name?"

"A close translation of the organization's name is Pervasive Justice and it is the same group," Jonathan replied.

"Doesn't exactly roll off the tongue," I said.

"Marny, are you buying this?" Tabby asked. "You're ready to just turn over *Intrepid* to these thieves?"

"Not all battles are worthy of blood," Marny replied. "I agree we should continue to look for a way out of this mess, but I don't believe we'd win in a confrontation with the Felio."

"I can't believe I'm hearing this," Tabby said and stormed off the bridge.

"I'll talk to her," Ada said, standing.

"Liam, we're receiving a hail from *Thunder Awakes*," Nick said.

Ada looked at me, torn between ship responsibility and personal accountability to Tabby.

"I've got it, Ada. Go."

Accept hail.

"Captain Liam Hoffen, pursuant to the charges filed with

Confederation of Planets under the code 146.12.40993, you are being instructed to voluntarily sail the vessel designated as *Intrepid* to the space station Chitundu. Any deviation from the provided plan of navigation will be interpreted as hostile and all necessary actions will be taken thus. Will you comply with the orders you have received?" The voice being interpreted was not Felio and it took a moment for the AI to catch up on translation.

"I do not understand," I said. "If this action is voluntary, why is it mandatory?"

"It is not within the purview of this office to offer legal interpretations. I will offer that as you are assumed to be the legal owners of the vessel *Intrepid* and as yet no judgment has transferred ownership, this is merely an expedient mechanism. It is outside of Strix jurisdiction to seize property before ownership has been modified." The voice was high and grating, almost screechy. "Please advise intent to comply."

"We will comply," I replied and ended the comm. It was ironic that I had to defend to the crew my unwillingness to get us all killed. I couldn't imagine an entire society that was willing to allow visitors to be so devastatingly preyed upon.

"Navigation path received, Liam," Nick reported. "It's a twelve-day burn to Abasi Prime."

"Plug it in," I said, defeated.

"What about the Cetacarians?" I asked, looking at Nick. "Can you think of any reason we shouldn't contact them?"

"I've already sent a query," he replied.

***

The sound of an incoming comm chirped in my ear and I awoke. I'd dismissed the rest of the crew from bridge duty, as we'd been going hard with little sleep. The Felio had dispatched four ships to accompany us to Abasi Prime. While I thought *Intrepid* might be a match for them, I was unwilling to set us to war with a people we'd observed to be so honorable, albeit misguided.

"I believe that message is from the Cetacar," Jonathan said, startling me. I hadn't noticed he was on the bridge when I awoke.

Play message.

"Greetings, gentle human folk of the mighty vessel *Intrepid*. It is I, Parlastio Stelantifi...," I couldn't understand the rest of what he said, but his name continued for many syllables, with more than a few breaks. I tried to focus. "... advocate representative of Pervasive Justice. I am most pleased to be considered to represent Liam Hoffen in the matter 146.12.40993. I have inspected the Confederation of Planet's claims against Liam Hoffen, Captain, and representative of the ownership of *Intrepid*. The claims made by the Chief Judicator are extraordinary in their scope and we have hope that an eventual positive outcome in your favor is possible. As time is of critical importance, I have transmitted a permission request that will allow Parlastio Stelantifi... to represent Liam Hoffen at the meetings of the Judicator of Confederation of Planets in your absence. I also invite Liam Hoffen to postulate questions related to this action, or others that might have arisen in the course of your arrival into this sanctuary of life we so lovingly embrace."

Record message.

"Parlastio Stelantifi, I apologize for shortening your name, but I have difficulty committing it to memory directly and will endeavor to do so in the future. As time is short, I'll respond directly. First, I grant you permission to represent me in front of the Judicator of the Confederation of Planets. I was given the impression by a party I would prefer to keep anonymous, that the Strix would be successful in seizing our ship. I am gratified to hear that you believe it is possible we may see a different, more positive outcome. I have many questions, although perhaps the most pressing is related to living arrangements for my crew when we arrive at the station Chitundu. Will we be allowed to sell the goods we brought along for trade to raise funds for the necessities of living?"

Send message.

"Captain, pardon us for listening in to your conversation, but we believe you might have misinterpreted the Cetacar's statement relating to the disposition of *Intrepid*," Jonathan said.

"Oh?"

"The Cetacar's phraseology, as translated, is not in conflict with Mshindi Prime's statements," he said.

"How is that?" I asked. "Parl said he thought the claims were extraordinary and that could eventually get them in our favor."

"The Cetacar are a long living species," Jonathan replied. "The word *eventually* is concerning. What if that time frame were to be forty standard years?"

"You think that's possible?"

"We have found support in Confederation public records for exactly this. Injustices are overturned so late as to be without value to the harmed parties," he replied.

I sighed. Just as hope reared its head, it was once again dashed. "I guess we'll know within forty minutes."

"Liam, there is another matter we would discuss with you," Jonathan said.

"Oh?"

"We will be separating from the crew of *Intrepid* when we reach Abasi Prime," he said.

"Oh? I guess I don't understand. Where will you go? Are you upset with us?"

"No, Liam. There is a matter we find we must attend to."

"In Dwingeloo? How is that possible?"

"It is of critical importance and we would appreciate your help limiting interest in our separation," he said.

"From the crew?"

"Yes," he answered. "Your crew would no doubt look to help us. If they were angry with us, instead, it is likely they would not speak of us for a period."

"I could tell them you've decided that since we'll be without a ship, you're moving on," I said.

"We agree this to be most expedient, although I regret the subterfuge," Jonathan said. "I trust you will find an appropriate time.

"I ask that you'd do one thing for me before we arrive at Abasi Prime," I said.

"Certainly. We are at your disposal and look forward to continued contribution while we are aboard."

"You can't tell anyone what I'm about to ask you to do," I said.

"If it is within our moral boundaries to do so, we will respect your wishes on this matter."

I nodded and explained my gambit.

***

"Anything shaking?" Nick asked after entering the bridge.

"We've only been under sail for two hours," I said. "You need more sleep."

"I can't sleep. I feel like we're walking into a trap."

"I just got another response from the Cetacar. They call themselves Advocates of Justice and it takes them a ridiculously long time to say anything. There's good news, really bad news and stuff somewhere in the middle," I said.

"Have you talked to Tabby yet?" he asked, ignoring my statement. "Marny said she found her in the gym crying. Ada was there."

"Crying?" I asked. It wasn't something Tabby did often and the thought weighed heavily on me. "No. Frak."

"We're about to go to hard-burn," Nick said. "I'll take the helm. You go talk to Tabby."

"I don't know what to say to her. Both Mshindi Prime and now this Cetacar, Parlastio Stelantifi, say the same thing. The Strix are taking the ship. The Cetacar is convinced they can get the ship returned."

"That doesn't sound bad," Nick said. "Tabby will love hearing that."

"Turns out that's the bad news; I just didn't tell you everything. Parl says we won't be successful in defending against the initial charges. The court is set up with a preference for the Strix Judicator. The good news is that I'm the only one being charged and even so, I can't be detained with the charges that have been filed," I said.

"How long before the ship is returned?" Nick asked.

"Minimum of fifteen standard years," I said. "Could be twenty-five."

"That's a crock of shite!" Nick said, spitting as he did.

"The trial is happening right now. They don't do it like we do; it's all motions being filed and passed around. They don't get together until the sentencing phase. That's why the Felio are escorting us back. Once I'm sentenced, I'll turn the ship over to the Strix."

"You said there was some good news."

"I'm the only one being charged," I said.

"The medium news?"

"We're each allowed to exit the ship with twenty kilograms of personal items, of which no more than a single kilogram may be in precious metals. The Cetacar are providing temporary housing and have reached out to the human settlement on the planet Zuri. They haven't heard back from anyone yet," I said. "Ironic, right? Here I was thinking we were coming to rescue another Belirand mission and they're going to end up rescuing us."

Nick grunted a laugh. "Ironic doesn't begin to explain it."

"What's Marny's mood about all this?"

"She's angry, but not at you," he replied. "She's worked with enough bureaucracies that she isn't surprised."

"I feel like I've let everyone down," I said.

"Let's take it one day at a time," he said. "It's a long trip to Abasi Prime."

"I'm going to go look for Tabby," I said.

"That's not necessary," Tabby said, leaning on the open hatch leading into the bridge.

It was my day for startling, as I jumped at her voice. I hadn't realized that Nick left the bridge hatch open.

"How much did you hear?" I asked, exploring her face and seeing red streaks. I started to get up, but she held her hand out to stop me.

"Nick, would you mind if Liam and I take this shift?" she asked.

"All yours, Tabby," he replied. "Sounds like I need to start collecting precious metals and making plans.

I nodded as Tabby got my attention by placing her hand on my chest and pushing me back into the chair. Once I was settled back, she climbed into my lap sideways and rested her head against my shoulder. I stroked her copper colored hair and pushed it back over her ear.

"I heard enough," Tabby said. "I'd make a fight of it, but I understand why you won't. I hate that they'll win and we'll just let it happen."

I didn't have words for her and knew she wasn't looking for them. She was always the warrior, unbending in her inability to compromise. It was my responsibility to protect her, even if it was from herself.

***

"We're dropping from hard-burn in three... two... one," Ada announced.

For most of the middle part of the trip, we'd fallen into familiar habits of taking watch, exercising and eating evening meals together. At mid-point, I'd informed the rest of the crew of Jonathan's intent to part from us once we arrived at the space station Chitundu. With all that had been heaped on us, it felt like minor news and he was wished well by all but Tabby, who had grown quieter the closer we'd come to our destination.

"Look at that," I gasped as the forward vid-screens displayed a view I wouldn't soon forget. We'd approached a huge, entirely water-covered moon in orbit around Abasi Prime. The system's brilliant white starlight reflected off deep blue water and bright white clouds. As it turned out, the Chitundu space station - our destination - orbited this moon. Sitting in dark relief behind the gorgeous gem of a moon sat Abasi Prime. The side facing us was in full night. At eighty-five percent the size of Earth, it was larger by at least twice than Mars. The continent we could see was completely illuminated by surface lights of cities still hundreds of thousands of kilometers from our position. For a moment, I wondered what life was like on Abasi Prime. What were the ordinary Felio families, sitting beneath those lights, doing just then? Were they sitting down for dinner or engaged in some sport I had never heard of?

"Receiving a hail from *Dew on Whiskers*," Ada said.

"One moment and then I'll accept. Friends, we've all had twelve days to deal with what feels like a lifetime of pain. But from this moment forward, we represent humanity. We will take what comes our way with dignity and we will pick our battles. I'm proud to be part of this crew and I'm proud to be human. Now it's time for this Confederation to learn just what humans are," I said.

"But haven't there been humans here already?" Jester Ripples asked.

"To that I say: they ain't seen nothing yet," I said.

Accept Hail.

"Captain Liam Hoffen, it is I, Mshindi Second. I am grateful you have complied with our requests and wish that there be no misunderstandings so close to our objective. Were that to happen, the results for your ship and crew will be devastating."

"Mshindi? Please share my gratitude with Mshindi Prime that she has honored us by sending her progeny as escort," I answered.

"The honor is mine, Captain Liam Hoffen," Mshindi Second replied, her face appearing for the first time on our forward video projector. Like Mshindi Prime, she had a dark brown coat with even lighter ochre-colored spots. "It is my responsibility to inform you that you may exit *Intrepid* with no more than twenty kilograms of material and a government agent will inspect the possessions you choose."

"I've been in contact with the Cetacar, Parlastio Stelantifi, and request his presence during this inspection," I said.

"Your request has been recorded and forwarded. Instructions for docking have been transmitted. Do you request any special services?"

"Our attitude controls have been acting up," I said. "Do you have the capability for manual tethering? I'm transmitting the points of *Intrepid* that will require lashing down."

"Understood, Captain Liam Hoffen. Mshindi Second will convey your requirement," she replied. "Are there further requests?"

"No, Mshindi Second," I said. "Hoffen out."

"Bring her in slow, Ada," I said.

"What was that about attitude controls?" Tabby asked. "What are you planning?"

"Let's wait until we're off the ship," I said.

"Liam?" Nick asked, warning in his voice. "Don't do anything stupid."

It was hard not to be awed by the Felio empire as we approached the space station. Like Mars, there were hundreds of ships of every conceivable size flitting about us. To my eyes, it appeared that we'd drawn attention that other ships of similar size did not have and I suspected word had gotten out about our arrival in-system.

Dew on Whiskers and the other two Felio warships ended up launching smaller, aggressive looking fighter craft to clear a path for us as the swarm of smaller ships increased with every kilometer of our approach.

Contact Parlastio Stelantifi, I instructed my AI.

"Liam Hoffen, I await with anxiousness the great pleasure of your arrival." I'd decided to call him Parl and hoped he wouldn't mind.

"Greetings Parl, we're almost there," I said. "Would you confirm for me that ownership of *Intrepid* has not been yet transferred to Confederation of Planets."

"I can most confidently assure you that until you stand in front of the Judicator of the Confederation of Planets, your ownership of *Intrepid* is without question," Parl answered.

"Is it offensive to you that I shorten your name to Parl, for expediency?" I asked.

"It is not offensive, Liam Hoffen."

"We'll see you in a few minutes then," I replied and terminated the comm.

"What was that all about?" Nick asked.

"He's planning something," Ada said, a mischievous glint in her eye. "We're landed. It will take the dock monkeys a few minutes to run out the manual tie-downs."

"You're not going to try to break out of here, are you?" Tabby asked, hope flooding her face.

"Nope. And you're all too darn suspicious," I said, standing up from the chair. "I believe our belongings are neatly packed next to the airlock. Remember, hold your heads high."

"You're driving me nuts with whatever you're planning." Ada smacked my butt as she hurried past me, catching up with Nick and Marny.

Tabby looped her arm into my own. "I'm in, you know, whatever it is."

"Hey, Cap, you're going to want to get a look at this," Marny said. "There's a three-meter tall blue giant on the other side of the airlock."

I set down the case I'd picked up and stared out through the armor-glass of the airlock. Indeed, there was a very sleek-looking blue humanoid giant towering over two Felio guards. The giant waved a wide webbed hand at me, the palm of which was dark blue. Its face had not a speck of hair, but was otherwise very humanoid, at least for the details I could make out at ten meters away.

"You know, I'm going to guess that's Parl," I said.

"I can confirm that is a Cetacarian," Jonathan said. "There is nothing to be alarmed about."

"I am afraid, Liam Hoffen," Jester Ripples said, holding his arms up after dropping the bag Nick had packed for him.

"Tabby?" I looked to her for help.

"Jester Ripples, up here, little frog," Tabby said, picking up Jester Ripples and his bag.

"We're green," Nick said.

"I'm right behind you." Tabby had stopped in the

130

companionway once she realized I wasn't following directly behind her.

"Just saying goodbye," I said.

I waited for her to clear the airlock and then turned back to the center of the ship.

Initiate scuttle program, deep cleanse, in twenty seconds, I said. Red lights flashed and the orange tail of Filbert disappeared around the corner of the passageway. "Frak!" I tipped over and laid into my grav-suit. I'd forgotten that darn cat so many times! It was an inexcusable mistake that I wasn't about to repeat. Fortunately, I scooped him up easily as he rolled over to have his stomach scratched.

I hastily retraced my path back to the companionway and closed the outer airlock door. As I closed the armored hatch and our last chapter aboard *Intrepid*, I caught a glimpse of bright orange and blue telltales of the oxygen-fueled fire that would consume the entirety of *Intrepid's* interior.

DON'T TOUCH THE CAT

"Greetings, gentle human folk. I find that I am humbled to stand in the presence of those who have traveled so bravely through the vast distances of our universe." Parlastio Stelantifi bowed his large head.

Standing a meter taller than any of us, Parl wore a shimmering, translucent cream-colored, sleeveless robe that was tied at his waist by a simple, braided gold cord. His form was basically humanoid except for a narrower build and ears that did not stand away from his head, but were embedded into his skull, leaving only an outline. With no hair, his face was smooth, as was the rest of the medium blue skin.

"Parlastio Stelantifi, it is nice to meet you in person," I said, retracting my grav-suit's glove and extending my hand.

Parl slowly extended his own, which completely enveloped mine. His skin was cool to the touch and the pressure he exerted was minimal. I looked up to the giant alien's face and wondered if the smile he wore was practiced for my benefit or natural to his species. Either way, the perfect symmetry of his facial features was, by any definition, beautiful. It was also unusual, with dark blue lips, eyelids and overly small nose.

"I, as a poor representative of the Confederation of Planets, would be pleased to recognize each of your traveling companions," he said after releasing my hand.

My ears popped as my AI's sound-canceling wave and interpretation circuits fired up again. It was the second time we'd been greeted with human-standard speech by an alien. In both cases, the speaker had been showing respect.

"Ambassador Parlastio Stelantifi Gertano Fentaril." A Felio gracefully strode into the impromptu reception area, still just one hatch away from the airlock where we'd entered. "I apologize for interrupting your greetings."

Parl turned toward the sound of the Felio's voice. "Mshindi Second. *Zakia*. It is refreshing to hear your voice and know you are well." I looked between the two of them. The second name he'd used, Zakia, had been spoken with considerable feeling.

"Judicator Yadingallie is most insistent that the human belongings be searched for contraband and weighed in accordance with Confederation policy and the matters in front of the courts," Mshindi Second said.

"While I can see no reason for the distrust shown to our esteemed guests, I honor your desire to keep the laws of our great society," Parl said.

I glanced at Tabby, who would be running low on patience for the loquacious alien. She had a slight grin on her face as we exchanged a look. I wondered if she'd figured out what I'd done to *Intrepid* and if she hadn't, what the backlash might be when she did.

"A room has been prepared and Judicator Yadingallie has sent two representatives to meet us. It is my duty to oversee the process," Mshindi Second said. "Crew of *Intrepid*, I respectfully request that you accompany me. We should have the capacity to resolve this matter shortly."

"Lead the way," I said.

"I have no items to declare," Jonathan interrupted. "While I find parting with friends distressing, I find no reason to delay. Liam Hoffen, I hope that our paths once again cross and that when you are in distress you would reach out."

"If you have no possessions to declare," Mshindi Second said. "You are free to depart. Are there others that would follow?"

Jonathan continued to express goodbye sentiments to the remainder of the crew.

Even though I'd been forewarned, I felt like I'd received a punch to the gut. I wasn't sure what the entire nature of the bond between me and the fourteen hundred thirty-eight sentients was, but I felt the loss of a friend all the same.

Ada, who'd been holding Filbert, handed him to me and exchanged a hug with Jonathan.

Jonathan's departure cast a pall on an already difficult moment and I sensed depression starting to settle over the group.

"Was it not the human William Shakespeare who first expressed that parting is such sweet sorrow?" Parl asked. "It is a heavy burden to experience such loss. Gentle folk, please bear with us for a short span longer and we will provide respite."

"Respite from having our ship stolen?" Tabby asked angrily.

"No, my new friend. Nothing I can do will repair the harm inflicted by an overzealous government," Parl replied.

"He's trying to help, Tabbs." I hoped to head off the fight Tabby had been itching to have since we'd arrived in the mine field.

She picked up her bag and then mine. "Let's get this over with."

"Tabitha Masters is sad." Jester Ripples grasped my free hand.

Wordlessly, we followed the Felio guard that had grown to eight, armed with either slug-thrower or blaster weapons, into a plain room adorned with nothing more than six tables. Standing to the side were two aliens that I immediately associated with pictures I'd seen of earth birds, called owls. Large round eyes, yellow beaks and some sort of covering that was either natural or worn and resembled feathers flowed from the top of their narrow heads down their bodies. The image was complete with hands that more resembled claws than any other species we'd been introduced to yet.

"The Judicator's representatives will not be introduced," Mshindi Second said. "Please extract all items from the containers and arrange them according to value."

"If the door is to remain closed, my companion Filbert would like to roam," I said as Filbert squirmed in my grasp.

"This is acceptable," Mshindi Second answered.

The two Judicator representatives, which I assumed to be Strix, started chittering at each other and then to Mshindi Second. My AI caught most of the protest, which was, in essence, that feral animals had no place on a space station and that Filbert should be terminated.

"Of course, most honored Quering," Parl intercepted the conversation. "A request for classification and termination is well within the purview of the Judicator's office. Parlastio Stelantifi Gertano Fentaril has requested formal status for the untested, pre-sentient form referred to as Filbert and I welcome your input to this proceeding. I have added your name to the investigation form and request your presence for the discovery process, as we currently are lacking Strix participation."

The resultant squawking was impossible for my noise cancellation to overcome and all I really caught were a few words that, poorly translated, sounded like insults.

I looked to Mshindi Second who answered my unasked question. "The Strix representatives rescind their original objections and your companion, Filbert, is welcome to prowl unattended." I couldn't help but notice that the Felio guard watched Filbert with more than a little interest and exchanged what I was sure were smiles.

With Filbert out of my arms, I set to unloading the case I'd packed with the items I felt we most needed. Nick had put together six blocks of precious metals, salvaged from otherwise very expensive components within *Intrepid*. Limited to a kilogram, mine was small as it turned out to be gold, which I lay at the left edge of the table. With only nineteen more kilograms, there wasn't a lot of room for other items, especially since Nick had spread the components of a replicator between each of our cases.

"The Judicator's office would like to challenge this unknown gem," Mshindi Prime announced to Parl, pointing at the quantum communication crystals we'd packed into Nick's bag. Of the items I was okay losing, the crystals weren't on that list.

"So noted. We request that the Abasi guard remove the items for further consideration and place them in escrow," Parl replied.

"Parlastio Stelantifi, we are uncomfortable losing those items," I said, stepping forward. "They are of significant personal value."

"The Judicator's office will have forty-five of your twenty-four hour spans to present a case for why the items are either unsafe for possession or have significant value to the Confederation of

Planets. If so deemed, they are subject to what human law recognizes as imminent domain," Parl replied.

"How do you know about Shakespeare and human laws?" I asked.

"It is part of the information the Belirand colony on Zuri has shared with our great society. Fear not, Liam Hoffen, I will work tirelessly to return your personal items."

"This substance is unknown," Mshindi Second said, waving a scanner over the two-kilogram bag on my table containing the remainder of the Aninonium we held.

"That, you can have," I said, bluffing. "It is sand from my home. If you take it, I get to go retrieve more items. I have things I'm starting to regret leaving behind."

"There is no negotiation possible in this process," Parl said. "You are not allowed entry to *Intrepid* until after a positive judgement has been made in your favor." I grimaced. If the judgement was in our favor, I'd made a horribly rash decision to burn out *Intrepid*.

The Strix chittered and reviewed the Aninonium's composition on the sensor. Silicate based, the Aninonium was indeed inert and closely resembled sand.

Unexpectedly, one of the Strix approached and chittered into my face. My AI struggled to interpret. "You are playing a dangerous game, *Human*. I sense deception, but cannot identify its source."

"Assistant Quering, it is inappropriate for you to directly interact with our guests as your office is pursuing formal charges against them," Parl said, stepping between us. "Liam Hoffen, I apologize for my esteemed colleague's breach in protocol."

"It's not hard to see what we're up against," I said. "Bullies and petty tyrants clearly aren't just a human affliction."

"Does the Judicator's office wish to set aside the item identified as sand from home?" Mshindi Second asked.

"We exercise our rights to seize the material," Quering, the Strix, replied.

So it went for the next two hours. In all, they confiscated a strip of grenade balls, the quantum communication crystals and, most significantly, the Aninonium.

"Your choices appear to have been well thought out," Parl said. "I regret the loss of your home-world material. It is regrettable to lose sentimental objects. I would now greet the rest of you as is our custom."

"Captain Liam Hoffen, it is now that we part ways," Mshindi Second said. "I express gratitude from House Mshindi for the honor you bestowed on us in recovering the Mshindi sword from Mhina. I hope that our next meeting finds us on level plains." With that, she bowed, her hand over her solar plexus. She led the Abasi guard from the room.

"Are there other formal requirements or are we free to go, Parl?" I asked.

"In two spans, Liam Hoffen is required to stand before the Judicator. I humbly request that I be allowed to stand next to you," he replied. "Otherwise, your companions are free to move about the Confederation of Planets territory unhindered."

"Why are you helping us?" Tabby asked. I could feel the agitation in her words. "What do you gain from this?"

"The Confederation of Planets is experiencing a misguided period of greed. The Cetacar people wish to demonstrate that this behavior is not representative of the vast majority of the citizenry. We are a long-lived people when compared to most species and have few material needs. It is our great joy to assist those in greatest need and provide an example," he said. "We only hope to gain friendship, Tabitha Masters. I understand your hesitance at such a proposal, but I assure you this is the case."

"Is it possible to find rooms on the space station?" I asked. "My crew and I are tired and need to figure out how to convert our metals into something that will allow us to purchase food."

"The Cetacar people invite you to retreat at our embassy on the moon, Rehema," he replied. "I have arranged for transportation if you are accepting."

"We accept your hospitality, Parlastio Stelantifi," I said.

"Are you sure, Liam?" Tabby challenged.

"No. If we are to survive, we need friends. Parl has shown us nothing but kindness," I said. "I'm going to trust him."

"I'm in," Nick said.

"My shuttle awaits," Parl said, taking us through the same door that everyone else had exited through. On the other side, we loaded our meager possessions onto wheeled carts that had been thoughtfully made available.

The space station, Chitundu, was huge and we soon found ourselves in a corridor every bit as busy as anything above Mars. One big difference, however, was that here it looked like we were attending a large, elaborate costume party. While the people around us were predominantly Felio, I located Musi and even a small pod of Norigans.

"Jester Ripples, do you see your family over there?" I asked, tapping him on the shoulder and pointing to the group of ten brilliantly colored Norigans. I'd learned from Jester Ripples that all Norigans considered each other family.

"What could they be doing here, Liam Hoffen?" he asked and jumped from Tabby's arms.

"Jester Ripples, wait," I called after him, but it was as if I was shouting in a vacuum. The look of surprise on the first Norigan to spot Jester was priceless. The chubby, slightly older Norigan back-handed the Norigan nearest him or her - I never could tell the difference - and trundled into the middle of the busy high-speed pedestrian traffic, causing Felio and Musi alike to leap and scamper aside.

"Parl, we'd better intervene," I said. "That whole group is going to frog-pile in the fast lane."

"I see your concern, Liam Hoffen," Parl replied. "Pardon me." Parl straightened and walked purposefully forward, his long strides eating the distance between us and the quickly forming knot of chaos. Deftly, he scooped Jester Ripples from the fast lane of the moving walkway and pulled the chubby Norigan along with him. Angry words from interrupted Felio and Musi were met with calm apologies as disaster was averted.

This day, which I had firmly believed would go down as one of the lowest points in my life, took an unexpectedly joyful turn. To be in the middle of a fur-ball of Norigans, reunited with a family member they believed lost, was incredible and caused me to tear up.

"Such a beautiful species," Parl said as he took a seat on the floor and looked upon the happy exchange. "Their focus is life affirming."

"He's so happy," Tabby said, handing the squirming Filbert to me. "I *do* understand, Liam."

"Understand?"

"Life is more important than a ship, even one as nice as *Intrepid*," she said. "I get that. I just think that if you let people take advantage of you, you'll always be their punching bag."

"I don't know how to do it any differently," I said.

"You're doing all right by us, Liam," Ada said, wrapping her arms around both Tabby's and my waist. The smell of her light perfume and the warmth of her embrace made me smile.

Tabby laid her hand over Ada's and held it. "We could learn a lot from those funny little frogs."

"Liam Hoffen, Tabitha Masters, Ada Chen, I must introduce you to my family," Jester Ripples said breathlessly as he approached. "Nicholas James, Marny Bertrand, please come closer."

I might have felt claustrophobic as the mini-horde of amphibious bipeds approached, if not for the silly grins plastered on their wide faces. Jester Ripples worked through the names as if he'd known them since birth and I still had no idea if they were just associates he'd never met, or lifelong buddies.

"What are you fellas doing here?" I asked.

"Please allow me to translate," Jester Ripples said as he turned and started enunciating each name he'd already provided. "Liam Hoffen does not prefer to use direct names, so it is often difficult to understand who is being addressed."

"We are on our way back home after a visit to Rehema," Booger Eye said. Okay, so that wasn't his name, but seriously, the situation was overwhelming and I couldn't keep track. "We were helping with a habitat restoration project after a minor volcanic eruption."

"The Cetacar thank you for your expertise and persistence," Parl said. "Your sensitive touch has restored the habitat of a beautiful species of Tentacled Polycyclids."

"I've been invited to return home with the expedition," Jester Ripples said. "I am now sad, as I cannot determine what I should do."

"Are you not concerned the Kroerak will learn of your return?" I asked. This was the reason Jester Ripples had given as to why he would not return to his home planet when previously pushed.

"The Kroerak have no record of which Norigans have been captured," Booger Eye replied. "This is a lie that has been promulgated to ensure cooperation by prisoners. Jester Ripples will not endanger his family if he returns."

"How can you turn that down, Jester Ripples?" I asked.

"Liam Hoffen, Tabitha Masters, Ada Chen, Nicholas James, Marny Bertrand, you are all my family now," he said. "I am being asked to choose and it is upsetting."

"Jester Ripples, if you return with your family, we will come visit you," I said. "Think of your family's joy when you are reunited. Would you deny them that happiness?"

"No, Liam Hoffen. And that is what makes me most sad," he replied.

"Jester Ripples, you can't be sad," Ada said. "I would give so much to see my mother again. What a wonderful gift you will bring to your family."

"Frak, does someone want to take my *cat* now?" Tabby said, reaching out for Jester Ripples. "I'm going to miss you so much, Frog-face." The nickname earned her a concerned look from Booger Eye.

"Tabitha Masters, you will always be my favorite sleeping partner," Jester Ripples said.

I laughed, but didn't say anything, which earned me a slug on the shoulder from Ada.

"We must leave now, Jester Ripples," Booger Eye said. "Our

transport will be departing in a few minutes."

I pulled the case we'd packed for Jester Ripples from the grav-cart. "Use this to pay for passage," I said.

"That will be unnecessary, Liam Hoffen. We are more than sufficiently funded. Thank you for taking care of our family. A grand celebration will greet you when Liam Hoffen travels to Norige," Booger Eye said. "We must travel quickly, Jester Ripples. I apologize for the haste that is required."

A flurry of hugs, more than a few tears and then Jester Ripples was off, running comically down the jetway with the gaggle of funny-shaped little aliens.

"Damn, I wasn't expecting that," I said, turning to Tabby, who was now clutching Filbert to her chest.

"Anyone touches my cat, dies," she growled.

"Our shuttle is just around the corner," Parl motioned. We were all just standing there, looking at each other, not ready to accept that we were down another crew member.

BREACH OF CONFIDENTIALITY

"You look like a child in that chair, Marny," Ada said as we settled into Parl's luxuriously appointed shuttle. The size difference between us and our host was made quite evident. I had to lift my arms to rest them on the armrests and I sank so far into the back of the chair that my legs were unable to bend at the knee.

"Parl, isn't the surface of Rehema entirely covered in water?" Nick asked.

"It is, Nicholas," Parl said. "Rehema is an uncommon jewel that we Cetacar treasure highly."

I looked through the glass of the shuttle at the broken cloud formations beneath. The dark blue water looked anything but inviting. "This shuttle is made to land on water?" I asked.

"I understand your confusion. I am not sure that translations between Cetacar and Human are yet perfected. The water's surface is not our destination," he said. "Before we continue our conversation, I would ask that you each secure yourselves with the emergency harness that is now available. Entering the atmosphere can be quite disturbing."

I exchanged a look with Tabby and we pulled straps around in a five-point harness. Fortunately, the fasteners weren't not difficult, as the buffeting of the ship began a few seconds later.

"Parl, surely the Confederation has inertial damping systems? Why not on your shuttle?" I asked.

"Perhaps our scientists are not as advanced as you would give them credit. Inertial damping systems are not available to most civilian ships. The machinery is too expensive and heavy," he said.

"I was under the impression that the Strix absconded with Belirand's colony ship," I said. "That would have had well developed inertial systems on board."

"There was little technology shared with industry from the Belirand ship," Parl said. "It is a source of much consternation within the species about this. The Strix have maintained that the systems were inaccessible and therefore much information was lost. There are others that say it has been withheld, either to support existing enterprise or because it is considered dangerous."

Nick grunted out a laugh. "It's nice to know that humans aren't the only species subject to conspiracy theories."

"What an interesting phonetic range you have," Parl said suddenly, obviously interested in changing the subject. "It is so narrow, yet you use it so eloquently."

The shaking in the cabin desisted and the shuttle broke into smooth flight, a red-orange glow that had formed around the windows quickly disappearing. I wondered about the training and specialization of the people sent by Belirand. Parl's shuttle had a fit-and-finish on par with the nicest ships I'd ever been on, yet it was devoid of armor-glass, inertial controls, and gravitational systems I took for granted on even the simplest of ships.

"Humans speak thousands of different languages." Nick obliged Parl's new line of conversation. "But everyone knows standard speech at a minimum."

"I am grateful for the translation provided by the one you call Jonathan," Parl said. "It does a magnificent job of translating your speech into Cetacarian, although, I confess to having previously studied human language on Zuri, where the Confederation settled our human guests."

"I was surprised not to see any humans at the space-station," Ada said. "After a hundred and fifty years, I'd have thought there'd be several travelers moving around at least. When I tasked my AI with locating a human, it came up empty."

"Most humans do not travel far from Zuri," Parl said.

My heart sank. "For a hundred and fifty years?"

"It has not been an easy transition for humanity," Parl said. "The loss of their ship upon entry to the system put them in the debt of many and they have not yet substantially recovered."

I exchanged a worried look with Nick. Something didn't sound right and Parl didn't seem like he was ready to fill in the details. I sat back and looked out the window, wondering what we'd stepped in.

"It sounds like slavery," Ada said. "In humanity's dark distant past, we robbed people of everything they had and then required them to work off a debt that would never be satisfied. After a time, we became so brazen that we simply skipped the part where the debt could be repaid and justified it to ourselves as benevolence."

"There is a small but strong presence within the Confederation of Planets that stand in opposition," Parl said. "We are ashamed of our actions and I wish to communicate to you our resolve in rectifying this matter."

As much as I might have liked to continue the conversation, I was distracted by the fact that Parl's shuttle was approaching the churning, watery surface of Rehema. My AI calculated the waves to be fifteen meters from crest to trough, something I couldn't imagine surviving in the small boats I'd previously used.

"Humanity is many billions of souls and I believe technologically superior in many ways," Ada said, not ready to give it up. "It is a dangerous precedent your Confederation has set."

"Uh, guys, we're about to crash land in the ocean here," I said. "This is an important conversation, but should we be doing anything?"

"The shuttle is well equipped for the oceanic environment, Liam," Parl replied. "Brace yourselves for entry, though. It appears our chosen entry point is experiencing a squall."

"I'm not sure our translation is working." My sentence was cut short as the shuttle tipped forward and plunged through the bottom of a frothy wave. The impact threw us all forward and our restraints strained to hold us in position. I was momentarily disoriented as the ship's tail section was impacted by the top of the wave, causing us to spin inelegantly. A moment later, however, the shuttle settled into a smooth flight.

"Why do you see danger, Ada Chen?" Parl asked, continuing the conversation.

"Because humans will vigorously defend what is theirs," I answered before Ada could. "If the Strix had taken a human government warship as they have taken ours, the action would lead to war. What if a scout ship from a human government had traveled through the Mhina gate?" I raised my hand. "Don't answer. I'm just guessing, but I'll tell you, the action would be considered an act of war."

"I don't understand how the Confederation was formed if it wasn't with the understanding that you can't steal from other species," Nick said. "How is it that you're able to trade goods and services without that trust?"

"You are asking me to defend what I believe to be indefensible," Parl said. "There is more to the Confederation than what you have been exposed to. Those in charge are utilizing their power to gain advantage and we have not been successful in exposing their corruption. Your arrival will once again shine a spotlight on this most troubling problem."

It was hard to pay attention to Parl as the shuttle slowly pushed its way through the viscous water. I'd never considered flying a ship in water. In fact, after my first meeting with Phillipe Anino, where I'd experienced swimming in a grav-suit, I knew traveling that way was way more difficult than sailing in the vacuum of space.

"Lights twenty degrees off starboard, Cap," Marny said.

My AI had picked up a feed of information from the shuttle and showed that we were traveling parallel to the water's surface at a depth of fifteen meters. We were shallow enough that the choppy water above still slightly rocked the craft and the star's light still illuminated the crystal clear blue water. Bright blinking lights were evident at a hundred meters ahead and the shuttled slowly arced to line up on them.

The structure we approached was like nothing I'd seen before. Tiny bubbles of glass were anchored to a stone reef where the moon's landmass reached upward, falling short of the surface by the slimmest of margins. It was as if a giant beast's last breath had been captured forever in these habitation bubbles.

"Is this a city?" Nick asked.

"It is our embassy to the Abasi," Parl replied "The closest translation I might consider is Dragon's Roost, as it is named for a great and noble creature from a world many light years from here. In searching Earth histories, your mythical dragons bear a striking resemblance to these beasts. It was the opinion of the builders that the reefs below resembled these dragons, an opinion I also hold."

"How many people are here?" Marny asked. I followed her stare which was fixed on two large fish swimming with speed toward the same twenty meter dome our shuttle approached.

"Seventeen at present," Parl replied.

"There are hundreds of domes," Marny said. "Is it always this deserted?"

"It is no secret the Cetacar people are in decline, Marny Bertrand," Parl answered. "Most Cetacar only reproduce once in their lifespan, which is several hundred of your human standard years. The last five hundred years of Confederation history has been wrought with civil unrest and unfettered violence. Many Cetacar have been lost while attempting to help young species come to the full understanding of the value of peace."

"And yet you keep trying?" I asked. "Have you no sense of self-preservation?"

"The Cetacar believe all life has value," Parl replied. "The countless lives that would be lost without our interaction is not something we are able to look away from. It is a noble objective and worthy of sacrifice."

"You need guards," Tabby said. "You shouldn't be traveling alone. The Confederation should provide protection for you."

"Host species take the responsibility of providing protection for us. Against our desires, the punishments for injury to a Cetacar are disproportionate. We are more likely to be assassinated by powerful entities than injured by common criminals."

"You mean the type of people who wouldn't be stopped by guards," Marny added.

"A perceptive analysis," Parl acknowledged.

As we'd been talking, I'd continued watching the two 'fish' racing ahead of the shuttle and realized that they weren't fish at all, but rather Cetacar. Their grace in the water was much different from Parl's lumbering gait on land. Long, narrow, pale-blue bodies, lithely slipped through the water at considerable speeds, erupting through the open bottom of a glass dome adjacent to the much larger dome our shuttle slowly settled next to. Like Parl, the two Cetacar were perfectly symmetric in their shape. The female was slightly larger than the male and by human standards, quite gorgeous and quite naked. Her full hips and rounded breasts caught me momentarily off-guard.

A slug to my shoulder brought me back to the moment. "Eyes forward, soldier." Tabby shook her head. "I really can't take you anywhere."

"My apologies, Liam," Parl said. "Have you found offense at the nakedness of my companions?"

"Hah. That'd be the day," Tabby scoffed.

"No," I replied too quickly, my voice higher than usual. Called out by Tabby, I decided I might as well fully commit to the conversation. "It's just that you are all so beautiful. I was distracted by how pleasant the Cetacar form is, especially that of your females. It's surprising to me. We're in a different galaxy and frak, if all the species look darn near human. Super human even."

Parl seemed to purr before responding. "I will pass along your compliments to Illaria Telleria Tesoro Luongia. She has a great love for the humans of Zuri and will be most pleased you recognize her beauty."

Tabby slugged me again and I winced at the repeated blow.

"Tabitha Masters, I do not understand your violence towards Liam. Has he offended by speaking of Illaria Telleria in such a way?" Parl asked.

"Nothing for you to worry about, Parl," Tabby answered. "Only Liam could make being a lech sound noble. I'm just reminding him that not all of us are buying what he's selling."

"I assure you Illaria Telleria will not be offended and she will also not seek to displace your position as Liam Hoffen's mate. In Cetacar tradition, it is acceptable to recognize all forms of artistic expression. It is considered high praise to be stimulated by another species' form, although as you have recognized, this often has side effects that are not desirable. I will share with Illaria Telleria that she should not seek to enjoy closeness with Liam Hoffen without first considering your relationship."

I closed my eyes and worked through math problems I hadn't considered since secondary education. Parl had just suggested something I hadn't considered. I wouldn't act on anyone's advances, but my mind and the rest of my body was considering things I needed to ignore.

"When do we meet with the Strix?" Nick asked. I looked at him and he returned my smile. Nick, of all people, knew I needed someone to throw me a shovel so I could climb out of the hole I'd dug. The mention of the Strix worked perfectly and all thoughts of the lovely Illaria Telleria fled my mind.

"Only Liam and I will be allowed within the chambers of the Judiciary," Parl replied. "Our presence is required in sixteen hours and we will host the meeting here in Dragon's Roost."

"The Strix are coming here?" I asked.

"Oh no," Parl replied. "There is no requirement for physical proximity. The Judiciary will communicate with us from within the confines of their fortified ship. To do otherwise would endanger them greatly."

"Why is that?" Nick asked.

"There are many who would seek to destroy those that adjudicate our laws," Parl said. "The Cetacar recognize the need for laws, but we also understand the sentiments of those in opposition to how these laws are applied."

"Seems like humans would be at the top of that list," Ada said.

"With your permission, we will disembark and be greeted by Ambassadors Illaria Telleria Tesoro Luongia and Gratio Lorosente Filientia Cesta," Parl said. "I would also be pleased to continue our discussion."

I looked to Ada who shrugged. I knew she was discontented,

but no doubt recognized that our hosts were either superb actors or were truly our advocates, just as they'd represented. My stomach growled and I realized we hadn't eaten in several hours.

"We will follow your lead, Parlastio Stelantifi," I answered, standing.

We exited into a dome that seemed small from the outside, but was indeed much bigger inside. The floor was made of a simple ground stone material and the walls were the rounded glass of the dome. The chamber we entered was twenty meters in diameter and completely empty, other than the central five-meter-wide cut in the floor that opened to the reef and ocean below.

Illaria Telleria and Gratio Lorosente had both donned the same shimmery gold translucent robes that Parl wore. The robes strategically blocked visibility to areas that humans generally considered not to be available for public display - if only barely.

Behind me, Tabby quietly tittered and I caught her and Ada eyeing Gratio Lorosente. Like Illaria and Parl, he too was magnificently proportioned.

"You are welcome to allow your companion, Filbert, to run freely." Illaria's voice was slightly lower than Parl's and had a musical quality to it. "We have made provision for his dietary needs, as communicated by Mshindi Second." She lifted a long arm and gently swept her broad hand toward a small mechanical object jumping erratically near the outside dome wall. "It is a simple machine, hastily constructed."

Tabby set Filbert down and he stayed next to her legs, but stared in the direction of the object. From experience, I knew he'd soon be chasing it once he was convinced the danger was less than his desire to pounce.

"We welcome you all to Dragon's Roost," Gratio Lorosente said, his voice higher like Parl's, but sonorous like Illaria's. "We have prepared a small feast in your honor and invite you to take your rest."

Gratio and Illaria approached, holding their arms out in a very human gesture, requesting permission to hug us in greeting.

"Welcome, Liam Hoffen." Illaria spoke softly as she pulled me in close. The warmth of her damp cheek surprised me as she bent to make up the significant difference in our heights.

"Your welcome is most appreciated, Illaria Telleria," I answered. "It was a difficult adjustment to have been received by the Strix as we were."

"Your predecessors have shown considerable resilience on the planet of Zuri and are most excited to hear of your arrival," Illaria replied.

"This is quite true," Gratio agreed, releasing Tabby from what I thought was an uncomfortable hug, although her scandalous eyebrow waggle at Ada made me question my assessment. Gratio embraced me much as Illaria had, softly speaking a welcome as our cheeks touched. "So much so that they have sent a formal invitation for you to join them on Zuri."

"There is no need to respond just now," Parl interrupted smoothly. "Let us join together in a feast from the seas of Rehema. Your parcels will be delivered to the accommodations we set aside for you at Liam's request."

"Parl, I intend to be direct," Tabby said.

"Please, Tabitha," Parl replied. "It is only with clear communication that issues are resolved."

"What do we owe you or the Cetacar people for your help?"

"A wise question, Tabitha Masters," Gratio replied. "We only ask for your consideration in utilizing our ambassadors when interacting with the Confederation of Planets Judiciary. Our mission is the betterment of our most excellent society. To be direct, without formal training, there are many missteps that the uninitiated are prone to making."

"Be candid with me, Gratio," Tabby replied. "Why would you do this? It is expensive for you and there is no direct benefit."

"I would modify your statement to – there is no immediate, direct benefit. Tabitha Masters, we are a long-lived people and recognize that for one species to succeed at the expense of another is to limit our potential. We *are* self-interested in our desire to help emerging species. Please walk with us so that we might continue this discussion while restoring our energies."

We followed Parl, Gratio, and Illaria into another domed room where stones of various sizes had been strewn about the room. Some had plates and silverware atop them, others were adorned with cushions and several had what appeared to be fruits and vegetables of unrecognizable varieties. The presence of plates, goblets and silverware caused me wonder just how many human guests they had previously entertained.

"It is in the tradition of the Cetacar to eat without hesitation. Please find a resting place and enjoy the bounty of our great home," Illaria said. "I believe Gratio interrupted Tabitha's conversation. Tabitha, please continue."

"If I'm to understand things correctly, the humans from the Belirand mission were sent to the planet Zuri where they were forced into debt."

"This is true," Illaria replied.

"If the Cetacarians are so wealthy, why wouldn't you simply replace the losses imposed by your grand society?"

"This idea was discussed at length by our people," Gratio replied. "With much input from the Belirand colony, we decided our best contribution was to help the colony secure loans and material in such a way that would allow them to survive and prosper. It is our long experience that wealth unearned is easily squandered. We have closely monitored our human friends and provided aid when most needed."

Tabby sat on a comfortable looking rock with a sloped back and considered the tall, blue alien. Gratio's answer had struck a chord common to Tabby's heart. The very idea of government handouts was the sort of thing that drove her nuts. Without work, she would often say, there should be no reward. It was a work ethic common on an asteroid mining colony.

"Your capacity for human standard is remarkable," Nick picked up the conversation as he did a plate. "How is it that you speak our language so well? Our translator AI's are barely operating when you speak."

"We have had considerable interaction with humans," Parl replied.

"Is that the only reason?" Nick asked. "Is it possible the reason the Strix won't meet with you in person is more complex than simply their safety?"

"Nick?" I asked. "What's going on?"

"You are most perceptive, Nicholas James," Gratio replied. "We have no desire to hide our capacity to sense thought patterns of sentients within a certain physical range. It provides a mechanism for improved communications."

"Some might consider it an invasion of privacy," Tabby said.

"Our only objective is productive peace for all sentients," Gratio answered. "Our ability to share your peaceful intent with the Judicator is as refreshing as it is fortuitous."

IT'S A FAIR COURT

Illaria released the belt around her waist and allowed her gown to slide to the floor and puddle at her broad feet. My cheeks burned red as I imagined her ability to read what flitted through my mind. She smiled wanly and gracefully dove through the opening in the floor that separated us.

"You're really not swimming, Ada?" I asked, looking longingly after our three hosts who beckoned to us from several meters away.

Ada raised her eyebrows at me. "After our last adventure on Curie with the Sephelodon? No, thank you." She scooped Filbert into her arms. "We'll be just fine right here."

"I don't see why you trust them, Liam." Tabby attempted to rekindle a private conversation we'd had after dinner. Gratio's admission of spying on us with some sort of telepathy had put her off entirely.

"I'm trying not to think about it too hard right now," I said. "I believe they mean well and they're honest to a fault. Gratio didn't need to tell us anything. Besides, it's just a swim."

"Fine," Tabby agreed and dove into the water. I followed her, with Marny and Nick close on our heels.

Seeing our acceptance, Gratio scooted off with a powerful flick of his legs and accelerated quickly. Parl and Illaria responded in kind and the trio were soon well away from our position. I nudged my grav-suit forward, taking the horizontal position I was most comfortable with, having learned to fly with AGBs. While I might look like I was swimming like the three Cetacarians, the principal was much different. Our grav-suits manipulated the micro-gravitational fields around us as we moved the water out of our way.

153

"We have never swum with any other sentients so graceful."
Illaria stretched out the words and delivered them in a manner
more like singing than talking. Her sonorous voice had changed
pitch slightly, but the inflections were all her own. Moreover, the
richness of the sound resembled instrumental music.

"Do you suppose they can hear our comms?" I asked.

"No idea," Nick replied.

"I'd be more worried about our thoughts," Tabby added.

"Please, do not dwell on our limited ability to interpret emotion
and intent. Even now, I only understand that you are concerned
with Gratio's revelation. Your communication is otherwise
secure," Parl answered. His voice, higher than Illaria's, was not
quite as melodious, but remarkable all the same. "Our ability to
communicate your peaceful intent will be well received by those
who seek to disadvantage you."

"You sound beautiful," Marny replied, uncharacteristically
changing the subject. "Do your voices combine?"

Instead of answering directly, the three broke into long-noted
song with more pitches than could be generated from the trio. I
realized we were no longer alone, having been joined by a group
of six more. Not unlike a wing of fighter pilots, they formed up,
following Gratio as he churned through the water, playfully
ducking around each other and weaving together a rich music I'd
never forget.

A bump from below alerted me to an adolescent male Cetacar's
arrival from the depths. His voice was deeper than Parl's. I pulled
up slightly to avoid him and lost much of my speed. He glided his
way through the group and placed himself next to Tabby, who
must have seen his approach as she didn't startle. I was caught off
guard as he ran a free hand along Tabby's leg and over her
bottom, smiling as he turned to face her, all the while maintaining
his speed.

"I think he likes you, Tabbs," Marny said.

"Beautiful human, play with me." The not yet fully-grown
Cetacar weaved his appeal to Tabby into the ongoing calls of the
Cetacarian pod.

"You cannot play with what you cannot catch. Point for Masters." Tabby reached across, tweaked his nose and rocketed forward, darting expertly through the frolicking group. Seeing the challenge, the youngster attempted to run her down. While he had strength and stamina, he was out-matched by our suit's technology.

"Don't take it personally," I said, rocketing past and bearing down on Tabby's position.

Simultaneously, Tabby and I broke through the ocean's surface and sailed up into the froth of churning water, only to be slammed by a breaking wave. Quickly recovering, we continued up above the stormy fray. I grabbed her foot gently. "Tag," I needled.

"What are we doing here, Liam?" Tabby asked as the violent spray of the angry ocean buffeted us.

"Looking for equilibrium," I answered. "We're taking losses at an incredible rate and we can't afford to alienate the only people who seem to be on our side."

"*Are* the Cetacar on our side?" Tabby asked.

"Until they aren't," I answered.

"Don't lose sight of that."

We were both caught off guard as the adolescent Cetacar exploded from the tip of a wave, only a few meters away. Too late, Tabby twisted out of his path, but he grasped her leg before releasing and diving back through the frothy surface.

"Oh, you did not!" Tabby exclaimed and dove in after him.

"Cap, you're going to want to see this," Marny called over the comms.

"Coming," I said, grateful for the distraction the playful Cetacar had offered.

I oriented on Marny's signal and flew to her position. As I approached from above, I caught sight of several dolphin-like animals porpoising along. When I dove back into the water, I discovered that the pod of Cetacar had been joined by a veritable host of sea life, including several giants, well over twenty meters long.

As I worked to rejoin the group, Illaria and Gratio gracefully peeled away from the animals and swam next to me. "We live for harmony between all creatures," Illaria vocalized, threading her words seamlessly into the song that had grown to a dozen and a half voices. She grasped my gloved hand with her own and swam along with me. It was hard not to be taken in by the sheer joy of being a part of this large group. I let myself exist in the moment, putting aside the worries that weighed so heavily on me.

I was both disappointed and relieved at seeing the lights of Dragon's Roost. We'd been swimming for a couple of hours, the Cetacar drafting along and even marrying up with larger fish, resting as they did. The group had thinned and by the time we arrived, we were down to our original group plus the adolescent male, who I was sure was crushing on Tabby.

My legs wobbled as my feet landed on the dome's hard floor. Even though the grav-suit provided most of my forward movement, I'd used untrained muscles and found considerable fatigue in my legs and torso. I turned away as Illaria, Gratio and Parl lifted onto the platform and covered themselves in their robes.

"Thank you for sharing that with us," I offered.

"It was our pleasure," Parl replied.

"Pleasure is too simple of a word," the adolescent Cetacar answered, staring unabashedly at Tabby. "Please, I must know your name." Standing at less than two meters, he was perfectly proportioned.

I felt a pang of jealousy as he reached his hand out to Tabby.

"Tabby Masters," Tabby replied. Her voice was higher than was usual and I realized she wasn't unaffected by his considerable charms.

"Why is it you demure? I feel your interest, Tabby Masters," he replied.

"Franceli Protunda Malater Babosta," Parl interrupted. "You must apologize. You have been told that humans have no capacity to shield their emotions and it is not our way to advantage ourselves as such."

"Why is the other human upset?" Franceli asked. "I simply share Tabby Masters' interest and would like to retire with her." With raised eyebrows, I looked from Franceli and back to Tabby. Somewhere, flirting had taken an unexpected turn.

"I ask that you separate yourself from our guests," Illaria said. "I will join with you before our rest cycle and explain the nuances of this interspecies relationship."

"My apologies, human friend," Franceli responded, turning to me. "I hope my misunderstanding has not offended too greatly. Tabby Masters, I consider with interest the expectations of our next meeting."

"Franceli Protunda, thank you," Illaria said and escorted the chastised Cetacar from the room.

"We have made arrangements for a rest cycle," Parl said, once Illaria disappeared with the obviously confused Franceli.

Tabby startled when I placed my arm around her waist. She was still staring in the direction Franceli had gone.

"Oh. Sorry." Her face flushed red as she turned toward me.

"Really?" I asked, annoyed.

"Don't be a hypocrite," Tabby retorted.

***

I awoke to a chirping in my ear. I'd set a movement alarm on the door leading into the communal room where the five of us slept. My jealousy over Tabby's interest in Franceli had taken me the better part of the night to recover from. I'd finally fallen asleep after accepting that she might not be wrong in how she saw it all, although I still felt she'd been close to crossing a line, even though she'd hadn't.

"Liam," Parl said quietly as I sat up. "It is time to speak with the Judiciary."

Tabby and I hadn't slept very close together making it easy to remove myself from the bed without jostling her. As I padded from the room, wearing only my suit liner, Nick got up and followed us.

Once outside, Parl addressed him. "Nicholas James, Liam Hoffen is the only one of your group that has been named in this legal action. As captain of your ship, he alone is liable."

"I would like to stand with him," Nick said. "We are partners in this."

"That will potentially open you up to further legal liability," Parl replied.

"Understood."

"I also share this responsibility," Ada said from behind us.

"The Strix have no capacity to understand noble gestures," Parl argued. "There is nothing that can be gained by this."

"Parlastio Stelantifi Gertano Fentaril, honor is found in the actions of a person when unobserved," Ada answered.

"A worthy sentiment, Ada Chen," Parl replied. "I have taken the liberty of preparing a light meal." He gestured to a table of flat stones that hadn't been here before we'd slept. I pulled a leafy wrap from the table and bit into it. Of the many great things we'd discovered about the Cetacar, their capacity for producing food that was anything but nutritional was not high on the list. I made a point of not inspecting the squishy contents of the wrap and quickly followed it with copious amounts of water. I finished the meal by selecting a citrusy fruit I'd enjoyed the previous day.

"I ask that you do not respond directly to Judicator Yadingallie," Parl replied. "He will make statements that you will find offensive. He will list charges that you will find unnecessarily punitive and you will want to question the validity of such. Allow me to prompt your responses."

"When will we discover if the Confederation of Planets will seize our ship?" I asked. "If they do, when will it be returned to us?" I was in the awkward position of betting against myself. After scuttling the ship, I'd feel like an idiot if the corruption of the Strix turned out to be a big hoax. I was also sure that the rest of the crew would have even stronger feelings on the matter and I wouldn't blame them.

"All will be resolved at the end of our meeting," Parl answered. "If you are ready, we may enter the communication chamber."

"Let's go," I said. Even though Ada grasped my hand as we walked down the corridor, I felt about as low as I could remember. I'd successfully pushed out thoughts about this meeting for the last several hours, but that was no longer possible.

The domed room we entered was simple, just like the rest of the complex. A projection device sat on a column of rocks and displayed a panel of three gaunt, beak-nosed Strix seated behind a table. A glass jar of wriggling worms sat in front of each of them as they busied themselves looking at what I assumed were reading pads. I looked on with disgust as the central figure snatched a finger-sized worm, dangled the treat above its narrow jaw and snapped off pieces until the entire worm had been consumed.

"Many pardons, Judicator Yadingallie," Parl said as Nick, Ada and I took our positions, standing shoulder to shoulder facing the projector. "It appears you are just beginning your refreshment period. Would you prefer that we reschedule for a more appropriate time?"

"Solicitous bastard. How did that stupid sea cow get involved in this?" The Strix on the left was speaking. With narrowed eyes, it swiveled its head, inspecting each of us in turn. "He seeks to delay the cycle of justice and deny possession of the new technology to our engineers."

"Why are there three?" The Strix on the right asked. "Which is the idiot, Liam Hoffen?"

I considered answering the question, but after Parl's warning, I simply looked on.

"Ignoring simple instructions," the middle Strix replied. "It affirms what we've heard of the limited intelligence of the species. It is remarkable they have developed such intriguing technology."

"More likely, they have stolen it," the left Strix replied, pulling another worm from the jar and snapping at it greedily. He was, apparently, uncaring of the viscera that splashed all over his brown tufted face. "Such a species could not possibly have developed the technology we saw evidenced when we seized the other ship."

I looked with interest at the Strix who'd said that, wondering what evidence led it to believe the Belirand crew had no ownership of the ship they'd arrived on.

"The blue cow talks simply to hear his own voice," the left Strix said, turning to address Parl. "Not all within our great society find what you offer as art to be pleasant. I find your screeching to be reminiscent of the function of my bowels."

"Have you nothing to say, Human?" the right Strix asked. "Are you even more stupid than your degenerate cousins?"

I looked over to Parl, having difficulty believing we had to put up with such insults from the high court of such an established society. Parl simply looked forward with a pleasant smile on his face. I wanted to reply, but bit my tongue.

"I believe they have become pets of the Cetacar," the middle Strix summarized. "You embarrass yourselves by hiding like children."

"Perhaps their minds are so weak they have fallen thrall to their new masters," the left one replied.

"I fear the condition of the ship. What mess they must have left behind. No doubt it will need scrubbing," the right Strix answered.

"It would appear the humans have no intent to respond," the middle Strix said. "For the charges of willful destruction of Confederation of Planets property, do you intend to file a defense?"

"Liam Hoffen, Nicholas James and Ada Chen have provided a full accounting of how it is they arrived at the Mhina gate," Parl replied. "It is our contention that they could have had no knowledge of The Confederation of Planet's placement of the Mhina gate minefield and that they are without guilt. Further, we argue that the damage caused to the ship, *Intrepid*, could have been prevented with a simple warning placed within the Mhina system. It is, therefore, the responsibility of this great society to repair the damage incurred upon entry."

"Is it too late to vote to remove the sea cows from our society?" the left Strix asked.

"Have you no memory of what occurred when Kroerak entered this gate?" the center Strix asked. "Of course you do, they obliterated billions of our citizens. We lost control of the planet Zuri and have yet to eradicate the Kroerak presence."

"There are those on the Judiciary that will agree with this assessment," the right Strix answered. "How have we come to a moment in our history that we would offer to repay damage caused by invading alien buffoons stumbling into our defenses?"

"Calm yourself, Lelbuggarra," the middle Strix replied. "After we have discovered all that the ship has to teach us, we will gladly return it to the sea cow's pet in full repair."

"What if this ship lacks detailed information of the systems, as did the ship of those who came before?" Lelbuggarra asked.

"An inspection of the mine field was conducted so the full value of the damages could be assessed," the middle Strix replied. I was astounded at just how brazen the discussion had become. I was equally astounded at how little input they required from us. "We find sufficient evidence of willful destruction of Confederation property to assess a one point four billion credit fine. What say Liam Hoffen, Nicholas James and Ada Chen in this matter."

"Respectfully, high Judicator Yadingallie, we object," Parl replied.

"So recorded. As the ship, *Intrepid*, is the only possession of value for the aforementioned humans, the Confederation of Planets requires the ship, *Intrepid*, to be held until a final assessment of guilt is reached," said Yadingallie.

"We request," Parl started and I cleared my throat, interrupting him. "Many pardons, honored Judicators. May I confer momentarily with Liam Hoffen?"

"It is allowable. I sit forward, awaiting knowledge of the genius that occupies the mind of your pet," Yadingallie replied.

"Perhaps it needs to void its bowels with the knowledge of its recent impoverishment," Lelbuggarra added.

"Do you suppose it has learned how to avoid soiling its clothing?" the left Strix asked.

I ignored the responses as Parl placed himself between me and the projector. "Liam, you are doing very well, it is critical that you maintain your composure."

"Understood, Parl. Yadingallie offered to return *Intrepid* to full working condition when it was returned to us," I said. "I didn't hear this stipulated; was he just blowing wind?"

"Blowing wind?" Yadingallie asked.

"High Judicator, this is a private conversation," Parl replied. "I will rephrase and ask the question, Liam."

"Yes. Yes," Yadingallie replied. "I heard the idiot's question. I hereby commit the Confederation of Planets to restoring *Intrepid* to full working condition, as I promised. That is, if you live that long. Do you submit that you have no further questions for this Judiciary, Liam Hoffen, Nicholas James and Ada Chen?"

"We do not," Parl replied. "The High Judicator seized five crystals that were declared as personal property and sand from Liam Hoffen's home. There is a limit of time in which their function and value must be assessed."

"We believe these crystals are used in communication. We expect to utilize a device located within *Intrepid* to establish this. If there is value for our great society, they will be retained," the Strix on the left replied.

"The communication function of the crystal that was discovered aboard the human ship was never confirmed," Parl replied. "There is no defense for retaining these objects."

"Tell him to shut his big blue jaws," the left Strix said angrily. "What do they care for a bag full of crystals and sand?"

"We are somewhat more limited in our actions with personal property," Yadingallie replied. "If we are unable to assess a proper function for these objects within forty days, they will be returned to the pets of the sea cow, as long as they remain in Confederation of Planets controlled space. Are there other issues that would be brought before the Judiciary?"

"We request an expedited appeal," Parl answered.

"This is acceptable. An appeal trial is set for fifteen standard years." I frowned at my AI's interpretation of the timespan provided by Yadingallie. The outcome of this judiciary process was exactly as Parl had led me to believe it would be.

"Thank you, most revered High Judiciary," Parl answered. "Your attention to these matters is most appreciated."

"See how it bows and scrapes to us even in the face of defeat?" the left Strix asked. "Why would we ever seek their destruction? We should instead bring them on as staff to the Judiciary. I would like a sea cow of my own."

"If only this were still possible, Chilkerney," Yadingallie replied as the projected image faded to black.

NOT EVERYONE'S A FARMER

"Is there something wrong with my AI translator?" Ada asked. "Or were those the most despicable, pompous, horrible creatures ever?"

"Your translation was most likely accurate," Parl said. "The Strix are well known for offensive language. If you look past this apparent character flaw, their single-minded pursuit of the interests of the Confederation of Planets has brought them to the position they now occupy."

"Have your citizens no sense of morality?" Ada replied. "Unchecked zealousness, greed, and taking advantage of visitors who are not strong enough to defend themselves is reprehensible."

"Your indignation is shared among billions of sentients who care enough to be informed on such matters. Unfortunately, the Strix are masters of manipulating a populace struggling to maintain a livelihood in a universe that contains such horrors as the Kroerak. Life is fragile, Ada Chen. It is not difficult to take advantage of this knowledge, if you are willing to bend truth to fit your purpose."

"What was your interpretation of the proceedings, Parlastio?" Nick asked. "The loss of *Intrepid* for fifteen stans is a setback we're still struggling to come to grips with."

"Perhaps this is a conversation best had with your entire party," Parl said. "I understand Tabitha and Marny have awakened and are engaged in vigorous exercise that closely resembles conflict."

"Did you apologize to Tabby yet?" Ada asked quietly, slipping her arm around my own as we walked.

"Apologize?" I asked, confused. "She was ready to go off with that kid!"

"Don't be dull, Liam," Ada replied. "The Cetacar obviously have the capacity to communicate more than words telepathically."

"What?"

"The child was taking advantage of her. Why else would Illaria remove him from physical proximity?" Ada asked.

"There would have to have been mutual attraction," Parl replied. "Ada is correct, though. Cetacar have the capacity to sway emotions of compatible sentients."

The sounds of martial combat announced that we were near to where Tabby and Marny were exercising. I smiled as we turned a corner and saw them using bo-staffs within a wide-open dome. A host of Cetacar had gathered and were observing the violent ballet, an activity I'd too often participated in - to the detriment of my physical being.

"Parl, can you explain why so many of the sentients we've discovered in our travels are so similar?" Nick asked.

"A great mystery, Nicholas," Parl replied. "The two leading theories are of a common creator or of seeding from an ancient, highly evolved super species. The simplest answer to your question is that sentient evolution prefers a bipedal form."

We entered the dome where Tabby and Marny were working out and I stood back, hoping not to be drawn in. Marny had been teaching me to fight with a bo-staff. While I'd learned a few moves, I was no match for either of them.

"How'd it go, Cap?" Marny asked, separating from Tabby and lowering her staff.

Tabby refused to look directly at me, instead lowering her eyes as I tried to catch her attention. Ordinarily, she was aggressive when we disagreed, unwilling to admit wrongdoing until I'd gone first. I'd learned this had more to do with her relationship with her own family than with me. She'd never heard an apology from her parents growing up. It was something I found confusing. Big Pete, while stoic in most matters, was honest about his own failings - if only well after the fact.

"We wanted to get together with everyone before discussing,"

Nick answered for me as I crossed the room to where Tabby stood. "Essentially, it is as bad as Mshindi Prime warned. The Confederation of Planets has found us guilty of willful destruction of Confederation property. They've assessed a one point four billion credit fine, which is ten percent greater than the assessed value of *Intrepid* and her contents."

"So they're taking the ship," Tabby said, looking at Nick before sparing a glance at me.

"We've filed an appeal," Nick interjected. "But, they won't listen to the appeal for fifteen stans."

"Justice delayed," Marny commented to herself.

"We believe you will be exonerated," Parl answered. "There is good reason to believe your ship will be returned at that point."

"Fifteen stans?" Tabby was unable to contain herself. "What are we to do without a ship for fifteen stans?"

"We've contacted the York settlement on Zuri," Gratio answered from behind me. "They have offered shelter for as long as you require."

"The Belirand mission?" Ada asked.

"That is correct," Gratio replied. "We offer our shuttle as transport."

I reached out and picked up Tabby's hand. "I'm sorry," I whispered. The events of the morning were settled and I couldn't allow the rift to remain between us.

She shook her head slowly, biting her lip. "You are right to be mad," she whispered back. "I let him touch me."

"When would we depart?" Nick asked.

"He tricked you, Tabby. He used his influence on you," I said. "It was not your fault."

"Departure is at your convenience," Parl answered.

"But, I wanted him. Part of me still does," she answered. A rare tear rolled down her cheek.

"The Cetacar are a beautiful people," I said. "I feel that same pull from Illaria and *she* works to suppress it. I can't imagine if she was to encourage those feelings. Tabby, I love you. Tell me you're with me and this is done."

"Of course I am." She dropped my hand and hugged me tightly. "I've never been so afraid of anything before. I thought you'd leave me."

I sighed. It was easy to forget that in her family, love had been sparingly shared and after all this time, she still didn't see herself as worthy.

"Wait, what about the comm crystals and the *sand*?" Marny asked.

"The crystals and sand are tied up for at least forty days," Nick said. "That is, as long as the Judiciary is unable to find sufficient value to desire to keep them."

Nick was offering a shaded truth. My comm crystal would certainly raise Mom, but that was only if they had a cradle. It wasn't a certainty that she'd answer without correct comm protocols, especially since humanity was at war.

I kissed Tabby gently on the lips and pulled her hand down with my own, turning to face the group. I grinned as Ada and Marny looked away, giving us the illusion of privacy. "We should take the York settlement up on its offer," I said. "We need a place where we can stop taking losses and get our feet underneath us."

"Yup," Nick said. "Let's go."

I laughed. "You know I hate it when you ramble on."

***

"What are you working on?" I asked, sliding down next to Nick. We'd been sailing in the Cetacar shuttle for eight days and had almost reached the Santaloo gate, which turned out not to be that far from the Mhina gate. Parl explained that the proximity of the gates wasn't a coincidence. Most believed the gates were natural formations of super condensed, ionized gasses. Others believed the gates had been placed by an ancient alien species.

"When I dismantled the replicator, I damaged the circuitry," he said. "I was just working through it to get a map of what needs repair. I'm building a pattern so we can get it manufactured on Zuri."

"I've been researching the trade routes around Zuri," I said. "They don't do much trade off planet. Why do you suppose that is?"

"They call it a sail-through system," Nick said. "Any ship capable of jumping in can make more credits by jumping through to Tamu and trading on Abasi Prime. It's a minimum of eight days to Zuri and only ten if they avoid Zuri and head straight through."

"There's trade on Zuri," I said.

"There is," Nick agreed. "It's just out of the way."

"That's opportunity," I said.

"We don't have a ship."

"Yet."

***

"Liam, I received a disturbing message from High Judicator Yadingallie while I was in my rest cycle," Parl said. We'd transitioned through the Santaloo gate and were six hours from the planet Zuri. The shuttle, while luxurious by any standard, was feeling like a prison.

"Oh? Has he decided to take the clothing from my back?" I asked.

"No, Liam. Had the Strix understood the potential of your suits, it very well might have, but they were not identified in the original assessment," Parl replied. "Your ship, *Intrepid*, appears to have suffered damage after the inspection by the Abasi Navy."

"Damage?" Nick asked, perking up. "What type of damage?"

"Per the engineering experts who arrived two days ago, there was extensive damage to all of the ship's systems. If I correctly interpreted the lead engineer's report, the ship's components were completely slagged. I believe this is a reference to what occurs to metals when they are heated to a point where they become molten," Parl said.

"Cap?" Marny asked. "You know anything about this?"

"Hold on, Marny," Nick answered. "Parlastio, what was the purpose of that communication from the High Judicator?"

"He wished to express his anger and believes the damage to have been purposeful," Parl replied.

"Yadingallie is suggesting we slagged our own ship?" Nick asked. "Was it not in the care of The Confederation while we stood trial?"

"There is evidence from nearby sensors that an event occurred shortly after your arrival at Chitundu Station," Parl said. "Yadingallie wants to communicate his great displeasure and that he will be looking to bring further charges against Liam Hoffen, Ada Chen, and Nicholas James."

"If I understand correctly," Nick answered. *Intrepid* was the property of Liam Hoffen at the time when this event occurred."

"This is true," Parl replied.

"Is it Yadingallie's assertion that The Confederation of Planets has jurisdiction over the treatment of private property?" Nick asked. "Or that Liam made any sort of statement as to the value of *Intrepid*? Finally, it seems that we have an outstanding question as to the ownership of *Intrepid*. That question should first be resolved before exploring these other questions."

"You have a fine mind for legal detail, Nicholas" Parl replied. "What you are implying is that the appeal process is available to High Judicator Yadingallie, just as it was for Liam Hoffen, Ada Chen, and Nicholas James. He has not yet filed an appeal and you are correct. The first issue, that of ownership due to seizure, must be resolved. Further, the timeline has been set for fifteen stans. Our response will be formulated at that future date."

"Liam?" Ada asked. "Did you slag *Intrepid*?"

"I wouldn't do that unless I felt *Intrepid* and the Tisons were about to fall into the hands of an enemy or corrupt government," I said. "I've sworn to Mars Protectorate that much."

"Damn," Ada swore. "I'm going to miss her."

***

I strained to get a good view out the shuttle's windows.

"Reminds me of Ophir," Ada observed. The primarily tan

landscape was dotted with bands of emerald green and turquoise blue.

"I think those are lakes," I said. "I don't think the green are trees."

"No, I wasn't thinking about the forest. Look at the settlement," Ada said. "It's walled. Like Ophir."

I switched back to the HUD's view using the ship's sensors and zoomed in on the rapidly approaching York settlement. Ada was right. The settlement was surrounded by a red-orange wall, which from our vantage point appeared to be fifteen meters high. Unlike Ophir, however, there was plenty of activity outside the walled portion of the city.

"That's a steel wall," Nick observed. "It's rusting, that's why it's red. Check out those towers and cannons. Talk about some firepower. Parl, why would York need such heavy defenses?"

"Historically, the Kroerak ran free on Zuri," Parl replied. "The war is long past, but periodically a warrior, long hidden in hibernation, awakes. York was originally at the forefront of defense for the planet's inhabitants."

"You're saying that not only did the Strix steal their ship, but they put the Belirand crew into an active war-zone?" Ada asked.

"It was unfortunate, but unavoidable," Parl said. "It was not without advantage to the human settlers."

"Like?" Tabby asked.

"The injustice drew considerable attention throughout the Confederation of Planets and much capital was raised," Parl answered. "Funds would not have been available to the settlement otherwise."

I was grateful when the shuttle settled on the ground as it short-circuited the tirade Tabby was winding up for.

The change to the energy level within the shuttle was almost instantaneous. We'd been trapped in the small, albeit luxurious craft, for far too long. Probably the most difficult part of the journey for each of us was the fact that we were headed into the unknown. Having landed, I think we all felt the same way; we just wanted to get on with it - whatever *it* might be.

The glass panels in the top third of the shuttle were designed for the much taller Cetacar and I was forced to bend down to look through the sections placed lower to facilitate a seated passenger's view. A crowd of humans, maybe fifty in all, had gathered at the bottom of a ramp leading up to the landing pad.

Without ceremony, Parl traced two fingers down a sensor pad, causing the panels of the exterior hatch to pull themselves into the ship's hull before disappearing. A brisk, sweet-smelling breeze cleared the well filtered cabin air in a single puff. Dust and flower pollen were my first impressions and I sneezed almost immediately.

A friendly hand clapped my back. "Nothing quite like being dirtside," Marny said. "It's enough to make a woman homesick."

Parl was first through the door, followed by Ada who was carrying Filbert, then Nick. I let Marny go around me and grabbed Tabby's hand, pulling her up from the chair where she sat. She'd been quiet for most of the trip. We'd found it impossible to talk privately, so I wasn't completely sure where her head was. I stopped momentarily at the top of the stairs and took in the settlement. The air was less humid than Ophir's, which I found odd given the ground water we'd seen during our descent. Unlike Ophir, where there were towering trees, Zuri's growth was shorter. Woody trunks fanned out into balls of gnarly branches five to ten meters in height. The plants resembled trees, but had no leaves to speak of.

We'd landed well outside of the rusting walls of the main settlement, but there were plenty of dwellings, most of which had been built into the side of the brown, rocky hills. The dwellings shared the same features; their entry doors were thick steel and their round windows didn't exceed two-thirds of a meter in diameter.

"Liam! Come down here." Ada's call broke me from my reverie. I located her at the edge of the crowd. She was speaking to a man whose size gave Marny a run for her money. He wore a broad grin and watched as Tabby and I descended. He stuck his hand out and when I reached to shake it, he slipped his hand past mine and grabbed my wrist. I'd seen people shake like this before, but it took me off-guard.

"Jackson Hagarson," he said. The man's shoulders seemed a kilometer wide and his forearms were as big as my legs. That said, he had a gut on him like nothing I'd ever seen. It stuck out past his barrel chest and I was dumbfounded. "They call me Hog and I'm the mayor 'round these here parts. I'd like to officially welcome you and your crew to York."

I smiled. The man had charisma. "Liam Hoffen," I said. "We appreciate your hospitality."

"Strix got you in a pickle, now didn't they," he said. "Best not to dwell on it, son. You're people and that's all any of us need to know. Ain't that right, Patty? And who's this pretty little thing?" Before I knew it, Jackson 'Hog' Hagarson was pumping Tabby's hand and giving her the benefit of his charm.

The woman standing next to him was petite with graying hair. She flashed a quick smile. "Hog's never short on words."

I offered my hand which she accepted with a smirk.

"Not sure I know what a pickle is," I said. "But he's probably right."

"Sure am," Hog clapped a meaty hand on my shoulder and I stumbled forward. "Careful there, son. You're a right thin one, aren't yah? Nothing hard work, sunshine and fresh food can't fix. Here, you need to meet the rest of the folks."

He steered me through the crowd with his hand still on my shoulder and a forearm behind my neck. After the third family, I lost track and was glad my AI was recording.

"Hog, you putting 'em up in the old Anderson 'stead?" a lanky, dark-haired man asked. My HUD reminded me that he was Curtis Long, married to a similarly lanky blond woman who seemed rather severe.

"I was thinking Anderson and Maresk," Hog replied. "No reason to crowd 'em up."

"You ever worked a farm, Hoffen?" Curtis asked.

"Asteroid miner," I said. "But we're traders more than anything."

"Not a lot of those here. 'Round here, person needs to be more than one thing," Curtis said. "Likely to starve otherwise."

"Now Curtis," Hog said. "Be plenty of time to talk about all that later. Not everyone's a farmer."

"Damn shame, if you ask me."

With a well-executed maneuver, Hog grabbed the attention of yet another middle-aged couple we hadn't met and continued the introductions. An hour later, I figured we had to have met everyone who'd come out and questioned if we'd met some of them twice. "Don't suppose they know how to drink where you're from?" Hog asked as the crowd started to thin.

"Hog. They've just sailed sixteen days. They might like a chance to get washed up," Patty chided, steering Tabby toward where Nick, Marny and Ada were locked in conversation with a pot-bellied dark-skinned man.

"Talking to Bish," Hog said. "Smartest fella in the whole damn city, unless'n it might be his kid." My AI pulled up the names Bob and Roby Bishop and updated Bob's name to include the potential nickname 'Bish.'

"What's goin' on with the brain trust here?" Hog asked, breaking into the rapid-fire conversation taking place between Nick and Bish. Bish looked over to Hog and raised his graying eyebrows, his eyes glittering with excitement.

"You ain't gonna believe it, Hog," Bish said. "Kid here says he brought along the guts to a replicator."

Hog swiveled his head over, locking on Parl's location. "Not so loud there, Bish. We got some big ears nearby."

"I already gave 'em the lowdown on that," Bish said.

"Cetacar make trouble?" I asked.

"Don't get me wrong, Hoffen," Hog said. "Good people as far as aliens go, but they got their own agenda and black-market tech ain't part of it."

"Frak, black-market?" I whispered.

"Best we talk about this after the big fella takes off," Bish said.

SETTLERS

"Sure sorry to hear about Earth being attacked," Hog said. Light was just starting to filter over the hills and my eyelids were heavy with sleep. We'd been the guests of honor at a raucous celebration and ended up at Hog and Patty's home, close to the center of York.

"Last we heard, they were making a push for the moon," Tabby said. She'd taken a liking to the enigmatic man, who seemed to enjoy the attention. "I can't imagine a force that could withstand the combined fleets of Earth and Mars. It must be horrible."

"You've seen battle," Hog said, patting Tabby's forearm patronizingly, but not without compassion.

Tabby ducked her head in an abrupt acknowledgement. "We all have."

"Wish I could say we didn't have any of that here," Bish said. "Kroerak all but took Zuri a hundred eighty years back." My AI projected a conversion showing that they'd adjusted their years to match the orbit of Zuri around the Santaloo system's star. "Abasi pushed 'em back, but they're still around."

"How much of Zuri is inhabited?" Nick asked.

"Now or back then?" Bish asked. "Today, maybe thirty percent of the land-mass and something around eight hundred million souls. Most of those Felio. Our eighteen-hundred forty-two doesn't even show up on their census."

"Eighteen-hundred forty-seven," Hog corrected.

"Right you are. Time was, there were two billion on the planet give-or-take," he said.

"Kroerak killed that many?" Ada asked, horrified.

"They got plenty of us," Bish answered. "Reports are a hundred million were killed in the initial invasion. York lost about half of

174

its original settlers. Zuri's population's been in steady decline ever since."

"But the Kroerak are still around? Why wouldn't they get hunted down?" Marny asked.

"Can't kill what you can't find," Hog answered. "Worse yet, they reproduce without so much as a dirty look."

"Now that's not entirely true," Bish interrupted. "It might be more like chickens, but there has to be a broodmare."

"True. Lay 'em and spray 'em," Hog answered. "Matter-a-fact Massey says he thinks he located a nest over past Blake's Run."

"What's he doing way out there?" Bish asked. "Good way to get killed."

"What's anyone do in Blake's Run?" Hog asked, looking at me. I shrugged at his question, as I certainly didn't know. "Salvage. Blake's Run used to be a good-sized city - can't recall what the Felio called it. Say, what did the Felio think of your little buddy there?" Hog gestured to Filbert who was stretched out on Ada. "I bet that made for some interesting conversation."

"Not so far," I said. "So Hog, tell us about replicators. Why didn't you want us to say anything in front of Parl?"

"Parl's not such a bad guy. Cetacar have always treated us well enough," Hog said. "Thing is, the Confed outlawed replicator technology back when we showed up. 'Course the military didn't have any problem taking 'em off our colony ship, back in the day. They must be shitting bricks about now since they don't have the tech to repair parts or make new ones."

"Sure they do," Nick said. "That's the first function of every replicator; to produce replacement parts."

"Not on a Belirand mission," Bish said. "Those Belirand bastards hobbled every piece of tech on the colony ship so it was useable but didn't give up its secrets if it fell into the wrong hands. Maybe the military has reverse engineered it by now. Who knows? Old news around here, though. Not to bring up a sore subject, but I bet they're loving your ship about now."

"Picking over her bones, is more like it," Ada replied.

"What do you mean?" Bish asked.

"Cap scuttled the ship," Marny replied. "Pretty thoroughly from what my little man here says." Marny mussed Nick's hair.

"Well, don't that beat all," Bish replied. "Took some balls, that did. How'd you know they were taking your ship?"

"Mshindi Prime told me it was going to happen," I said. "As did Parl."

Bish and Hog exchanged a look. "You know those Mshindi are from around here," Hog said. "A hundred kilometers that-a-way." He pointed over Ada's shoulder.

"I hate to break up the party," Bish said. "But I'm gonna be worthless today and I figure these kids would appreciate getting settled in."

"About that," Marny said. "How is it that you live outside the walls of York if there are Kroerak around. We have some weapons, but nothing that'd bring down a warrior."

"Well, first, we haven't had a mature warrior through here in more than a dozen years. Mostly, we just see juveniles," Hog answered, crossing his arms atop his considerable paunch. "Second, every homestead is equipped with a mounted blaster. If you're not caught out in the open, they're easy pickings and there's a bounty on 'em. Works out to ten Confed chits for every kilogram. Can't make a living at it, but it's something."

"Full disclosure," Bish interjected. "Andersons and Maresks were killed by wild Kroerak hatchlings. These wild Kroerak aren't well organized, but every once in a while, they can cause quite a lot of trouble. They're damn near impossible to track, especially the little ones."

"Rent?" Nick asked.

"For the homesteads?" Hog asked. "Outside the wall is free. Hell, we outta be paying you," he said, with a twinkle in his eye. "But we won't. You'll want to find jobs. We're headed into the cold season, plenty of work around here. Sounds like Curtis would like some help out on his farm."

"We're traders, Hog," I said. "We're looking for a ship."

"Tall order, that," Bish answered. "If one were available, how in the seven stars of Tardarius would you pay for it?"

"That's a detail to work out," I said.

"Nothing wrong holding some cards back. Wish I had a lead for ya on a ship," Hog answered. "Bish, you heard of anything?"

"I'll have to talk to my boy, Roby," he answered. "He's been doing work for Goboble. I seem to remember him saying something about an old freighter."

"You don't want to be sending these kids over there," Hog said. "Nothing but trouble around Goboble."

"Are you all still up?" Patty asked, walking into the room they called the parlor. "Hog, you need to fix that cooler today or my cream is going to sour, and you were supposed to show them to their new homes. They have to be exhausted." She'd excused herself at some point in the evening last night, citing the fact that she had to get up early to open the restaurant she and Hog owned.

Hog pulled his petite wife over to him, wrapping his arm around her waist. "You're right, dear. You know how I get."

Patty smiled affectionately at her husband, straightening his hair with a free hand. "You go take a nap and I'll stop by the homesteads on my way over. Massey can take care of opening for breakfast this morning. I'll bet most of my regulars are hung over as it is."

"That was one helluva welcome party, wasn't it?" Hog smiled widely, looking around the table for confirmation.

"Sure was, Hog," I answered. "I have to ask. Why the red-carpet treatment? We're nobody special to you."

"Not one to mince words. I like that," Hog turned toward me and I felt the pressure of his full attention, different somehow from the command presence I felt from Commander Sterra or Admiral Alderson. It was more that he carried the room when he talked. "Humans are a minority population on a backwater planet. We're the proverbial small fish in an even smaller pond and we're fighting for our very survival here. We've been here a hundred eighty years and we're still considered guests of the Confederation, which means we have no representation."

"I'm not sure how we change that," I said.

Patty gave Hog a look part of impatience and stood up.

"You might not," he answered. "But I'm willing to take a risk on five young bucks like yourselves. The simple fact is we're stronger together."

I stood and extended my hand. "Your generosity is appreciated."

Patty placed her hand on Hog's back and gently urged him from the room. "We've stocked your bungalows with necessities," she explained as we followed her through the elegant home. "Talbot Jenkins runs the commissary if you find you're missing anything."

Hog kissed his wife at the back door and we exchanged handshakes one last time before they headed back toward the main part of the house.

"Everything run on Confederation chits?" I asked.

"That's right," Patty answered. "Some species call them credits or notes. It depends on your translation device, but they're all the same thing. The Strix require that every member nation, species or guest utilize the same valuation and the Confederation gets twenty percent of every transaction."

"That's quite a tax," Nick said. "Local governments tack on top of that?"

"Abasi get another fifteen percent," she answered. "York takes another five."

Nick whistled in appreciation. "Forty percent is steep."

"There's a lot of bartering," Patty answered, winking. "Now, we can do this a couple of ways." She changed subjects as we approached a white building that looked much like her and Hog's home, but was a fifth the size. "We can take a few trips with my carriage or you can walk and I'll carry your parcels."

"Carriage?" Ada asked, quietly enough that I was sure she was getting information from her AI. We'd seen plenty of pneumatic wheeled vehicles the day before and I'd already heard the term carriage used in reference to the vehicles.

Patty opened a side door to the small building. "It's how we get around. Eventually, you'll need to see about getting one from Bish or Roby." There were two, four-wheeled vehicles parked in the bay. Both were two-seaters with sizeable, covered storage areas in back. "We don't haul many people around, but between Hog's feed-store and the restaurant, we need to move a lot of material."

"I think Ada's about to pass out," I said, rubbing my hand on Ada's back. She lifted her shoulders in appreciation. "The rest of us can follow along easily enough."

Ada didn't put up much of a fight. She settled in the front seat, holding Filbert, as Marny and I loaded the back of Patty's carriage with our packages.

"It'll be a good walk. The bungalows are three kilometers out on the other side of Quail Hill," Patty said. "If we run into Kroerak, you'll need to take cover in the closest homestead. Don't knock, just go in. Every home has auto-targeting guns that'll provide cover. I don't mean to alarm you; it's unlikely to happen. I can provide some cover with the carriage, but if there's more than one, it's better to be safe."

Marny pulled out the katana she'd carried ever since Anino had presented it to her and strapped it comfortably across her back. Patty lifted a wide bay door, exposing access to the cobblestone road that ran past her and Hog's home. When Marny caught me looking, she smiled. "Like she said. Better to be safe." Tabby, who'd been rummaging through our own parcels, handed me my Ruger blaster and strapped on her own.

"I'll go slow," Patty said as she jumped in next to Ada.

"No need," Tabby answered. "We'll keep up. Four meters per second should be about right. And, no grav-suiting, Hoffen."

The Santaloo system's star threw long shadows as we jogged through the center of town toward the main gate. My HUD displayed the external temperature at three degrees and my breath fogged as I exhaled. The oxygen-rich air smelled sweet as my lungs worked to adjust to the sudden burst of physical activity. I didn't look forward to the first few minutes, when my body would fight the change, but I knew the exercise was long overdue.

The heavy gate swung open at our approach. We'd learned that it was always manned, but sometimes, especially late in the evening, it might take a few minutes to rouse the watch. Apparently, the early morning watch was already up and about, as a lone figure waved to us from her high perch at the top of the rusty walls.

"No bug activity this morning," she called as we passed below. "You should be clear. And welcome to York."

I turned and waved as we passed through onto the same path we'd arrived on from York's landing pads. About twenty meters from the wall, however, we veered left and up a wide, gravel road.

"I guess Parl took off," I said.

"Bishop said the Cetacar are like that," Nick answered. "They prefer not to stay in remote outposts. Apparently the threats on their lives are common knowledge."

I nodded in acknowledgement and the four of us continued to follow along behind Patty's carriage. The whine of the vehicle's electric motor and the crunching of our feet on the path adding to the whispering of a light breeze through the branches of the vegetation that had been denuded in preparation for the coming winter.

"Must be a lot of mineral deposits," Nick said as we rounded a rocky bend that placed us on a forty-meter-long bridge. Underneath ran a ten-meter-wide crystal clear river whose water had a blue-green cast to it. "I'd bet there's copper upstream."

"Think it's safe to drink?" I asked.

"Patty will know," Marny answered. "We should be careful though, there could be parasites or bacteria our bodies aren't ready for."

On the other side of the wooden bridge, the slope of the path took a decidedly upward turn and I found that four meters per second was getting harder and harder to maintain. As a result, my desire to talk was reduced considerably.

"I found a download from the Abasi data stores with map data for this area," Nick said. His lack of breathiness was a dead giveaway that he was using the grav-suit to lessen his running load. I considered doing the same, but knew Tabby would bust me on it. "This road is called Blake's Way and our new homes are just over the ridge. Your AI should be able to pick that up now."

Sure enough my HUD started filling in details. We were twelve hundred meters from York and had another thirteen hundred to go. The next six hundred meters would take us up in elevation at a rate my AI figured I could take, but would put me at ninety-percent of my capacity. Basically, I was going to be hurting when we got to the top.

By the time we reached the summit of Quail Hill, my breath was ragged and my vision narrowed to just the path under my feet. The relief as we started down the opposite side was considerable as the muscle groups in my legs shifted to slowing my descent instead of dragging me upward.

"Are you seeing this?" Tabby asked.

I lifted my head and fought back the nausea that had been induced by working too hard on the climb. Slowing for a moment, I took in the valley below. The star's bright light illuminated the countryside several kilometers ahead of us, leaving only the valley directly in front in the shadow of Quail Ridge. The natural beauty on display was awe inspiring. Aqua green ponds were connected by a widening stream that lazily wound its way down the slope. Nestled within were thick growths of stubby trees, many of which still retained their green leaves. I sailed upward with my grav-suit, knowing that my attention was not on the path. As tired and distracted as I was, I'd risk stumbling on a rock or missing a turn and plunging into a ravine.

"This is amazing," I said as Tabby joined me.

She took my hand and squeezed it. "Nice job on that hill."

"I could really use a suit cleaner," I confessed.

"First priority is getting that replicator working," Nick offered, sailing up next to us. Tabby, seeing that Marny had been abandoned, dropped my hand, set down next to Marny and urged her to speed up.

"How hard is that circuit going to be to create?" I asked.

"Bish said there's a pretty good bazaar not far from here in

Azima. He said he'd run us over there tomorrow and help us trade out some of the platinum we brought along. If we can get parts, I should have it going in a few days," he answered.

My AI brought up a local map and showed that the city of Azima was a hundred kilometers away on the other side of York.

"Azima, that's pretty close to where Bish said Goboble is." As I said it, my HUD zoomed in on Azima and showed a location six kilometers out labeled Jorg Outpost.

"Might want to take that one a little slower," Nick said. "Hog thinks Goboble's trouble."

"What if he has a ship?" I said.

"Where would we go?" Nick asked.

"Wherever we have to," I said. "I'm not getting stuck here."

"It's not that bad," Nick said. "People are friendly and once Anino fixes TransLoc, they can send *Hotspur* for us."

"What are you saying, Nick?"

"I guess while we're stuck in Dwingeloo, maybe this could be our home base."

"Sure," I said. "I'm in. I just need a ship."

BAZAAR

I awoke to the smell of food cooking. As it turned out, the first bungalow we were offered, which had been dug out of the rocky hillside, had three bedrooms. We'd decided, at least for now, to stay together. Having lived on a ship with considerably smaller private spaces, the house seemed quite roomy for the five of us.

The room Tabby and I ended up in was three by four meters and at the back of the house. The bed linens were clean and while I was distracted by the smell of the dust within the room, at least the bed was comfortable.

"The mechanicals are self-contained," Nick informed me as I entered the common space - technically called a family room. It was the room adjacent to the heavy front door and the only space with windows and direct line of sight to the outside. All other walls in the single-story home were the rough, solid rock of the mountain. "They're like ship's systems, except spread out. The generators are capable of serious power output. It's like these systems were salvaged from old ships."

"Anything you can scavenge for the replicator?" I asked.

"Some, but not everything. I'd prefer not to tear things up too much, though."

"What smells so good?" I asked as we traipsed into the kitchen, almost tripping over Filbert who raced through the hallway erratically chasing dust bunnies.

Marny stood behind a three-meter-long island and smiled as we entered. "I'm not sure what it is, but it cooks and smells like bacon. They set us up with a few weeks of food, especially if the other house is outfitted like this."

"Any coffee?" I asked.

"I looked, but didn't find anything along those lines," she

answered. "There's tea. Not sure how it tastes though."

"Marny and I have been talking," Nick said as Ada padded into the room and slid onto a barstool. She was wearing a loose night shirt that I wasn't a bit surprised had made it into her twenty-kilograms of essentials.

"Oh?"

"We like your idea of getting a ship," Nick said. "There's no reason we can't run trade from Zuri."

"Do you think they have anything here that's worth trading?" I asked.

"It's a whole planet," Nick said. "There has to be something interesting."

"Won't know if you don't look," Marny said.

Tabby came in behind me and slid into the chair next to Ada, her hair still wet from the shower. "You're not forgetting that the Kroerak are attacking Earth, are you?"

"What can we do about it?" I asked.

Tabby raised her eyebrows but didn't answer.

"We get ourselves into a position where we're ready. When an opportunity presents itself it, we take it," Nick said. "And that means not relying on the kindness of strangers. Even human ones."

Marny slid two plates across the smooth stone island so they landed in front of Ada and Tabby. My stomach growled loudly as the smell reached me. "Are those real eggs?"

"The Belirand mission came with quite a bit of Earth livestock," Nick said. "They have cows, chickens, pigs and even some horses."

"How is it the Kroerak don't wipe them out?" I asked.

"Have to ask Bish," Nick said.

"There's your export," Ada said. "It'd be a specialty."

"I'm not hauling livestock," I said. I was saved from further conversation as Marny slid two more plates over to Nick and me. Ada's idea wasn't bad. The bacon and eggs were delicious, but marketing something nobody'd ever heard of wouldn't be easy.

"What about gravity sleds?" Tabby asked. "What's with all the wheels on everything?"

Nick leaned back, obviously searching for information with his AI. "Inertial systems and gravity sleds would both work," He finally said. "Much of what we take for granted is covered by patents and copyright, so I can't get clean rights from our database. The inertial systems and grav-sled patterns have reasonable public domain patterns available."

"How would you build them without an industrial replicator?" Ada asked.

"Manufacturing is something that's been around a lot longer than replicators," Nick said. "We'd just need to figure out what's available. We could build a decent prototype with the replicator we already have once we get it running."

"What time is Bish coming tomorrow?" I asked, looking through the hallway and out at the amber-colored sky. We'd gotten off-sequence with the planet's sleep cycle.

"He said first thing tomorrow."

"What does that mean?" Tabby asked. "Like oh-dark?"

"Earth terminology," Marny answered. "First thing generally refers to some time after sunup."

"Sounds like we need to get a card game going," Tabby said. "Patty leave any beer?"

Turns out she did.

***

Having lived most of the last few years on four hour shifts, the idea of going to bed at 0200 local and being expected to get up at 0800 seemed like a dream. I was startled when Tabby pushed on my shoulder, waking me.

"Someone's at the door," she said. "I'm going out."

"Hold on," I said, pulling at my grav-suit. Somewhere along the line, Nick had figured out how to heat the bungalow, so there wasn't any real reason to be wearing the grav-suit around the house. Still, it was comforting to put the suit on. The idea of being on a planet covered with atmosphere seemed particularly foreign to me. I picked up my Ruger and clipped it onto my waist where it was less conspicuous than my favored chest position, but still relatively easy to get to.

The young man at the door looked like a younger, thinner version of Bish - with a full head of hair.

"Hello?" Tabby said, opening the door.

The smile on the man's face was immediate. "Roby Bishop." He stuck his hand out to Tabby. "Engineer extraordinaire. We met at the party." I checked the time, it was 0630. At least I now had some reference for what first thing meant.

"Tabby Masters," Tabby replied.

"Oh I know your names. Dad couldn't help babbling all afternoon about the mysterious five who showed up from Sol," he said. "I always figured Sol was just a cosmic joke old people played on us. But here you are. Ready to get going?"

"We can be," I said. "I don't think Nick's up yet. I'll go get him."

"Figures. Dad's not big on details. Told me to be here before the crack of dawn. That you were itching to get over to Azima first thing."

I shook my head. There was that phrase again and it wasn't helpful.

"I'm up." Nick padded up to the door, his hair sticking straight up and the side of his face still red where he'd been lying on it. To his credit, he was wearing his grav-suit.

"How much room do you have?" I asked.

"We can take three," Roby answered.

"Let's go," Nick said. "I left a message for Marny."

"Any chance there's food where we're going?" Tabby asked.

"If you have the chits, there's nothing you can't find in Azima," Roby answered.

"Any problem with weapons?" I pointed to the Ruger at my side.

"Damn. Look at that," Roby said. "Mind if I take a look?"

I pulled the weapon from its holster, locked the firing mechanism and handed it to him. "Manufactured on Earth," I said. "Government doesn't allow them to be replicated."

"Dad said something about how replicators are commonplace

in Sol," Roby answered. "Is it true you have one with you?"

"The important bits," Nick said.

"This is replicated on Earth?" Roby asked, turning the gun over in his hands. "It looks machined to me. It's perfect. You could make this?" He handed the gun back to me and I holstered it.

"Not this exact weapon," Nick replied. "But a similar weapon is within the capacity of the replicator we've brought along. Something like Liam's weapon would take several hours."

Lights flashing on the path caught my attention. The darkened carriage lit up from inside illuminating Bish waving his arms impatiently.

"Maybe we should talk as we go," I said, pointing out at the vehicle.

"Oh. Right. Dad's probably cussing me out about now," Roby said.

"I'll grab the trade material," Nick said and turned back into the bungalow.

Tabby patted her abdomen. "I have it."

"Are you sure that's a good idea?" Roby asked as we walked out to the carriage. Unlike Patty's hauler, this carriage had a second row of seats as well as a sizeable interior cargo space. "Azima can get pretty rough and you'll have to leave your guns in the vehicle. Oh, Dad wants Nick to sit in front, if that's okay."

"We have to bring it along; how else would we trade it?" Nick asked, climbing into the seat.

"I don't mean to be offensive. But should we really be bringing a *girl* along and should she be carrying your stuff?" Roby answered.

Tabby stiffened next to me and I laid my hand on her arm. "I got this, Tabbs." There might have been a hint of a chuckle in my words.

"Choose your words carefully, Hoffen," Tabby growled.

"Think of Tabby as a Felio," I said. "You know, top of the food chain and all."

I jumped into the vehicle and sat in the center, forcing separation between Roby and Tabby.

"I didn't mean anything, Ms. Masters," Roby answered, flustered. "There are a lot of Felio where we're going and they might see you as a threat. We've had trouble with women getting pushed around."

"I think we'll be okay," Tabby answered sarcastically.

Bish typed onto a glass panel between him and Nick and the carriage started moving, slowly at first, as it turned around and drove away from our new home.

Roby started to talk, no doubt to defend his position, but was interrupted by Bish. "Son, your heart's in the right place, but you need to learn how to read people. I believe our new friends from Sol can handle themselves just fine."

"Humans aren't like Felio," Roby argued. "Felio women are just more dominant. How could they know that? She's going to get challenged in the market if she carries herself as equal. I'm just trying to keep her safe."

Tabby snorted derisively in response and I recognized that both Bish and I had done as much as we could for Roby. He was now on his own.

"Little man, there's no possibility I'll *carry* myself as your equal." Her voice dripped with sarcasm as she looked out the window.

"It's a biological fact that human men are physically superior to women on average," Roby replied. "There's no shame in it. I don't understand why this is upsetting."

Tabby sat forward in her chair and I knew she was done talking. She would be moving on to more convincing lessons if I didn't do something.

Fortunately, Bish rescued his son. "Roby, you're being insensitive. You need to apologize. Tabby, I'm sorry. My son is a brilliant engineer and would likely have been a leading scientist in any field he chose back on Earth, but the intricacies of human interaction escape him, especially sarcasm."

"I'm sorry," Roby replied sulkily. "I was trying to help. You're in a new galaxy and your worldview is likely skewed by previous experiences. I mean no offense."

Tabby grunted and leaned back into the chair.

"I noticed there was no coffee in the bungalow. Tell me you guys brought coffee plants with you," I said. "I can't bear the thought of only having public IP synth coffee."

"Public IP?" Roby asked.

"The replicators have unbreakable rules about intellectual property," Nick answered. "Our AIs carry the entire library of publicly available replicator patterns. Synth-coffee has a bunch of different varieties. The public stuff is pretty bad."

"Your entire economy would have to be based on intellectual property since your replicators make everything," Roby said. "That's incredible."

"And probably why replicators aren't allowed in the Confederation," Bish answered. "The impact to jobs would be severe."

"It's very efficient," Nick agreed. "Mostly trade involves raw or unique materials: fresh foods, iron ore, oxy, water, precious metals and natural fiber materials like wood."

"Don't forget alcohol," I said.

"Bish, does York have any exports?" Nick asked.

"With other species?" Bish asked. "Not really. We do, however, receive assistance from the Abasi government."

"Financial?"

"It's not a great deal, but they help with hard-goods to help keep our defenses in order. It's beneficial for them as there aren't a lot of Felio left on Zuri. We don't have anywhere else to go and by helping us, they're able to keep the local population of Kroerak down."

"Down? Are they breeding?" I asked.

"Not in the sense you're thinking," he answered. "The first thing an immature female Kroerak does is to throw off an egg sack. They are tiny little things, like fish eggs - the eggs, not the juvenile bugs. Those damn eggs can sit for decades before they're fertilized. Once a planet's been infested, it's nearly impossible to decontaminate it."

"What if I said I had public IP that'd change the way these

carriages work?" Nick said. "Get 'em up on a hover plane instead of rolling along on wheels."

"Sounds interesting," Bish answered. "Probably get the attention of Strix, though. They'd come down hard on anyone using replicators to manufacture goods."

"Patterns aren't that complex," Nick pushed back.

"You're saying we reverse engineer it," Roby jumped in. "Is that possible or are the components impossibly small?"

"It's public domain," Nick answered. "We won't be able to manufacture it as elegantly as a replicator, but our AIs can break the process down into components that could be built by people."

"A real export," Bish replied. "What do you think you'd need?"

"Prototype," Roby said. "The Abasi have a similar idea to IP. If we make a couple of prototypes we could hire a solicitor to protect the idea."

"How far is it to Azima?" I asked.

"Eighty kilometers," Bish replied. "Takes us about sixty minutes. The road smooths out after we pass through Kuende."

"Roby, tell me about the ship Goboble has," I said.

"I'm having trouble with the main engines," he replied. "It's actually an old sloop class Abasi Navy ship that was retired eighty years ago and converted to a freighter. Light armor, but big fricking engines. All the turrets were stripped and it leaks air like a colander."

My AI replied to my raised eyebrows by displaying a picture of a perforated metallic bowl with water running from the holes.

"He's looking for a sucker. Said there's no shortage of 'em."

My heart skipped a beat. The ship sounded perfect. Nick groaned as I patted him excitedly on the shoulder. I sat back and closed my eyes. I was going to have that ship.

I must have fallen asleep, because the next thing I knew, we were stopping and the sounds of a busy city filled my ears.

"They call this The Bazaar," Bish said. "At least that's standard translation. We'll park and walk in. You'll need to lock those guns up under the seats. We don't need the type of attention they'd give us."

"What specifically do you need, Nick?" Roby asked.

"Electronics," Nick said. "It'll take my AI a few minutes to analyze what we're looking at."

"Abasi technology isn't that different from human," Roby answered. "There are some differences, however."

I shut out what was very likely a thoughtful description of the technological differences and gazed out over the city. I felt like I was in some sort of weird vid. People were walking all over the place going about their business, but they weren't human. It felt like they were just wearing costumes. While most were Felio, there were many other species represented. There were meter tall, black and gray furred rodents, heavyset reptilians and even those who looked almost completely human, but with small modifications.

The smell of The Bazaar hit me hard when I stepped from the carriage. Unlike the impeccably clean, colorful tents of the open-air markets of Puskar Stellar, the Bazaar was dirty and crowded. Smells of filth and food mixed, causing my empty stomach to roil. Like Puskar Stellar, there were tents everywhere, but the fabrics were faded.

"Takes a bit of getting used to," Bish said, clapping me on the back. "The smell isn't usually this bad. I think they're having trouble with septic."

"Should we exchange for Confed currency?" I asked.

"Not right away. Trade with your hard currency first. Exchange at the end so you have funds in your accounts," Bish said. "Everyone accepts legal tender through the terminals, but prices are lower if you exchange hard currency."

"Precious metal work?" I asked.

He nodded affirmatively. "Best not to say much about that. Plenty of thieves and cutthroats in Azima."

"I'm starving," Tabby said as she stretched. "Oh. What's that smell?"

"I know a good place," Roby said. "It's not that expensive."

"I'll buy this morning," Bish said. "You can pay me back once you've converted funds."

We fell in behind Roby as he worked his way into the bustling throng and through the streets. My eyes fell on a pair of meter and a half tall gray-brown furred aliens, their gnarled hands tiny, but sporting thick claws. Memories flashed to mind of the dunes of Musi bones on the second moon we'd visited in the Mhina system, picked clean by Kroerak.

"What are you staring at human?" My AI translated the squeaky voice.

"Nothing. Sorry," I said and attempted to move around the pair. A flash of steel in the morning light warned me of danger. Before I could respond, a black baton batted the sharp blade to the ground.

"Mine," Tabby growled and just as quickly stowed her telescoping bo-staff.

"No kill." Aggression gone, the Musi was now pleading with Tabby.

"Keep moving," Tabby said and pushed me forward.

"Mine?" I asked. Looking over to her. My grav-suit would have easily absorbed the Musi's blade. She shrugged and smiled.

"Don't apologize," she said. "It makes you sound weak."

Roby opened his mouth and closed it again without a sound, his eyes wide.

"We should keep moving." Tabby nodded to Roby.

"Right. We're almost there," he said.

As we walked, I tried not to look like a tourist, but I gawked at the goods that were for sale: clothing of all kinds, rugs, pots and pans… everything imaginable. Most of the wares could easily be produced by a replicator. The vendors were all kinds of pushy, doing whatever they could to draw us into their spheres of influence.

"Mornings are busiest." Roby had to yell to communicate over the din of the crowd. "I wanted to bring you to a Pogona restaurant called Koosha's. Pogonas are the most human-like I've met and Koosha makes the best breakfast around."

My eyes followed Roby's to the back of a woman dressed in a light beige robe that hugged her slender, shapely body. Her pale white shoulders were visible through a curtain of bright white hair that hung to her shoulder blades. She must have felt my eyes on her, because she turned. Shock must have registered on my face as I took in her alien features. A protruding jaw with wrinkled jowls and slits where her nose should be stopped me in my tracks. For a moment, her brilliant blue eyes locked onto my own and then she turned back to whoever she'd been talking to.

"Roby, Roby, my dear boy." A male of this same species greeted Roby as we approached the popular food cart in front of which several tables had been set out. "You are back and you've brought friends. Koosha welcomes all."

I quickly recalled that Roby had referred to Koosha as a Pogona. Unlike the female Pogona, Koosha's skin was light brown, almost the color of the female's robe. He spoke with a slight hiss as a long, narrow tongue flitted in and out of his mouth. Like the female, however, his proportions were very human.

"Thank you, Koosha," Roby said. "I couldn't bring visitors to The Bazaar without stopping by for breakfast. They're off-worlders, after all."

"Aren't we all." Koosha gestured grandly, placing his hand on Nick's shoulder. "Then Jala will present our finest proteins. Jala, my dear."

"Yes, Koosha. I have been listening." Jala's voice had the same hiss.

"What brings important off-worlders to Azima?" Koosha asked as he ceremoniously wiped dust from chairs around an open table.

"Roby," Bish warned.

"Electronic scrap," Roby answered. "We're trying to piece together some old equipment."

"Then you'll wish to visit Mangusi," Koosha answered. "His attics are full of scavenged Abasi technology."

No sooner had we sat than Jala set bowls of noodles in front of us. I smiled and nodded in response, which caused her to intentionally blink back at me.

"Careful, Hoffen," Tabby said. "We don't know the customs."

"We could be betrothed, no?" Jala asked, running reptilian-skinned fingers along Tabby's arm. "A simple joining of Pogona and Human?"

"Amusing," Tabby replied, although I was curious as to who the 'we' might be in the betrothal. Jala hadn't made it clear if she was interested in Tabby or me.

"The food is compatible with human physiology," Roby stated as he enthusiastically slurped noodles from the side of the bowl. Hunger won me over and I joined him. The noodles turned out to be fibrous and required quite a lot of chewing, but the chunks of protein and the broth were delicious enough.

"You think we should call Goboble for an appointment?" I asked once everyone had settled in to eating.

"I let him know we'd be by later today," Roby said.

"I still feel this is a bad idea," Bish said. "There have to be other ships available and you don't want to be involved with Goboble."

"He's not that bad, Dad," Roby answered. "He's very logical."

"He's a thug, Roby."

BATTLESHIP GRAY

"This will work." Nick pulled a red painted box from a stacked pile of assorted Abasi electronics. "We should get extras though. It's likely we'll ruin a few of them."

We were using a subroutine Nick's AI constructed to search the myriad of junk electronics strewn haphazardly across shelves, stacked on each other, and lying all over the floor. After two hours, I wondered if we'd ever find what we needed. The differences between human and Felio technology were considerable.

"Mangusi, how much for this?" Roby asked, pointing to the red device.

The dark green-skinned Pogona looked more alien than had Jala and Koosha. His jaw protruded significantly and the loose skin beneath it hung in great folds.

"Very rare," Mangusi replied. "They were salvaged from a military installation at great expense."

"They're probably paper printers," Roby grumbled under his breath. "It's always drama with these guys."

"A hundred credits for the five we're looking at," Roby said louder, so Mangusi could hear him.

"Ten thousand credits," Mangusi replied. "Each."

"That's crazy," Roby answered. "These things are everywhere."

I typed a message to Tabby who stood next to me, asking her to hand me five platinum fingers, each worth six hundred Confederation credits.

"You will not find them," Mangusi replied. "These units were used by Abasi military in the manufacture of ammunition. They are very rare."

Tabby slipped me the platinum and I approached Mangusi. He

had a peculiar smell, like something had stuck in the great folds of his chin and was decaying.

"We are not interested in spending the day shopping and I would leave with five of them," I said. I held up three of the platinum fingers. "It is plain to me that these items have been here for a long time. You aren't likely to get such a generous offer again, especially in hard currency."

Mangusi's bright blue eyes looked greedily at the platinum fingers I held.

"Twenty grams each. Ninety-nine point ninety-eight percent pure. Easy to transport and universally accepted."

He reached for them and I pulled my hand back. "Not so quickly, Mangusi. Do we have a deal?"

Mangusi's tongue flicked forward, tasting the air, like a primal reaction to the presentation of the platinum. "Your offer is intriguing," he hissed. "But it is not enough."

"Would you make us browse other purveyors of salvage today? Our time has value, but your initial offer was insulting. My pride also has value," I answered. "Would you see my platinum leave with me or find a common ground?"

"Eight of your platinum delicacies," Mangusi replied. He was asking for the equivalent of thirty-six hundred Mars credits. "With understanding they are as pure as you represent."

"They are pure," I answered. "I will give you a single finger each for five devices once you have delivered them to our carriage in good shape. And only after they've been loaded. We leave Azima in an hour."

"Each of these fingers is of the same volume and quality as what you have shown?"

"Let me be clear, Mangusi. One hundred grams of pure platinum for five of your worthless office machines," I said.

"This is acceptable."

"We're done here," I said, pointing to the stairs that would lead us down to street level.

"That's highway robbery," Roby said once we were alone. "I've seen hundreds of machines just like that all over the place."

"He knew he had us," I said. "We'd spent too much time searching."

"Hog asked if we'd pick up twenty liters of light blue wall stain," Bish said." Patty is going to make him freshen up the restaurant. Then we should stop by the mineral exchange."

"Lead the way," I said.

As we walked, a request for a tactical comm channel opened in my peripheral. I blinked acceptance. Two red dots perfectly mirroring our speed and heading showed on a tactical display of the street.

"Bish, Roby, keep cool, but we're being followed," I said. Roby started to turn, but I hurried to his side and wrapped an arm around his shoulders. "Best not to look, my friend. No need to alert them."

"What's the play here?" Bish asked. I appreciated his question, but he was hardly in any shape to contribute to combat and I suspected the same could be said of his inquisitive son.

"How far is the paint store?" I asked.

"Fifty meters," Roby answered.

"Good," I said. "Nick, you go on with Bish and Roby. Tabbs and I will lead our other friends off."

"Don't," Roby said. "I've been mugged a few times. If you just give them your money, they don't do too much damage."

"If they're looking to jump us, they're probably armed," Bish said. "We shouldn't split up."

"Have you seen much combat, Bish?" Tabby asked.

"I've fought off my share of Kroerak," he said.

"It's not the same. You two go with Nick. He'll have us on comm if we get in trouble," I said. "Don't come out of the shop until we give you an all-clear."

"Yup," Nick answered.

I looped my arm into Tabby's and we turned abruptly, Tabby laughing freely and pointing at something colorful that caught her eye down the street. If our tails followed Nick, we'd double back and fall in behind. If they stayed with us, we'd lead them away until Nick and the Bishops had cover within the paint shop.

"Looks like we've picked up a third," Tabby said. Her AI's security program identified a group that, while physically separated, moved together as a loose team. "How do you want to play this?"

"Take this alley." I pointed down a narrow opening between two tall stone buildings. "Let's just be blunt. They see humans as soft targets."

It didn't take long for two of the reptilian-faced Pogonas to round the corner. It was hard to determine if they were sneering as they approached, given their elongate jaws and unusual faces.

"Some chance number three is circling around behind us," Tabby said. We stopped about fifteen meters in.

"Shite, this is the wrong way," I said and abruptly started heading directly toward the aliens. "We're two hundred meters over that way." I pointed over the top of the two approaching males. I chuckled as one of them followed my point with his eyes.

"Where are you going, little humans?" the one who hadn't followed my point asked as we closed to within a couple of meters.

"New to town," I said. "Got turned around. Excuse us."

"Why don't you hold up a moment," he replied. "Perhaps we can be of assistance."

"Liam. We need to go, these guys look scary." Tabby pulled in close to me.

"There is a tax for the usage of this street," the Pogona replied. "It will cost you platinum bars." When he opened his mouth, I realized he lacked teeth, but rather had jagged ridges running along the inside of his mouth.

"Seems like someone has been talking out of turn," I said. "Does this mean our deal with Mangusi is off?"

"I know of no Mangusi," he replied.

"Then how do you know about the platinum?" I asked.

"We are very observant."

"It's not the word I'd use," Tabby said and crossed in front of me.

"Don't be so human," he replied. "Detain this one." He reached his hand behind his back as his compatriot tried to grab Tabby. She'd neatly blocked them both from me and I used the distraction to extend my bo-staff. Tabby spun quickly and slammed her elbow into the henchman's face, the crunching sound reminiscent of my own poor experiences with bones breaking.

I thwacked the speaker's snout with the end of my staff, choosing a sure strike over power. I didn't drop him, but his blinking eyes conveyed pain. As his arm came around with a pistol, I crashed the staff's end across his wrist, disarming him.

"Might have us confused with someone else," Tabby said, sweeping her now extended staff through the legs of the one she'd smashed in the face, dropping him to the street.

"You have poorly planned your assault," the lead Pogona said from the ground. "There are three of us and you are now in the weak position."

I looked to the end of the alley. Sure enough, the third Pogona was running toward us with a long-barreled weapon in his hands.

"Hold on, Tabbs," I said.

"Nah," she answered, grabbing a fist full of the speaker's loose jowls and rotated over his head, as would only be possible with a grav-suit. "I'll just aerate this one's neck and call it even." The Pogona struggled against her, but her grip was strong.

"How did you…," he started, but Tabby choked off his speech by pulling violently to the side.

"Tell your buddy to put down his gun or I'm going to empty your gizzard," she said.

"Release me," he answered. "This is just a misunderstanding."

I turned to face the menace with the rifle. I gestured to raise my face shield and jumped back over the top of the first Pogona Tabby had knocked down.

"Tell him to drop the gun or everyone's going to be misunderstanding you," Tabby answered and again wrenched on the loose skin beneath his jaw. This time a howl of pain escaped from between his thin lips as his head jerked violently to the side.

"I will not drop this weapon," the Pogona down the alley said. "I care not if this fool is unable to speak."

"Right. I was afraid you were going to say that," Tabby answered and brought her bo-staff up across her captive's chest. Once there, she let go of his waddle, grasped the other end of the staff and lifted up with her grav-suit. She sailed directly at the obstinate, would-be thief. I took the opportunity to crack the second, already injured henchman in the stomach, retrieved the pistol on the ground, and followed after her.

"What are you doing?" the remaining gun-wielding thug asked too late, as Tabby plowed him over and followed him to the ground.

In the confusion, his rifle came loose and I snatched it up.

"Tell whoever sent you, humans are off the menu," she spat, violently twisting his arm as more cracking sounds occurred. "Next time, you'll be going back in a box. Understood?"

I swung the rifle into the side of the building, shattering the stock and then dropped it on the ground. Finding a loose stone, I similarly destroyed the pistol.

"You've just made an enemy," he said.

"Seems like we already had an enemy," I said. "I believe we've just sent a message. Now, if Mangusi would like to keep his deal, we'll see him in thirty minutes. Otherwise, he can keep his junk."

It's hard to turn your back on even vanquished enemies, but I wasn't about to back out of the alley. Tabby and I turned and moved with good haste back to the main street where the crowds of people had thinned considerably since the morning rush.

"That didn't look good," Nick said as we entered the paint supply shop. "I almost called the security forces."

"They're probably on the payroll," Bish said. "Azima is a forgotten town on a forgotten planet. It's not likely you'll see the best and the brightest here."

"Except for House Mshindi," Roby corrected.

"We've had some interaction with Mshindi," I said. "Why would they stay on Zuri?"

"Honor," Bish said. "House Mshindi was well respected for their part in pushing back the Kroerak and defeating them on Zuri. They could no more abandon Zuri than change their names."

"We should get going," Tabby said. "Especially if we're going to the mineral exchange."

I wasn't thrilled at the rate the exchange gave us, but we had nineteen hundred grams of platinum and ended up placing fifty thousand Confederation credits into a company account Nick established. We still had four more kilograms which should net us an additional hundred thousand credits. It seemed awfully short for purchasing a space-worthy ship and preparing it to sail.

"I understand you ran into difficulties after you visited my place of business," Mangusi said after he exited a flatbed vehicle, loaded with more than five of the devices Nick had picked out. "It was not my doing, but I fear our meeting played a part in your troubles."

"You think?" I asked, sarcastically.

"I do think so," he replied, not grasping the sarcasm.

"I will offer two additional machines for the price of five, as remuneration for the actions of an employee who no longer finds employment with Mangusi."

"We should leave and forget about you, Mangusi," I said. "Nick, check the machines and make sure they haven't been tampered with."

"Thank you, Liam Hoffen," Mangusi replied. "I am embarrassed by this breach of trust."

"They're good, Liam," Nick answered after he carefully scanned the machines.

"Let's be done with this." I extracted the five platinum fingers and handed them to him once he and the driver of the truck had loaded the machines.

"I think Mangusi was sincere," Roby said as we pulled away.

"Don't be naïve," I answered. "Those machines aren't worth a tenth of what we paid and if he couldn't steal the platinum from us, he sure wasn't going to let it leave without finishing the deal. He's a scum-ball, Roby. Now, let's go talk to a man about a ship."

***

Jorg Outpost was nothing like I'd expected. In the back of my mind, I'd constructed a seedy, barren hangout, complete with musclebound thugs carrying automatic weapons behind tall fences topped with razor wire and mounted turrets on military-styled vehicles. I chuckled to myself as we arrived at a veritable oasis in the semi-arid, rocky terrain that made up most of my experience on Zuri.

Tall trees stood as the only sentries along the outside of the town of which row-houses formed the only fence. I'd come to understand that any settlement on Zuri relied on a physical barrier to separate the residents from the constantly spawning Kroerak. A pristine, metal gate stood open and a uniformed Felio sat alone in the guard shack that separated coming and going lanes of traffic.

"Hiya, Semper," Roby called out the open window as Bish pulled to a stop.

"Are you working today, Roby?" The younger Felio asked. She gave us a once-over. "Who are your friends?"

"This is my Dad. Say hi to Semper, Dad," Roby said.

"Greetings, Semper," Bish answered. "Call me Bish."

"Chill. Hi, Bish."

"These guys have a meetup with Goboble," Roby said. "They want to look at his starship."

Semper set down a reading pad. "No kidding. You're pilots?"

"Came all the way from another galaxy," Roby said.

"Roby," Bish warned.

"I read about that. Welcome to Zuri," she said.

"Thanks," Tabby replied, smiling.

"I guess you know where you're going," she said. "Best not to keep Goboble waiting."

"True enough," he said. "See you next eight-span."

"Okay," Semper replied as Bish pulled away.

"Girlfriend?" Tabby asked, needling.

"What? No," Roby said. Like Ada, his darker skin didn't give away what I was sure was a full-on blush. "Humans don't have Felio girlfriends."

"Why's that?" I asked.

"Survival of the species," Bish replied. "Without our young reproducing, our population will stagnate."

"Sexy," Tabby responded, sarcastically.

"Simple matter of numbers," Bish answered. "Humans and Felio have no possibility of procreation. A romantic relationship is pointless."

"But they're compatible otherwise?" I asked.

"Liam!" Tabby backhanded me in the chest and I watched as Nick covered his face, hiding a grin.

"What? Everything else is so similar," I said. "You're not even a little curious?"

"No!"

"Most of the humanoid species are physically compatible," Roby answered. "But Dad is right, there's no record of productivity."

"Relationships are more than sex," Tabby said. "And this is officially a messed-up conversation."

"Call me a romantic," I said. "But the heart wants what the heart wants."

"I'll stay with the carriage," Bish said. "I want nothing to do with Goboble or this conversation."

Bish had stopped the carriage just outside of a compound separated from the rest of the outpost by a three-meter-high wall. Like the rest of the community, dense trees and shrubbery separated the dwelling from the driving paths, but due to the approaching cold season, they'd lost most of their foliage, just as those around York had.

"Pressure barrier?" I asked, my eye tracing the glimmer of a yellow pressure barrier that soared up from the wall and looked to cover an area a hundred meters or better in diameter. Within the barrier, dark green leaves hung from thick trunked trees and colorful birds flitted between branches draped with vines.

"Goboble is Golenti," Roby explained as the four of us stepped out onto the flat driving path. "Everything inside the dome is from his home planet or at least reminds him of it."

We were met at the gate by two Felio, both carrying long guns. They wore similar uniforms to Semper's. Olive-drab shorts and halters were also similar in style to what Mshindi Prime and her crew had worn aboard the Abasi Battleship *Thunder Awakes.*

"Roby Bishop, you do not work today." A female Felio stepped forward, looking down at an armband that had an embedded, flexible vid-screen.

"Off-worlders want to take a look at Goboble's ship," Roby replied. "I messaged him earlier."

"We were not informed," she replied tersely and extended three narrow claws from the ends of her furred fingers. "I will make contact." The tips of the claws flew across the screen as she typed.

"If you carry weapons, they will remain here," the second Felio, also female, announced.

"No weapons," I said, holding up my hands and turning around. Technically, I was lying. I carried a nano blade and a bo-staff, but both were flattened and well disguised on my grav-suit.

"You may enter," the first guard answered. "Goboble has informed me that he will meet you at the ship."

My heart skipped as adrenaline surged through my body. Looking at ships was one of my favorite things and I needed to tamp down expectations.

"You can see it, just over there," Roby said, pointing through the lush, jungle-like flora that crowded the interior of Goboble's compound. My AI projected a red triangle on a gray section of steel that was barely visible. We followed a meter-wide, red-graveled path along the interior of the outside wall and were curving around the periphery of the sprawling main structure.

"You said something about the main power plant," Nick said. "What's the issue?"

"Parts," Roby said. "The Abasi government won't sell the couplings we need and I haven't found the right scrap. These old Abasi ships are tough as nails and way overpowered. We've blown all the couplers we've pulled from civilian ships."

"Have you tried to manufacture them from nano-steel?" Nick asked.

Roby tilted his head and frowned. "Not sure what you're saying."

"Nano crystalized steel," Nick answered. "Hardest stuff we know how to make."

"Titanium is what we need and getting a machine shop to work with titanium requires us to ship from Abasi Prime. The cost is astronomical."

I had a difficult time tracking with their conversation as we emerged from heavy jungle and the unnamed sloop came into view. It was forty-two meters of battleship gray glory. Dual rectangular engines were tucked neatly into the back third - sexy, like pistols on a woman's hips. One engine, thick and stubby, was mounted on the upper side of a longer, narrow engine. The heavy carbon buildup at the back of the larger engine fairly screamed of inefficient atmospheric operation. Forward of the engines, a narrow waistline joined with boxy - dare I say, buxom - cargo and living spaces.

"Easy, big boy," Tabby purred in my ear. "You're panting."

WHAT A VIEW

"Did they actually use tools when they removed the turrets or did they just hook her up to an asteroid and make a run for it?" I asked as we flitted over the exterior.

"These engines have been used hard," Nick observed. "I can see light through the cowl. I bet it leaks like a sieve."

"No way." I sailed around to the starboard atmospheric lift engine where I found only Nick's feet extending aft.

"Yup," he answered. "Look here." He prodded a beleaguered panel that was so thin it flexed and showered rust onto the ground below. "And look at those nozzles." The powerful lamps on his suit's helmet illuminated carbon covered brass fittings. "They're completely corroded. I think Roby's being optimistic that power couplings will get this girl back into space. I'd bet it won't even hold vacuum."

"That is a bet I would be interested in procuring." The voice was deep and rich, like a singer's might be.

I slid back out of the engine to find a blocky, dark gray alien standing next to Tabby and Roby. He was short, only coming up to Tabby's chest, but thicker in every other dimension than the heaviest human I'd seen by at least twice. From a distance, his skin looked like stone and he wore what resembled a business suit from an old vid, only the coat just reached down his thick arms two thirds of the way and there was no collar, nor lapels. He was accompanied by two Felio guards, one male and the other female. More concerning, however, was that two of the lizard-chinned aliens we'd run into in the alley stood to the side, guns leveled at Tabby and Roby.

"What's this about?" I asked, rotating and gliding over to Tabby, poised for action.

"Is this the one who attacked you, Peretop?" The man, who must be Goboble, asked.

"We were following them as you required. The squik," he nodded to Tabby as he said the word, "got a jump on Norateg and broke his appendage."

"I'd have broken more than that if he hadn't been such a Gunjway," Tabby retorted. I caught a slight grin forming on the female Felio's face at the seemingly well applied insult, but my attention was drawn back to the lizard-chinned aliens who advanced, adjusting their weapons.

"You will lower your weapon, Peretop," Goboble said. "*If* there is action to be taken, it will be at my discretion."

The Pogona looked from Tabby back to Goboble, but didn't immediately lower his weapon. In response, the female Felio hissed and dipped her head menacingly.

"These squiks cannot be trusted, Master Goboble," Peretop answered, but lowered his weapon all the same.

Goboble stepped forward and raised his hands, showing his empty palms. "I am Goboble. Master of Jorg Enclave. I apologize for a rude welcoming."

He hadn't stepped close enough for me to touch his hands, so I mimicked his behavior. "Captain Liam Hoffen," I replied, showing my own empty palms. "This is my fiancé, Tabitha Masters, and my business partner, Nicholas James." To their credit, both Tabby and Nick raised their hands.

"And these are my most trusted. Hakenti and Charena." The two Felio raised their paws, the female's claws slightly extended.

"Well met," I replied.

"I demand you address my complaint, Goboble," Peretop said. "While in your employ, we were attacked. The Musako Syndicate will not abide your lack of action."

Goboble moved his lips in a way that I found distracting. It was somewhere between a purse and frown. His lips were dark gray and resembled the texture of stone, possibly adding a strong sense of malice to his expression. "So you claim," Goboble replied. "Liam Hoffen, do you have anything to say on this matter?"

"Simple self-defense," I replied. "These two and another attempted to extract payment for our use of a public road. When we refused, they drew weapons and threatened us. When they refused to listen to reason, we had to convince them with more physical means."

"Lies from a squik," Peretop said. "You can believe nothing they say. We were following them and they jumped upon us, looking for monies. They are blood-thirsty aliens who injured Norateg."

"This does present a problem. The Musako will want an accounting," Goboble said. "Liam Hoffen, do you have any mechanism that would support your assertion?"

"Can't you just make him replay his data-stream from that time?" I asked.

"I am not sure of what you are referencing," Goboble replied.

"Data-stream. The log of his activities for the day," I said.

"He has no such thing," Goboble said.

"Well, I do," I said. "So does Tabby, for that matter. And Nick has data from when they first started following us."

"You knew they were following you? How?" Goboble asked.

"Personal security routines in our suits," I said. "It keys in on figures that are moving with us, even when we can't see them. We've had enough trouble that it's a useful routine."

"Suits are these clothes you wear that are so tight on your bodies?" Goboble asked.

"Right," I said. "If you'll permit, I can show you a replay." After pulling my earwig from my ear and detaching it from along my cheek bone, I stepped forward and held it out to Goboble. I must have been nervous or perhaps I stepped more quickly than the guards appreciated, but I was met with two paws on my chest as the Felio stepped in front to protect their boss. The female, Hakenti's, claws extended and poked at my grav-suit which hardened in response to the contact.

"Most interesting," Goboble replied. "Is it this suit that allows you to fly around as if there is no gravity?"

My stomach got an all-too-familiar sensation as I recognized that I was over-sharing. I hadn't seen anything like a grav-suit or even regular vac-suits with AGBs since we'd landed here. The idea that the technology might be valuable had escaped me.

"The suits are customized to the wearer," I said. "They cease to operate in the case their owner is incapacitated."

A deep rumbling emitted from Goboble and I realized he was laughing. "A poor attempt at deception. Hakenti, Charena, allow Liam Hoffen to approach. I would experience this technology he has removed from his face."

"Your physiology is considerably larger than human, but it should adapt," I said. "It's a little uncomfortable at first, but will project images to your eye and sound to your ears."

"I have heard of technology like this," Goboble said, plucking the device from my hand. His skin was rough as it scraped my palm, and the earwig was dwarfed in his oversized hand. The device expanded into his ear, but was unable to attach to the skin along his cheekbone.

Replay incident in alley with the Pogona to Goboble's earwig.

"Remarkable technology to be recorded at all times and with such clarity," Goboble said, tugging at the earwig. "Peretop, you are relieved of your contract with me and I will send an accounting of this action to the Musako. If I had wanted the humans assaulted, it would have been in my requirements."

"You overstep your authority," Peretop snarled.

"You will cease to address me," Goboble replied, giving the earwig another tug. Unfortunately, the earwig didn't recognize his skin as a touch and refused to disengage. I started to step forward, but he got just enough purchase on the device to pull it from his ear, crushing it as he did. Without apology, he handed the device back to me. "A captain without a ship is a peculiar thing, don't you think, Liam Hoffen?"

I accepted the broken earwig and stuffed it into a pocket. In my haste to clear our names, I'd lost a piece of technology that would certainly be difficult to replace. "The Confederation has an interesting way of welcoming guests to the system," I said.

"It is a simple matter of survival," Goboble replied. "The big prey on the small. It is the way things have always been. What is it that I can help you with, *Captain*?"

"We have interest in your ship, Goboble," I answered.

"It is not for sale."

"Everything is for sale," I said.

"A cynical perspective," he replied. "Perhaps I have misjudged you. The price is one-point five million Confed credits."

"For a ship that doesn't sail?" Roby spluttered. "It's not worth half that."

"Roby. If you would like to remain in my employ, you will join your father in his vehicle," Goboble said, seemingly unperturbed.

"Yes, Master Goboble," Roby replied.

"Is he in any danger from those Pogona who just left?" I asked.

"Not within Jorg Outpost," Goboble replied. "I am the master of my domain and they would suffer greatly."

"I'll walk him out," Tabby replied.

"As you wish," Goboble said.

"Would you allow a walkthrough?" I asked.

"Certainly," Goboble said. "But, you must understand. The ship is not for sale."

"Let's talk once we get a good look," I said.

"I will leave Charena to accompany you," Goboble said. "Bring them back to the viewing room once they have completed their inspection."

"Yes," Charena said, nodding his head.

Charena approached the ship and tapped a code on a mechanical security pad obviously designed for Felio claws. An iris-style hatch in the belly slid open and a ladder descended at forty-five degrees to the ship, settling on the ground. He nodded and stood aside.

"Six hundred ninety-two cubic meters," Nick announced as we arrived at the top of the stairs and into a rectangular cargo hold. "Fifteen percent larger than *Hotspur*."

"Smaller than I'd have expected."

"No airlock on this hatch," Nick said, ignoring my observation.

"Planet-side entry only," I responded. "Sure has seen some

wear. The deck plating is beat to shite." I kicked at the floor and dislodged a rusty sliver of metal.

"It's a side loader," Nick said, pointing at the bright red and yellow warnings in a language I didn't recognize.

"How do you load her without a dock?" I asked. I was concerned that the deck where we stood was two and a half meters above ground level.

"Elevator here." Nick walked over to a mechanical control surface that was reminiscent of the ancient freight elevator in his mother's equipment rental business. My eyes sought out and found the break in the deck where a three-meter square section could be lowered.

"A lot of storage for a military ship," I said.

"Same as *Sterra's Gift*," Nick countered. "Long range military ships are used to resupply outposts."

"Not in a lot better shape than *Sterra's Gift* was either," I observed.

Nick was already moving aft. "I'll check out the engines."

I raised my grav-suit's helmet so I could use the HUD and inspected the elevator's controls. It was a simple mechanism and my AI translated the worn instructions. The controls for power required Felio claws. Nick had foreseen this issue and, while clumsy, we'd brought a couple of small pieces of metal to insert into the mechanism. To my delight, the metal worked as well as did the elevator. A gust of wind and a wash of bright light filled the hold as I lowered it.

"Well, that's something," I said.

"What's something?" Tabby asked as she flew up through the opening.

"The elevator works. Want to check out the passenger spaces?" It was more of a statement than a question and we made our way over to a ladder that led up to what I assumed was the crew area.

"Charena, would you mind?" I asked. The iris style opening at the top of the ladder was closed. Charena had been standing passively toward the edge of the hold, watching us with mild disinterest.

"I will open," he replied.

"The security locks are all mechanical?" I asked, hearing the clunking of tumblers as he worked the mechanism.

"They are," he replied, stepping back.

"Not extra chatty, is he?" Tabby asked as we started up the ladder.

I laughed and opened a hatch that ran forward between the top deck and the cargo deck. The smell of ordnance wafted out, although I was unable to locate anything resembling ammunition. That said, broken crates and debris covered the meter and a half tall tween deck.

"How'd you like to be in there during a fight," I said.

"What do you mean?" Tabby asked.

"Take a whiff. This was ammo storage once upon a time," I said.

"Then what's that hatch?" Tabby asked, pointing to another tween deck entrance just above.

"My nemesis," I answered.

"What?" She chuckled, pulling open the hatch. I hovered up next to her and wasn't the least bit surprised to smell the reek of a poorly maintained, most likely broken, septic system. "Oh. Frak, that smells." She slammed the hatch shut.

"Let's at least check out the bridge before we get into the septic," I said.

"I'm not going in there," Tabby said, losing interest and climbing up.

We'd arrived on the top deck on the starboard side. Directly opposite, on the port side was an airlock that led to the second hatch Nick and I had seen from the outside. Just before the airlock entry, the hallway T'd off, forward and aft.

Deck One's design was rectangular and straightforward. The T junction was dead-center of an eighteen by ten meter layout. The hallway ran from the bridge at the bow and aft to the galley/mess combination amidships. I felt like there was missing space in the design, but decided to pay attention to that later. Six bunkrooms included two generous officer's quarters and two heads. The bathrooms, while not disgusting like those we'd found on *Sterra's Gift*, didn't appear to be any more functional.

The five-meter square bridge was well designed and I immediately fell in love with it. At the extreme fore, sat two pilot's chairs. Directly behind the pilots was a single captain's chair. The pilot's chairs were lowered into the deck so the remainder of the bridge had a clear view through the heavily mullioned glass.

While the bridge also had a view both port and starboard at the bow, it was through glass panels and a three-meter gap. Curious, I looked down through the gap and discovered more seating.

"What do you suppose that is?" I asked as Tabby joined me, looking down into what I'd have thought were the tween decks.

"Gunner's nest," she replied. "Looks like something ripped out all the controls - and not too gently."

"And that?" I asked, pointing to an aft hatch on the bridge. It was adjacent to the hatch that led back into the main hallway.

"It's locked," she said, trying the door.

Wordlessly, Charena padded across and opened the door. I expected to find an entry to the gunner's nest, but instead found a two-by-four meter room with four workstations, one of which was a pilot's yoke.

"Emergency bridge?" I said. "Charena, do you know how they get into the gunner's nest?"

"Yes," he replied and lifted a panel in the floor of the bridge near the portside pilot's chair.

I walked forward to the open panel and slid down into a cluttered, junk strewn area. The gunner's chairs had been pulled out and now lay on their sides, the metal legs bent and torn. At two meters tall and two meters deep, the space felt close, although it ran the entire width of the bow of the blocky ship. In the wells that were open to the bridge above was more junk.

"None too gentle when they removed those turrets." I shone my beams at giant steel patches on the bow that looked like they'd been applied by monkeys.

"Did he really say a million and a half?" Tabby asked. "This ship has seen better days."

"Not sure what that was about," I said. "I've connected to Zuri's market, such as it is. There are a few ships out there - none this big - and they're priced in that range. I can't believe they're in this bad of shape, though."

"How are we going to make this work?" Tabby asked. "We have what, a hundred fifty thousand in platinum between all of us. We'll need some of that just to survive."

"Agreed," I answered, slithering through the hatch and onto the bridge. "Let's see what Nick's found and then we can talk to Goboble."

"You don't want to look at the septic field?" Tabby needled.

I ignored her jab, knowing in all likelihood I'd be up to my elbows in alien crap if we ended up procuring this ship.

We glided back down into the cargo hold and through a wide, already open hatch that led further aft. We finally found Nick, lying head-first in the starboard engine.

"What are you finding?" I asked.

Nick rose up, startled, and banged his head on the bulkhead. He swore quietly and slid out from his awkward position. "Just about what you'd expect. These engines have been used hard. They have some life left in them, but yeah, they're pretty beat."

"Can't run without the parts Roby needs?" I asked.

"No, she'll sail, alright," Nick answered. "The big problem is with the atmo-entry engines. She'd be okay for short hops planet-side, might even be able to escape atmo, but no way would I trust her to re-enter. Most of these systems are purely mechanical."

"What do you mean?" I asked.

"No AI control," he replied. "You'd have to have an engineer back here or you'd be asking for trouble. What kind of crew can she hold? I bet it's more than *Hotspur*, have to be."

"Twelve would be comfortable," I said. "Eighteen or more if you hot-bunked. Biggest problem I saw is every door, hatch, and panel is designed for Felio claws."

"You mean beyond the fact that every surface is worn, cracked or ripped up? This ship is a rust-bucket," Tabby said. "I can't see why you love these project-ships."

"I suppose I have a soft-spot for the aged ship," I admitted. "Thing is, we either make an opportunity or we wait for one. I'm not much for waiting."

"Master Goboble invites you to his viewing room." Charena spoke, unexpectedly.

"You do the strong, silent thing well, Charena," I answered.

Charena nodded forward to the exit. "It is best not to keep Master waiting."

We followed Charena off the ship and back through the secondary fence that segregated the lush foliage of Goboble's compound and the sandier, native ground of Zuri where the ship sat. Thick, mustard yellow adobe walls surrounded the sprawling compound and a wave of hot, humid air pushed on us as we entered. The slight smell of rotting vegetation reminded me of the time we'd spent on Grünholz.

We followed a natural stone path through well-tended shrubbery and found Goboble resting in a pool of water, with nary a stitch of clothing on his body. Upon seeing our approach, he stepped out of the pool with his back to us and accepted a towel from Hakenti. I was mesmerized by the sight of the alien's thick, bony structure that made up most of his back. It was as if he wore armor, but it was obviously part of him as it was covered by the same dark-gray, stone colored skin.

"Thank you, Hakenti," he said as he donned the tailored slacks and suit coat we'd met him in. "I trust your inspection of *Fleet Afoot* was satisfactory. I would very much enjoy your truthful assessment."

"I'm not sure we're that good of friends, Master Goboble," I said. "*Fleet Afoot* is deficient in just about every way imaginable."

"Is this your assessment as well, Nicholas James?" he asked.

"Without significant maintenance, the star-side engines and other mechanical systems are nearing their end-of-life," Nick answered. "The life-support system is operational, but well outside of safe tolerances. The hull appears to be capable of holding pressure and I believe the planet-side engines lack the power coupling as described by Roby Bishop. Beyond that, the interior is dilapidated and not suitable for long-term habitation. I see no justification for your assessment of one-point-five million credits."

"Were you able to run a power to weight ratio on the star-side engines?" Goboble asked, unperturbed.

"Just a moment," Nick replied, his eyes searching the HUD we couldn't see. "Mercury in retrograde," Nick exclaimed. "Is this correct?"

Goboble smiled like he'd just told a dirty joke. To say it was disconcerting on the powerful-looking alien was an understatement. "I believe you have a suitable answer for my valuation."

"Nick?" I asked, raising my grav-suit's helmet so I could review the data I knew Nick would be sending me. I gasped as I looked at the readout. If the data was correct, the ship was seventy percent faster than *Hotspur*.

"Master Goboble, I apologize, I believe we have wasted your time," I said. "The price you are asking is more in line than I had expected, but it is well beyond our reach."

"It is not so," Goboble replied. "We have much in common. Please sit." He gestured grandly to rocks that looked out over the jungle compound.

We did as he asked and for a moment the four of us sat peacefully, listening to the chatter of wild birds and the gurgle of water flowing into the pool next to us. A million ideas floated into my mind, but I knew speaking early would give up any chance of positioning we might have.

Finally, Goboble spoke. "I have no interest in selling *Fleet Afoot* to you." He paused and allowed his words to sink in. "I would, however, entertain a joint-venture. A partnership, you might say."

"Go on," I encouraged.

"It is unusual to run into unaffiliated crews," he continued. "Those not bound by clan or governmental loyalties. I see value in this. I would hire your crew to run a shipping business for me. Completely legal, of course."

I knew from experience that most negotiators tip their hands in the first few moments of every negotiation. The fact that he emphasized legal cargo was important and likely a shading of the truth.

"You started by talking of joint-venture and partnership and ended with an offer of employment," I said. "Partnership is possible, but we have no interest in employment."

"But you have nothing to offer to the partnership, where I bring a ship worth a million and a half credits."

"Goboble, I have been negotiating deals for many years," I said. "Let's stop dancing. We have something you want, otherwise you wouldn't be talking to us. You also understand we're not going to accept employment."

"You remove much of the joy out of the conversation, Liam Hoffen," Goboble said. "Perhaps it is the way of humans. I propose we form an agreement, a company, as I believe you humans call it. I own seventy-five percent, your crew owns twenty-five percent, split any way you see fit. For this, I will add *Fleet Afoot* and you will turn over your space-suits to me."

"No way," Tabby said, unable to contain herself. "These suits are worth a couple hundred thousand a piece, minimum."

"You have a counter proposal, Tabitha Masters?" he asked.

"Ship for suits, seventy-five percent to us and you're a silent partner," she said.

I raised my eyebrows. It was a good counter.

"*Fleet Afoot* for five of your suits," Goboble said, running a thick finger beneath his chin. "And a twenty-five percent stake. I can do this, but I require one final thing."

He'd caved too quickly and I knew the zinger was incoming. "What's that?" I asked warily.

"I am allowed to place items on your ship, without charge and without question," he said.

"Legal items?" I asked.

"Not in every corner, but certainly on Zuri," he replied.

"Are we to be smugglers?" Nick asked.

"We need a buyout," I said.

"So to remove Goboble from our arrangement?" Goboble asked.

"Yes."

"One point-five million credits," he replied.

"Give us a day to discuss this with the rest of the crew?" I said.

"Yes. Take the ship out for a test run," he replied. "Return either the ship or the suits in three star cycles with your answer."

***

"Are you sure you can fly this thing?" Roby asked. It had taken some work, but we'd convinced Bish and Roby to ride back to York in *Fleet Afoot*.

"If you can get those engines running, I can sail her," I said, working the controls with the Felio claw simulating gloves Goboble had supplied. The controls were stiff, but functional.

"She'll start," he replied. "I'm telling you, this old girl just needs those power couplings and she's one-hundred-percent."

"All the same, shouldn't you be back in the engine compartment, just in case something goes south?"

"York is north of here," Roby said over his shoulder as he exited the bridge.

"I'll go with him," Nick said.

"I see no good coming from dealing with the likes of Goboble," Bish said, flopping into a chair at the back of the bridge.

"He'd be a silent partner," I said.

"He's a criminal," Bish said. "He'll have you smuggling contraband. You'll be criminals."

"As if the Strix gave us another option," I said. "Bish, Earth is under attack by the Kroerak and we're stuck in another galaxy. Frak these guys, but I don't give a shite about Confed laws, especially when they steal my ship. I can't believe you feel any other way, given how you've been treated. I have two priorities. Figure out how to survive here and see if we can help Sol in any way possible."

"Sol gave up on us a hundred eighty years ago," Bish replied. "I think you have your priorities upside down. You've been abandoned just like we were."

"That's just it, Bish," I said. "We were the crew sent out to find you. We might have been late in coming, but there are people trying to help."

"Too late," Bish replied. "I have a nice home and I certainly don't need help from Sol."

"Liam, I'm going to start the atmo-engines," Nick called over the suit's comm.

"Go ahead, Nick," I replied.

A deep throbbing started in the back of the ship and the hands of four of the eight gauges on the panel in front of me swept from zero to a hundred. A moment later, the ship shuddered to a stop and the gauges dropped back to zero.

"One more," Nick said. "We're adjusting." Over Nick's comm I heard Roby chattering instructions. "Okay, this will be better. Trying again."

The ship vibrated and the gauges spiked, then dropped back fifteen percent. A cloud of dust swirled around the front of the ship, momentarily obscuring our view.

"You sure the carriage is tied in tight?" I asked.

"She's lashed in good," Bish replied. I appreciated that, while he disagreed with our decisions, he wasn't overly grumpy about it.

"Hold on, Nick," I said and applied power to the heavy atmo engines, slowly at first and then all at once to escape the ground effect. The forty-two-meter ship popped up, surprisingly nimble, and I rolled us to the port to limit the amount of engine wash to Goboble's compound.

"Well, I'll be," Bish said, optimism returning to his voice. "What a view that is."

HEAD SWEATS

"She's a bit slippery," Tabby mentioned as I handed controls of *Fleet Afoot* over to her.

Bish tapped on a gauge. "Hard on fuel too."

"Any idea where we can come up with fuel?" I asked.

"One of the advantages of being on a planet no one wants to live on," Bish said, "there are fuel dumps all over the place. Abasi abandoned them when they took off. Not worth hauling back to Abasi Prime."

"First good news I've heard since we got here," I said.

He couldn't take his eyes off the scenery passing beneath us. "Sure is pretty from up here."

"Is Zuri so sparsely populated that no-one has a grav car?" I asked.

"That's high-value-tech," Bish said. "Too expensive for settlers on a backwater planet. You'd see plenty of them on Abasi Prime, though."

"Bish, tell me, why didn't the Kroerak continue invading?" I asked. "You can't tell me the Confederation defeated them militarily."

"You know, that's been the source of quite a lot of conversation over the years," he answered soberly. "Confed says they were defeated, but the news that's available from that time shows the Kroerak just pulled out."

"You mean after ruining Zuri," I said.

"Sure. And the hatchlings just aren't that tough," he replied. "Ravenous little buggers, all the same. Rumor is the Confederation found a way to run 'em off."

"Like a weapon?"

"Something like that. Happened real quick too, about the same time those settlers were brought back from the Mhina system," he said.

"You think they discovered a weapon in the Mhina system?" I asked.

"Could be," he replied. "Sure would explain a lot."

Tabby broke into our conversation. "Looks like there was some excitement down there." We'd followed the road back from Azima, past the abandoned town Kuende Run, alongside York and finally over the top of Quail Hill. The excitement Tabby was referring to was in the form of eight dead tiny Kroerak warriors, each under a meter tall, all lying dead on the ground.

"I guess Marny figured out how to run the defensive turret," I said.

"That's a big group," Bish said. "We haven't seen that many around here in a few years."

"Liam, set her down next to the other homestead," Nick called up from the engine room. "I was thinking we'd convert it to a workshop."

"Copy that," Tabby answered and gently set the ship down so the aft section was close in on the bungalow we'd yet to explore.

I waved to Ada and Marny who had come out of the house. There was little chance they missed hearing our approach. Ada immediately sailed to the ship and started giving her a once-over.

"You bought a ship?" Ada asked over the comms.

"Maybe," I replied. "Comes with a price and some strings. We'll have to talk about it."

"Doesn't everything," she replied. "Kinda beat up, don't you think?"

"If you think she's rough on the outside, wait till you see the inside," Tabby replied, shaking her head.

Ada laughed. "Liam and his pet projects."

We made our way down to the cargo hold and offloaded the carriage. "Stay for lunch, Bish?" I asked.

"I'm under orders from Patty to bring you all to the restaurant," he said. "She has her famous harvest chili and sweet rolls cooked up."

My shoulders had to have fallen in disappointment. "I was hoping to dig into these ship systems."

"I probably made that sound negotiable," Bish said. "That's not the nature of Patty's invitations. The woman gets what she wants one way or another."

"We'll have lunch in York," Nick agreed.

I smiled at Nick's quick turn. I could tell he wanted to work. Now that he had his replicator parts, he'd want to get after it. Thing was, we weren't about to start burning bridges with our new friends.

"What happened here, Marny?" I walked over to the dead grouping of baby Kroerak warriors and kicking one with my boot.

"Bungalows are well set up," she said. "We got a warning when they were about two hundred meters out. Nice little targeting system. I wasn't sure of our range, so I waited until they were in nice and close. There were three different groups."

"That's odd," Bish said. "Good creds though. You have four thousand lying there."

"How do we collect?" I asked.

"Tell Hog. He'll send someone out to pick 'em up," he answered.

"Where does that money come from?" I asked.

"Abasi government. They encourage Kroerak eradication so they can resettle Zuri."

It didn't take long to load back into the carriage and we were soon headed back to York. The town bustled with activity and we received more than our share of attention as we arrived. I was ready to dismiss it to the fact that we were new when Bish noticed it as well.

"You're going to be the talk of town," he said. "As if you weren't already. We haven't seen two starships in York in the same week for as long as anyone around here can remember."

"Bish, how long is a week?" I asked.

"Eight days. Just like everywhere." He shook his head like I was being intentionally dense.

I laughed, but didn't push it.

"Now, Patty's chili can be a little spicy, not that you could tell by how much of it my boy packs away. Don't show any fear, just ask for a glass of milk. It's the only thing I've found that'll put out the fire. Seasoning comes from a native tuber, called selich. It has a great taste, but like I said, it can be a little overwhelming at first. Trust me, though, you'll get used to it and you don't want to be offending Patty. You'd break her heart."

"Back from the big city?" Hog welcomed us. "Looks to me like you found more than you were looking for."

I shook the big man's hand as he welcomed us into Patty's restaurant. Restaurants pretty much looked the same no matter where in the universe you ended up. The décor was best described as log-cabin with various farming, hunting, and fishing implements hung from the outside walls.

"It was a good trip," I agreed.

"Made a deal with the devil is more like it," Bish grumbled, switching back into the pessimistic persona I didn't enjoy so much.

"Goboble is a hobgoblin," Hog agreed. "He's treated Roby all right, though."

"Because the boy's a genius," Bish argued back.

"That he is, my friend." Hog clapped Bish on the shoulder and shut down the conversation in a single smooth move I envied. "You're going to love Patty's chili. She has a new batch of rolls coming out in a few minutes. I guarantee you won't leave even a crumb behind on that plate."

"I know I'm starving," Tabby said.

Hog seated us at a large, central table. I might have accused him of showing us off, but his brilliance was soon obvious as a steady stream of interested people walked by the table, introducing themselves or in some cases, reintroducing themselves.

"You all are celebrities around here," he said. "Might as well get used to it. You're giving people hope and I don't care if it is with Goboble's ship. It's high time we stopped thinking of ourselves as the bottom of the food chain around here. You find the parts you were looking for, for that *special* project?"

"Sure did," Nick said. "Paid more than triple their worth, but no matter. We need to get a line on some raw materials, though."

"What kind of raw materials?"

"Chlorine, titanium dioxide, magnesium, iron ore and a basic carbon-like coal," Nick spooled off.

"First two are harder," Hog said. "The other three should be easy. Take some labor though."

"Salt will get you chlorine," Roby argued. "Titanium dioxide is found in rutile and the sand pit is loaded with it. How much do you need?"

"A few tonnes each," Nick said. "I'd like to stockpile the materials next to the bungalow we're not using. We'll convert that into a machine shop. I'd also like to get a line on steel sheet."

"Curtis Long has the equipment," Hog said. "He'll want something for it, though."

"Credits work?" I asked.

"With Long?" Bish asked, scoffing. "Once he hears you have credits burning a hole in your pocket, he'll be your new best friend. Roby, can you show Curtis where to find that rutile?"

"What's a good wage?" I asked. "Could we hire you for a while, Roby, what with *Fleet Afoot* no longer out at Jorg Outpost and all? We could also use a little help from a Felio if you know any."

"Thirty creds a day is what Goboble is paying us temps," he said. "I bet I could get Semper to come over. She's only part-time at Jorg."

"I'd go fifty creds and as many days as you want," Nick said. "We probably only have two days a week for Semper and it won't last that long. I'm planning to switch out all of the Felio controls to something more usable by humans."

"Hate to break up the big party," Patty announced as she approached holding a platter filled with steaming bowls and frosted rolls.

Hog jumped up and took the heavy burden from his wife, allowing her to pass out the food. One whiff of the rolls drew me in. I was used to cinnamon rolls and while they smelled similar, the spice was different.

"Careful with the chili. It's wicked hot today. I brought fresh milk for you virgins."

"Thank you, Patty. This smells unbelievable," I said. "And thank you for the eggs and bacon. Marny whipped up the best darn breakfast this morning."

"It'll take you all a bit of getting used to how things work around here," Patty said. "Can't have you starving. And, Hog, that refer unit is still acting up."

"We're missing a part," he said. "I've got it on order, but the supplier says he might not have one on Zuri."

"So, what? We get a new refer?" Patty shot back, her ire raised.

"No. Let me work on it."

"Well, do something. I won't have my cream curdling again. Dig in, kids. Don't let our bickering stand in your way." The enigmatic woman switched from whip-cracking spouse to benevolent host in the blink of an eye.

I dug out a spoonful of the meat-laden, red soup. At first, I thought she'd overstated the spiciness of the mixture. I was digging in for a second spoonful when a bloom of pain tugged at the back of my throat and the top of my head started to itch.

"He's got scalp itch," Hog laughed as I reached for my head. "Head sweats are next, I'm telling you."

I sputtered, unable to speak as Bish handed me a glass of creamy white liquid. I don't recall ever having milk in my past, but when it hit my throat, the fire momentarily quenched and then lit up once again. The crazy thing was, the taste of the chili was such that I wanted more, even though I knew I was asking for trouble. I set the glass down and grabbed another bite, but couldn't do it. With my throat now on fire, I had to set the spoon down.

"He's hooked." Bish was pleased, looking from Hog to Patty. "Don't worry, you'll be able to take on more of it later."

Tabby sputtered next to me as she grabbed for a glass of milk. Soon, the entire table - except for Marny - was sucking from glasses of milk, terrified of the delicious bowls of pain.

"This is fabulous," Marny said. "It's spicy and amazing. How did you get this flavor?"

Patty handed a couple of potatoes to Marny. "Selich root. Native plant our Abasi friends turned us onto. Over time, you build up a tolerance to the spice. Although, it looks like you're already there."

"Oh, it's plenty hot," Marny said, finishing her bowl and swapping her empty one with Nick's. "I've always enjoyed a good burn."

"Now for the best part," Hog said. "You've taken your medicine, it's time for the pleasure." As he spoke, he picked up a thick, frosted roll and took a bite.

I joined in and experienced the same enjoyment I'd had when first introduced to cinnamon rolls back on Jeratorn station with Tali Liszt. The taste wasn't quite the same, but every bit as delicious. I reflected back on Hog's assertion that humans were at the bottom of the food chain. As far as I could tell, the people of York had built a pretty good life for themselves.

***

"Hold that panel." Nick pointed to the Frankenstein contraption we were calling a replicator. He and Roby had been working on it for the better part of three weeks. What had once been a Class B replicator shaped like a two-thirds of a meter cube had grown to fill much of the bungalow's main room. Nick had left the control surfaces behind on *Intrepid*, planning to utilize his grav suit's HUD. The problem was we'd parted with those suits when we'd signed documents with Goboble and formed the new company, Zug Enterprise - a name Goboble ended up choosing.

"What's your first run?" I asked. We'd had several false starts, each failure caused by power surges, poorly routed logic circuits or any number of issues. The theory we were working under was that the device was designed to replicate replacement parts for its own repair. We didn't have license to replicate an entirely new machine, but Nick had brought enough of the original that it respected his right to manufacture.

"The case," he replied, firing up the now terrifying machine. "It'll stabilize the replication process to have a solid frame."

"That'd be nice," I said. "Any ETA? I'd kill for a meal-bar."

"Seriously?" Nick asked. "With all this home cooked food, you want a meal-bar?"

"You can take the boy out of the asteroid fields... " I replied, wondering just how warm the panel was going to get under my hands and looking around for something that might provide insulation.

"Any chance of fixing my earwig?" I asked. It had been a long time since I'd been disconnected from my AI for more than a day, much less three weeks.

"We'll see if it came with repair IP," Nick replied. "Probably did."

We stood in silence, both holding parts of the machine as it labored to push out a familiar looking panel. As was common, replicators had no trouble manufacturing simple items and the panel spit out onto the makeshift apron.

"Perfect," Nick said. "Three more of those and we'll be able to let it run on its own."

It was well past 0200 in the morning when I slid into bed next to Tabby.

She turned and threw a leg over me and pulled me close. "Are you mad scientists making progress?" She smelled fresh and clean and I relaxed as I breathed her scent in.

"It's making Patty's refer part right now," I said. "After that, it's going to scan my broken earwig to see if it has any repair provisions."

"That's a good idea," she said. "We need a suit freshener, not to mention vac-suits. I feel so darn exposed in these natural materials. The air moves right through them."

I tipped my head down and blew onto her chest. "Like that?" I asked.

"Don't be starting something you don't want to finish," she said.

I slipped my hand beneath her shirt and ran it up her ribs, looking for the comfort we often shared. I might not have as much endurance as Tabby, but I wasn't dead either and I never looked away from an offer freely given, at least not where she was concerned. "Did you go out for a run this afternoon like you were planning?"

Needing little provocation, she sat up on top of me and pulled off the nightgown she'd purchased in town. It wasn't an overly practical material, but without grav-suits, we were down to suit-liners and they were little more than underwear. I marveled at her again, still wondering why someone as beautiful and capable as her would pair up with me.

"Your pillow talk needs work," she laughed and playfully batted at my hands as I reached for her. "I ran down the Quail Ridge for a few clicks. Ended up bagging another half-dozen baby-Ks. I feel bad shooting them. They're just hungry."

"It's going to get busy the day after tomorrow," I said. "Nick has a plan for all the tools he's replicating. We have a team from town coming out to raise the machine shop. I was hoping you and Marny would go to Azima and deposit the rest of the platinum."

"Seriously, Hoffen. This stuff doesn't turn me on."

"What if I told you we'll have meal-bars by tomorrow?" I said.

"Okay. No." She plunged her hands beneath the covers and grabbed me.

"Oh. Right." That was quite a successful redirection on her part.

SKITTERING HORDE

"Fifty kilograms of poly powder and see about any of these chemicals in liquid or powder form." I handed the list to Semper on a reading tablet we'd replicated the night before. The young Felio had shown up the day after we'd suggested to Roby we might have work for her and hadn't missed a day since.

"I know where we can get all this stuff," Roby said, attempting to pluck the tablet from her paws. She easily maneuvered it out of his reach and batted him on the nose for his trouble. Filbert, who'd found he both loved running wild through the hills of Zuri as well as the attentions of his energetic - albeit evolutionarily distant – cousin, took the opportunity to jump onto her.

She gave him a perfect feline scowl. "I do not need your help in procuring these items, Roby Bishop."

"Isn't Nick installing the new power couplings this morning, Roby?" I asked.

"They're done? I didn't know he even had the pattern finished. I was out installing those Kroerak monitors in Long's field. Why doesn't anyone tell me anything?" Roby looked around excitedly and bolted off, his spastic energy spooking Filbert who jumped away from Semper's loose grasp.

Roby stopped suddenly, turned around and ran back. "Sorry. I gotta go, Semper. Good luck in Azima. I wish I could go with you." He gave me a guilty, lopsided grin and ran off.

"Mud on that one's tail," Semper said, her own tail flicking with agitation.

"I think you confuse him," I said. "Do you have enough room to haul everything on that list?"

Semper drove a three-wheeled trike that had some room for cargo on the back. Fifty kilograms of powder was pushing it.

"Breezy days," Semper said, nimbly jumping onto her tricycle. "I will return in four fingers." The Felio split the day into sixteen chunks, each represented by finger or toe. It wasn't unusual for them to make time references to their toes for night hours and fingers for daylight hours and she was communicating a six-hour span.

"Need any help this morning, Cap?" Marny asked, walking up behind me.

"You picked the wrong guy to ask," I said. "I've pushed all the muck out of the tween deck and I'm going to use Nick's new power washer to clean it. I'd kill to have my grav-suit back."

"I've been in worse holes," Marny said cheerfully, wrapping her muscled arm around my shoulder and walking toward the ship with me.

In the three weeks since we'd fired up the replicator, it had been churning out parts non-stop. As for the septic field, I'd decided to completely replace the current system. I had absolutely no idea what the original design had been and suspected that whatever the configuration, it had long ago been abandoned. The poly powder Semper was bringing back would allow us to finally start laying out our newly-designed system.

"I'd kill for a renno bot," I said.

"I hear you," Marny answered. "My little man wants a structural scan of both tween decks once we spray them down."

"Copy that," I said, holding up the scanning unit Nick had handed me only a few minutes ago. "So I have a tough question for you."

"Shoot, Cap," Marny said, swinging up through the open hatch and into the cargo bay.

"You and Nick do any more talking about taking things down a notch?" I asked.

"We have," she answered.

"What's your take on that?"

"Feels like a conversation the two of you should have," she said as we slid into Tween Deck One, which I'd misnamed the Poop-deck, for obvious reasons.

"I think he wants me to tell him it's okay, but I have," I said. "I just don't want to break up the team."

The two of us worked in silence for a while, rustling long water hoses to the far end of the deck. Once we got the spray head working and bad things started flying aft, Marny took up the conversation again. "Thing is, Cap, those are different ideas. Nick would never deny you the stars, but that's not what he wants. Take a look at what's happened to York since we arrived. There's a constant stream of people at the door, looking for ways to improve their lives. The thing is, Nick has answers for them. Sure, a lot of that's because of the replicator, but you know as well as I do, it's more than that."

"I see it," I agreed. "And you're right, he sees solutions where everyone else sees problems. What's the right answer?"

"Keep doing what you are," Marny answered. "But give him some room too."

"How?" I asked, drilling in on a particularly stubborn piece of grime. The power washing device he'd supplied peeled back decades of grime and left a tale of woe behind now that previously covered metal rot was brought to light.

"How bad do you need him to sail milk runs with you?" she asked.

"Not at all. If Roby's interested, he knows those engines better than Nick," I said.

"That's your conversation, Cap," Marny replied.

"Where's that leave you?" I asked.

"Never did buy into the idea of a ball-and-chain relationship," Marny said. "I'm a Marine and need to be on the move. My little man knows that, just like I know we're holding him back."

My mind spun as we doggedly chased every last bit of grime from the compartment. The idea of Nick not always being at my side was disconcerting, but Marny was right. He'd become an enigma since getting his workshop put together. When he wasn't working on *Fleet Afoot* or repairing a piece of equipment for a York resident, he was hard at work on his pet project: building an inertial damper system that integrated with the current Felio gravitational systems. If you ask, he has even more plans after that.

"Break for lunch?" Ada called over the comms.

"We're just finishing up," I called back, sliding the hoses out of Tween Deck Two, where the once war-oriented ship's ammo had been stored.

"Anything serious going on in there?" Nick asked as I dropped to the floor of the cargo bay.

I looked guiltily at Marny and realized he was asking about structure. If he had any clue, he didn't let on. My AI had been recording the scan data and while there was significant pitting and even places where a well-placed foot could poke through deck plating, all of the structural members were in good shape.

"Nothing a renno bot couldn't fix in a couple of months," I quipped sarcastically, flicking the data to him.

"I hired Bud Stagnar to install our septic plan," Nick said. "He'll be by first thing tomorrow morning. Think you could get these brackets welded in before that?" He flicked a layout back to me. If there was one thing I'd become better at than scooping crap, it was welding to the exacting specs of one of Nick's plans.

"Easy," I said. "I'll do it after we eat."

"You should show me how." The voice belonged to Semper, who I hadn't heard approach.

I ignored her request for the moment. "Can we afford to pay someone? I can do the installs."

"Bud is doing the work in trade for a few parts I made for him. He had two machines down because he couldn't get replacements."

"Master Hoffen. Please hear me. I am small and strong and I learn quickly," Semper pushed, her wispy voice insistent. A staccato tapping on the deck drew our attention. Looking down, we discovered a single, thick claw had protruded from Semper's right foot and was oscillating. "Hik." She sucked in a quick breath as her eyes followed my own and she ran from the deck.

"What the frak?" I asked, surprised.

"Skittish, I suppose," Nick said. "Seemed embarrassed."

"For the love of all that's holy. Go after her, Cap, she was embarrassed," Marny said.

I looked to Nick, who shrugged helplessly at me.

"Double frak." I jogged over to and jumped through the cargo bay's open elevator. It was only a two meter drop to ground level, although without the grav-suit, I found the landing jarring. I crouched and spun around, trying to locate Semper.

"What's going on?" Tabby called.

"You see where Semper went?"

"What'd you do, Hoffen?" Tabby asked.

"Nothing!" I replied defensively, my voice rising.

Tabby pointed toward the back of the property, uphill to the hogback that gave Quail Ridge its name. I caught a brief glimpse of orange fur about thirty meters out and took off in pursuit.

Since we'd been here, we'd taken out sixteen Kroerak hatchlings. Small they might be, but in groups the size we'd been running into, they were extremely dangerous. The fact that Semper might not be aware of the increased threat concerned me enough that I hastened my pace.

"Semper, wait," I called, trying to catch sight of her in the thickening brush. There was a fork in the path. One trail led straight up the mountain and the other ran parallel to the ridge I knew was several hundred meters above. I stopped and heard nothing.

"This way, lover." Tabby, who I hadn't heard approach, breezed past onto the lower path, jogging easily. She and Marny had been patrolling the paths around our new home and her familiarity with the terrain was considerably better than my own. I pushed and caught up with her.

"Did you see her?" I asked.

"No, but I would have if she'd taken the other path," Tabby said, handing me my Ruger. I accepted the gun and slid it into my jacket pocket. "Marny and I saw signs of Kroerak this morning. Stay sharp."

Even with all the action, I'd yet to actually see one in the wild for myself. The closest I'd come was a warm cleanup a couple of days back when Tabby had been confronted while running on the road three clicks down the mountain.

"I talked to Marny about Nick," I said, knowing she and Marny had already been through the conversation.

"Good."

"I don't see any reason why he has to come along on every run," I said. "I just don't get how he isn't lonely if Marny does."

"Yeah. I think you're missing the conversation," Tabby said.

"I don't think so," I argued. "Marny doesn't want to give up shipboard life. Nick wants to run the business from Zuri. What'd I miss?"

"How many places have we called home in the last few stans?" Tabby asked.

"Two or three? I don't know; it's kind of a moving target." As I said it, I looked sideways at her. She had a point and I suspected I was nudging my way there.

"Right. Every time we get things settled down, off we go," Tabby said. "Nick can't sink his teeth into any long-term projects."

"What about Petersburg?" I asked. "Last time we were there it was amazing. We had pod-ball courts, a diner, armor-glass kilns, a foundry, sheet stamping and the nano-steel factory was nearly complete. Heck, if we weren't cut off from Tipperary, I'd have bet Mom would have had us running back to pick up the Lichts so they could start working the nearby asteroids for ore."

"I bet you're right," Tabby said. "But what's Nick part in that?"

"He started it all. Petersburg was totally his idea." I caught her point as I said it and she was more than willing to let the realization wash over me.

"There she is," Tabby said, pointing.

The small Felio had slowed to a walk ten meters ahead of us and turned at our noisy approach.

She looked at us in panic and with a strangled shriek bolted off. The behavior was odd, even for an alien, most of whom we had learned shared similar emotions to humans.

"Flighty little thing, isn't she," Tabby said as we once again gave chase.

"Semper, please stop," I called. "Tell us what's wrong."

If there's one thing a Felio can do, it's run. And Semper was no exception. I was already winded from the exertion of running uphill and I'd only just started to recover. Tabby, on the other hand had no such limitations and even Semper's natural ability for speed had nothing on Tabby.

"I'll get her," Tabby said and streaked forward. I marveled at the raw speed and grace with which she moved. In moments, the two of them disappeared from view on the path ahead. I slowed my pace to something I could maintain.

My rest wasn't long, as blaster fire soon broke through the quiet of the mountain. I surged forward and fumbled for the gun stowed in my coat. The garment had turned from keeping me warm to keeping in too much heat and hampering my movements. The whole idea of changing clothing based on variable planetary temperature was still new to me and I added another item to the list of reasons I missed my grav-suit.

"Stay still, Semper," Tabby ordered as I rounded a bend.

Two Kroerak hatchlings were on the trail, jumping at one of the low growing trees of Zuri. At a meter in height, there was nothing on these babies that wasn't designed for poking, tearing or consuming. Fortunately, however, they lacked the intelligence of their older brethren. More importantly, they lacked an impenetrable carapace. It wasn't exactly easy to kill the little beasts, but doable. We would never have approached an adult Kroerak with only blaster pistols.

"Liam, please don't let her kill me," Semper pled, her voice constricted with fear.

"The bugs, Semper," I said, having trouble processing what she was saying. "They're keyed in on your movements. You need to be still."

"She'll shoot me," Semper replied, obviously looking at Tabby. It was then I realized her movements were not as much to stay away from the bugs as they were to stay out of Tabby's line of fire.

"What?" Tabby bellowed. "I'm trying to help you, you silly girl."

"Tabby won't shoot you, Semper."

"Why is she chasing me?"

"We're worried about you," I said. "You ran off. It's dangerous back here; the bugs are everywhere." I gestured to the bugs that were clamoring to reach her as proof.

"You're worried?"

"Oh, for frak sake," Tabby said and placed her pistol in the holster at her waist. "Don't move, Semper. I'm not hurting anyone but these bugs."

Tabby ran past the tree and veered off, up into the light underbrush and loose soil of the mountainside. With free hands, she gracefully scrabbled up the slope. Almost as if pulled with a leash, the two bugs turned from the still squirming Semper and gave chase.

With Semper no longer in the direct line of fire, I pulled up my pistol and stitched a pattern of crappy shots into the hillside. I was still breathing hard and the bugs were bouncing all over the place, trying to catch up with Tabby. Interestingly enough, however, they made poor progress as they gave chase, their limbs flailing as they tried to climb the rocky terrain.

I finally beaded in on one of them and on my fourth direct hit, I found pay-dirt and it dropped. Tabby, hearing the shots, turned and drew down on the remaining bug and opened fire.

"At least we know your gun works," Tabby said as I approached, verifying the bugs weren't getting back up. When I gave her a quizzical look, she smiled. "Sounded like a lot of shots. I wondered if it was misfiring."

"Very funny." I turned and slid down the embankment to where Semper was still three meters up in the tree. "Semper, please come down."

The young Felio placed a furry forearm over her face and looked away. "I may not, Master Hoffen." Her voice cracked and I noticed the fur on her leg was quivering. She was shaking.

I climbed up into the thick-trunked tree and she shifted away from me as I did, but finally allowed me to get close. I rested a hand on her back. It's easy to think of aliens as not really being people, when you look at them from afar. The Felio are really just big cats, after all. Up close and personal, however, is another thing entirely. I'd learned a little about the girl in front of me. Her coat was spotted orange with dark brown swirls and, therefore, her nose, lips and eyelids bore the same dark brown color. She wasn't a dominant, like a lot of the female Felio and she spoke with a soft, wispy voice. When my hand touched her back, she flinched, but didn't move further away.

"Semper, please tell me what is bothering you," I said. "We do not want to hurt you and we don't want you getting hurt by running away."

"She will kill me," Semper said.

"She will not," I said. "Tabby is my fiancé and I know her better than I know anyone in the universe. She will not hurt you." I stroked the fur on her back, straightening it.

"You should not do that," Semper said.

I removed my hand. "I'm sorry, is that inappropriate? I was just looking to comfort you."

"It is not always inappropriate," Semper replied. "And it feels nice, but you will make your mate more jealous."

"Hoffen, get down here," Tabby said.

"Just a minute," I said. "Tabby, do you intend to harm Semper?"

"No. Of course not," Tabby replied. "Seriously, Hoffen. We have trouble."

I jumped from the tree and landed hard, absorbing the shock with my knees. Two kilometers out, past our homestead, an angry horde of Kroerak spawn boiled through the valley. Their heading was clear, as they moved straight toward the house.

"Contact Marny," I said. "Semper, there is danger. Please, come with us."

To the young Felio's credit, she did as I requested. I felt her paw slide into my hand as she looked out at the approaching army and gasped. I gently squeezed back.

"We go now," I said.

The slope of the path was slightly downhill and I found it easier to make good time. We arrived in the compound to a flurry of activity as supplies were being hastily stashed in the ship and pulled into the bungalow-turned-workshop.

"One minute!" Marny shouted a warning. "No exceptions. Ada, take your position on the workshop turret now. We might have scouts."

"Semper!" Roby ran up to us as we assessed the chaos. "I was so worried."

I scanned my HUD. Nick had already prioritized the critical items and I claimed the boxes of poly powder Semper had retrieved earlier in the day. They should have been brought right into the shop, but I suspected she didn't know any better. I cursed for our lack of a grav-cart as I attempted to pick up the fifty-kilo bundle from the back of the tricycle.

"Tabby!" I shouted. Unfortunately, she was nowhere to be seen, but Roby arrived and we struggled together to move the material inside. Turns out, a minute is a really short period of time and by the time we'd dropped the third bundle of material, we were out of time.

"Ah, frak," I said. A trickle of Kroerak had arrived and were being plucked off by the deceivingly small turret. *Fleet Afoot's* elevator had been left halfway down and at least one bug wormed its way inside. "Stay here and lock this!" I ordered Roby as I pulled the bungalow's door shut behind me. Apparently, he needed no other prompting and the door's locking mechanism closed.

I scanned my HUD's tactical display. Marny had each of us identified. Semper was in *Fleet Afoot*, which is what I'd subconsciously recognized when I'd seen the bug or bugs make their way into the ship. Tabby, Marny and Nick were hunkered down in the bungalow we were using as crew quarters.

"Cap, what are you doing?" Marny asked. "That group is eight seconds out."

"Something stupid. Stay put!" I raced out across the courtyard-turned-shipyard and dove up onto the elevator. I rolled to my feet, sprung up onto the deck and came face to slobbering proboscis with a Kroerak spawn.

To say I've been in a lot of tight positions would be a bit of an understatement, but this moment would go down in the record book. The angry little critter's immediate response was to grab the sides of my head with its pointy claws. I've heard that a kitten's claws are sharpest when they're young and I immediately suspected this to also be true of the Kroerak. My head was pulled forward and I experienced excruciating pain as the claws bit into my skin.

"Aieee!" I caught the merest glimpse of a figure in flight as I fumbled for my pistol. The gun dislodged and dropped to the deck of cargo bay. I inwardly cursed as my hand found the pistol, only to send it even further away.

My head snapped violently back and I was lifted from my knees and flipped over. Together with the Kroerak, I fell backward and down a meter to the elevator's half-way retracted floor. I heard a cracking sound as the bridge of my nose gave way under the force mashing it into the nasty little bug's maw.

The din of chittering and scraping at the edges of the elevator's platform filled my ears. The horde had arrived and I'd attracted a lot more attention than was wise. The first thing I noticed was that the bug atop me was no longer moving, although its claws remained well attached to my face. I swiveled, pried the claws away from my head, and kicked out with my boot at the bug that had dragged me backward. I managed to dislodge the unwelcomed visitor, but others sought to take its place. I spun quickly and kicked another clear of the platform, but I was being overrun.

"I'm coming, babe," Tabby called.

"No! There are too many," I replied. "Give me a second, I've got this." I wasn't sure that my statement was true, but I sure wasn't going to allow Tabby to wade into the onslaught of chittering death to rescue me. Even with her physical prowess, there was no way she'd get through them to me.

"Up here."

My eyes landed on Semper who leaned over the edge of the deck, holding onto a support and waving my Ruger at me.

I snagged the gun and fired at the bugs making progress

getting up onto the platform. I knew better than to think I'd successfully repel them, but I just needed an opportunity to gain my feet. Semper had given me that. I side-rolled and popped up, narrowly avoiding the grasping arms of the bugs.

"Deck One," I ordered as I regained footing on the cargo bay. Ideally, I'd like to have closed the elevator, but there was no time to raise the lumbering lift.

Semper just looked at me, not understanding. She was holding a half-meter-long spanner, the very device I suspected she'd used to crack my face-buddy on the back of its head.

"Up the ladder." I grabbed her arm and pulled her across the deck. It didn't take much convincing and she jumped lightly onto the ladder and gracefully raced to the upper deck.

I took a couple of shots at the spawn in pursuit and followed. It wasn't inconceivable the Kroerak could climb a ladder. Their older brethren had no troubles with passages of any type, beyond slippery floors, complete vacuum and empty spaces. I wouldn't rest until we had steel between us. Together, at the top of the ladder and on the top deck, we slammed the hatch shut and spun the new locking mechanism Nick had invented, which was friendly to both Felio and human alike.

"You came for me," Semper said.

"Of course," I replied and before I could say anything else, she ran her cheek against my neck and laid her head on my chest. The move caught me off guard, mostly because of its intimacy. The heat of her body against my own and the rumbling sound within her chest was all I could think about for a few seconds as she wrapped her arms around me.

SHIP SHAPE

"Liam!" Tabby called over the comms. "Sitrep. Your BP and respiration are spiking."

"We're safe, Tabbs," I replied. "Semper and I are locked in the passenger compartment. All good." I wasn't about to admit that the physical closeness with the petite alien contributed to the readings.

"You're hurt," Semper said, inspecting the blood that had transferred to her fur. The bug had broken my nose and savaged my face. No doubt I was in need of a med-patch or three.

"Stay put, Cap," Marny cut in. "They're swarming the ship, but Ada's got a good line on them and she's picking 'em off."

"Anyone call York?" I asked.

"Nick's on the horn with the wall," Marny said. "They're clear, but closing up shop."

Semper looked up into my face, not giving up the spot she'd taken next to me. It became clear that she had more than post-stress recovery on her mind.

"Hey, Semper, will you answer a question for me?" I asked.

"Yes, I certainly will," she replied, staring into my face.

I searched her yellow eyes and marveled at just how beautifully made the Felio were. "Why did you run off earlier?"

"I was embarrassed," she replied. "My claws. I lost control of them."

"Were your claws showing an interest that you find embarrassing? I'm not familiar with Felio tradition."

"It is acceptable, now," she said.

I was on dangerous ground and wanted to be careful how I moved forward. I considered my words carefully and finally responded. "You know I find you very attractive."

"I smell your response to me and understand."

"Do you also understand I am betrothed?"

"Will she wish to fight for you?" Semper asked.

This was the strangest conversation I could possibly imagine having while a horde of Kroerak attacked my ship, but here we were.

"Semper, humans don't have the capacity to control their pheromone production where attraction is concerned. I wonder if that's a skill the Felio have developed," I said. I'd heard something along those lines from Hog or Bish.

"I am not certain what you are saying to me. Do you not find me attractive?" She pushed away, her face downturned. She was moments from either tears or a fit.

"You are attractive, Semper," I said. "If I were not promised to Tabitha, I would be interested in exploring a relationship with you."

"I would accept temporary comfort and offer that I will challenge Tabitha Masters to gain position for a stronger claim," she replied.

"There are those who would find your offer workable," I said. "I can't, though. Tabitha has been my friend for as many years as I can remember. Our relationship is one that I wouldn't risk for temporary comfort."

"I understand, Master Hoffen," she replied. "Tabitha Masters is a fierce warrior. I have seen her sparring with the big one. You are wise to align with one such as that. I will remove myself from your presence."

She moved to get up and I grabbed her wrist. "Semper. There is no lack of honor in your offer. A smart and beautiful Felio like you needs an unencumbered mate, but I don't want to see you leave us simply because you expressed interest in something you didn't understand."

"Tabitha Masters will require it," she said, emphatically. "Will you not tell her of our conversation?"

"I will," I said. "But she'll understand and will not seek to cause you harm. Trust me, I know this for certain."

"How can you know this?" Semper asked, her arm growing limp as she no longer pulled away.

"She is my best friend," I said. "I trust her in everything, as she does with me."

"I will try to remain."

"Good, because I really need to stop bleeding onto my jacket now," I said. "Apparently, blood is hard to wash out."

"Your outer clothing is ruined. Hand it to me," she said.

I stood and removed my jacket, then handed it to her. Together we walked to the bridge, which was starting to look like it would be functional. We'd replaced the flight controls with the twin stick configuration I preferred and applied patches to the ripped material on the seats. It wasn't pretty, but it was comfortable.

"Nick, do we have any med-patches aboard?" I asked.

"Yup. In my toolbox, back in the engine room."

"I'm afraid that's not within reach just now," I said.

"There's a catwalk above the main hallway." he replied. "Access through Tween Deck Two." A circuitous route appeared on my HUD.

"What kind of progress are we making against the invaders?" I asked. I needed first aid before attempting a long crawl like that.

"Down by half," he said. "That's the good news. The bad news is a lot of them are out of range or obstructed. Marny thinks we'll have 'em mostly clear by morning."

"Copy that," I said.

"How bad are you?" Tabby asked.

"Bent nose and some scratches," I said. "I'll be okay."

"Hunker down, we'll clear 'em out," Tabby replied.

The sound of tearing cloth caught my attention as Semper turned my jacket into strips with her claws. I was about to object when she placed a paw on my chest and pushed me to sit.

"Hold still. This is not what it will appear to be," she said.

I looked at her, confused, as she placed her paw on my face and pushed it to the side, holding it against the back of the chair. Before I could object, she leaned in and licked the side of my face, her course tongue running along one of my wounds.

"Ouch. What the heck?" I struggled.

She'd anticipated my struggle and held firm, coming in for a second run.

"You will become infected if it is not treated until tomorrow," she said and lay a strip of my jacket on the wound. "I have cleaned it and will stop the bleeding. It is necessary."

I allowed her to wrap the wound but stopped her when she turned me to work on the other side.

"Hold on," I said. "Just stop the blood. I have med patches in the back."

She ignored me and pushed my head over firmly. "Do not be a kit. It is well known that cleaning a wound prevents problems." I closed my eyes and accepted the moment. I wasn't about to argue and, at least, we'd moved past the crush phase of our relationship. "Perhaps you will see how strong of a mate I could be for you."

"Semper," I said with mild disapproval and pushed her away.

She batted at my nose playfully, which caused me no shortage of pain.

"I have deceived you, Master Hoffen," she said. "It was as Roby says – a joke."

***

"Wakee, wakee." The smell of synth coffee filled my nose. I smiled as I awoke to Tabby's face not far from my own.

Semper jerked and pushed away from me awkwardly. We'd fallen asleep against a couple of cushions on a bulkhead that overlooked the starboard gunner's well.

"I meant nothing by my closeness," Semper defended, when Tabby looked over to her.

Tabby chuckled. "Don't be so skittish. If this one strays, it will be him who pays the price. Coffee?" Tabby handed Semper my coffee cup and I watched it transfer longingly, hands to paw.

"It smells foul," Semper replied. She spluttered as she sipped and handed it back. "And it tastes like dung. What is that?"

"A poor substitute for real coffee, but most welcome," I

answered, snagging the cup from Tabby's hand before she chose to give it away again. "We're clear?"

"Two hundred six," Tabby said. "York sent a patrol at first light and helped us clean up the stragglers. "One hundred sixty of them are crew killed. It's a quick eighty-thousand in bounty."

"Curtis Long will be happy," Nick added as he joined us on the bridge with Ada right behind.

"Why's that?" I asked.

"He hauls the corpses and buries them. He's getting fifty credits apiece," Nick said. "Not only that, according to Hog, this group probably cleared the valley. Apparently, if the bugs clump up like that, they draw 'em in from a long way off. Curtis won't have to worry about his livestock this winter."

"They see a big group like this very often?" I asked.

"Not since Hog's been alive," Nick said.

"Some people have all the luck," I said. I caught Tabby's eye. She was smiling and cut her eyes to the side. Semper had slid up next to me, although a step back. "You sure you want to throw in with us, Semper?" I brought my hand around and rested it on her back, pulling her into the conversation. "You can count on our luck being like that just about every time. We tend to bring out the best in those around us."

"Yes, Master Hoffen," she replied. "I would like to be part of this. You are all so brave and have seen so many things."

"Nick, how hard would it be to get one of those welders outfitted with Felio grips?"

"Piece of cake," he replied. "If Semper comes with me, I can get one fit in a few minutes. Stagnar is due this morning to start hanging pipe. I know we got put off by the bugs, but maybe you could get ahead of him."

"I'm on it," I said.

***

"You're getting pretty good at this," I said. "That bead isn't pretty, but it'd hold an elephant." Semper and I had been working for the better part of the day hanging brackets for the new septic field.

As predicted, Stagnar arrived right on time, but he was easygoing and started in the aft-head first.

"It is very hot," Semper replied. She'd burned much of the fur from the ends of her right paw. Something about hot metal that wasn't actually on fire gave her trouble and she was learning the hard way, even with the welding gloves Nick had manufactured.

"Bud, the deck is all yours," I said. "Give us a ring if any of those are out of place."

"Can do, Liam," he replied. "I should finish up by tomorrow afternoon and we'll give it a right-thorough test. The system is intriguing. You say the only output is sand?"

"That'd be true if we could get the right bacteria. Problem is, closest critters are likely back in Sol," I said.

"What about the Belirand landing ship?" he asked.

"What about it?"

"Still some scrap left over there. Who knows, you could get lucky," he said. "They kept it all covered up, but Hog can getcha some access. But, like yah said, they're likely all dead."

"Can't hurt to check. System works either way," I said. "Tell you what, I'll get Nick to make a detector. We'd pay a pretty penny for a liter of those microscopic little bugs if they were to be found."

"I might be willing to dig through. Seems to me this here system might have some commercial appeal," he said. "Been a lot of talk about that sort of thing in town, now that we have traders for neighbors."

"I'm starting to work on a run to Abasi Prime," I said. "You know of anyone who has anything they'd want to ship that direction or back?"

"I hear there's interest in Long's beef," he said. "You might see about that."

"I'd have to be pretty desperate to haul livestock again." If I never had to haul another cow through space again, it would be too soon.

"I might be wrong, but I think he was talking frozen."

"That we could do. I'll talk to him and don't forget to grab that detector from Nick. I'd pay a thousand credits for a liter of those bugs."

He gave me an appraising look. "That much? What would you charge for the plans for this here system?"

"Ask Nick. It's a public domain pattern back on Sol, so I'd think he'd be willing to share it."

"What now, Master Hoffen?" Semper asked, hauling her welding rig up from the far end of the tween deck.

"If you're crawling around in the bilge, you definitely get to call me Liam," I said. "Or, if we're on the bridge, call me Captain. No 'masters' around here. Why don't you knock off for the afternoon? We've been at it pretty hard. Go check in with your family or whatever you do in your spare time."

"I could use some help," Roby said as he walked beneath us.

Semper looked at me with raised eyebrows.

"Go." I turned and climbed up to the main deck.

When Bud was finished with the bilge, *Fleet Afoot* would be as ready as she was likely to get without the attention of a true shipyard. I heard Semper's wispy voice as she excitedly explained to Roby how she'd learned to weld and started to go into detail about her experiences. Initially, we'd received complaints from a couple of the townsfolk for employing a non-human. Apparently, the citizens of York liked to keep to themselves and preferred to employ only humans. Fortunately, Hog fielded the complaints and explained that we were bringing a lot to York and rocking the boat probably wasn't the best idea.

Raise Goboble, I instructed my AI. I wasn't sure it would work and was a little surprised when Goboble answered.

"Captain Liam Hoffen. It is a pleasure to hear from you," he replied. "I understand our ship is nearing completion."

I bristled at the *'our ship'* part of his statement. He had exactly two rights in our company. The first was a reservation of twenty percent of our cargo space that we were not allowed to disturb, beyond what is normal. The second was a twenty-five percent share of profits. Nothing in our arrangement gave him any ownership of corporate assets and we were allowed to buy him out at one-point-eight million credits.

"I'm looking at a run," I said. "I'd like to leave in ten spans. I'm open to destinations, although Abasi Prime is toward the top of my list."

"I have been researching human words with the help of the suits you traded," he said. "Your plan is audacious. Yes, I would speak for my twenty-percent reservation and if you are willing to make a small side-trip, I would add an additional twenty-percent."

"What kind of side trip?"

"A smuggler's drop," he said. Talk about audacious, he wasn't even hiding his intent. "You will match a course and velocity provided by a representative of my own who will accompany you. At the correct moment, you will release the load."

"What are you paying for a smuggler's drop?" I asked.

"In that you will not be subject to government inspections, the rate should be unchanged from Series-B cargo."

"I will get back to you," I said.

"Understood." He terminated the comm.

I sat back. I was already in bed with the devil. Was I on a slippery slope? And when we finally did come up with a million point eight - which was already three hundred thousand more than I thought we'd negotiated - what then? Would he accept the business deal? I settled on the one fact I knew; if I didn't fill the ship, it would all be academic.

I'd stopped being surprised by the similarities in trade between the various ports of call in human space and what I was discovering on Abasi Prime. Trade is trade and shipping is shipping. If you want to be a shipper, you have to be willing to buy a bond. Unlike TradeNet, there were a multitude of bond agents between Zuri, Fan Zuri, Abasi Prime, Abasi Second and Abasi Prime's settled moon, Rehema. The four planets covered two solar systems and were host to forty-two billion souls. Most of the inhabitants were Felio and all were within reach of the

Abasi government, which belonged to the Confederation of Planets.

One difference was the idea of purchasing a discounted bond. In Sol, a bond was collateral held against the safe delivery of goods. If the load was lost; the bond was forfeit. Oddly enough, we'd seen our fair share of lost loads and bonds collected. The idea of a discounted bond allowed a company to purchase a half a million credit bond for a hundred thousand credits. Given our cash position, it was an intriguing concept.

"Nick, what do you think about this?" I shot him the bond I was looking at. The agent appeared to be well respected and was offering a five-to-one bond which converted to a non-bankrupt-able note for full face value.

"Twenty-five percent return on their money, plus interest," he said. "But really not a horrible gamble. We could do that while we're getting started, then buy it out." He was referring to a provision in the bond that made it convertible to a full-face bond for a fee and additional filings.

"You mind if we burn capital on it?" I asked.

"Nope. Can't move forward without it," he said. "I'll take care of it this afternoon."

My next task was to learn how the different ports dealt with stevedores and then I'd start lining up cargos and destinations.

***

"Are you coming to bed?" Tabby's voice woke me. I'd fallen asleep in the pilot's chair. The last thing I remembered was signing a contract with Barika, a stevedore company in the city of Nadira. If everything went as expected, we'd fill our hold in Nadira and return home to Zuri with a bundled load for Azima.

"I'm coming," I said, rousing myself and walking from the bridge.

My hazy mind registered a funny smell as I walked back to find Tabby. My first thought was that Roby had burned through more of those plastic wires he was so fond of. This smell, however, was pleasant. I caught a glow from within one of the officer's quarters at about the same time Tabby stuck a long, bare leg out the door. A moment later, she swung her head into the hallway with a silly grin on her face. An outstretched finger beckoned me forward.

The room's transformation was perfect. The mattress had been repaired and somewhere Tabby had found - or had Nick manufacture - linens. A desk had been installed in one corner next to a small table with enough seating for four. Small candles were lit and placed on every conceivable horizontal surface.

"It's awesome." As I took it in, Tabby wrapped long arms around me from behind. "We're back in business."

"We sure are," she whispered huskily.

BUG GUTS

I pulled a suit liner from the trunk lashed to the deck. In secret and in cahoots with Tabby, Nick had manufactured three basic liners and a public domain vac-suit, complete with AGBs. The shower Bud Stagnar installed on board didn't have quite the flow of the showers in the bungalow and the walls still wept with iron rust, but it was *my* head on *my* ship and that meant something to me.

The fit of the vac-suit was good, although the available smart-fabric wasn't nearly as nice as my previous vac-suit - much less, the grav-suit Anino had produced. No matter, it reminded me of my beginnings on Colony-40 with Mom and Dad when we had to use a similarly inexpensive material.

We'd spent the last ten days working feverishly on *Fleet Afoot*. While she was barely functional compared to *Intrepid* or *Hotspur* or even *Sterra's Gift*, she was in good enough shape for our maiden voyage.

"Looking good, Cap," Marny said as Tabby and I entered the bungalow's main gathering room. It didn't escape my attention that while she and Ada had switched to vac-suits, Nick still wore planet-side clothing.

"Nice surprise this morning. Thanks, Nick," I said.

"Yup. Can't be sailing off into the deep dark without a good suit," he said. "Roby's installing a suit-cleaner and coffee station this morning."

"I'd like to bring him and Semper on as crew," I said. "That ship is going to need a lot of love while we're spaceside."

"You just want to bring a back-up girlfriend," Tabby said, slugging me in the arm.

"She's a good kit," I said, borrowing the term Semper had

251

introduced. "And she's turning into a heck of a good welder."

"Loyalty is also an admirable trait," Marny said.

"Are we doing the smuggler's drop?" Ada asked, changing the subject as Marny slid a plateful of bacon onto the island for general consumption.

"I told Goboble I'd need to inspect the packages before making a decision," I said.

"He's okay with that?" Ada asked. "I thought it was a no-questions-asked type of thing?"

"I told him that everything on our ship was subject to inspection," I said. "The fact is we rarely inspect packages from normal shippers."

"If we're going to be smugglers, are we at least getting a premium?" Tabby asked.

"The ship will clear twenty-five thousand credits on this trip."

She scowled at me. "We make better money killing Kroerak spawn."

I laughed. "I'd like to think that's not a continuing adventure. Don't you think it's curious these Kroerak are coming out of the vents just as we arrive?"

"I've never doubted our capacity to draw a crowd," Marny said.

"Nick and I changed the way we're paying out," I said, looking at my life-long friend. "We're going to set shares based on Mars standard rates. With a ship like *Fleet Afoot*, we need extra crew and they need to be paid."

"The twenty-five thousand Liam mentioned is above and beyond crew payouts," Nick added. "We'll load the rest into our Confed company account. The company took on a half-million credit bond, of which we've only paid twenty percent. It's acceptable risk today, but over the long run we'll want to reduce it by buying out the remaining four-hundred thousand. We'll also work on building up a nest-egg so we can buy Goboble's portion of our company." He took a breath. "I also need capital for the inertial-damper system venture we're working on with Hog."

"Are you making progress on a prototype?" Ada asked. "We've kept that replicator running constantly since it came up."

"That's the other thing I wanted to talk about," Nick said, looking to Marny for support. "I'm not planning on coming on the first run. I'd like to take that time to work on the prototype."

The eyes of the room shifted from Nick to me. I smiled as broadly as I could manage, even though I felt a flutter of uncertainty in my heart.

"Can't say I won't miss having you on board," I said. "But that's where your heart is and I'm all in. Besides, until we're able to get back to Petersburg Station, this is our home. Marny, this puts you in a position of having to choose. I hope you know we're all good with whatever you decide."

"Doesn't change a thing for me," Marny said. "Sailors have been leaving their loved ones at home since the days when they hollowed out canoes with fire. We talked about it and we're resolved. I will however, feel bad about leaving this lovely refer and grill behind."

"Ouch," Ada said, picking up her tea and hiding behind the cup.

Nick feigned agony. "I'm not sure how that makes me feel."

"Are we all in agreement to hire Roby and Semper as crew?" I asked.

"I'll second," Ada answered.

"Any nay votes?" I asked.

Tabby raised eyebrows, but I saw the smile on her face.

"Motion carries. I'll approach them this morning. Ada, we're looking to do an atmo-test and pick up Goboble's cargo. You in?"

"Of course," she replied. "I've been itching to get my hands on her. Word is she's got some real nuts."

I swiveled my head toward her sharply. She wasn't ordinarily one for coarse talk, but her impish grin told me I'd heard her right.

"Frak yah, she does," Tabby replied.

"She'd better," Marny said. "Without a single pea-shooter, our options are pretty darn restricted."

"I'd like to set sail in an hour," I said. "Goboble is expecting us at mid-day and I'd like to have our shake-down out of the way. After that, we'll pick up a load in Azima."

"Aye, aye, Cap," Marny replied. "I'm afraid we're going to be sailing on meal-bars, tea and coffee for the majority of the trip. I built up some frozen stock, but the fresh material won't make it past the third or fourth day. Eggs, ham and bacon are about it."

"Breaking my heart," I answered.

"Roby and Semper just pulled up," Nick observed. "It's short notice to offer them crew positions, but I think Roby already talked to Bish."

"Talked to Bish about what?" Roby asked as he entered the front door.

"Crewing for us," I said. "We'd like to offer you an engineering mate level three position."

Disappointment crossed Semper's face. "And Semper, we'd like to have you along as a cargo handler level three."

"What's level three?" Roby asked.

"Pay grade," Nick answered, flicking a schedule from his HUD to Roby.

"I'm at least a level one," Roby said. "Heck, I almost had this bird in the air before you got here."

"You're about the most instinctive engineer I've seen," I replied. "Thing is, you have gaps in your knowledge. Like, can you tell me what the correct level of jeperson bacteria is in the algae O2 system?"

"No," he replied sullenly.

"No such thing," I said. "I just made it up. Don't take it personally. You just lack experience with our systems to be the expert I'd expect from a level one."

"Like you have any experience," he replied.

"Couldn't agree more," I said. "We've all a lot to learn and we need intelligent, motivated crew to help us through. Are you on board?"

"I already talked to Dad," he answered. "He isn't crazy about the idea. Thinks you guys play it fast-and-loose. His words not mine. But, heck yah, I'm in."

"Semper, are you interested? Have you checked with your family?"

Roby took a sharp breath.

"I am unencumbered," Semper answered, crossing her arms and wrapping them around her own waist. Once again, I marveled at how similar Felio body language was to human. "I do not understand why you would offer this," she replied. "I am not a powerful warrior and I have few skills."

"It is your promise we value, Semper," Ada slid from the stool where she sat at the counter. "*Your* promise to protect the crew and ship just as we promise to protect you."

"None has valued my words before," Semper said. "I will do as you say, Ada Chen."

Tabby smirked at Ada. "And get me coffee in the morning."

"As you wish," Semper said.

"Tabby!" Ada swiped at Tabby as Tabby cowered away. "No Semper, there is no such requirement. Tabby will fetch her own coffee."

"Nick, how long before we could have vac-suits for Roby and Semper?" I asked.

"They're in the shop," he answered. "I'm not completely sure how Semper's tail will work, but I borrowed a design we saw when *Intrepid* was boarded."

"Marny, would you mind getting Roby and Semper checked out on vac suits and settled into crew quarters? Ada, Tabbs, please work through the pre-sail checklist Nick and I put together."

"Copy that, Cap," Marny replied. "This way, my friends."

"Aye, aye," Tabby gave me a mock salute and followed Ada.

"Are you sure you want to stay back?" I asked Nick, once the room had cleared.

"I am," he replied. "Frankly, I'm grateful you're not pushing me on it."

"You should have said something earlier, buddy," I said. "We can make this work."

"There's something you should know," Nick said. I could tell by the tone of his voice that it was a serious problem. "I got a message from Parl last night. Strix figured out a way to keep our comm crystals."

"What? They can't do that!" I said, clamping my jaw shut. I wanted to scream at Nick. Well, technically I already had, but I wanted to blow my top. Our only mechanism for communicating with home had been stolen. "Did they give a reason?"

"They argued it is in the best interest of Confederation internal security. Parl explained it's a delaying tactic that opens Strix to a counter suit, which he filed," Nick explained. "I told him we didn't want a payout – we just wanted our crystals back. He's on it, but something's up."

"Crazy bastards," I said. "Those crystals are useless to the Strix or even the Confederation for that matter. What are they thinking?"

"They are delaying our ability to contact Sol," Nick said calmly. "I have difficulty believing that's a coincidence, but for the life of me, I can't figure out why."

"You've never been one for conspiracies," I said.

"I didn't say I was unaware of their plan," Nick said. "As long as the Kroerak are focused on Sol, they're not focused on the Confederation. I just don't know what we could communicate home that would make a difference. We're missing something. I'm missing something." He sounded frustrated. Nick didn't miss much.

"Work it through, little buddy," I said, mussing his hair. He rolled his eyes at me, but appreciated the contact. "We'll be back in sixteen days; give or take."

"Keep my girl safe." He punched me in the arm as we both walked out and over to the waiting ship.

I looked up at *Fleet Afoot*. She was about the homeliest ship we'd ever sailed - by *any* reasonable standard. The scarred and pocked armor exposed a willful lack of care for the ship's integrity. Removing turrets, sensory packages, antennae and just about anything of even minimal value had been done like an angry child experimenting with a trapped bug.

That said, she was my kind of broken. The damage, to my way of thinking, was all superficial. Sure, we'd love to have the weapon systems back and the pocked armor wouldn't put up with half of what we were used to taking. The thing was, she was faster by far, than any ship I'd sailed before. I couldn't wait to get her star-side and try her out.

"You really do drool a little when you gawk," Nick said. It was his equivalent of a hair-mussing and he grinned.

We climbed up the ladder and into the cargo hold where we found Marny giving Roby and Semper the run-through of ship-board life. It was a familiar conversation that I found comforting. I acknowledged her with a nod of my head and continued up the ladder to the top deck.

"How goes pre-flight?" I asked, entering the bridge. Ada and Tabby occupied the pilot's chairs that looked out through the expansive glass covering the entire bow.

"Plenty of systems aren't behaving," Ada replied. "Your septic and O2 are both in good shape, however. We're waiting for Roby to run checks in the engine subsystems."

"All hands, prepare for departure in ten minutes. All stations check in, please."

"Liam?" Roby's shaky voice called over the comm. I heard Marny correct his address and he started over. "Er. Captain. Engines are at sixty-two percent efficiency. Atmospheric systems are eighty-three percent and gravity system is eighty percent."

Ada had already given me the updates, but I was interested in how he'd present them.

"How about fuel reserves?" I asked.

"You helped load them," he replied with some exasperation. I waited for Marny's correction. "Er. We're loaded one-hundred twenty percent, Captain."

"Thank you, Engineering Mate," I answered. I looked out the window to see that Nick had disembarked and was standing in front of his workshop.

"Cargo specialist, Semper. Is the cargo bay secured and ready for departure?" I asked.

"I am not sure, Captain Liam," Semper replied.

Tabby swung over the arm of her chair. "I'm on it."

"Hold on, Semper. Tabby's on her way," I said.

A few minutes later, Semper's voice came back over the comm. "Captain, the hold is secure. Our status is green."

"Copy that, Semper," I answered.

"Ada, the honor is yours." I flicked the simple navigation plan to her that would take us to Jorg Outpost.

"All hands, prepare for immediate departure," Ada announced.

"Request to be about the bridge," Tabby called from the bridge door. Instinctively, I knew she'd brought Semper up with her, as the door wasn't locked.

"Permission granted," I answered. "Better get clipped-in though."

I smiled as Tabby led Semper to the starboard pilot's chair and helped her fasten the five-point flight harness. "Now don't touch anything," Tabby said. "And if you throw up, it's your responsibility to clean it."

Wide-eyed, Semper nodded her head in agreement.

Slowly, Ada added power to the atmospheric engines. After a thorough grinding, filing and fairing of the engine's control surfaces, the engines no longer sounded like fabric stuck in a high velocity station atmo fan. She now sounded like something more becoming of a big-boy spaceship. Semper gasped and her claws fully extended into the arms of her chair as *Fleet Afoot's* nose dipped precipitously to the starboard and Ada struggled against the poorly balanced power distribution of the parallel engines.

"Relax, little one," Ada said patronizingly, as she gently compensated and brought the nose back to level. "Roby, can you give me a little less on the port? I think you're burning a little hot."

"I got you, Ada," Roby replied. "We've got a race condition on the tertiary governor. I should have it in a second."

"Just give me a warning before you ..." Ada quieted and her hands flew across the virtual keyboard in three-space in front of her. The ship reared up and she fought for a moment, finally leveling out our flight. "Damn it, Roby, you just gave me a forty percent boost on the starboard."

"Right, sorry," Roby replied. "It turned out I still had the injection ports turned down."

"What about the race condition?" I asked, unable to stay out of the fray.

"I was wrong," Roby replied. "Port's running fine."

"We'll talk about this when we're on the ground," Ada said. "For now, no more adjustments while we're mid-flight."

"Yeah, sure," Roby replied defensively.

I could imagine Ada's eyes rolling even though I couldn't see her face. I didn't know many pilots who could have kept flying under the conditions she'd just encountered and Roby had no idea the danger he'd placed us in. Even though Ada was one of the nicest, most even tempered people I'd ever been around, Roby was about to see a side of her that most people didn't know existed.

A soft mewing sound from Semper was the only external indication of the stress she was feeling. Well, that and the holes she'd dug into the aged, synth-leather arms of her chair.

Ada took us up to five kilometers and accelerated toward Goboble's compound.

"Steady at three hundred meters per second," Ada announced. We were just under the speed of sound, which Ada wisely avoided as it would introduce a considerable amount of turbulence. The trip, which had taken hours in a carriage, took us fifteen minutes. I couldn't understand why everyone didn't want a spaceship.

***

"My associate, Ferin, will accompany the cargo," Goboble said.

"On the smuggler's drop?" I asked. "What if the receiver misses the pickup?"

"Ferin represents the party to whom the material will be delivered. It is in their best interest to make the rendezvous," he said.

I took a deep breath. "Okay, where's my bill of lading?"

"There will be no bill of lading," he said.

"What am I supposed to show when we're stopped?" I asked.

"You will not be stopped," he answered.

I wasn't thrilled about not having a bill of lading, although to my way of reading the Confederation laws, it was not within the scope of a planet's authority to inspect a ship in deep space. It was trickier, however, once you got within a million kilometers or so.

"If I don't know what we're carrying, it doesn't go on the ship," I said.

"I could have manufactured a falsified bill-of-lading," he said. "If we are to be business partners, you must learn to trust me."

"We are not partners, Goboble," I said. "We purchased your ship with our grav-suits. You retain a right to reserve twenty percent of our hold. There is no provision for asking me to break laws."

"There is no law being broken," he replied.

"You will show me or you can forget this deal," I said.

The two Felio bodyguards stiffened at my snappy tone. In response, Tabby and Marny adjusted positions. I hadn't seen Felio fight before, but I still liked my odds, at least until the remainder of Goboble's guards arrived.

"You are a frustrating human," Goboble replied. "I will show only you. Your friends must stay behind."

Tabby stepped forward. "No way."

"It's okay, Tabbs," I said. "I have this."

I followed Goboble into the shed where the crates destined for Nadira on Abasi Prime were already being moved to *Fleet Afoot*. With a single wave of his hand, the laborers scurried from the building. Goboble led me to a stack of crates well to the back. Atop the stack sat a lizard-chinned Pogona idly whittling on a stick.

"Ferin. Our young captain requires an inspection before these crates are loaded," he said. It was impossible to tell if Goboble was annoyed or happy, as his tone of voice was always the same rolling deep bass.

"Ah. The impertinence of our youth." Ferin stood up and jumped down from the stack, grabbed a crowbar and handed it to me. "There are things best left alone, Captain."

"I don't *need* to look in there," I said, not accepting the crowbar. "I'm just not willing to put them on my ship otherwise."

Ferin flicked a look at Goboble who nodded almost imperceptibly. Ferin shrugged and violently jammed the flat end of the crowbar between the lid and the wooden box. After some work, he finally lifted one corner and a putrid smell washed across us. I coughed at the unexpected stench.

Ferin tipped his head to the side and shook it in disgust at me. "Go ahead, Captain. Inspect. Please."

I was already committed, so I approached and peered into the container. My stomach lurched as my eyes fell on a morass of Kroerak hatchling bodies already well into decomposition. My AI outlined several intact bodies on my HUD, picking the details from the slimy ichor.

"What the frak?" I asked. "You're hauling bug parts?"

"No, you simple git," Ferin said. "That's just a convenient mechanism to discourage inspectors. Dig down about arm's length. You'll really need to get into it."

I looked at the Pogona, his face unreadable aside from an irritating smirk. I closed my eyes in disgust and reached down. My hand hit something hard and I slowed, tracing a series of rounded objects with my fingertips. I closed around a single object and pulled it out of the goo. I held up a reddish tuber and shook it free of the slime.

"Potatoes?" I asked.

"Your word does not translate," Goboble said. "The root is called selich. It is not allowed to be transported from Zuri."

"The vegetable used to make soup? That's the big secret?" I asked. "This has to be the lamest smuggling run, ever."

"Says the idiot with bug guts on his sleeve."

GREASED LIGHTNING

"Take this." I shoved my reading pad at Semper in frustration. "Make sure every crate on this list is accounted for. The pad will do the work."

Semper looked up at me, ears rolled back. She had no idea why I was yelling at her, but to her credit, she took the pad.

"Stop!" I stepped in front of a pair of Pogona who'd just dropped four fifty kilogram crates against the outer wall of the hold and were headed back to the elevator. They stopped and looked at me resentfully. "The load plan I gave you has these running on the center line."

This earned me a look of hostile non-comprehension, as if my translator circuit was speaking gibberish.

"What is the problem?" barked the heavy-set lizard-chinned Pogona named Mesti, who only half an hour ago had seemed so amenable. He looked up through the lowered elevator platform. "Do not impede my workers."

"You're not following the loadout plan," I said. "You put all that weight against the bulkhead, we won't be able to fly."

"We move the crates to your ship," Mesti replied. "You must move out of the way."

I growled under my breath, stalked over, jumped onto the elevator and squared off with the chubby lizard face. The Pogona had a smell about them that wasn't always unpleasant, but Mesti was particularly ripe. I suspected it reflected the poor sanitary habits as evidenced by his stained beige tunic. I pulled half of a platinum finger from my belt, worth about three hundred credits. "I don't have time to argue with you. Load to my plan and this is yours." I held the nugget up for him to see and deposited it back in my belt.

"What is this plan?" he asked.

"Semper, join us. I need that pad for a moment," I said over comms.

"Yes, Captain Liam." A moment later she appeared at my side, handing me the reading pad. I turned it so Mesti could see the loadout I'd already transmitted to him.

"This is most unusual," he said. "I was not aware of such a requirement."

Show contract, I instructed my AI which switched the pad's readout to show the agreement I had with the Azima shipper, presumably Mesti's boss.

"I have seen no such thing," he said.

"It is our agreement and you will abide by it. Otherwise, you will unload the cargo and we will continue without it. Carrot or stick. You choose." I pulled the platinum nugget out as I emphasized the word carrot.

Angrily, Mesti exchanged harsh words with his crew.

"You will need to direct them," he said, finally.

I turned to Semper. "Do you have an inventory of what has been loaded?"

"I'm not sure," she said, her ears flattened against her head again. I glanced at Marny, who I often relied on to ground me.

"Excellent training moment, Cap," she said. "Simple tasks offloaded reduce cognitive burden. Trust your crew."

I blew out a hot breath and laid my hand on Semper's shoulder. Inwardly, I chastised myself as Semper flinched at what I'd hoped to be a friendly gesture. I'd damaged the minimal trust I'd built with my newest crew member.

"We'll get this, Semper," I said, forcing a calm into my voice I didn't yet feel. "I need you to do exactly one thing. Rescan the crates that have already been loaded. Once you're finished, we'll start loading again. You scan every crate that enters and remove any crate that is taken off. If things move too fast, you call stop and I'll back you up. Is this something you can do confidently?"

"I can," she said, accepting the pad from me. Her voice didn't carry much confidence.

"Would you feel better if Ada helped?" I asked.

Semper looked at me, clearly assessing if I could be trusted with an answer that might make her look less than confident.

"I think I can do it," she said, although, once again, her voice carried a question more than an answer.

"Semper, my anger is not at you," I said. "This is an alien planet to me and people do things differently here. I'm frustrated with myself. Would you accept Ada's help if she were here?"

Semper nodded in tacit agreement and I had a decision to make. If I called Ada down to help, I'd be telling Semper I didn't trust her. If she failed at the task, I'd be annoyed and probably make the situation worse. The blood rushed in my ears as I ground on the conversation, feeling everyone's eyes on me.

"Go ahead and rescan the current cargo," I said, finally. "If you need help, ask for it. We'll back you up."

"Yes, Captain Liam," she said and scurried into the hold.

"You are wasting my time," Mesti said, argumentatively.

"You've wasted mine, Mesti," I snapped back. "I've been in this business a long time. Never have I had a shipper ignore loading instructions."

"You are no longer at home, Human."

I turned away from the greasy lizard chin and instructed my AI to build a plan to reorganize the crates that had already been loaded.

After twenty minutes, Semper called from the hold that she'd finished her inventory.

"I'll need your workers in the hold," I said and stepped onto the elevator platform. "Bring your lifting devices."

Grudgingly, Mesti and his crew rearranged the crates and we got back to the business of loading. Without making a show of it, I scanned each crate as it was loaded and directed the Pogona crew.

In the end, Semper proved herself to be a quick study, even discovering that two crates were mislabeled and stopping a third crate from being offloaded.

"Marny, close it up," I said, plunking the platinum nugget into Mesti's outstretched hand.

"A pleasure, Human," he said, his voice indicating much the opposite.

I didn't answer beyond swinging up into the hold.

Once my eyes adjusted to the lower light, I found Semper had already started pulling thick cargo straps from bins along the aft bulkhead. *Fleet Afoot's* limited inertial control threatened to topple anything that wasn't strapped down while in atmospheric flight. We worked in amiable quiet, throwing straps over crates and securing them to heavy lugs built into the floor.

"What a piece of crap," Tabby said as she and Marny joined us in the hold after securing the exterior hatches. "I can't believe you paid him to do his job."

"We're all learning," I said. "Semper, I apologize for allowing my anger at Mesti to be directed at you. It wasn't my intent."

"I understand," she replied simply.

I nodded. I'd damaged my relationship with her and would need to do better.

"You saved us credits today by discovering those crates," I said. "Thank you."

Her ears pricked up at the praise. She wouldn't be much of a card player. Her emotions were too easy to read.

"What did you think of your first flight in a ship?" I asked, looking to engage her further as the four of us worked our way up the ladder to the bridge.

"It was exhilarating," she said. "I did not know if I should be afraid or happy. The land is very beautiful, though. I am glad to have seen that."

"Wait until we get into space," Tabby said. "Zuri is gorgeous from five hundred kilometers up."

"You are certain this ship will keep its air?"

Marny laughed. "Put that at the top of the list of things we take seriously."

"Ada, we're on your go," I said, sliding into the captain's chair behind the two pilots. It was difficult for me to allow someone else to fly my ship out of the atmosphere for the first time, but Ada was every bit the pilot I was.

"I believe that honor belongs to you, Liam," she replied. "We're clear on the warm-start checklist. The helm is yours."

"Captain has the conn. All hands, prepare for immediate departure," I announced.

"Roby, I need a green from engineering if you're ready to go," I prompted. Without response, the engineering status flipped to green.

I applied steady power to the atmospheric engines and finally the ship lurched, tearing itself from the gravity of the planet. This time, however, it didn't attempt to flip as I added power evenly to the parallel engines and veered away and up from the small trading town.

Establish comm channel with Nick and all ship, I instructed the AI. "Heya buddy, we're about to take off. We'll see you in a few days," I said.

"Copy that," Nick said.

Cue Greased Lightning, I said, to groans on the bridge.

The sound of an ancient musical play filled the public address of the ship.

Go Greased Lightning, you're burning up the quarter mile.

Go Greased Lightning, go greased lightning.

I leaned back and throttled up, enjoying the moment as we rocketed skyward.

"You're a nut," Nick replied. "Safe travels all."

It took only a few minutes to escape Zuri's gravity and we eased forward in our chairs as *Fleet Afoot's* gravity system responded positively to the single problem of thrust not complicated by planetary gravity.

"Liam, there's an Abasi frigate adjusting course on intercept," Ada announced as we cleared three hundred kilometers.

"Roby, fire up the star engines," I said. "But leave the atmo engines online."

"That's not advised, Captain," he replied. "The exhaust of the atmo engines could impede the star engines."

"Watch and learn," I said. "Please advise when the star engines are online. Ada, set a navigation plan for the Tamu gate."

"Copy that," Ada replied.

"Won't you stop for the Abasi ship?" Semper asked.

"That's a planetary patrol," Marny replied. "Without direct orders there's no reason."

"Star engines impede communications," I said.

"Liam, they're spooling up on an intercept course," Ada announced.

I pushed the atmo engines to a ninety-percent burn and was more than pleased at how quickly we were adding delta-v between us and the planet - as well as the Abasi cruiser.

"We're being hailed by the frigate *Claws Extended*," Ada said.

"Wait one," I answered. "And, that's not a particularly subtle name."

"Roby – where are my star engines?" I asked.

"We're online, Captain," he answered after a moment.

All stations prepare for hard-burn.

"Ada, nav plan?" I asked.

Ada tossed a plan onto *Fleet Afoot's* simple navigational system. I simultaneously killed the atmo-engines and engaged the star engines, quickly ramping them up to hard-burn.

"They're giving chase," Ada said.

The ships both appeared on the small vid-screen to my left. I missed the gorgeously rendered holo displays of *Intrepid*, not to mention the full wall of high resolution vid-screens. What I loved, however, was the fact that we were adding delta-v like gang-busters. If *Claws Extended* didn't change something, we'd be well out of their range in short order.

After twenty minutes, Ada announced, "I think they've given up."

"Nicely done, all," I said.

***

"Twisty little freak!" Tabby exclaimed as Semper slipped around her in the main hallway running down the centerline of the main deck.

We'd introduced Roby and Semper to pod-way, a variant of pod-ball that utilized the close spaces on a ship under sail. Tabby was right, Semper's body twisted impossibly as she maneuvered the hallway. For someone who'd spent no time in zero-g, she'd adjusted rather quickly. Between her twisting and judicious use of claws to add friction, the little Felio moved in a most unpredictable manner.

Roby, on the other hand, was lost, especially when the hallway was turned down to zero-g. The kid had little muscle mass and no inherent physical skills, at least that I could identify.

"I have a point!" Semper exclaimed as she gently released the pod-ball into the slightly open hatch of the bridge.

"No way," I laughed, tipping back one of the precious few bottles of ale Hog had sent along. We were at the point of circumvolve and were coasting without aid of the star engines. Marny had held back a feast's worth of frozen foods and had been baking all morning. "Add that to the list of things I didn't expect to see this trip."

"She's so graceful," Roby said, mesmerized.

I wasn't sure exactly who he was talking about, because both Tabby and Semper were beautiful in flight. While Semper might have natural abilities, Tabby was both powerful and agile beyond any I'd seen. I'd ask her later if she allowed Semper the point, though I doubted it.

"Hate to break up the fun," Marny said, "but we're ready for our feast."

"Do you know any combat forms?" Tabby asked as she and Semper padded back down the hallway.

I grinned as Tabby rested her arm companionably over Semper's shoulders.

"It is not allowed for my caste to train in combat," Semper answered.

Tabby looked at Semper and then at me. "What the frak? Are we living in feudal Japan?"

"It is a matter of resources," Semper explained. "Someone must harvest the crops and prepare the meals. When I was very young, my temperament was determined to be too mild for combat."

"That's shite," Tabby said. "We'll start on that tomorrow."

"Roby, tell me about the engines," I said as we helped move plates and dishes to the end of a long mess table. "Are they showing stress?"

"Not as far as I can tell," he said. "We lack decent diagnostic tools. We'll have to wait until we land so I can do a manual inspection."

"We could do it after our feast," I said. "Nothing wrong with an EVA."

"EVA?"

"Extra vehicular activity," I answered. "Australians from home call it a walkabout."

"Outside the ship?" he asked, horrified.

"Yup. I'll take both you and Semper out," I said. "Need to start getting used to those AGBs."

"It's one of the reasons we play pod-way," Marny said. "Games sharpen the mind by providing a focused objective. Best not to do all your learning when we're in a real tussle."

"Invitation still open?" Ferin asked, standing at the open hatch to the mess.

"Everyone on the ship is welcome," Ada answered.

We hadn't seen much of the surly Pogona since we'd assigned him to the third and smallest bunkroom. I got up and pulled a corked ale from the ice chest we'd been nursing along and handed it to Ferin. "Halfway to the Tamu gate," I said. I received a rare smile as he accepted the beer.

"There's been a change of plan," Ferin said. "Our rendezvous has been updated." He pushed a reading pad across the table to me.

"Goboble will confirm this?" I asked.

"Goboble doesn't know and can't be trusted," he replied. "Remember, I'm responsible for the crates and you work for me."

I nodded. He was right, it was his signoff I required to clear the delivery and while I didn't like last minute changes, it was a reasonable precaution to keep the actual drop location a secret from as many people as possible. The location was roughly halfway between the Tamu and Mhina gates. Even with *Fleet Afoot's* poorly maintained engine, we'd be only a few hours on hard-burn from the mine-field next to Mhina.

"Problem, Cap?" Marny asked.

"No," I answered. "Nothing I can put my finger on, anyway."

***

"Liam, there's a ship ahead," Ada, who had the helm, pointed out what I'd already seen. We'd transitioned through the Tamu gate the day before and were slowing to match the vector required by the navigation data Ferin supplied.

"Marny, would you escort Ferin to the bridge?" I asked.

"Aye, aye, Cap," she replied over the comm.

A few minutes later Marny knocked on the hatch to the bridge. "Request to be about the bridge?"

"Permission granted," I answered. "Ferin, what's the meaning of this?"

He looked at the ship's signature on my vid-screen. "I guess they're early,"

"You guess?" I asked. "Is that the ship we're meeting up with or isn't it?"

"Why don't you call them and ask?" he answered, sarcastically.

"Because if they mean to do us harm, I'd like to change course," I answered.

"Looks about right," he said. "Won't know until we get there. It's not like I've actually met them."

"That's a military cutter," Ada said. "She's trying to raise us on tight beam. We're not resolving it though. We just don't have the gear."

"Military, you say?" Ferin perked up. "Didn't see that coming."

"Should we abort?" I asked.

"The fact that they're not ordering you around should tell you what you want to know," he said. "Abasi aren't exactly known for their stealth. I'd have to say that's our pickup."

"Widen our scans, Ada," I said.

"Already at maximum," Ada replied. "That cutter's the only thing as far as we can see."

"Take us in," I considered warning her to be ready for action, but that was unnecessary.

The hour of deceleration was uncomfortable as we approached the smaller, but significantly better armed ship. It didn't escape me that a single well-placed missile would stop *Fleet Afoot* dead in her tracks.

"We're receiving a request to heave-to and accept a cat-walk," Ada said.

"Put them on comm," I said.

"Can't. They sent the message on a tight-beam to my vac-suit," Ada replied.

"That's ridiculous," I said. "Nobody has that kind of control from another ship."

"What do you want to do?" Ada asked.

"Ferin?"

"Welcome to smuggling," he said. "If you're wanting a warm, cozy feeling, that's just not going to happen."

"Heave to, Ada," I said. "Marny, lock Ferin in his quarters."

I pulled a blaster pistol from a cabinet in the forward bulkhead and placed it in front of Ada. "Shouldn't come to this."

"That's not the deal," Ferin said, unsuccessfully resisting Marny as she escorted him from the bridge. "You're to deliver me with the goods."

"As long as everything goes well, you'll be fine," I said.

He turned to call from his forced departure. "They'll need to see me."

I didn't answer and allowed Marny to continue dragging him aft. "Marny, join us when you're free."

"Aye, aye, Cap," she replied.

The sour taste in my mouth and overall jittery feeling warned me of the increase of adrenaline in my system. If I were honest, it was these moments I truly lived for - the unsettled moments before contact.

"Positive contact," Ada said. "There are three inbound in the catwalk."

I cussed quietly to myself as I wished for an armored glass look-through on our airlock. Instead, I waited for the pressure gauge to cycle.

"Ready?" Marny and Tabby, who stood directly behind, drew their blaster pistols and leveled them directly ahead.

"Go," Marny answered.

I spun the manual airlock handle, pushed the door forward and dropped my hand to my blaster pistol's grip in preparation for whatever might be on the other side.

"We are short of time, Liam." The voice belonged to none other than Jonathan, who - even more curiously - stood next to Mshindi Second, the daughter of Mshindi First, the captain of the battleship *Thunder Awakes*.

IT'S ALL IN THE CHILI

"There is not a moment to waste, Liam Hoffen," Jonathan instructed as he entered the hallway and rigidly accepted a hug. It wasn't lost on me that he returned the hug, albeit awkwardly. The rush of adrenaline followed by the sudden appearance of a friend I thought I'd lost caused my eyes to water.

"Welcome, Mshindi Second – Zakia," I said, using both her title and common name. Releasing Jonathan, I offered my hand. She accepted it in a most Felio manner, which was to lay her paw on my outstretched palm and gently extend claws until they brushed skin.

"Captain Liam Hoffen, I thought it not possible that you would be sailing this ship. I find even less understanding that Abasi records list a business entity with your ownership," Zakia said.

"Wouldn't be much of a captain without a ship, now would I?" I asked, smiling. It was a much longer conversation than I wanted to have in the hallway. "Please, come aboard."

"Liam, I am afraid that matters are most urgent," Jonathan pressed.

"Understood. Join us in the mess and we'll get right to it," I said, weaving my way through the knot that had formed. The hallway leading to the starboard airlock, the only airlock accessible from Deck One, was adjacent and directly forward of the mess and galley space. As I turned into the mess, I heard banging on bunk room three's locked hatch. Ferin, apparently, didn't appreciate his unexpected confinement.

"We must run the Mhina Blockade," Zakia said before we could sit.

I looked to Jonathan for confirmation.

"Mshindi Second's assessment is correct," he answered my

unasked question. My mind spun and I desperately wished Nick was here. It was the sort of thing he'd have anticipated and already have an answer for. I closed my eyes and pushed away the confusion. A heavy hand came to rest on my shoulder. Marny's, no doubt. She knew I had trouble when too many confusing things bombarded me at once.

"One step at a time, Cap," she guided.

I nodded at her and then said, "Explain. Why would I endanger my crew and ship, Zakia?" I opened my eyes and looked directly at her. It was a challenge, but she had it coming.

"The Kroerak have invaded your home worlds," she said, ignoring or not recognizing my challenge. "They will continue until they have ravaged your planets and annihilated your species, just as they attempted with the Felio peoples."

"I have disturbing news. News that I fear will cause you great distress. I request that you are seated," Jonathan interjected.

"Just say it," I said as my stomach turned to ice and dread filled me.

"I have been in contact with Thomas Anino," he said. "The combined fleets of Earth and Mars Protectorate have failed and the Kroerak have taken all but the center mass of the continent of North America."

Involuntarily I sucked in breath. "Taken? They were fighting for the Moon."

"Earth's moon was lost when a second Kroerak fleet reinforced the original invasion," Jonathan said.

Ada dropped into a chair, her whole body sagging. "But there were a billion people."

"Mass evacuations saved many," Jonathan said. "The loss of human life is estimated in the low hundreds of millions. It is believed the Kroerak are holding most of the people captive."

"How? Anino shut down TransLoc," I said. "How did the second fleet arrive?"

"Unknown," Jonathan replied. "It is also an unproductive conversation. There are fourteen point two billion people within Kroerak controlled territory."

"It's The Cradle all over again," I said. "We're their food source." I was referring to the planet where we'd rescued people who'd been raised like cattle by the Kroerak.

"We believe the Kroerak are responsible for the extinction of fourteen entire species over the last eight hundred stans," Jonathan said.

"How can we help?" I asked. "We don't have guns or even TransLoc engines. We're hauling potatoes for frak sake."

"What I am about to tell you is considered treason by the Strix," Zakia said. Her words brought instant silence to the room. "One hundred eighty spans previous, the Felio people faced a similar invasion. We had thought that by abandoning the Mhina system, our people would be safe. You see, the Kroerak had no capacity for building jump-drives required for travel through the wormhole. What we failed to realize is that there are Kroerak capable of pulling information from their captors. In short, we had only two years of peace before a Kroerak fleet arrived in the Tamu and Santaloo systems and initiated war with our people.

"The war was particularly devastating, but nowhere more so than the planet Zuri, which had fewer defenses than Abasi Prime and Abasi Second. It was the decision of the Confederation that all resources were to be given in defense of the Felio home worlds in Tamu and to allow Zuri to be taken.

"There is no treason in this," I said. "We know most of what you're saying."

Zakia continued, undeterred by my interruption. "The Kroerak quickly gained control of Zuri and settled in to the task of population control. The loss of life was incomprehensible, but there were pockets of resistance. Just when the light seemed to be extinguished, a most important discovery was found. A group of humans who'd been exiled and forgotten were being avoided by the Kroerak."

"The Belirand mission?" I asked.

"The very same," she answered. "As you might imagine, this drew considerable interest from Confederation scientists. The root of the selich plant was adopted as a food staple by the humans of

Zuri. It is a native plant and widely ignored by the Felio people, as even in small doses it causes considerable discomfort and an inability to eliminate in a predictable manner."

"I think humans have a similar reaction," I said. "I tried the York Chili and was unable to eat more than a single bite. It is too spicy."

"You would have been wise to endure the discomfort," Zakia said. "Ingestion of the selich plant causes human and Felio flesh to become poison to the Kroerak. The very smell of ground selich is a significant deterrent to the Kroerak."

"Is this why the Kroerak didn't feed on the personnel of the Felio fleet that rescued the Mhina settlers?" Ada asked.

"No," Marny interrupted. "That timeline is wrong. The discovery of selich happened after the rescue."

"The Felio fleet knew they were unlikely to return home and were given instructions to honorably discharge themselves if capture was likely. We have long known how to poison ourselves in a way that Kroerak cannot consume. It is unfortunate that this poison also kills those that ingest it."

"Discharge, as in suicide?" Ada asked.

"Yes. It was their sacrifice that allowed so many to live. To this day, we celebrate their lives each cycle," Zakia answered.

"Why would the discovery of selich be kept a secret?" I asked. "Wouldn't you want to tell every sentient species possible?"

"The Strix argue that by withholding this information, the Kroerak will turn away from Confederation space. You see, selich plant is poison to more than Kroerak, it is also poison to thirty percent of the species that make up Confederation membership."

"Including Strix, no doubt," Tabby added.

"This is true," Zakia said.

"But not Felio and not humans ," I said. "If we make it back to Mhina will Anino reactivate TransLoc?"

"Not like it matters, we don't have any Aninonium," Tabby said.

"We do," I answered. "I smuggled a small portion in my grav-suit. It's not much, but it's enough to get Fleet Afoot back to Sol."

"Why then was the Belirand comm crystal on *Cold Mountain Stream*?" Marny asked.

"We were attempting to contact the human corporation, Belirand," Zakia said. "We were trying to warn them of the Kroerak's discovery of human technology in the Mhina system. The Kroerak are relentless in tracking down new species' home worlds. To my knowledge, no contact was made until your arrival."

"We need to go back and get Nick," Tabby said. "If we make it to Sol, there's no guarantee we'll be able to return for him. He could be stranded forever."

"There is no time," Marny said. "Every minute we delay, the Kroerak are murdering people. We can't lose twelve days of transit time."

"We could TransLoc to Santaloo," Tabby said.

"We don't have enough Aninonium for two jumps," I said.

"We estimate the Kroerak forces are killing seventy thousand people each twenty-four-hour period," Jonathan said.

Clarity of mind is a luxury in tense situations. There was no way Nick would accept the blood of seventy thousand a day for the twelve days it would take for us to retrieve him. Even with sufficient Aninonium, the loss of several hours delay would be unacceptable to him.

"Ada, I need you on the bridge. Prepare for hard-burn to the blockade. Zakia, I assume you have a point of entry, or some plan for avoiding the minefield. I need you to accompany Ada."

"We do, Hoffen Captain," Zakia answered. Under the circumstances, I wasn't about to correct her backward address. "Mshindi Prime has been slow to reactivate the mines along *Intrepid's* escape route. The fleet will still respond to your proximity and there is no guarantee you won't be destroyed."

"Understood. Jonathan, please head down to engineering. The engines we have suffer from poor maintenance and our general lack of understanding. Any additional power you could give us might make the difference in survival," I said.

"Zakia, before you go, what would you have us do with the

Pogona, Ferin, who accompanied the cargo?" I asked.

"Ferin is a criminal. My crew will take him into custody," she replied.

"Don't let her," Marny said. "If you turn Ferin over to the Abasi, you could endanger Nick."

"You have no choice," Zakia said, literally bristling as she did, preparing for confrontation.

"Zakia, you are already breaking your own laws to help us," I said. "Allow us one more transgression. I would not want to endanger our friend."

"Ferin was specifically chosen due to his criminal activities," Zakia said. "Our success hinges on his delivery to the Abasi courts. This is not negotiable."

"Success?" Marny asked, stepping into Zakia's personal space.

To her credit, Zakia did not back up.

"Yes. There is but one reason a guard might be out of position while patrolling the blockade," she said. "And that is in the pursuit of a criminal trespasser. Ferin's presence on the shuttle will provide legal safety for the patrol. Without this, the Captain will not participate."

"Damn it," Marny spat.

"On my honor, Ferin will not be heard from for forty-five cycles," Zakia said. The period of a cycle referred to Abasi Prime's rotation or twenty-eight hours.

"Marny?" I asked.

"I'll take him over," she said.

"Tabby. With me," I said. "Marny when you're done, we'll need you in the hold."

"What's going on?" Roby asked as we barged in and interrupted a conversation between him and Semper. I'd momentarily forgotten about exiling them to the engine room when we'd docked with the shuttle.

"Semper, Roby, this is Jonathan," I said. "Roby we're in an emergency. I need you to provide Jonathan with full access to the engines and systems. Help him with whatever they request no matter how ridiculous it sounds."

"Seriously? This is my engine room," he replied.

"Roby, don't test me just now," I said.

"Frak that. I'm tired of being pushed around," Roby said.

I pulled my pistol from its holster and leveled it at him. "Roby Bishop, I am captain of this ship and this is not a democracy. I expect my orders to be obeyed. If you find this to be too much, you can spend the remainder of the trip confined to your quarters."

Roby stumbled backward at my abrupt shift and raised his hands. The notion that I was pushing him harder than was reasonable flickered through my head and I justified it with the urgency of the situation. It was one of those moments I knew I might later regret.

"No. I'm sorry," he cowered. "Please, don't shoot me."

I holstered my gun. "Make your choice, Roby. Semper, you're with Tabby and me." I spun and exited the room.

Semper followed behind us, her ears flattened and brows pulled back in a subservient posture. I knew she felt I was a madman and the next several minutes weren't going to do much to disabuse her of that notion.

"Lock the interior hatches," I ordered as I approached the hold's console.

Tabby responded by scampering up the ladder to Deck One. I pointed Semper to the hallway leading to engineering. To her credit, she moved about as fast as I'd ever seen her. As the two of them locked things down, I dialed down the gravity in the hold to 0.05g. It was enough that we could feel the orientation. Crates already in place wouldn't just up and slide away, as when suddenly exposed to zero-g.

"Ada, I'm cycling O2 from the hold," I said. "I'm dumping any cargo other than the selich plants."

"Copy that, Liam," she answered. "The shuttle is disembarking."

I grabbed a reading pad from the storage compartment on the console where I stood and hastily blocked off all extraneous cargo. It wasn't hard to identify, as we'd segregated the smuggled goods from the legit, knowing we'd be dropping the potatoes and bug-guts first.

"Captain Liam?" Semper asked as she approached.

"Seal up your suit, Semper," I said, lifting my helmet and pressurizing. I added a command link with Semper and Tabby's suits and verified that we were all secure. "We're going to offload all of the goods from Azima. The crates we loaded from Jorg Outpost are staying."

"I don't understand. Won't you be penalized for losing this cargo?"

"Yes. We're not going to Abasi Prime anymore," I explained as the O2 cycled from the hold. I'd selected the quickest decompression even though it would end up venting some of our precious oxygen. "We're going to need to sail as light as possible."

Once I received a ping from my AI indicating the hold had been successfully vented, I opened the main cargo hold door which we hadn't been able to use on Zuri. We'd loaded from the ground at each location.

"Push these out, Semper," I directed, waving my arm over the crates my AI highlighted as unnecessary.

Together, the three of us worked feverishly to drop the load from the hold. More than once, Semper lost track of the fact that high mass objects are just as hard to slow down as they are to get moving. Fortunately, I didn't care about the ultimate disposition of the crates and allowed them to crash into the bulkhead and break apart. Twenty minutes and forty tonnes later, we'd cleared most of the cargo that would cost us three hundred thousand in lost bond.

"Ada, we're clear. Execute your burn plan," I said, sweeping the hold's door jamb of debris that blocked its ability to close fully. I jetted up to the console and raised the elevator, this time successfully.

"Copy that, Liam," she replied.

"What do we do now?" Semper asked as I re-filled the hold with atmo.

I'd cooled considerably since my run-in with Roby and I owed him an apology. "Would you work at placing a second set of straps on the remaining crates. I have a feeling we're in for a bumpy ride. I'll check on Roby."

"Were you really going to shoot him?" Semper asked.

"No," I said. "He needs to learn about ship's discipline, but that wasn't my finest moment."

"He is very smart, Captain Liam, and he gets angry when he is dismissed," Semper said.

I nodded. She was taking a risk I wouldn't have expected and I realized that Roby's interest in her might be reciprocated.

"I think we all feel that way," I agreed.

The ship shifted as the star engines spooled up and the three of us stumbled in unison. *Fleet Afoot* might be quick, but she wasn't particularly subtle.

I spun the airlock open and was greeted by a cloud of gray smoke. There was just about no good reason for smoke on a space ship and I bolted back to the engine room.

"It wasn't me." Roby looked up with hands raised defensively.

"What's going on?" I asked.

"A necessary purge," Jonathan replied. "Unfortunately, we had no option but to utilize a chemical reaction to re-establish the correct gap in the selenium chamber. The smoke you observed is harmless enough if nanite cleansing is applied within twenty hours.

"Nanite cleansing?" Roby asked, eyes wide.

"Med-patch," I said, pulling two of them, as indicated by my HUD, from the first-aid kit I'd mounted to the wall. I activated a patch, reached into my suit and applied it to my chest. "Open up." I pointed my finger at his chest.

"Seriou ..." He cut off his complaint before completing it and opened his suit, exposing his chest.

I activated a patch and pressed it in place. "About before, Roby. I was hasty with my weapon. Don't get me wrong. An order is an order, but I understand I took you off guard by springing Jonathan on you."

"I don't understand what's going on," he said, looking at his feet.

"Earth is being invaded by Kroerak, Roby," I said. "We might be able to help, but we need to get there as fast as possible."

"What can we do?"

"Stay   alive."

DECOMPRESSION

"All hands," I announced. "Strap in. This is going to get bumpy."

With Zakia's help, it had only taken two hours to navigate to a spot on the edge of the patrolled space around the Mhina blockade. The cutter's captain, a hero I hoped I'd someday meet, would sail across the sensor range of the patrol's path and attempt to flee once they'd been discovered. Ideally, the cutter, which had been chosen based on its power-to-weight ratio, would engage three of the patrols on constant surveillance duty.

"Nastere reports the patrol has given chase," Zakia announced.

If we'd been sailing *Intrepid*, I'd have given the controls to Ada. Her ability to sail the larger ship was well beyond my own. *Fleet Afoot*, however, was a third the length of *Intrepid* and more importantly, its mass wasn't anywhere near forty-five hundred tonnes. At forty-two meters and eight hundred tonnes empty, *Fleet Afoot* sailed like a mid-sized sloop and the responsibility fell to me.

"Roby, give me combat burn now." I grinned as the engines immediately responded. He'd been waiting for my request.

Fleet Afoot jumped as we streaked forward, accelerating just as her name implied. At this rate, we'd make contact with the minefield in eight minutes. And for a full minute, the plan worked exactly as we'd hoped. The real problem came to fruition as we started reeling in the second patrol, who'd only tacitly redirected their route to run down our distraction.

"Liam, we're being hailed," Ada said.

"Do not answer," Zakia said. "They will attempt to gain access to your shipboard systems as they communicate."

"Jonathan, are you in any position to defend against a hack? We're being hailed by the second patrol," I asked over the comm.

"Yes, Liam," Jonathan replied. "You may allow the communication."

"You should not do this," Zakia said. "Our ships have considerable cyber warfare capacity. There is little to be gained."

"Remind me later to tell you the story of the Goose and the Gander," I said.

Accept hail. "Go ahead, Abasi patrol," I said as lightly as I could manage.

"This is restricted space and you are ordered to immediately desist operations and prepare to be boarded." The voice belonged to a Felio male, whose furry face appeared on my vid-screen.

"I'm afraid that's not possible," I said. "It appears we left something in Mhina and need to retrieve it."

"Perhaps you are unaware that a mine field separates your position from that of the Mhina wormhole," he replied.

"I'm showing your delta-v as insufficient," I said. "Are you sure you want to waste your fuel?"

"We have successfully infiltrated," Jonathan said. I detected a slight elevation in the pitch of his voice and realized that was the sound of pride.

"What'd you do?" I asked.

"It is technical in nature," Jonathan said.

"Can you summarize?"

"Yes. The Abasi cyber-attacks provided insight as to what they felt were ship vulnerabilities," Jonathan replied. "We crafted a counter-attack mimicking their own and we were able to find a deficiency in their defenses."

"Impossible," Zakia said.

"Best bet is to listen to him, Zakia," I said. "I am certain they will share the vulnerability with you so you can patch it in the future."

"The ship will only be disabled for five minutes," Jonathan said.

"That's enough," I answered as the mine field entered the edge of my vid-screen's display.

In and of themselves, the mines were nearly impossible to identify, but our AIs had recorded the locations of the mines when we'd been through them previously. Our entry point was to be the narrow corridor *Intrepid* had plowed free. The debris of the broken mines showed up on our sensors, unlike the actively hidden mines that occupied the remainder of the field.

Abasi command employed a layered approach. The first two patrols represented only the outer layers of the onion. Unfortunately, the next layer presented more of a challenge, as a wise Abasi captain positioned her frigate between us and the field.

"Zakia? We have trouble," I said, sailing past the ship *Winter Leaves* just outside targeting range.

"Daraterest First," Zakia said with both dread and pride in her voice. "A brilliant tactician, she has anticipated our gambit. I will contact her and ask for mercy."

"Hold on a second," I said. "What are the chances she'll respond to that?"

"I believe she will only listen to my communication. By now, she is aware we employed sophisticated cyber warfare and she will not risk a similar failure," Zakia said.

"Put yourself in her shoes," I said. "Will she allow us entrance if she's convinced we are on an important mission?"

"I would not," Zakia answered. "I would notify Abasi command and await orders. To do otherwise is to remove oneself and their family from service."

"Those mines are forty meters apart," I said.

"Liam," Ada warned.

"No. Listen," I said. "We know their locations and we're only fifteen meters wide. We'll fit. They're not deployed to stop a sloop."

"They're magnetically attracted," Ada replied. "To stay ahead of them, you'll have to move too fast to avoid them. There's no margin for error."

"We can't stop now," Tabby said. "People are relying on us."

"This is insane," Ada said.

"Are you with me?" I asked.

"This might be a colossally bad idea," Ada said. "But I don't see an alternative."

I flipped *Fleet Afoot* over and applied an emergency burn, bringing our relative velocity in line with the field.

"Seems like an understatement," I said as I swept *Fleet Afoot's* tail around and decelerated into the mine field, angling back to the open corridor we'd left behind last time. "Ada, Tabby, mark 'em as you make 'em out."

It was one thing to rely on our sensor logs from a couple of months ago. It was another thing to make visual contact with the mines and cement their real positions.

"Down and starboard!" Ada exclaimed. To the outsider, it might have been confusing. Did she mean there was a mine down and starboard or was I supposed to navigate down and starboard?

Turns out, this is the sort of thing crews with experience work out in advance. Ada was giving an order, not pointing something out. She was reducing the mental work I needed into two simple statements. In response, I pushed the stick over and dodged a previously invisible bogey.

It was a close miss, but I'd already moved on and rolled over smoothly, giving just a little more acceleration in response to the mine that had been tugged in our direction. As soon as it trailed off, I reduced our speed to what felt reasonable.

"The grid is off. We're shifted. Starboard again," she said.

I rolled around the inertia I'd added to the mine and flung away harmlessly.

"Jonathan, any help on this?" I asked.

"We're working with the sensors," he replied. "Ada is correct, the field is askew from our original recording. There must be a force in effect we haven't accounted for."

More outlines appeared on my HUD. The display had been adjusted so that sensor-identified mines were solid and predicted mines were outlined.

"Full stop!" Tabby said, but it was too late.

At the last moment, I adjusted and only succeeded in causing the mine to detonate against the hull at our vertical centerline. Without warning, the glass in the bridge imploded and then was sucked through with the quickly escaping atmo.

I managed to stop us as a sharp pain in my left shoulder warned that something very bad had happened. I looked down to see that a finger width, steel wire had impaled me and embedded itself into the seat behind me. I reached for the wire and tried to remove it, but lacked the strength.

"Tabby, are you up?"

"Copy," she answered, leaning over and slapping some sort of patch onto Ada's visor. Frak and double frak, Ada's life signs were flagging.

"Marny, report," I said.

"I'm up, as is Zakia," she replied.

"Tabby, take control of the ship on the combat bridge. Zakia, help with navigation. Semper, report to combat bridge immediately," I ordered. A quick twist of Zakia's head caught my attention, but just as quickly, she was on the move. "Marny, tend to Ada."

"Cap, are you hurt?" Marny asked concerned, although she moved deliberately to Ada.

"I'll be all right," I said. "Tabby, we've got to get through this."

"Tabitha, we've discovered the offset," Jonathan reported. "We're updating." I watched as the entire field of outlines rotated. We weren't anywhere near where we'd expected to be. "The mines are orbiting the wormhole."

I groaned as I shifted in my seat, reaching into my belt to grab my nano-blade. The smallest movements were excruciating and the edge of darkness crept across my vision, as I flirted with blacking out. I flicked the blade out. At first, the steel wire resisted my attempts. Turns out, too much of my biological material had splattered onto - and continued to splatter onto – the metal. I shifted and reopened the hole in my vac-suit, allowing atmo to blow out into the vacuum of the bridge. Nano blades won't operate on anyone or anything attached to the wielder, so I wiped at the wire with my glove in an attempt to clean it. A fresh wave of pain washed over me.

"Cap, you gonna make it?" Marny asked, grabbing the sides of my helmet. I'd apparently passed out and fallen forward.

"Ada?" I asked, groggily.

"Triage," Marny replied. "I need to get her aft, but you can't blink out on me like that."

"Take her. I'm not critical," I said, through gritted teeth. My suit sealed up next to my shoulder, but the public domain vac-suit had no nanobot medication to apply, not even pain killers. With Marny's help, I gained my feet and stumbled back through the abandoned bridge. The rapid decompression had caused the bridge hatch to seal and I grunted at the predicament of evacuating the atmo from the remainder of Deck One where doors had been left open. There was no helping it; I wouldn't be able to apply a much-needed med patch otherwise.

"All hands. I'm blowing the atmo on Deck One," I announced. "We have wounded on bridge. Roby, Semper – check in."

"Hold took a direct hit, Captain," Roby replied almost immediately. "I'm sealed in the engine room with Jonathan. The hatch is jammed. We think it's external."

"Tabby, did Semper report to the bridge?" I asked.

"Negative. Ship shows her in the cargo hold," Tabby replied.

I shook my head. The news was bad. If the cargo hold was breached, we might have lost her and, even worse, those damned potatoes that our entire frakking species might depend on.

There's a difference between recycling and blowing atmo. In one scenario, you wait for the ship's strong vacuums to capture the atmo. You always lose some in the exchange, but it's relatively efficient, more so on some ships than others. In this case, I'd set the vacuums to recover what they could and was giving them a ten count. I'd recover maybe a third of the atmo, but I'd gain a lot of time - time that Ada and Semper might desperately need.

"Go, Cap," Marny said over the comms. I didn't even turn back to her as I smacked the emergency seals and blew the lid on the deck. Someone had been paying attention to our plight, as gravity reduced to 0.2g. The change made carrying Ada's unconscious body much easier for Marny, and I could navigate with arc-jets and allow my arm to hang limply. I blew the seals on the captain's quarters and swung the hatch wide. Once Marny passed me and entered the quarters, I pulled the door shut and restarted the pressurization sequence for the room. "What gives, Cap? You're injured."

"No time, Semper is missing," I said.

"Damn it, Cap. I'm up," she said. "I could have done that."

I'd already turned the corner in the aft hallway and dove headfirst down the ladder tube into the cargo hold. My shoulder hurt like a beast, but I wasn't in danger of passing out again. The mine I'd hit had blown out a three-meter square chunk of the starboard bulkhead and a single crate lay trapped next to the opening, pinned by twisted metal at about mid-deck. Otherwise, the hold was completely empty. The brown arm of Semper's vac-suit hung limply down from atop the crate.

Frak! I arc-jetted up to her. One of the reasons I'd always chosen dark colors for my vac-suits was they didn't require cleaning quite as often as the lighter colors. Semper's suit was covered by dark splotches and my heart sank. No one, alien species or not, could survive that much blood loss.

"Semper!" I cried out, dropping my face shield onto her own. I could have cared less at the pain I was causing myself. Shite, I'd been the cause of it and earned whatever pain I felt.

"Captain Liam?" Semper's eyes fluttered open. "Did I catch it? Are we okay?"

I raised up and ran my arm over the back of her suit. The lights of my helmet caught the green tinge of Kroerak ichor. "Catch it?"

"The crates, they were being sucked out," she said, slapping the top of the crate where she lay, testing it. "I could only save this one."

I used my command override to access her suit's biological readout. I wasn't exactly sure what I was looking for, but she was very much alive. It took me a second, but I did realize that was obvious, since she was talking to me.

"You did good, kid," I said. "Better than good. Are you hurt?"

"Big headache." Just as she spoke an explosion rocked the ship and rocketed through the opening, tearing a furrow through the side of the crate.

"Tabby, what was that?"

"They're blowing the mines. They know we're onto their layout," Tabby said. "I don't know if we can keep taking these hits."

"Semper, move this crate clear of the opening and find something to seal it back up," I said. "I'm going to have to lock you in down here."

"Yes, Captain Liam," she answered, her voice trembling.

"You can do this, Semper," I said, placing my hand on her shoulder. "You may have just saved millions of my people with your quick thinking. Tough it out for a few more minutes. We'll get through this."

"Go, Captain," she replied.

I jetted around to the ladder and spun the cargo hold's airlock closed once I was through. *Pressurize Deck One,* I instructed the AI.

Where depressurizing can take up to several minutes, depending on the level of recovery required, pressurization occurs relatively quickly. By the time I made it to the Combat Bridge, there was enough pressure for an emergency hatch pop. That is, I opened the hatch in advance of perfect equalization and caused everyone who wasn't sealed up quite a bit of discomfort.

"*Thunder Awakes* and the response fleet are on approach," Mshindi Second announced, ignoring my entry. "There is conflict. Dissension."

"Explain," I demanded. Against the advice of my AI, I peeled back my vac-suit. We were in L-1 space - occupying a room directly next to vacuum – and removing a vac-suit under those conditions was a recipe for danger. I figured the amount of blood running down my arm and back was higher priority.

"You're hurt," Tabby started to move away from the standing position in front of the combat bridge's pilot controls. She'd brought *Fleet Afoot* to a complete stop three kilometers into the giant mine field.

"I have it," I said. "Mshindi – Zakia, explain dissension."

"Daraterest has interrupted our communications. There is only one reason for this," Zakia explained. "She is preventing *Thunder*

Awakes from communicating. Daraterest has discovered House Mshindi's deception and will attempt to unseat my mother from command of the fleet."

"Missiles inbound!" Tabby announced.

"Frak!" With my suit down, I wasn't able to get information from my HUD. I scooted next to Zakia and tracked the six heavy missiles bearing down on our position.

"I can't move," Tabby warned. "She'll blow the mines and we can't take another hit."

"Who fired?"

"It was *Thunder Awakes*," Zakia said, defeat in her voice. "Mother must have already been taken into custody."

"I'll make a run for it," Tabby said. "We can't take six missiles any more than we can take those three remaining mines."

"Wait," I said. "Track them. Make sure, Tabby."

With little time left, we had just one chance.

"Missiles have now been fired from *Winter Leaves*," Zakia announced.

"Tabby, on my mark, I want you to head for that closest mine at a quarter combat burn," I said.

"That's not enough by half to escape them," she said. "It's already too late."

"I have this," I said.

Fortunately, we had only to wait a few seconds for the first raft of missiles to arrive.

"Go!" I ordered as the deadly missiles from *Thunder Awakes* streaked past our ship at no more than a few meters off our starboard and exposed their intended route.

"Aieee!" Tabby yelled in anticipation of contact and jammed the throttle forward. I could only imagine her eyes were closed as she followed my last instructions, still not believing we'd survived.

Without my HUD, the only evidence of *Thunder Awakes* contact with their intended targets was the tinkling of debris against the heavily armored bulkheads of the combat bridge.

"Emergency burn, Tabby," I said. "There's no way *Winter Leaves'* missiles are targeting mines."

I stumbled, unable to stand against the acceleration. Tabby and Zakia were strapped into the standing chairs while I'd been trying to work my way over to the medical station. I grabbed at the lock on the medical cabinet and managed to paw out a handful of med-patches as I crumpled to the ground.

"Jonathan, prepare worm-drive for transition," Tabby ordered.

I grimaced as I activated the first med-patch I could find and slapped it on my shoulder. Relief was instantaneous as pain-numbing nanites flooded the wound. I only partially applied another patch to my back. I'd been operating on adrenaline and my body was starting to shut down in response to injury. Sagging against the aft bulkhead, I rested my head in the corner under the narrow desk. My eyes followed Zakia's twitching tail as she worked with Tabby to get us out of harm's way. I smiled dopily, recognizing that the second phase of the patch was starting to work – drugs – the really good kind. The nanites had decided I'd had enough and were sending me down the happy path.

Minimal narcos, I instructed the AI. Well, that's what I tried to say and I'm pretty sure that's what the AI translated my mumbling into. A moment later, my head started to clear about the same time my shoulder started to throb.

"You hanging in there, love?" Tabby called, not looking back.

"Nothing better than these med-patches," I said. "Whooo!" I exclaimed as a shiver of euphoria worked through my body. Regretfully, the nanites would shortly clear my system.

"All hands, brace for impact. Missile danger close," Tabby said. "Jonathan, wormhole transition on my mark. Five. Four. Three."

For as much whining as I've done about fold-space, the wormhole jumps felt like something of a fraud. About the most I felt was a flip-flop of my stomach and we were through it. A moment later, a violent explosion rocked the ship and *Fleet Afoot* started tumbling ass-over-elbows through the Mhina system.

THAT OTHER PLACE

"Roby, report. We've lost starboard engine control," Tabby ordered. I clawed at the narrow counter attached to the forward bulkhead of the combat bridge and attempted to gain my feet. Our tumble was slow but accelerating. Fortunately, my head was starting to clear from the narcotics, although the pain had also returned.

"Hold on," Roby replied, his voice lacking its normal confidence.

"Roby, that engine is pushing us further and further out of control," Tabby argued. "It will be lethal in forty-six seconds."

I gingerly jammed my arm back into the sticky-wet sleeve of my vac-suit and pulled my helmet back up. Tabby was right, our rate of spin was increasing and we would shortly overwhelm the ineffective inertial systems of *Fleet Afoot*, at which point we'd be plastered to the bulkheads with no hope of recovery.

"No good," Roby replied, his voice high and panicky. "The circuits are jammed. We took a direct hit starboard side. I think it's fried."

"Let me take the helm, Tabbs," I said.

She looked at me and assessed, obviously trying to determine if I was in my right mind. She must have seen what she needed, because she unclipped and helped me into position.

"Roby, forget the starboard. Give me port control," I said.

"I can't. It's not working."

"You can do it, Roby," I said. "Just relax and focus. You know this ship. Block everything else out."

Precious seconds ticked by as I searched for alternatives with my AI.

"Roby, ignite the atmospheric engines," I said.

"What? That's crazy," he said. "We won't have enough fuel to land."

"Do it!"

A moment later, my AI sounded a chime to let me know of Roby's success. The thing about the atmospheric engines utilized by the Felio was that they burned a horrific amount of fuel. The fuel wasn't particularly expensive, but the volume required was ridiculous. That said, it was intensely powerful and when not pushing against the gravity of a planet, it had more raw thrust than our star engines.

"You're online," Roby informed me. My shoulders hurt where the harness dug in, preventing me from flying away from the center of our rotation. The trick with unwinding a tumbling ship was locating that center point and applying thrust in reverse, against it. Unfortunately, the starboard star engine was continuing to add to the already precarious position.

"You have to get that starboard engine shut down," I said. "I'm only going to be able to buy us a short amount of time with these atmo engines before we run out of fuel."

"I can't. They're not responding," he answered.

It was tough focusing on reversing our spin and walking him through basic survival, but I had no other choice. "Frakking break it if you have to, Roby. We're dead, otherwise."

For several minutes, I struggled against our tumble and managed to slow us against the engine's chaos. I felt nothing but relief when finally, Roby managed to disable the rogue engine and we settled back into level flight.

"Nice job, Roby," I said.

"We're screwed, Liam," he answered sullenly. "I broke it good."

"Jonathan is helping him," Tabby said. "I think it's going to be okay."

"Work on the port engine control," I said.

"Won't help," he said. "These engines are designed to be run as a pair. You saw what happened when they delinked. It'll just be that all over again."

"Report back to me in two hours." I terminated comms and

turned to Tabby and Zakia. "Zakia, would you accompany me? I have a crew member in the hold and there's a good chance she's in trouble. Tabby, see to Marny and Ada, they're in our quarters."

It took every gram of discipline I had not to stop and check on Ada as Zakia and I flew past. I still had no idea what shape she was in and feared the worst. Last I'd seen, she'd received a nasty head wound.

"This crew member," Zakia interrupted my train of thought. "She is a Felio from Zuri?"

I noticed as we approached the hatch leading to the airlock separating Deck One from the cargo space, that there was vacuum on the other side. We'd have to find another route.

"Yes," I answered. "You good with a spacewalk?" Even though we were traveling at great speed relative to the system's star, we were doing so in vacuum and with no acceleration. It was no different than being on an asteroid.

"I am competent," she answered.

I palmed open the airlock and closed the hatch behind us. Unlike evacuating an entire deck, the airlock cycled atmo efficiently and quickly.

"We picked Semper up on Zuri," I said as we worked our way around to the breached cargo-hold. The jets on Zakia's suit were decent, but nothing like the arc-jets I took for granted. "Found her working for an undesirable type and figured we'd be a better option. Not sure that was a good call. I may have killed her."

"Then she will have died heroically," Zakia said. "This mission is more important than ten thousand lives."

I jetted into the hold and visually swept the room. Adrenaline surged through my system as I found neither Semper, nor the remaining crate of selich roots.

Locate Semper, I instructed. Immediately, my AI projected a blue contrail. The smoke trail curved away from my location and up into the ladder tube that was an airlock between the two decks.

I zipped around to where the smoke led. "Over here." At the top of the shaft, floating next to the hatch that opened to the top deck, we found Semper.

Medical diagnostic. Override authorization, Liam Hoffen. I turned the young Felio over and peered through her face shield. I couldn't make out any signs of life. A moment later, however my HUD displayed her status. She was merely unconscious.

"Most curious," Zakia said as she slid up next to me.

"We need to move her back to the living spaces," I said. "I don't think it's curious that she's unconscious. This was a horrible place to ride out that tumble. She definitely got banged around in here."

"It's not that," Zakia said, as we worked our way out of the tube and jetted back around to *Fleet Afoot's* airlock.

"Oh?" I asked.

"Semper is family," she replied.

"Mshindi?"

"No. Mshindi is a title only given to the nobility in our family. Semper's temperament was not suitable to service House Mshindi." She placed her arm under Semper's knees and cradled her as we stepped from the airlock.

"Must be a high standard." I led her to my quarters where she laid Semper on the couch.

"How is she, Cap?" Marny asked.

I finally allowed myself to look at Ada. She was on the bed, her vac-suit pulled down to her waist, leaving just the tight suit liner. I focused on her chest and sighed in relief as she drew breath. A large med-patch lay over the entire left side of her face.

"Not sure." I looked over to Marny momentarily and then returned my attention to Semper. "She was floating loose in the cargo hold. It was my fault."

I accepted a medical scanner from Marny and retracted Semper's face shield. The scanner indicated a specific med-patch, which I applied.

"You could not have anticipated a missile following us through the wormhole, Hoffen Captain," Zakia said.

"What about Ada?" I asked.

"It's not good, Cap," Marny replied. "She took a piece of glass to the orbital socket. Her eye is damaged beyond repair. It's past what even *Intrepid's* med-tanks could have repaired."

"Frakking hell." I sat down hard against the wall next to Semper and rested the side of my head on her arm, not willing to let go of her paw. I felt that if I let her go again, she might just slip away. It was pointless wallowing, but things were lined up heavily against us and I was finding it hard to breathe.

"Cap, she's alive," Marny reassured me. "Take a deep breath. We'll get through this."

"The selich root is gone," I said weakly. "This entire trip is for nothing."

"Damn," Marny said beneath her breath. "No matter. We'll go back and get more." She was trying to sound upbeat, but even she felt our loss.

"How much do you need?" Semper asked, drawing in a deep breath and trying to sit.

"Lie back, little one," Zakia said, smoothing the fur along the smaller Felio's brow.

"Mshindi Second?" Semper's eyes flew open.

"Yes, little kit. I am here," she replied. "You must rest. You have taken injury."

"My pocket." Semper freed her paw from my hand and unzipped her vac-suit at her waist. She extracted a single, paw-sized selich tuber and held it up.

"Is that enough?" Marny asked.

"It will have to be," I said.

***

"How are you feeling?" I asked Ada who stirred beside me on the bed.

Roby and Jonathan had restored control of the starboard engine sixty hours ago, and we'd been underway on a modified burn ever since. Our current estimate was that we'd arrive at the ghost fleet in three more days.

Ada placed her hand on the med-patch that covered her eye. "Unreal headache," she whispered. "How bad is it?"

"You've lost your left eye and your skin is badly burned," I said. "You'll need a synth-skin graft. The damage to both is bad."

"Engines feel unbalanced," she said. "Did we clear the mine field?"

"Yes. We're in Mhina," I said. "We're sailing on the starboard engine."

"Did we lose anyone?"

"There were a few other injuries, but you took the brunt of it. You've been down almost three days. Medical AI had you in a coma and you weren't supposed to wake up for another hour. Tabby's going to be pissed, she's got the helm," I said.

"How are we going to get this mission back on track?"

I smiled. Ada and I were cut from the same cloth. "Roby and Jonathan believe they can repair the engine with access to the machine shop we saw on *Cold Mountain Stream*. We'll patch the bridge and cargo hold with salvage from the fleet. We're planning to turn around repairs and take on fuel in ninety-six hours. Think you'll feel up to sailing by then?"

"My depth perception will be off." Ada waggled her one functional eyebrow.

I shook my head, unwilling to take the bait. "You'll never believe it, but Semper and Zakia are related. Apparently, Semper is a Mshindi that didn't make the cut."

"What's that mean?"

"The females are put through tests. If they pass, they get to be Mshindis. Otherwise they're sent off to make their own way, completely without the benefit of the family name or resources."

"That's horrible. She's Zakia's sister, then?" Ada asked.

"More like a second cousin. At least that's the way I understand it. Zakia was pretty happy to see her, though," I said. "I guess they grew up together. Semper was like a kid sister."

"House Mshindi has taken quite a stand helping us," Ada said. "What do you suppose will happen?"

"According to Zakia; Mshindi First will take the blame and essentially be tried for treason against the Confederation. She could be executed," I said.

"That's incredible."

"Mshindi Second – Zakia - said the entire Mshindi nobility is in on it. One hundred officers and politicians serving at every level within the Abasi government. They're all standing with Mshindi First. Zakia thinks there's possibility of a civil war against Strix control of the Confederation. It isn't just the Mshindi that are unwilling to be part of allowing another civilization be torn apart by the Kroerak."

"It's happened before?"

"According to Zakia, the Confederation has refused to help several non-member species that were under siege. She's not particularly talkative, however," I said. "I better go get Tabby, she's been waiting. Think about strapping on your big-girl flying pants. We're going to need all the help we can get."

"Cap?" Marny pushed open the door to the captain's quarters-turned-medical bay. "Ada! You're awake."

"Thanks to you, I understand," Ada replied, pushing her hands into the bed as she attempted to sit up.

"Hot skippy, it's good to see you up," Marny replied. "Cap, we have a problem and you're needed on the bridge. Sorry, Ada. Lousy timing. I'll come back."

"Kroerak?" I asked once we were in the hallway.

"Worse," Marny replied. "Abasi."

"They sent a ship through the wormhole?" I palmed the combat bridge's secure entry. Zakia and Tabby stopped what sounded like a heated conversation.

"Liam. Our sensors resolved twenty-three ships entering Mhina through the wormhole ten minutes ago," Tabby said. "Jonathan has identified them as Abasi ships."

"Can we identify the ships? Are they hostile?" I asked.

"Your sensors are too limited," Zakia said.

"That's shite," Tabby replied. "Those ships are sailing without transponders."

"Why would they do that?" I asked.

"Common practice in combat," Zakia answered. "Abasi ships utilize a combat identification system."

"That's our answer," Tabby argued. "If they're friendly, they wouldn't be sailing quiet like that. We'd never have picked them up without Jonathan sifting through our sensor data. They're emitting virtually no electro-magnetic radiation beyond what their engines leak. And those engines are frakking efficient."

"It is technology we developed when battling Kroerak," Zakia said. "The Kroerak had the capacity to intercept, locate and decode signals we thought secure. Early in the war, they pinpointed our command structures with ease and anticipated our strategic movements. That advantage led to the fall of Zuri."

"When will they overtake us?" I asked.

"A cutter has broken free from fleet," Tabby said. "It's moving faster than anything I've seen and will intercept in less than four hours."

"Armed?" Unanswered questions hammered at me, each vying for priority. I closed my eyes, working to order the chaos within. We'd burned about halfway to the ghost fleet and that had taken sixty-two hours. *Fleet Afoot,* the fastest ship we'd every sailed, might have accomplished the same in twenty hours if well repaired. The idea of a ship capable of that sort of transit in four hours was mind boggling.

"The *Wind* craft are combat capable," Zakia said. "Standard complement is a light turret, although they can be retrofitted to carry a single missile. They are not usually deployed on combat missions and are more commonly used as personnel transports."

"Surely Daraterest scanned *Fleet Afoot*. She'll be aware we have no offensive capacity," I said. "A light turret is all it will take."

"What can we do?" Tabby asked.

"The next move is up to the Abasi," I said. "Ada's awake. You should go see her."

***

"Captain Hoffen, the Abasi cutter is one point eight kilometers astern and attempting to establish point-to-point communications. How would you like to proceed?" Jonathan called from the engineering bay. For most of the trip, he and Roby had been confined to the engineering bay as we were separated by vacuum and it required evacuating the atmo from their space to transfer personnel and supplies.

"Patch it through to the combat bridge."

"Communication established and transferred to bridge."

"Go ahead, unidentified Abasi ship," I said. "This is Captain Liam Hoffen." I was ready to argue that we were sailing in the deep dark and that neither the Confederation nor the Abasi had any legal standing to molest my ship or crew. It was a weak argument, but it was all I could come up with.

"Captain Hoffen, I request that you desist motion. We have personnel to transfer."

My vid-screen displayed a fluttering image of none other than Mshindi First.

"Adahy - mother," Zakia said quietly.

"Zakia – daughter. It gives me pride to see you well."

"Mshindi First. Our hold is open to space, as is our primary bridge," I said.

"Your primary engine is venting electromagnetic radiation much like celebration lights at winter's end," she replied. "My engineers have diagnosed your failures and we convey appropriate remedies."

I chuckled. For some reason the AI translation for Mshindi First always came through overly formal and with odd word choices. "I am powering down." I stopped our remaining engine's burn. I hoped she was right about fixing our starboard engine, otherwise we'd overshoot the ghost fleet if we spent more than an hour in repairs.

"Marny, Tabbs, we're about to receive company. Please meet me at the airlock," I said, allowing my AI to route the comms appropriately.

"What is going on, Hoffen Captain?" Semper asked, catching me as I turned in front of the mess hall on the way to the airlock. I felt a twinge of guilt at not having made an all-ship announcement about the ship that had been quietly pursuing us for the last four hours.

"Good time to learn about boarding procedures, Semper," I said. "We'll be accepting a boarding party from an Abasi ship. No matter who we're allowing aboard, we need to be careful. Each person allowed entry has the potential of endangering our crew and our mission."

"Roger that, Cap," Marny said, pulling up behind me.

"Semper, you'll stand just behind me to my right. If anything goes wrong, you are to duck down and not interfere with Marny or Tabby," I said.

"Are you expecting trouble, love?" Tabby asked.

"I am not," I answered.

"Captain, the *Wind* vessel is extending a gangway and requesting docking permission," Roby announced over comms. I appreciated that he was paying attention to our communication protocols.

"Granted," I said. Just behind Tabby, Zakia now stood. I had a momentary flash of insecurity with the knowledge that two Abasi I knew very little about would shortly be flanking us. I comforted myself with the knowledge that the cutter could easily destroy us if it came to that. Maybe 'comforted' wasn't exactly the right word.

"Cap," Marny said. "I need you in the here and now. Focus."

"Copy that, Marny," I agreed. I wanted to argue, but she had a knack for sensing when I was distracted.

"They're at the door," Roby said over the comms.

I palmed the security pad and allowed the outer hatch to unlock as the airlock chamber aboard *Fleet Afoot* equalized with the gangway. Once green, I pushed and set in motion the retracting iris hatch. A moment later, I stood face to face with two of the largest Felio I'd ever seen – one male, the other female.

"You will make way," the female growled. Even beneath the vac-suit, the muscles in her shoulders tensed just as her claws tightened on a medium-length blaster rifle.

"You don't give orders here," I said, reaching for the blaster pistol at my waist.

It was at this point the world of sanity gave way to that other world – the place where time slows and bad things occur that will later cause great pain. It's a world where consequences are added to the tab but are, for the moment, ignored. The female Felio was insanely fast. I'd barely placed my hand onto my pistol when the butt of her rifle lashed out and met the side of my face.

LOSING THE WAR

Thanks to the near-constant training I'd received from both Tabby and Marny, I managed to raise my forearm into the path of the rifle's butt, despite my surprise at the attack. I wasn't fast enough or strong enough to completely block the blow. I did, however, cut down on the blow's impact and instead of dropping to the floor like a sack of potatoes – strike that, selich – I instead rolled to the side, accepting the Felio's power, and allowed the force to turn me. My next move, brilliant in conception, was to continue around and bring a side kick into the Felio's midsection. Unfortunately, speed, strength and training are three critical components to martial combat and I lacked everything but a great concept. As 'great concept' wasn't on the short list of critical components, I wasn't overly surprised when the Felio executed a sweep of her own, taking out my stable leg and dumping me to the deck.

Turns out, against the two Felio guards, I was considerably outmatched - a fact that didn't escape me as I looked up from the deck. The second fact that didn't escape me was that I was not alone. No sooner had I hit the deck but Tabby sailed across the now vacant space above my body and piled into the still advancing Felio.

"DESIST!" I heard a translated cry from the airlock.

"Disengage!" Another translated cry from the hallway.

Within each of us – Felio and human alike - lies an angry beast. It's the part of us that answers the first call to the fight-or-flight response. Whatever this primal reaction is, words, especially those yelled, have little impact. If anything, those heated words encourage, if only momentarily, the excited beast to further action.

On average, a Felio gives up ten percent of body mass to a spacer human. In the case of the female that had cleanly laid me out, she was well above average and out-massed Tabby by ten kilograms. Ordinarily, this would have been a significant difference, but Tabby is anything but ordinary. I'd like to say the powerful Felio female and her male companion were well-matched opponents for Tabby and that they'd battled mightily to the end. The fact was the female had made a critical mistake by dropping me.

Tabby, well in front of Marny, jammed the side of her foot just below the slightly turned female Felio's leg and used the sideways momentum to spring into the surprised male. In flight, Tabby raised her knee and drove it through the male's chin as she wrapped her outstretched arm around the female's neck. Gravity and time - both of which Tabby seemed to momentarily defy - returned. A cracking sound came from the male Felio's neck as he fell back to the deck. At the same time, Tabby landed in a crouch, still holding the female.

Not without martial skills and undeterred by the chaos of battle, the female twisted from Tabby's grip and reared back, ready to re-engage. There are moments in battle, when something occurs that I find so confusing, that later I find myself replaying the incident, trying to reconstruct the sequence. What happened next was one of those moments as a waft of smoke curled up from the Felio's chest. She stumbled backward, confusion on her face, and the sound of a blaster round followed. Right – sequence – I told you, I'm still working to reconstruct the details.

"Tabby, no!" Marny had arrived half a second behind Tabby and was trying to corral her against the airlock's bulkhead - no easy task.

"Hoffen Captain, are you injured?" Zakia asked, coming to my side.

I looked back at her with some confusion. "Yes. Why are they attacking? Are you taking the ship?" It still hadn't registered if we'd won the battle in the hallway, but without any ship defenses, we would still be sitting ducks for the Wind's attack. A plan to board and overpower the crew started to form in my mind.

"We are not enemies," Zakia said, raising her paws defensively.

Marny pushed around Zakia and dropped to her knees, inspecting the fallen Felio male. "Get a med kit. His neck is injured," she said. The Felio's labored breathing and bloody drool was concerning.

"I'll go." Semper jumped up from the crouched position she'd taken when the melee began. I felt a small amount of pride at her having listened to my instructions about getting out of the way if the shite started to meet the rotary circulation device.

"Captain Hoffen, I most modestly apologize for this adverse interaction." Mshindi First advanced, ignoring her fallen warriors. "I am aghast at my guard's escalation. I find fault within for improperly calculating the impact to my warrior guards' hearts of our chase in *Dusk Wind*."

"I'm not sure I understand," I said.

"Hoffen Captain, if I may help," Semper said as she handed a medical kit to Marny.

"Please, Semper," I said.

"Abasi warriors are trained to hunt prey. Mshindi First is expressing regret for not recognizing they remained on the hunt," she said.

"I accept this apology, Mshindi First," I said. "I hope we have not caused irreparable injury to your people."

"It is their guilt," Mshindi First said. "My guard must maintain control under all conditions, even if the short span has been troublesome for us all."

A smaller Felio slid through the knot of people and joined Marny as she worked on the fallen male. A groan from the female guard echoed through the hallway as Zakia helped her to her feet, all the while quietly chastising her for attacking the ship's captain. The offended Felio guard's defense was simple – I was a male and how was she to know I was the leader. Even with adrenaline still urging Tabby into combat, I caught the slightest grin on her face as she listened to the translation.

"I would request you do not punish your guard for their diligence," I said. "If we are to defeat the Kroerak we will need those who are quick to action."

"I will consider your words, Captain Hoffen," Mshindi First said. "Action without discipline brings about madness."

"Marny, will he be okay?" I asked.

"I don't know," she answered. "Their bodies are so different. I'm not sure what's supposed to be where. A human couldn't have survived that break."

"Aganath will fight another day," the smaller Felio who was helping Marny answered. "He will not like that he has humans to thank for his recovery."

"Send him back any time he wants to discuss it," Tabby said as two more Felio arrived to help move the fallen guards off. Marny stood and walked Tabby away from the airlock. As she disappeared, I could just hear her mumbling. "Frakking asshats. Bringing that weak shite over here."

I placed a smile on my face that I still wasn't sure of and extended my hand. "Welcome, Mshindi First. It is our honor to have you aboard," I said, repeating the words I'd wanted to initially greet her with.

"It is my gratefulness," she said. I would have to talk to Jonathan about cleaning up her translation, as I was positive we didn't want further confusion. "Zakia, we see damage to *Fleet Afoot*. Has your mission failed? What of the hot tubers?"

I turned away as she addressed Zakia. "Jonathan, can you do anything for Mshindi's translation? It is difficult to understand."

"Yes, Liam," Jonathan replied. "We noticed and believe she uses a more formal speech than other Felio. We're uploading more appropriate dialogue interpretation as it becomes available."

"Our mission remains successful," Zakia replied. "It is to the honor of your sister's unproductive daughter."

"This was the child you played with in your youth? Semper?" Mshindi First asked. "How is it she is aboard *Fleet Afoot*?"

"Hired on as crew," I said, reinserting myself into the conversation. "Please, join me in the mess. We have few spaces where we can meet that are not exposed to vacuum."

"With your permission, Captain Hoffen," she answered. "Our engineers have brought supplies and expertise capable of ship repair. We will successfully bring function to *Fleet Afoot*. They are most concerned with the energy signatures of your engines and believe it is possible they will soon desist from operation."

"Engineering help would be most appreciated," I said. "Roby, would you coordinate with House Mshindi engineers?"

"What's going on, Liam?" Roby asked over the comm.

I bristled at his response and decided I couldn't ignore his lack of protocol. "Future responses should sound a lot like – aye aye, Captain," I replied and cut the comm.

"Captain – would you query the honorable Mshindi First on the success of her secondary mission?" Jonathan said.

"Without success, further engagement would not have been viable. Our presence in Mhina is affirmation of our gambit's success," Mshindi First said, accepting a small pouch from an aide who'd remained relatively hidden behind her. She handed the soft leather pouch to me. When I opened it, I found it contained the missing communication crystals.

"You've recovered these from Strix control?" I asked.

"Once we exposed our support of your entry to the Mhina mine field, we were forced into decisive action," she answered. "With instruction from the ones you call Jonathan, we equipped our vessels with the necessary machinery to traverse fold space. As such, we have withheld the material referred to as Aninonium."

"I don't understand how you knew to do this and how you recovered our materials," I said.

"Your crystals and Aninonium were being held by Abasi. It was a simple matter to retrieve the objects," Mshindi First said. "It was with instructions from those you refer to as Jonathan that we modified our ships while in transit."

"Is this why you separated from us, Jonathan?" I asked.

"Our observations in the Mhina system led us to believe Abasi had found a mechanism for denying the Kroerak the food source required," he said. "By separating from *Intrepid's* crew, we were able to contact those who were capable of providing aid. It was not until we reconnected with Thomas Anino that he was able to suggest the plan we are currently employing."

"How is it that you can talk with Anino? The crystals were seized," I said.

"We have a quantum communication crystal buried within our being," he said.

Two Felio showed up in the gangway with full grav-carts. It wasn't lost on me that, once again, the military had access to technology rank-and-file citizens were denied.

"Bridge?" A small Felio asked.

"Captain Hoffen," Mshindi First interrupted. "With your permission, my crew will stay aboard until we reach the disabled fleet. I humbly request you allow *Thunder Awakes* and her sister *Lightning on Plains* the privilege of first arrival with anticipation that a sleeper Kroerak might still reside."

"You want to go first?" I asked, smiling. "Oh, heck yah. We've as much firepower aboard as a toothless mouse."

"Until that moment, I request we keep communication at nil," she replied. "I will share our plans upon arrival and hope they meet with your approval."

"Until then," I said and gave her a mock salute that I immediately wished I could undo.

"Zakia - you will accompany me for the remainder of our journey," Mshindi First said, leaving no doubt in my mind she wasn't used to others mistaking her orders for requests.

"Bridge?" One of the engineers who'd been left behind asked as soon as Mshindi First retreated to the cutter.

I've had the good fortune to often be in the presence of excellent engineers. I suppose that says something about the shape of the ships I often sail. The fact was, however, the two Felio engineers, both female, were about as nerdy as any I'd met, human or otherwise. The idea that nerdy makes for good engineers is yet one more idea that translates between human and Felio particularly well. Bumha and Vuhma – oddly unrelated – quickly set about restoring function to the bridge. Apparently, blown out glass and holed cargo bays were right in line with their expertise and after deploying semi-autonomous instruments, they formulated a repair plan.

"Buhma is asking if you'd be willing to do some cutting," Jonathan called me from the engineering bay.

"I'm standing right here," I answered. "Can't they just ask me?"

"We believe Tabby and Marny make them nervous," Jonathan said.

"Have them send a plan. We'll make the cuts."

It took three hours for Tabby and me to cut out the ruined portions of the bridge, tween decks and cargo hold. The plans provided by the Felio engineers were precise and I wondered just how they'd go about repairing the remaining damage. As we worked, Vuhma and Buhma left us to help Roby and Jonathan with the damaged engines.

"Jonathan, tell me more about Anino's plan," I said as we worked. Cutting steel, while tedious, wasn't particularly difficult and Jonathan had more than enough processing power to hold several simultaneous conversations.

"The plan is diverting substantially from Thomas Anino's original," Jonathan replied.

"How so?" I asked.

"Initially, we were surprised by your oversight in not mentioning a need for Aninonium to transmit *Fleet Afoot* along the trans location wave," Jonathan said.

"I smuggled a small amount off *Intrepid*," I said.

"There are many of us who suggested you might have done this," Jonathan said.

"What about the Abasi fleet?" I asked. "What are they doing here? Two battleships, five cruisers and eight or better destroyers is overkill."

"We simply do not know," Jonathan admitted.

"Does Anino?" I asked.

"He might," Jonathan answered. "An Abasi operative retrieved the quantum communication crystals seized by the Strix. Mshindi First has been in direct contact with Thomas Anino ever since."

"This plan is why you left us on the space station?"

"Yes. We initially contacted Mshindi First while aboard *Thunder Awakes*. In addition to recognizing the significance of the poisoned Felio, we needed to find a viable mechanism for returning your crew to Sol without attracting too much Confederation attention," he said. "You returned to space much more quickly than we had anticipated and we found we had to act accordingly."

"In just a few weeks, you were able to start a civil war?" I asked.

"There are more beings like us who are working toward a greater good," Jonathan said. "The Abasi were already well informed as to humanity's plight. They are an honorable people and when confronted, they responded as such. Master Anino can be most convincing."

"Let me guess, Anino is promising them some serious tech for their help," I said.

"It is true," Jonathan replied. "He has offered intellectual property that will give the Abasi advantage when dealing with the Strix. There is no dishonor in this."

"Right," I said. "Would you mind telling the 'Umah twins we're done cutting off the waste."

"Always so clever," Jonathan replied. "I have communicated such. They request that you retrieve the patch material as was left next to the cargo bay on starboard side."

"Patch material?" I arc-jetted over to the starboard side along the outside of the ship. A machine, half a meter square and a meter long, was just finishing a weld on a glass and mullion replacement that looked like it would fit perfectly in *Fleet Afoot*.

"They request you secure with light welds so that their manufactury may finish the process of installation," he said.

"Sweet machine," I said. "Should we take it over with us?"

"Affirmative."

"Get things worked out?" Tabby asked.

"Help me move this," I said, gesturing to the new robot I desperately wished I owned. "You know I never thanked you for coming to my rescue."

"Your awe was all I needed," Tabby answered. "That and a really satisfying cartilage crack from the big guy."

"You could have killed him," I said. "Doesn't that bother you?"

"Not even a little," she answered. "First, I pulled my knee and didn't think he was in any real danger. Second, he attacked *my* crew on *my* ship. I have no compunction about defending what is mine."

"You're a little scary sometimes, you know that?" I said.

"Good thing to remember."

***

We were in the final six hours of deceleration when the Abasi fleet, led by the two massive battleships *Thunder Awakes* and *Lightning on Plains* roared overhead. Okay, technically they didn't make a bit of noise, but I personally hadn't been exposed to quite so much firepower all in one place and I could *feel* their presence, if only emotionally. I'd seen larger fleets of ships, but never more than a single battleship in any location and especially not flanked by four battle-cruisers and half a dozen destroyer sized vessels.

"Are those all Abasi, Jonathan?" I asked.

"Yes. Although the ships belong to differing Abasi houses," he answered. "House Mshindi has been joined by two others; Perasti and Gundi."

"What kind of chaos is that causing back on Abasi Prime?" I asked.

"This is unknown," he answered. "Abasi government is much like the Confederation of Planets. It is a coalition of smaller nations – called houses. Three powerful houses have gone against the will of the Confederation and there will be a reckoning. It is a gamble that they will achieve enough to warrant their actions."

"The Abasi intend to jump to Sol with us," I said.

"Sixty-eight percent of us believe this to be the most likely scenario," Jonathan said. "It would rectify the presence of the excess of Aninonium."

"Anino isn't telling you what's going on?" I asked.

"I believe Thomas Anino to be under considerable stress, as we are unable to raise him with any regularity," Jonathan replied.

"How will he turn TransLoc back on?" I asked.

"The Kroerak have re-established Trans Location," Jonathan replied. "This is how the second Kroerak fleet was able to arrive at Sol."

"If the Kroerak have TransLoc, who can stop them?" I asked.

"There is a failsafe," Jonathan said.

"It doesn't appear to be working," I said. "If it was, he'd have stopped that second fleet before it arrived."

"There have been difficulties," Jonathan said. "The control of Master Anino's consciousness has been tenuous."

"What the frak does that mean?"

"Thomas Anino has been captured, tortured and killed on four separate occasions since the occupation of human space by the Kroerak. The technology that allows his continued existence is failing. He flees by entering fold-space and moving to a new location. The Kroerak are able to locate him utilizing Belirand Corporation's locator technology."

"We've lost the war," I said, realization seeping in. "You're saying the Kroerak can control any location they want."

"That is not quite correct," Jonathan said. "Humanity has many strongholds on each of their continents but the Kroerak control the majority space. If the Kroerak were to focus on any individual stronghold, they might be successful, but for now they are content because they have achieved their first objective."

"Which is what?"

"To secure a food source."

THE HUNT

When we finally arrived at the ghost fleet's location, the area had been entirely transformed. Small shuttlecraft zipped about, large ship repair tenders had been deployed, and it looked like a mass of crazy, frenetic activity.

"Liam, we're being hailed by *Thunder Awakes*," Ada said. She'd insisted on taking her pilot's seat to bring us in. If I'd been worried about her injuries, I needn't have been. She brought us in easily.

"This is Captain Hoffen," I replied.

"Captain Hoffen, I request your presence aboard *Thunder Awakes*. Is this amenable?" Mshindi First asked, her signal strong and her picture on the vid screen unwavering. It occurred to me that the 'Uhma twins had installed an Abasi combat communications device.

"I accept," I answered.

"I will dispatch a shuttle immediately," she replied and terminated the comm.

Ada flicked a navigation path at me. "We're also receiving orders to this location."

Somewhere along the line, the command structure of our mission had been modified. I'd worked around enough high achievers to recognize the behavior. I'd need to make a push for more autonomy or Mshindi would simply assume she could continue to give orders.

"It is planned to install *Intrepid's* TransLoc engines," Jonathan said. "That location is where repair tenders will be located."

"Jonathan, Tabby, you're with me," I said. "Ada, you're in charge."

We were met at the airlock door by the engineers Buhma and Vuhma, tools loaded on otherwise empty grav-sleds. Instead of waiting for the gangway to be extended, the five of us exited into space and arc-jetted across to the waiting shuttle where we met Zakia – Mshindi Second.

"Greetings Captain Hoffen, Jonathan, and Tabitha," Zakia said. "We will join Mshindi First for a strategy session."

We offloaded onto *Thunder Awakes* and she led us through crisply painted, well maintained passageways. I felt a pang of regret at having bricked *Intrepid*. I missed her clean lines and impeccably maintained systems. It was the sort of thing you didn't know to miss until you no longer had it.

The room Zakia led us to was set up with a gallery of two rows of chairs encircling three sides of an open floor. The chairs were separated from the open center by a thin railing. The room had seating for forty, although only half that many were in attendance; some wearing vac-suits, others simply wearing uniforms. The different houses quickly became evident by their various color schemes. As recognition of our arrival spread through the room, the volume of chattering diminished.

"Captain Hoffen. Jonathan. Tabitha Masters." Mshindi First greeted us as she walked into the room. "Please recline everyone."

A male Felio stood forward and addressed the group. He had a full mane of thick fur that started in the middle of his chest, wrapped over his shoulders and bristled unyieldingly atop his head. "We have made sufficient statement. We must return to Tamu with our dead ancestors and abandon this false promise of glory. Today we have embarked on a mission most valiant and we may yet recover our position with the Confederation."

"Drop, Gunjway coward." Mshindi Tertiary erupted from the galley and streaked across the open section of floor.

"Majida! Decorum." Mshindi First deftly cuffed the quick-moving Felio on the back of her head just before she reached the male speaker. While lacking any real power, Mshindi First's blow stopped the faster, younger Felio in her tracks.

"We are committed, Adahy. There is no span for shirking," Mshindi Tertiary defended, turning her full attention to Mshindi First.

"We reserve violence for our enemies. You will desist," Mshindi replied, her quiet words daring the younger Felio to disobey. Mshindi First turned to address the fidgeting but still orderly group. "What say you, House Perasti? Has Gundi Second's separation from our preparations poisoned also your minds?"

Where the male Felio wore dark green uniforms, the female who stepped forward wore bright, medium blue. Grayed fur around the muzzle was the only clue I had concerning her age. The reaction from the room was immediate. The nervous movements and whispering ceased as everyone held still in anticipation.

"House Perasti has awaited one hundred eighty spans to recover our ancestors from their place of rest. I find myself reflecting on the great sacrifice of those most noble warriors who went before us. Those of Perasti, Mshindi, and also Gundi. When House Perasti was approached with this bold plan, I slumbered. My warrior self had fallen to sleep and been replaced with a politician. Here, at this moment, sharing space with my kinsmen as they are retrieved to our holds, I am reminded of their courage and honor.

"No, Gundi Second. House Perasti will not balk today. We will not allow our tails to curl beneath. We will not scrape to the mighty Kroerak empire, for we are Abasi!" As Perasti First's voice rose, so did the members of her house with left paws held firmly over their chests.

"Abasi do not run from battle - we are warriors first." Almost imperceptibly, she nodded her head at the end of the sentence and her house responded with an exhalation. I might have mistaken the sound for a cough if only one Abasi had done it. The entire group was clearly adding an exclamation point to her speech.

"The span has long since passed to repay the mighty Kroerak for their assault on our peoples. While we are a patient people, we choose to be a people of courage."

Zakia stood next to me, paw on her chest and responded with a chuff at the same time as Perasti.

"We choose to be a people of honor." In seeing their second in command rise, the remainder of those wearing House Mshindi uniforms stood and chuffed in response.

"And today, if the battle so wills it, we choose to be a people of sacrifice." Once again, the room responded with a chuff. I looked over to Gundi Second who stared at the floor in front of him.

"No, Mshindi First - my good friend Adahy. There is no poison in the minds of House Perasti. We will join you on one last great hunt and we will hide no more behind mine fields and weak-willed Strix cowards."

Having said her piece, the diminutive Felio matriarch, Perasti First, raised her own paw slowly to her chest and held it in place firmly. Mshindi First responded by bringing her paw up to her chest and bowing slightly at the waist.

When Mshindi First straightened, she turned back to the smaller group of green uniformed Felio, most of whom were standing. "House Gundi, does your second speak for you?"

"I desire to say that Gundi Second has spoken out of turn." The Felio who stepped from behind the railing and faced both Mshindi and Perasti was indistinguishable from the other Felio around her. She bore shorter, dark brown fur and beige tiger stripes. Unlike Gundi Second, she had no mane, which appeared to be a solely male trait.

"He has not," she continued. "He has merely expressed the concern shared among my ranks and fostered by my own indecision." A murmur rolled through the crowd at her admission. "In our beings and taught to us over the span when we were kits, we both know and have learned that to run from battle is without honor. The graveyard of my ancestors speaks to my existence and has brought forth resolution and excitement I thought no longer possible. House Gundi stands with House Perasti and with House Mshindi. We will not flee from our duty." As she finished speaking, she raised her paw to her chest and turned back to her own people, causing those still seated to rise.

I'd like to report that this was the end of the speech making. Turns out, Felio really enjoy talking about glory, honor, past deeds and all that. The fact of the matter is, it all started to sound the same after a while, especially when the people or places were unrecognizable to me. I spent most of the next three hours observing Felio body language and not listening so much.

"Captain Hoffen, what do you say?" Mshindi Prime asked.

I looked up at her and then around the room. I had no idea what she'd asked of me. Fortunately, this was not new behavior for me and my AI recognized my quandary. It quickly summarized Mshindi Prime's question as to how we planned to deliver the selich root.

"We'll jump in two hundred thousand kilometers below the ecliptic plane. The reports we have are that the Kroerak have space superiority over Earth. We believe the combined fleets of Mars and Earth have been driven off to the location we'll share with you shortly, before we enter TransLoc space. Once there, our objective will be to locate what remains of Earth's government and explain the discovery of the selich root. We believe we will have twenty minutes before the Kroerak are aware of our arrival."

"Explain how the Kroerak will be made aware?" Perasti First stood from where she'd been reclining against the railing and approached.

"TransLoc travel is all tracked through a central system on Earth," I said. "This facility has been seized by the Kroerak. We believe this is how they re-enabled TransLoc travel for the second fleet."

"How many vessels were in the second fleet?" Gundi First asked.

"Jonathan?" I turned to Jonathan who was sitting next to me.

"Imprecisely, eight hundred. What is known, however, is that planetary defenses have successfully defended the combined fleets and that the Kroerak have suffered great casualties. The Kroerak now engage in a land war on all continents and are satisfied to leave the human fleet alone, as it no longer has strategic value. They seek to restore themselves by feeding on a captured population."

"The time to strike is now," Perasti First brought her arm up quickly and raised it above her head. "The fatigue of the Kroerak warriors will be at its greatest and their fleet will be at its weakest. When will these ships be prepared for transport?"

"Abunda, stand forward," Mshindi First demanded, stepping up next to Perasti First. "Provide to us a time frame."

"The main fleet is prepared in this hour to venture forth," a thin Felio holding the equivalent of a reading pad said, not looking up from the pad but stepping into the center court. "I have learned from our esteemed visitors that the modifications we have made to our own wormhole engines require a small amount of catalyst they refer to as Aninonium."

"What of our ancestor's ships?" Mshindi First asked. "You have shared that many of these ships would be capable of making the journey with us. We have brought many supplies and machineries for this purpose. What say you?"

"It is as you understand, Mshindi First," Abunda said. "With an additional seven days we will fully return thirteen ships back to function." I appreciated my AI for translating the Felio time back to something I could understand. "We also understand that transit on the fold-space wave will require ten days. It is quite simple. The fleet will arrive in seventeen days with thirty-seven ships."

I stood and stepped over the railing, apparently breaking some sort of rule of etiquette. I heard chuffs and saw more than one Felio angrily lunge in my direction. Mshindi First saw the disaster I was creating and intervened. "Captain Hoffen, please stand forward and report."

"My apologies," I said, to which Mshindi First nodded. "TransLoc waves are affected by mass. Abunda's calculations are completed based on *Thunder Awakes*. Smaller ships such as *Cold Mountain Stream* or, even more so, *Fleet Afoot* can transit much more quickly. It is not linear, but the differences are significant. With planning, you could launch your ships in waves. Send the battleships immediately and repair progressively smaller ships, in order."

"Is this true, Abunda?" Mshindi First asked.

"I am not aware of this," she replied. "The mathematics he infers is within logical bounds."

"My sisters, remove yourselves from *Thunder Awakes* as we will journey forth within the hour. Mshindi Second, make preparations to remove your crew to our grandmother's presence aboard *Cold Mountain Stream*. I expect to see you in the field of battle, by my side."

The room erupted into chaos as the Felio began talking all at once. Abunda dodged more than one as she wove her way over to Jonathan, Tabby, and me. "How have I made such a grievous oversight?" she asked, looking up from the reading pad, holding a stylus between two thick fingers and pinning it in place with a single, outstretched claw.

"Your mathematics are correctly applied," Jonathan answered. "The bubble effect of TransLoc can be modified such that each ship may create its own event wave. We have transmitted an update to your display pad and wish for your review."

"That is outside of possibility," Abunda said. "My compute machinery has significant protections. How have you modified my datum?"

"Perhaps this is an issue we might address at a future moment. We have provided you a schedule of launches and believe with existing personnel, you might launch six more ships as a result of rearranging your repairs," Jonathan said.

"Captain Hoffen, we must desist from this location," Mshindi Second had found her way back to us, as the room had thinned considerably. "I will transfer you to *Fleet Afoot*."

"Abunda – when will *Fleet Afoot* be ready to sail?" I asked. "We do not plan to travel with the fleet."

"Your ship was minimally damaged," she said. "You are ready to sail. We have taken liberties to restore weaponries and have reinforced the bridge and cargo structures."

"We've only been here three hours," I said. "How is that possible?"

"Most of ship repair is preparation. House Mshindi has significant capacity for which we take great pride," she replied. "Buhma and Vuhma were quite thorough in their preparation while completing your traversal."

"Time is limited previous to departure," Zakia pushed.

"Wait," I said and fished out the original Belirand quantum comm crystal. "We need to retrieve this crystal's cradle."

"It is non-operative," Zakia said. "Our ancestors tried for many months to cause it to function."

"It works and I have its mate," I said. "If Mshindi Prime brings it aboard *Thunder Awakes* and we are successful in contacting Earth's defenses, she will have instant communication, even while in TransLoc."

"This would be a significant strategic advantage," Mshindi Second agreed. "We must add speed to our stride."

"Go!" I said.

The lithe Felio sliced through the crowd at a speed Jonathan, Tabby, and I found difficult to match without causing offense to those we brushed past. As we ran through the hallway, Zakia's rank became more than a little useful, as a simple command caused the bustling crew to part, leaving a clear path. No sooner had we arrived on the busy flight deck and loaded into a shuttle than it lifted off, punching through the blue energy shield that separated the deck from vacuum.

"I don't know how to thank House Mshindi for helping my people," I said. "I feel that you are entering a fight from which many of you will not return."

"The cost of honor must be more than words," Zakia said. "This is something House Mshindi, House Perasti, and House Gundi believe has been forgotten by the Abasi people. We will awaken our kinsmen with bold action."

The transformation aboard *Cold Mountain Stream* was remarkable. The landing bay, originally containing a single fighter and the Musi ship we had commandeered, was filled with sleek new fighters, stacks of missiles, and crates of supplies. Missing were broken hatches and corpses. Even though Zakia was destined to take command of the ship, she didn't pause for even a moment to inspect the changes. Instead, she streaked through the hallways on her way to the bridge, where the largest transformation of all had occurred. The bridge's function had been fully restored and engineers were just finishing repairs on the entry hatch we'd cut open.

My eyes immediately fell on the captain's chair. For a moment, it seemed that the original Mshindi had somehow been resurrected, as a red furred Felio stepped from the chair.

"Where is the communications device?" Zakia demanded.

I pointed at the location where it had previously been located. The cradle was missing.

"Mshindi Second. Please explain. What is this you speak of?" the Felio who'd occupied the captain's chair asked, placing her paw low on her chest and bowing slightly.

"An alien device," Zakia replied. "It was located where the human indicates."

"Quiart. I require a report. Where is the device Mshindi Second indicates?"

An engineer stopped working to explain. "It was not part of the original bridge design and has been removed."

"I task you with locating this object," Zakia said. "It is of critical importance."

"As you require." Quiart bowed before racing off.

I held the crystal out to Zakia. "Make sure Mshindi First has this and the cradle. We should get going. Jonathan will transmit schematics for the cradle's design. Worse case, your engineers can repair or manufacture a new device."

Zakia accepted the crystal. "Distinguished Mate Hearni will see that you are returned to *Fleet Afoot*. Captain Liam Hoffen, House Mshindi bids you good hunting."

"Mshindi Second, it is our good fortune to have found trustworthy allies. I owe you a debt of gratitude that I fear cannot be repaid. Good hunting, Zakia," I said and placed my fist over my chest and bowed as I had seen so many Felio before me do. Zakia returned the gesture and then we were off, racing through the hallways of *Cold Mountain Stream*.

"That you, Liam?" Ada asked as our shuttle closed on *Fleet Afoot's* location.

"Copy that, Ada," I answered.

"I'm initiating evac on the airlock," she said. "We're through our checklists and all statuses are green."

Fleet Afoot had gained two forward facing turrets, a missile tube and a rear-mounted belly turret that looked like it had good visibility aft.

"Ooh," Tabby exclaimed. "Baby got some teeth."

I've always had trouble looking at the small things around me when something big is looming on the horizon. It wasn't that I wasn't excited about the upgrades to *Fleet Afoot*. Fully working airlocks, turrets, repaired engines and a functional bridge were all excellent upgrades. The problem was, I knew what we were up against was bigger than anything we'd faced before and I wasn't sure how we were going to make it through to the other side.

"We'll transition to TransLoc on your command," Ada said as Tabby, Jonathan and I joined her and Marny on the bridge.

"Engage!"

***

"We're taking fire!" Marny exclaimed slightly before we completed exiting from the TransLoc wave.

"Hard starboard," Ada said. "Twenty-degree ascent." I pulled on the stick and adjusted to Ada's instructions.

A volley of Kroerak lances sailed across the bow of *Fleet Afoot*. Miraculously, we were not struck, something I attribute to Ada's uncanny ability to resolve details several moments before I could whenever we exited TransLoc.

"Frak," Tabby said. "We landed in the middle of them."

My vid-screen showed the truth of her statement, as no less than two dozen Kroerak ships were finally resolved by our sensors.

"Weapons hot, Marny," I said. "All hands. Combat stations!"

COUNTING LEGS

I cursed under my breath. I'd become reliant on holo projections for close combat and *Fleet Afoot* wasn't equipped that way. I tore my eyes from the vid-screen and swept the battle space in front of me. We'd taken the Kroerak off guard. The volley of lances - clearly the work of a startled gunner - had imbedded in a nearby Kroerak ship, causing it to vent gasses and list to the port as it attempted to adjust to the friendly fire.

Jamming the starboard throttle wide open with slightly less on the port side, all the time twisting the port stick, *Fleet Afoot's* response was immediate and crisp, something we'd not previously experienced from the aging ship. I wasn't sure how we were getting out of this nest of vipers, but I knew one thing: the ship that had taken fire was causing its own chaos and I was taking advantage of it. From dead start, we accelerated at an incredible rate. I desperately wanted to compare the numbers to those of *Hotspur*. Instinctively, I knew we were out-performing the old girl, but I had little mental capacity to dedicate to the idea.

I blinked on the targeting reticle and painted the damaged Kroerak as my primary target. "Light that maggot up!"

Tabby and Marny had slipped into gunner's chairs that sat half a deck below the bridge and on opposite sides. The gunnery stations were protected on the sides by armor collets that bumped out from the ship like high collars on Chinese business suits. In normal flight, the chairs and collets retracted and an armored panel covered the openings. In combat, the raised chairs provided three hundred sixty degrees of visual freedom. In an emergency, the chairs could be retracted at the expense of visibility.

The sound of a missile launching directly beneath my feet gave me momentary pause. We were accelerating faster than I was used to and, for a moment, I wondered if we would outpace the Abasi missile - a bad idea. I was quickly disabused of this notion, as the missile streaked forward from our position, its spent propellant momentarily frosting the glass in front of me. If there's one thing I've learned, it's that nobody willingly stands in the path of a missile if they can avoid it. In this, we find commonality with the Kroerak. Add to this a barrage of blaster fire stitching the area around the missile and you have about the best outcome you can hope for. While I didn't have time to completely assess the battle group surrounding us, I suspected we weren't in the same weight class as most of the enemy. Our flurry of offense would only buy us so much. As such, it was up to me to make hay while the sun was shining. As an aside: that was one of my dad's favorite sayings, but it never made much sense.

Battles in space, just like brawls in bars, generally start with a lot of posturing, followed by more of the same. When the fists start to fly, the duration of the event is short-lived. Unfortunately, we'd skipped the posturing part and had jumped straight to fisticuffs. In a marginally well-matched fight, the first to draw blood generally has an advantage. In our case, none of this applied beyond the momentary tussle we were having with the ship that had received friendly fire. Just what we were going to do with the remainder of the Kroerak fleet was something I had to consider as I followed the missile in.

"Captain, launch imminent, starboard side, aft," Jonathan announced, just as a fusillade erupted from the ship that had missed us the first time.

We continued toward the failing Kroerak ship, rocketing through the explosion we'd caused. I pushed hard on the sticks while simultaneously rolling us over. A significant chunk of the Kroerak ship had split away and I shot around the side, using the debris as a shield. The lances had been too late or too slow to catch us.

"I'm receiving a hail from *NAS Saratoga*," Ada said as the ship we'd separated from the flock shuddered under the impact of a second barrage of lances.

Accept hail. "Captain Liam Hoffen, *Fleet Afoot.* Tell me you've got a solution to this game of duck-duck-goose I'm playing." I lined up on the next largest ship I could find and pressed down hard, making all possible haste. If Tabby and I had learned one thing, it was that the big Kroerak ships had virtually no solutions for close-in, small ships. Although the revelation that they didn't mind shooting at each other dampened much of my excitement.

"You're deep in enemy territory, Captain Hoffen." The flickering bust of a Mars Protectorate naval officer appeared on my vid screen. "You need to make all possible haste in extracting yourself from your current locale."

I grit my teeth and turned hard so that the top of *Fleet Afoot* skimmed over the Kroerak ship. As I did, Tabby and Marny lit up the surface of the ship with blaster fire.

"Starboard!" Ada said. I rolled out of the way of an opening weapon's port on the battle-cruiser-sized ship.

"Are you frakking serious?" I screamed into my comm. "Your advice is to get away from the frak-tonne of ships that are shooting at us?"

I glanced down at the vid-screen. The Kroerak battle group was starting to organize. I twisted the display. We were almost dead center and the smaller ships were organizing to cut off the most likely escape route. Instinctively, I jammed both sticks forward and peeled away from the battle cruiser. I twisted and tipped over, following the rocky skin of the cruiser like we were embedded between the threads of a screw.

"Captain, this is General Brownie Walkden. You need to make all possible haste to the attached coordinates." The calm woman's voice had a ring of authority. "We are under hold-fast orders and cannot intervene."

"Hold fast? Whose orders?" I asked, flipping *Fleet Afoot* horizontally and pushing hard against our current vector. As it was, we were going to slide past the aft of the cruiser, but at a reduced speed. "Marny. One shot at those engines is all you're going to get."

"Copy that, Cap," she answered.

"Operational security prevents sharing that information over unsecured channels," she said. "You mind sharing where you dropped in from? We're not getting a clean read on your ship's signature or transponder."

"Liam, now!" Ada warned me. I spun the ship back over as Marny's missile escaped forward.

"Roby, give me an emergency burn," I said into the comms, pushing forward so hard on the sticks I was afraid I might snap them off. I was also afraid I couldn't afford not to squeeze out every possible newton of force.

"Ship's not from around here, General Walkden. Best we have this conversation in person," I said. "Operational security and all."

"Copy that, Hoffen. You make it to those coordinates and we'll peel back the fleas," she said.

The ship lurched forward and started to tumble. I fought the spin and leveled out our flight, but we were losing power.

"Roby, what's happening back there?" I called.

"We've been holed, Captain. Jonathan is dead." Roby's voice was high and unfocused.

"Roby, listen to me," I said. "You gotta calm down. Otherwise, we're all dead. I know you. You can do this. Why are we losing power?"

"A shaft impaled the engine room," he replied. "It's the one that got Jonathan. We're exhausting tetroxide."

"You have to patch it up, Roby," I said.

"With what?"

"One step at a time, Roby. First, blow out a big breath." I dodged behind a frigate-sized ship that was trying to turn toward us. We were moving fast and the Kroerak were having difficulty reacting to my juking and jiving, but if we continued to lose power, I'd have to level out our flight path and they'd have no trouble dialing us in.

"But Jonathan…" he said.

"But nothing, Roby," I said. "You give me power back or we're Kroerak food."

"Shite," he replied "Okay. I got this."

"Now, Roby." I rolled behind a frigate that was attempting to turn toward us. Chips of armor exploded from its surface as Marny and Tabby focused their fire.

"I got it," he whooped, sounding surprised. "But it won't hold for long."

"Hold on, everyone. We're making a run for it." The engines responded to whatever Roby had done and I'd found an exit where only smaller ships were nearby. It was a now-or-never moment.

Rarely is running from a close-in battle a good idea. Turned out, this time was no exception. Our gyrating through the fleet had caused both chaos and confusion, but more than a few gave chase. I watched my vid-screen tensely, looking for positive delta-v trails superimposed on our pursuers. The staccato thub-thub-thubbing of the aft turret was small comfort as we were ejected like a glob of lava from a volcano, pulling a stream of ships behind us from the writhing mass.

I've sailed ships with speed and ships with armor. For me, *Intrepid* was a perfect mix of both. That said, in a similar situation with *Intrepid*, we'd have been toast. *Fleet Afoot* is built for exactly one thing - running flat-out. Not only were there no ships with a positive delta-v, we were quickly reaching a point where we'd be out of range for the lance waves of the bigger ships.

"Impact imminent," Ada warned and flicked a corrective vector at me. The joy of sailing with people you trust is that there is no need to doublecheck their information. If Ada saw something and had a plan, I wasn't about to argue. I adjusted immediately. She had. A cruiser-sized ship released a wave of destructive lances and her path provided cover, placing us behind one of our smaller pursuers. It wasn't perfect protection and I braced for impact, wincing as the hull breach klaxon sounded simultaneously with the impact of lances on our belly.

"Damn good flying, Cap," Marny said.

"Ada – Jonathan," I said.

"I'm on it," Ada said, pulling her combat harness off and rushing from the bridge.

"Semper, report," I said.

"There's so much blood," she replied.

"Are you hurt?" I asked.

"No. It is Jonathan," she replied. "I have never seen someone die. It is horrible."

"Ada is coming. Do as she says," I said.

I flipped through the pressure leak warnings on my vid-screen as we continued to accelerate. The thub-thub-thub of our rear turret warned me that something had, once again, come within range. I flicked my screen back to the delta-v projections and discovered two small craft, possibly missiles, reeling us in from a considerable distance.

Hail General Walkden.

"Go ahead, *Fleet Afoot*." General Brownie Walkden's flickering image appeared on screen.

"We're coming in hot," I said. "I have two bogies on my tail and I'm not sure we're going to make it."

"We're tracking them," she replied. "You need to shoot them down. You're too far away for us to help."

"Marny, you have any *rocks* left in your bag of tricks? *NAS Saratoga* says they're not going to be able to help with those bogies."

"You've got distance, Liam, burn 'em." Tabby urged. "We've got this."

I didn't need any further prompting. I flipped *Fleet Afoot* end-for-end and reversed our engines which, like *Intrepid*, were just as powerful in either direction.

Set five second warning if we're going to re-enter weapons range for remaining Kroerak Fleet.

The ships in pursuit were tiny for Kroerak, no more than a hundred tonne each. If the inequity of the fight occurred to the bugs, it never became evident, as they didn't divert from their attack vector for even a moment.

"Cap, incoming fire," Marny warned a moment before my HUD outlined streaks in the otherwise dark space ahead of us. In response, I reversed our engines again and rolled to the side. The streaks sailed past us harmlessly only moments before I lined up on the lead ship. Marny and Tabby immediately tore it to pieces as the second ship sailed past us, not even firing. I spun over in pursuit and watched in amazement as the remaining ship turned and fired on us. It was tricky for a moment, but I avoided the missile just as Tabby picked up a lock and obliterated the ship's engines.

"Bugging out," I said and realigned with the coordinates given to me by the North American general. I watched as Tabby and Marny stitched space around the crippled enemy ship, unable to finish it.

"You suck, Hoffen," Tabby complained just as the hull breach klaxon turned itself off.

"Status, Ada," I said.

"You need to come down here, Liam," she said. "Jonathan's in bad shape and we need help."

"I've got the helm," Tabby said. She left the gunner's station and emerged from the hatch in the bridge's floor in a matter of moments.

With assist from my arc-jets, I sprinted down the passageway and careened into the shorter hallway that led to the tube which joined the forward two decks. I spun open the hatch and flinched as the pressure differential popped it open violently. Fortunately, there was atmo on both sides and the action had equalized the two spaces.

Running through the cargo hold, I observed at least five Kroerak lances piercing the hull, stuck in various bulkheads. Sloppy patches of both quick sealing foam and welded plate adorned each of them. It was more than I could focus on, so I spun open the remaining hatches and arrived in a scene straight from my worst nightmares. Jonathan was impaled, suspended on a lance in midair as Ada and Semper attempted to help. Blood pooled on the engineering bay's deck beneath him. The pointy end of the lance had also pierced a pressurized gas line, but two orange bags had been pinned around it with long, telescoping poles.

"Frak. We've got to get him off there," I said.

"I have a plan but you're not going to like it," Roby said.

I looked hard at the kid. He'd been nothing but a pain in the ass for the entire trip. He was right. I didn't even like that he was talking while I was trying to find a solution.

"Quiet, Roby," I said. "Let me think."

"Listen to him, Liam," Ada said. "It's crazy, but it might be our only chance."

Somewhere along the process Ada had lost the med patch from her face. The burns had left her beautiful face disfigured. Breath caught in my throat when I realized she'd removed the patch to aid Jonathan.

"What do you have?"

"The gas in the line is cooled so it's in liquid form. It will boil on contact with the atmo."

"How does that help?" I asked.

"When gas transitions from liquid to gas it releases energy."

"You want to freeze the lance?"

"With enough force it'll shatter," he said.

"Quick. Lay something on Jonathan. We can't afford to get any on him," I said.

From a nearby storage compartment, Roby grabbed welding blankets we used to protect machinery when welding nearby. The blankets seemed inadequate, but we were short on time, if not too late already. Together we spread them carefully onto Semper, Jonathan and Ada.

"I'm going to use this to deflect the stream of gas," Roby said, holding the ruined lid of a tool box in his hands. "Pull the bags and then use that big spanner to break the lance when I say go."

I shook my head in disbelief, but grabbed and released the telescoping legs in turn, allowing the bags to fall to the floor. As described, the spray of gas quickly filled the room with an eerie mist, but Roby moved in and placed the lid into the stream.

"Your hands, Roby," I said as frost covered his gloved fingers.

"Hit it," Roby exclaimed, standing firm.

I swung the spanner and it deflected. "Frak."

331

"Again!" Roby urged.

I grabbed the spanner with both hands and swung it overhead as hard as I could manage. The top portion of the lance shattered and Roby fell to the ground, dropping the toolbox lid.

Together, Semper, Ada and I lifted Jonathan's unmoving body from the lance and lay him on the deck. The hole in his abdomen gaped as I cut the vac-suit back.

"Captain. The gas, you have to stop it," Roby said, holding his hands awkwardly in front of him.

The system of bags and poles seemed to have worked before and I jammed a bag into place and allowed the pole to telescope to the deck.

"He's dead," Semper said, laying her forehead on his chest.

After extending two more poles, I placed my hand on Semper's back to comfort her as Ada worked with the med scanner and applied an array of patches and material from the emergency kit we'd brought along.

When I finally allowed myself to focus on a blinking message on my HUD, I smiled.

"Well, shite," I said.

I flicked the message to Semper and then to Ada. The message simply read; Jonathan vessel shutdown was successful and will require six hours for full operations to be restored. We thank you for your efforts.

"What are these bags and how'd you know how to use them?" I asked as I gently pulled Roby's gloves from his blackened fingers.

"Semper found them in the ship's catalog," he said. "Standard equipment aboard Abasi ships. The bags are supposed to be good for fifty-five hundred kilopascals."

"This is going to pinch," I said as I pulled the gloves completely off. Roby yowled as I spread a nanite salve around his fingers and wrapped them back up.

"Love, we're being hailed again," Tabby said.

"On my way," I said. "You have this, Ada?

She nodded. "Go."

"Go ahead, *Saratoga*," I said.

General Walkden's voice came through. "Captain, congratulations on your escape. Are you in need of assistance? We read several small breaches along your hull."

"General, we need an audience with whomever is in charge. We have urgent communication," I said.

"Captain, we're going to need you to heave-to and be boarded."

"General, we don't have time!"

"Only way you're getting past this point," she replied. "Kroerak have been getting awfully creative lately."

Just then I arrived on the bridge. The North American battleship *Saratoga* filled the view screen in front of us. Its pitted, burned, and scarred armor told the tale of battles, the scale of which I couldn't even imagine.

"Copy that, General," I said. "I'd recommend vac-suits. We've a leaky gut."

A wry smile crossed the Flag Officer's face as she nodded her head in agreement. "See you on the other side, Captain."

***

Turns out, getting boarded by Marines was old hat for me and mine. The firepower difference between *Fleet Afoot* and the complement of ships surrounding the *NAS Saratoga* was such that we had just the one option. All but Ada and Jonathan were assembled in the mess as the North American Marines entered through the airlock. Upon contact, I raised my hands and interlocked my fingers behind my head, a gesture mirrored by the crew.

"We have an alien aboard," the lead Marine announced and leveled a heavy rifle at Semper.

"Careful, Soldier," I cautioned. "She's on our side."

"Quiet," a second Marine snapped. I felt fortunate that he didn't take a liberty shot to emphasize his point.

"No. More like a cat." The first Marine was obviously talking to someone in command.

"Cat." He repeated after a moment. "Think skinny tiger." I

furrowed my brow. I couldn't imagine why they weren't projecting video.

"Any more aboard?" The first Marine asked. His uniform's name patch read Stolzman.

"There are two more people aboard," I said. "They're in engineering. One of them is wounded."

"Copy that, Captain Hoffen," he replied. "Mary – keep the crew here, we'll check out the remainder."

"Aye, aye, Sergeant." A female Marine in full body armor stepped forward, her heavy rifle pointed at the ground in front of us. "Keep it clean and quiet, kids, and we'll be out your hair in a few minutes," she instructed.

True to her word, no more than ten minutes later, Stolzman and the other four Marines returned to the galley.

"We're clear. Welcome to hell, Captain," Stolzman said and directed his Marines back through the airlock.

TELL ME IT'S REAL

"What do you mean there are forty alien warships bearing down on our current position?" Admiral Buckshot Alderson asked. I'd be lying if I said I was surprised to see that the tough old bird had survived. What *did* surprise me, however, was that he was aboard the dreadnaught *Bakunawa* surrounded by the remainder of the combined fleets of humanity. So far, we'd learned that the second wave of Kroerak had nearly finished the war the first wave had started.

"The Abasi were attacked by the Kroerak over a hundred fifty years ago," I said. "You won't be shocked to hear it was shortly after a failed Belirand mission discovered the Felio people and a coalition government called The Confederation of Planets."

"Nothing shocks me about Belirand Corporation," he said. "But then I thought you were done with surprises also. What are you inferring about Belirand? Come out and just say it. We don't have time to be coy, son."

I grimaced. Alderson had a way of getting under my skin. Around him, I tended to say things I didn't want to – or probably shouldn't. I loved the man's brilliance, but I wouldn't enjoy working for him.

"I think it's possible Belirand put the Kroerak onto the Abasi," I said. "The timing is too convenient. Shortly after Belirand discovers Confederation space, the Kroerak show up in force. Why else would Belirand abandon a mission of such importance?"

"Sounds like speculation," Buckshot said.

"Well, here's something that's not speculation," I said. "The Abasi figured out a way to make their bodies poisonous to the Kroerak. The bugs can't feed on them and won't go anywhere near their planets. It ended the Kroerak siege."

The impact of my words was immediate; the entire remaining military elite of humanity took a collective gasp. I made eye contact with Greg Munay and gave him a quick nod. Last I knew, he'd been cut off in the Ophir system.

"Bullshit," Alderson exclaimed.

"I can prove it. You have any captive Kroerak?"

"What are you doing, Cap?" Marny asked.

"They want proof. We brought it. The fate of humanity rests on this," I said. "Even with the Abasi fleet, humanity can't stand against the entirety of the Kroerak force with what remains. This fleet won't last another six months. We have to show them before it's too late."

"What do you want us to do?" Admiral Alderson asked.

"Bring in a Kroerak warrior. The hungrier, the better," I said. "Keep everything but its mouth restrained."

"You better not be wasting my time, kid," Alderson said.

I gave him a small smile. "When have I ever wasted your time, Admiral?"

"It's the only reason you're sitting in this room," he growled back. "Do as he says."

I pulled a quantum communication crystal from my pocket and placed it on the table in front of me.

"Who is on the other side of that crystal?" General Walkden asked.

"Mshindi First, leader of House Mshindi. She is the commander of an Abasi fleet and aboard one of two battleship classed ships that will arrive in local space in five days, three hours and twelve minutes," I said.

"We've never been at a weaker time in our history," a high-ranking officer I didn't recognize cut into my conversation. "How do we know these Abasi haven't come to pick over our bones once the Kroerak soften us up."

"I can't speak for their intent," I said. "I can, however, repeat what they've said to me, which is they're coming because they believe it is their duty to stand. The Abasi lost three billion souls to the Kroerak. It's a matter of honor. And, it is not the entire

Abasi, but three houses. It is my belief they expect to lose this war."

"That's a lot of honor," Alderson said, sarcastically.

"They have been in contact with Thomas Anino," I said. "I believe there is promise of a technology exchange."

"Now, that's something I can believe," Alderson said, grunting appreciably at his discovery that Abasi nobility was a ruse. I had no desire to debate him, as I knew I had neither the skill nor the patience. I also knew he needed all relevant information to make decisions. He might be arrogant, but he was smarter than me by an order of magnitude – at least where military planning and politics were concerned.

Conversation was interrupted by the entry of a full-sized, energetic Kroerak warrior. It was dragged into the meeting room by two Marines in mechanized armor, standing a full three meters tall. They were attempting to control the angry bug with flexible leads affixed around its thorax and some sort of metallic wrap around its upper limbs. A heavy hood had been dropped over its head. The sound of straining motors could be heard as it pulled against the Marines, although they had it well under control.

"Hungry enough for you, Hoffen?" Alderson asked as the hood was lifted and the warrior thrashed about, attempting to bite at the Marines who held it. The Marine on the left lashed out suddenly and smashed the bug on its beak. I winced as greenish goo squirted out. The warrior, instead of cowering, pulled at its lead and snapped.

"Holy shite!" Roby exclaimed.

"Sack up, son," Alderson guffawed. "It ain't going to hurt you."

There's something that happens to a team in battle. Ten hours ago, I might have found Roby's exclamation annoying, even embarrassing. That changed when Roby stepped up to save the ship and help save Jonathan.

"Back off, Alderson. Roby doesn't need your shite," I said. My outburst earned me a surprised look from Marny and an eye roll from Alderson.

"Is this female a Felio?" General Walkden asked.

"Semper is part of my crew and a Felio from the planet Zuri," I said. "Both Roby Bishop and Semper are natives of the planet Zuri and have inadvertently been inoculated by a naturally occurring tuber known locally as selich."

"The people of Earth welcome you, Semper and Roby Bishop. I apologize for my colleague's impertinence. We are understandably raw in this moment," Walkden said.

"Holy crap, Brownie. I don't need you apologizing for me. Hoffen is angling for something, we just haven't heard what it is yet," he said. "I assume you're going to blow our minds with all this?"

I looked at Alderson. The once larger-than-life man was thinner than I remembered, his face haggard. I searched his eyes, which failed to convey the disrespect of his words. They begged for good news that he refused to believe might exist.

"Roby, I need you to do something for me," I said.

"Why is that man yelling at us?"

"He's afraid, Roby," I said, placing my hands on either side of his head, so he could only see me. "He knows that without a miracle, humanity will be lost. Roby, you're going to be his miracle."

"I don't see how. I don't know anything about Kroerak," he said.

"I need you to trust me, Roby. Patty's chili is the reason the Kroerak hatchlings stopped attacking York," I said. "It's in your blood, Roby. You're poison to them."

"Chili?" Roby asked. "Selich. That's why we were smuggling crates of selich?"

"Any time now, Hoffen," Alderson needled.

"I need you to be brave," I said. "And I'll go first."

With Roby's hand in my own, I slowly approached the Kroerak warrior. I recognized the name patch on the Marine who'd punched the Kroerak – Stolzman.

"Sergeant Stolzman, what's your experience with these warriors? If I put my hand up there, will the Kroerak try to bite it off?"

"Copy that, Hoffen," he replied. "I hope that's not your plan here, because this old girl hasn't been fed in better than a fortnight."

"Any reason you could imagine why she wouldn't?"

"Nothing I can think of."

"Okay, I'm going to raise my hand, so we can get a baseline," I said. "I'd appreciate you holding her back."

"We got her," he replied, tightening up on the lead.

I exhaled a nervous breath and stared at the bug. Its beak snapped at nothing as it tasted the air in front of it. I waved, then jabbed my hand into its space, narrowly avoiding the lunging beak as it strained against the mechanized Marines who held it.

"Roby, I'm going to step back. I need you to demonstrate those same for the Admiral."

"Frak, Liam, er… Captain. I don't know," Roby said.

"Take it slow," I said. "Those Marines can hold her and they'd love nothing more than to take her apart. Am I right on that, Sergeant Stolzman?"

"Copy that, Captain Hoffen. We got her, kid. Do your thing," Stolzman replied.

Roby looked back to Semper who approached and placed her paw into his outstretched hand.

"We'll do it together, Roby Bishop," she said.

He nodded and together they raised their hands in front of the warrior. Initially, the warrior swung its head from side to side, beak open, but not snapping. As the pair gained confidence and closed the distance, the warrior reversed and attempted to back away, closing its beak violently and twisting its head to the side.

"Well, I'll be," Alderson said, quietly. "Just the human kid. What was your name again?"

"Roby Bishop," Roby replied, his voice wavering.

"Roby Bishop, make me a believer. Have the cat girl back up," he said.

"Felio," Roby answered.

"Right you are, Roby Bishop. Would you ask your Felio friend to back up and show me that it's afraid of you?" Alderson said, sitting forward in his chair with a smile. The transformation on the Admiral's face was amazing; he was intensely interested and, more importantly, looked like he was seeing a light at the end of a very dark tunnel.

"Go ahead, Semper," Roby said as he leaned in and exhaled loudly toward the Kroerak warrior, which continued to try to flee.

"I don't suppose we could get a blood draw," Alderson said.

"Alderson," I said, coming to Roby's defense.

"No. He's right," Roby said. "We need to see this through."

A few minutes later, a medical technician showed up and drew a phial of blood from Roby's arm.

"Sergeant, think you can get that into that bug's gullet?"

"Thought you'd never ask," Stolzman replied. He pulled a nano-steel prybar from the side of his leg armor and swept the legs of the Kroerak so it fell on its back. I felt pity for the bug as the two Marines restrained it, pried its beak open, and crushed the phial into the back of its throat. We'd lost any sense of the humane and I felt lessened by my part in it.

For several minutes, nothing changed beyond the thrashing of the warrior as it fought to escape.

"How long does it take?" Alderson asked.

"No idea," I said. "We just learned about this five days ago, and spent most of that time trying to survive long enough to get here."

"Sergeant, take the warrior back to its cell," General Walkden ordered. "Captain Hoffen, we understand you've taken damage to your ship. We'll send a crew over to help with repair. I propose we reconvene in six hours."

We all stood as General Walkden and her staff excused themselves.

"Hoffen, I need you to see this," Alderson said as he walked over to a bank of windows that were opaque until he motioned with his hand. I gasped as I looked at the gorgeous blue planet. I'd seen it so many times in vids, but never in person. Alderson flicked something to me and the outline of the darkened North American continent showed on my HUD, a stripe of bright lights illuminating the center third.

"Before this war started, that entire continent would have been lit up. Kroerak control more than three fifths of all the landmasses of the entire planet. We're holding on by a thread, Hoffen," he said. "Tell me this is real."

"It's real," I said.

"Admiral." General Walkden's voice called from the door. "You're going to want to see this."

"Walk with me, Hoffen," he said.

I followed him to where Walkden stood. She handed him a reading pad showing live video of the warrior, lying dead on a medical table.

"It died on the way down to the holding pen. Intelligence wants to open it up," Walkden said.

"Any chance your Sergeant put it down?"

"Not a chance."

"What do you want to do, Brownie?"

"Kroerak are on the move," she said. "If we're to have any chance, we need to get this crew down to Stratcom. They need time to reproduce this. No doubt the Kroerak know what we're up to."

"When did you say those Abasi were going to show up?" Alderson asked.

"Five days, Admiral," I said, holding the crystal out to him. This time he accepted it.

"Then we'll hold on for five days," he said. "Brownie, can you get this crew to Nebraska?"

"Kroerak have already set up a blockade. Not even that tin can Hoffen arrived in is making it past. We'll have to send scans to the surface," she replied.

"No good," Alderson said. "They're going to need biological material."

"Give me five mechanized suits," I said.

"You have any idea what you're talking about?" Alderson said. "Those mechanized suits aren't toys, son."

"Good thing my crew is trained," I said, not expanding on the fact that neither Roby nor Semper had been in a mech suit before.

"Even the kid?" Alderson asked.

"No. Leave Semper and Roby here," Marny said. "I've been eating selich root since we arrived on Zuri. I'd been wondering why Tabby only ran into hatchlings when I wasn't running with her."

"You're saying you think you're inoculated?" I asked.

"Be worth a test," Walkden said. "Keep us from dropping all our eggs in one basket." I looked at the older General and raised an eyebrow. She smiled wryly and nodded.

***

Two hours later, five of us were streaking through space with nothing more than mechanized armor between us and vacuum. The plan was that Sergeant Stolzman, Private Goodman, Tabby, Marny, and I would silently sail past the Kroerak that had placed themselves between the remainder of the fleet and Earth.

"Why isn't anyone surprised the Kroerak decided to set up a blockade now?" I asked on a point-to-point comm with Stolzman.

"We took a risk feeding the poisoned blood to that warrior," he replied. "Kroerak brass know when warriors are killed. We don't know why, but that's how it is. It's why Alderson bought your story so quickly. He wanted to see what the bugs would do in response to the warrior's death. Now, we just need to keep you alive long enough to save the human race."

At least, that was what I think he was going to say. Just as he pronounced the word 'human,' his suit exploded.

"No comms." Private Goodman ordered and rolled over, firing arc-jets and blasters at the Kroerak ship that'd taken interest in us and killed Sergeant Stolzman. "I'll draw them off."

I watched helplessly as Private Goodman gave away her position and angled away from us, firing at the ship without mercy. For a moment, I believed she might make it out as the heavy ordnance from her suit tore into the ship. My hopes were soon crushed, as she blinked from existence.

CONTACT

We watched helplessly as a third wave of lances were fired on our position. We'd already lost two of our number and I couldn't help but wonder if this was the end. I reflected on the sense of loss I felt in conjunction with the likely failure of our mission. We were so close. But having been discovered, I believed it would only be a short time before the Kroerak dialed in on us. I breathed a sigh of relief as the lances sailed past ineffectively. Only my AI was fast enough to track their path and an ember of hope flared as I recognized the wave had missed our position by a hundred meters.

Part of the plan was that we were to make periodic adjustments to our glide path by firing our arc-jets. It was the sort of thing where small adjustments would be magnified greatly in where we landed, but I made a last-minute decision to abandon the plan and signaled Marny and Tabby to follow my lead. The Kroerak were looking for us and I couldn't draw any attention, even if it meant putting us at a disadvantage groundside.

For the next hour, we glided along quietly as Kroerak ships cast about in orbit high above Earth and the morning sun pulled around the beautiful planet. I felt exposed, but our tiny shapes were impossible to pick out of the vastness of space. My heart was sick with the belief that my conversation with the Sergeant led to the Kroerak's discovery of our location. It was an action that was impossible to take back. For Stolzman and Goodman, there would be no coming back from it. For me, it was a burden I'd have to find a way to live with.

I was relieved from my internal monologue of self-destructive thoughts when my boots started glowing and throwing small flames. We'd reached Earth's atmosphere and were falling like the meteorites we'd become. Of all the things a mechanized suit is good for, atmospheric insertion was high on the list. There was little that could be done to mask our entry. We'd been assured that, while it would seem like a big deal to us, even Kroerak sensors couldn't scan enough of the sky to pick up three falling objects as small as we were. A few minutes into the atmosphere, our arc-jets fired, slowing our fall and making course adjustments.

"We're not going to make Nebraska," Marny said, the background noise in our suits making it difficult to parse her words.

I punched up my map. I wasn't familiar with any of Earth's political territories, much less North America. Marny had transmitted a predicted drop zone and we'd land somewhere in Kroerak controlled space, most likely eastern Iowa or possibly western Wisconsin. Each second we fell, the prediction became more accurate. If I wanted to dial it in further, we'd have to utilize more energy and create a larger signature; something I was unwilling to do.

I can tell you, it's an incredible rush when your brain finally resolves the ground beneath you as more than just a large patchwork of fields, towns, rivers, and the like. It's something about the realization that an actual hard surface is speeding toward you at an impossible rate. You understand you're about to be firmly embedded into its surface and will be nothing more than a small puddle in the bottom of your boots. Fortunately, it all happens very fast and the mech suits – Popeyes, as my dad used to call them - take care of the hard work, including damping just enough of the impact so that you're left with a painful jolt, but nothing more.

I lowered my visor and approached Marny and Tabby. We'd landed in an unharvested field of wheat, next to a copse of trees. My HUD showed the nearby town as Chetek, Wisconsin.

"Sorry about the location," I said. "After Stolzman and Goodman, I couldn't risk any more exposure."

"Damn shame," Marny said. "Not sure how they locked in on us."

"It was my fault, Marny," I said. "Stolzman and I were talking on point-to-point. Kroerak must have detected it."

"You can't take that, Cap," Marny said. "Point-to-point is undetectable."

"Ordinarily, I'd be all in for some handwringing and wallowing," Tabby said. "But just in case you didn't notice, we're eight hundred kilometers from where we're supposed to be."

"We'll avoid population centers," Marny said. "Twin Cities are due west, but we'll run into the Rochester corridor. Safest route would be to go north, though it'll add three hundred kilometers."

"None of this works if we get captured," I said. "The Kroerak know what's at stake and they'll be coming for us."

"North it is," Marny said and started jogging through the field.

A well-conditioned mechanized marine can move for hours at roughly the speed of the fastest human sprinter without significantly tiring. That said, we were looking to cover twelve hundred kilometers and were talking about significantly more than a few hours of extended effort. I hoped I was up to the task.

We'd landed early in the morning and as most things do, our journey became routine. We weighed speed against caution and settled in to a comfortable pace with Marny at the front, Tabby next, and me bringing up the rear. In the first few hours of the morning, we saw little evidence of the Kroerak invasion beyond the complete lack of human population. Just like on the moon in the Mhina system, equipment had been carefully stored, the owners obviously taking pride in how they left their homes, hoping they'd be able to return to their farming operations soon.

"How are you holding up, Cap?" Marny asked. We'd been going for three hours and I was starting to flag. It wasn't that I didn't think I could keep going, but looking at the route Marny had planned, I was confident I didn't have another thirty-two hours of non-stop effort in the tank.

"Hanging in there," I answered. "I could use something to drink, though."

"There's an M.R.E. stream in your suit," Marny said. "Make sure you're keeping up on it."

"MRE?"

"Meals Ready to Eat," she replied. "We're burning a thousand kilo calories an hour, Cap. Don't be ignoring the nutrients."

"Tube next to your chin, starboard side," Tabby said.

Somehow, I'd ignored this in our training. I sucked on the tube and a stream of slightly sweet liquid poured into my mouth. It was about the best thing I'd ever tasted and relief was immediate. Suddenly, the beauty of the landscape came back into focus. For the last hour, my vision had been narrowing and I'd become one with the task, falling into the rhythmic clunk of our boots, placing one foot in front of the other. With the boost of energy, I suddenly found myself deep in a pine forest, leaping over small streams, startling deer and flushing small flocks of birds from the cover of tall grasses. Earth was beautiful.

It wasn't until well past 20:00 when Marny pulled up. We'd been on the run for fourteen hours and even with MREs I was beat. The strain was evident on Marny's face too, as sweat poured from her brow.

"We'll hole up in that barn," Marny said, pointing at a ramshackle building sitting abandoned at the edge of an untended field. "It's too risky to keep going in the dark."

"Goodman said the Missouri River is the front line," Tabby said. "North American military was holding everything west of there to just past the Rocky Mountains. She said the fighting on the ground was intense. We might want to try to slip into the Dakotas."

"Do they even know we're coming?" I asked. "Alderson made it sound like comms aren't secure."

"That's right, Cap," Marny said. "But for the first time in human history, the enemy isn't another person. We make it to the base, they'll let us in."

"How long are we here for?"

"Six hours downtime. I'll take first watch," Marny said.

You might think it's hard to fall asleep in a dilapidated barn in the middle of Minnesota after running all day. Turns out, once your body is worn out, sleep comes easily.

"Cap, wake up," Marny shook me gently.

"Did I miss anything?" I asked.

"Spotted a patrol twenty clicks out," she said. "Two bugs moving west to east."

We'd moved from forest to rolling plains in the last hours of the day and visibility had increased considerably. Something I was sure wasn't to our advantage.

"Get some rack time," I said. "I've got it."

"Aye, aye, Cap."

I carefully exited the barn and slowly scanned the horizon. A hill behind the barn obstructed my view so I climbed up, but was careful not to stand directly on the ridge, choosing instead to stop just short of the top. Tactically, the area wasn't great for defense. We were open from every side. That said, we had no limits on the directions in which we could run, if pushed.

I settled in and allowed my suit's passive sensors time to adjust to the terrain. The trick of operating on a short amount of sleep is keeping your mind and body active. Out in the open, I found the task more difficult, but the stakes were high enough. About thirty minutes into my watch, my sensors picked up on what I suspected was the same patrol Marny had seen on a returning trip east to west. Beyond that, the two-hour shift seemed to take an eternity and I was glad when it was finally time to wake Tabby for her turn.

Almost no time seemed to pass when Tabby's voice woke me again. "Wakee, wakee," she said.

"Make sure to hit the MREs hard to start with," Marny said. "Your AI will load a stimulant. We'll want to be more diligent today. There'll be increased patrols and once they find us, you can bet they'll bring a crowd. According to the intel Walkden shared, there's a fort at Waubay, South Dakota.

"That's only three hundred kilometers," I said.

"I'm hoping they'll be able to provide transport," Marny said.

"And not shoot us," Tabby added.

"And that," Marny agreed.

There's a well-respected saying that no plan survives contact with the enemy. Whoever said that was either a genius or had seen combat. I'd bet the latter. We'd covered two hundred kilometers when we popped up over the top of a hillock and ran straight into a patrol station that consisted of eight warriors. Either they'd seen us coming or their reactions were finely honed, because my first warning came as a warrior charged into and knocked Marny over - a feat I'd not have thought possible against a mechanized suit. Tabby, next in line, barely had time to brace for the impact of the next two.

I had just a moment - which I didn't squander - to raise my weapon and fire an armor piercing stream into the melee. In close combat, friendly fire is a concern. The mech suit's AIs were particularly attuned to friendly targets and utilized the combat data streams of a squad to synchronize positions and movements such that injury is very unlikely. For me, the idea that Marny and Tabby were being mauled by the warriors was more important than the unlikely event they'd be hit by my rounds. The Kroerak, given sufficient time, could break through the suit's armor and it was imperative they be removed post haste.

An explosion from Marny's position rocked me back, although my suit easily absorbed the shock wave. I'd made progress peeling off one of Tabby's attackers and was preparing to fire explosive rounds at the advancing horde. The explosion separated the fur-ball that was Marny and the warriors and she rolled to her feet. It took her only a moment to free her weapon and the two of us continued tearing into the crowd. Only twenty seconds later, the sound of a third weapon joined the din and then, as abruptly as it had started, the attack was over.

"So much for stealth," I said.

"Change of plan." Marny updated the route we'd carefully planned to something significantly more direct. The three of us took off at a dead run, which under perfect circumstances, would put us at Fort Waubay in ninety minutes. While I knew I wasn't capable of keeping the pace for ninety minutes, I was willing to put distance between us and the mess we'd made.

There's something particularly invigorating about running for your life in a mechanized suit. You make ridiculous time, chewing up the ground, leaping over gullies and clawing your way up the side of hills. After fifteen minutes at an all-out sprint, my lungs burned with exertion. While I tried to conserve my arc-jet fuel, it became increasingly difficult to keep up with Marny and Tabby without bursts of help at critical moments.

"Take cover!" Marny exclaimed. We'd just crossed into an open field, at the end of which was a rocky outcropping where the ground dropped off. I'd fallen back a hundred meters from Tabby and Marny. While they were close enough to successfully utilize the available cover, there was no way I'd make it in time to outrun the three bogies now on my radar.

I urged my lead-filled legs to move and at the last moment, jumped and twisted around so that my back landed in the soft earth. The move jostled my aim, but as I slid along on my back, I opened fire on the Kroerak attack craft. The ground around me erupted with a hail of explosions. I'd taken worse than I'd given in the exchange, but I was still functional. Using an Aikido roll, I turned over my shoulder and popped back up to my feet. My legs refused anything more than a jog, but it would be enough and I caught up with Marny and Tabby on the downhill slope of a shallow ravine.

"You have eyes?" I asked Marny. To be clear, those were the words I intended but my ragged breath made the words come out unintelligible. Turns out, there aren't many questions three ground soldiers have when they're being attacked from the air and Marny made a reasonable assumption.

"We clipped one and I marked it," Marny replied, also breathing hard. "They're lining up for another run at us. They'll try to keep us pinned down so they can bring in reinforcements."

"One thing at a time." I flopped onto my belly on the opposite bank, lining up on the incoming craft. Two more thuds in the soft mud told me of Tabby and Marny's acceptance of my basic plan.

One thing I'd learned about Kroerak was that they have little sense of self preservation. For them, the mission is everything. This is a fault, in my opinion. Sure, there are a million other

Kroerak who will fall in behind them, but their unswerving approach made lining up on them easier than it should have been. I checked Marny's tactical view and aimed at the primary target. My role was simple, pump as many armor piercing shells into the ship's fuselage as my mech suit could manufacture.

The ground in front of us exploded and we had to duck back into the gully as the craft buzzed across our position at high speed. Of particular interest, however was that one of the three was now cartwheeling through the field behind us and a second had thick black smoke billowing from its tail.

"One more pass and we're up again," Marny said. I immediately regretted the efficiency of the mech suit's killing capacity. I'd have loved nothing more than to spend just a little more time in the mud and allow my body to recover. Unexpectedly, the remaining ship peeled off while its smoking buddy turned back for a final, suicidal pass. "Cap. Try to make contact with Fort Waubay. We're about to be overrun."

I saw nothing in the area that supported her assertion, but I'd also not seen the amount of combat she had.

Transmit on all channels. "North American forces at Fort Waubay. This is Captain Liam Hoffen. We're in dire need of help and are about to be overrun by Kroerak forces. I'm transmitting our mission parameters and authorization. We request immediate assistance."

We'd been given the authorization that would allow for secure identification when we arrived at Stratcom. We had no authority to request help, but it didn't matter. I couldn't make another sixty minutes of sprinting and Marny was certain we were about to be set on by something big.

"Make for the town," Marny said, highlighting the small town of Morris, five kilometers from our position. So far, we'd gone out of our way to avoid population centers.

Mud flew from our suits as we raced across the damp soil of a field and jumped onto the hard surface of a roadway. The war had long ago arrived in Morris, as evidence of a skirmish quickly came into view. A once proud school, a college, lay in ruin, disgorging the remains of a citizenry that had attempted to resist the invaders. Skeletal remains littered the grounds next to ruined military hardware, centuries out of date.

"There." Marny highlighted a fortified position that looked to be where the defenders of Morris had made their last stand. We jumped through a hole in the stone wall in front of which were piled sandbags and a dirt berm.

"What did you see?" I gasped for air, glad to have stopped moving.

"Those planes were sent to locate us for an attack force," she said. "Believe me, they'll overrun us easily." As she spoke, a squadron of Kroerak aircraft flew over our position.

"Won't take them long to figure out where we've gone," Tabby said.

Marny nodded in agreement. "They'll roll in armor."

"Or just overrun us with warriors," Tabby said. "We might be able to take down as many as fifty or sixty, but after that, who knows."

"We've been in tougher spots," Marny said.

Tabby and I both laughed. It was a ridiculous statement and we all knew it.

"You're good people, Marny," I said. "Can't imagine any two people I'd rather spend my last hours with."

"How long do you think it'll take for them to find us?"

"Those planes will figure out pretty soon that we're not in the open," Marny said. "After that, they'll send out scouts. We've probably bought ourselves three or four hours. This place is well enough defended, we should be able to make our stand until we run out of ammo. You hear anything back from Fort Waubay?"

"Not a peep," I said. "Far as we know, they've been run over too."

"Meal-bar?" Tabby asked, pulling one from her side pack. "Strawberry?"

"Yup," she said and tossed it to me.

"My favorite."

SPOILED SPINACH

Waiting for the Sword of Damocles to fall is about as much fun as pulling metal splinters out after a grinding accident. That is, not at all. It's not that I didn't appreciate being alive, it's just that waiting is painful.

"Contact," Marny whispered. On the tactical display, I located the warrior she'd tagged. It had been running through town and stopped at the location where we'd exited the field and entered the roadway.

"Frak," Tabby said as it turned toward us and accelerated in our direction.

Just before it entered the darkened opening to what we'd decided was the school's gymnasium, it stopped abruptly and swung its beak back and forth. A motion I'd seen before.

"Marny," I whispered over the comm. "Lower your face shield."

"What?" she asked.

"Do it!" I whispered back.

The noise of her face shield lowering caught the warrior's attention and it advanced. Once again, however, it stopped and then retreated. Finally, it turned and ran off.

"What the frak was that?" Marny asked, uncharacteristically cussing.

"You stink," Tabby whispered.

"I have an idea." I pulled the one remaining selich root from my pack and cut it in thirds, hoping I wasn't damning humanity out of existence. But if we didn't survive, what I had in my pack wouldn't do anyone any good. "Tabby, eat this." The tuber I handed her wasn't in great shape, having been over-handled and exposed to Kroerak hatchling guts.

"Are you insane?"

I popped my own piece into my mouth and chewed on it. My mouth felt like I'd bit into lava. I coughed as I sucked on my MRE stream and swallowed. There was no amount of liquid that would put out the fire in my mouth. I wiped tears from my eyes and, too late, realized I had residue on my fingers.

"Cap, are you okay?"

"Help me get this into my pack." I handed her the remaining piece of selich.

Next to me, Tabby's coughing fit alerted me to the fact that she'd done as I requested. We wouldn't be safe from an aerial attack, but what could I say, we'd take whatever advantage we could get.

The sound of heavy machinery moving in signaled the beginning of the end. A stream of warriors poured around the end of the street, funneling through the ruined buildings toward our location.

"Conserve ammo and pick your own targets," Marny said. "See you on the other side."

I stood next to her and Tabby joined us on the line at the broken opening to the school.

Braapp. The sound of machine gun fire prompted me to raise my face shield and I switched from full auto to three shot. Even with the heavy guns of the mechanized suits, each Kroerak cost us about two percent of our remaining ammo load. It was a funny thing I could do while both flying and fighting - calculate useless pieces of information.

If the selich had gained us anything, it was that the Kroerak weren't climbing all over themselves to get to us. They were compelled to advance, but something in their DNA caused them to balk when they got within five meters of the building's opening. I might have felt guilty for the slaughter, but then, they were coming for us and there was little we could do about it.

"I'm out," Tabby said, unclipping her nano-steel pry bar from her leg armor. Like all things made for Marines it would serve just fine as a club and in the hands of a mechanized Marine, it was a darn fine one at that.

"Hold on," I said. I still had twenty percent of my ammo remaining. We'd made quite a pile in the last ten minutes and there was no reason to wade into the mess until we were all out.

"Out," Marny said, discarding her rifle.

A moment later, I too was out. I plucked my pry bar from its holster.

"Stay between us," Tabby said and leapt into the never-ending mass of warriors. I wasn't sure who she was talking to, so I jumped up next to her and swung my bar into the first bug I could find. Marny joined us and together we stood in a semi-circle, using the entrance to the school's gymnasium as a funnel.

The reluctance of the warriors to attack became the only thing that stood between us and being instantly rolled over. It was as if I could see their compulsion to attack warring with their revulsion of us. The best way I could think to explain their behavior was like how I felt when I found a large spider in my sleep quarters. You know you have to stay until you find it and squish it. You can't leave the room or go find a better means of disposal. If you fail, it will be hidden in your bed one night – waiting. You also have no desire to get anywhere near the thing in case it's figured out how to jump on you and sink its fangs in.

The dance between us became rhythmic, even predictable in its repetition – a lunging warrior is met with an up strike, bashed in and kicked to the side only to be torn away by eager replacements. The death toll on the warriors stacked up and for a few minutes, it appeared we were making headway. That is, until a fresh wave of hundreds poured into what is now the school's old parking lot.

Swing, jab, kick. Our motions were fluid and deadly in their efficiency. After twenty kills, my knowledge of the perfect location to strike a Kroerak had grown and while the mechanized suit did most of the work, my limbs started to tire from the simple exertion of repetitive movement.

For minutes, which seemed like hours, we fought, causing a stalemate. I knew it worked against us, as the Kroerak strengthened in numbers more quickly than we could dispatch them. It came as no real surprise when a wave of warriors crashed over the pile of bodies we'd stacked and bowled us over, back into the gymnasium.

"Form up!" Marny exclaimed. From the corner of my eye, I saw her struggle to fight her way clear of a swarm. This time, there would be no explosive charge from her depleted ordnance pack. I'd been lucky and had rolled clear of the wave that pushed us inward.

I rushed to Marny's aid, hacking at a heavily armored back. I scrabbled for purchase and jammed the pointy end of my pry-bar beneath the soft linkage of the bug's neck. It twisted its head defensively and wrenched the bar from my hands. I was in such a frenzy that I hardly noticed, simply balling my armored fist and mashing it into the side of the bug's head with all the might I could gather. It was an immovable object meets irresistible force moment. The bug's heads are heavily armored. It was as if I'd struck iron and I felt the bones of my hand snapping, the inertial systems of the suit unable to adjust sufficiently.

"Incoming!" Tabby yelled and confusion clouded my thoughts as I felt myself lifted over Marny's bug pile.

An explosion tore into the gymnasium and the ceiling collapsed, sending massive chunks of steel-reinforced cement onto us. Two seconds later, a second explosion ripped up the floor and I was tossed like a ragdoll ten meters to the opposite wall, along with a healthy dose of debris, pinning me in place. It became clear that the bugs had given up on their bread-and-butter swarm offensive and had switched to just finishing the job with good old fashion explosives.

I tried to flex my hand and smiled. The pain was there, but it had become a distant idea, almost like a memory. Intellectually, I knew it was narcotic injections from the suit's AI. It was programmed to keep me functional even in the face of bodily damage. With both hands, I pushed at a boulder that lay on my chest. It was more than I could lift, even with the suit. After a few tries, I laid back and looked for another idea.

A blinking light on my HUD caught my attention. How long it

had been blinking was anyone's guess. I'd been consumed with the rage of battle, and blinking lights had been pushed off the list by more primal impulses. As my vision cleared, I focused on the light. It was a request for squad communication. I found the idea odd. We'd been on a tactical channel for days. I blinked acceptance.

"Stay down. Help's coming." The ebony face of a woman, obviously concentrating on other things, showed in my HUD. The skin on her face shook as the sound of automatic weapons fire transmitted through the channel she'd left open.

"They're blowing the building," I said. "Make sure you get my pack if you don't get here first."

A grim smile broke out on her face as I watched her eyes searching the combat displays. "Look schmuckatelli, answer the phone once and we wouldn't have to drop baby-deuces in your hole. And, we ain't bringing back no spoiled spinach. Now, get your ass up and do something. You copy?"

"Copy," I said and started punching at the rock that held me down. I had no idea what she'd said, but frak if her confidence wasn't inspiring. Chips of cement fragmented from the block, while deep down something told me I was doing horrible things to my damaged hand. Frak if I cared, it was time to live. The rest of the conversation was noise. Damn it, but was I ready to tear off some bug arms.

***

"CAP!"

Marny's face came into focus as I struggled to free myself.

"Cap, are you hearing me?" she asked.

"What the frak?" I asked looking to the sides. I was being held against a wall by two Marines in Popeyes. "Get off!" I attempted to shrug off my captors.

"He's level, Patty Cake," the Marine on my left announced.

"Captain Hoffen?" The ebony skinned Marine who'd contacted me looked over Marny's shoulder.

"Copy," I said.

"Let him go, boys," she said. "He's CRS." A term I later learned meant 'Can't Remember Shite.'

"What the frak happened?" I asked, looking at Marny.

"Sergeant Patricia Casien." The woman lowered her visor and popped my shoulder with her open glove. "I might have hit you with a little too much go-go juice. No apologies, though. You're a crazy man. Anyone ever tell you that?"

"It's come up. What's the plan here, Sergeant?" I asked.

"Cake! We got Hangers inbound," an excited Marine interrupted.

"Go!" She grabbed my shoulder and dragged me along until she was sure I was following.

"Love, you sure you're okay?" Tabby asked as we jogged through the wreckage that used to be the small town of Morris. Hundreds, if not thousands, of Kroerak warriors lay strewn about. A small transport ship sat atop a pile of debris.

"Not sure what happened back there. I think I broke my hand though," I said.

"In you go." A Marine turned me about brusquely and lifted me onto a bar that stretched along the length of the transport ship. The shoulder of my suit clamped onto the bar and I immediately lost most suit functions.

The scene below was bedlam. I counted five Marines being carried off, their suits ruined, missing arms and legs. The price of our extraction had been high and I hoped what we carried would be worth the loss. I'd mourn the fallen. There was little else I could do.

The ground rushed by beneath us as we flew low and fast. The contradictions between the natural beauty of the patchwork landscape and the ruined cities was not lost on me. As we closed in on our destination, we gained elevation and flew over a great fight in progress. A horde of Kroerak were attempting to breach great earthen walls that looked as if they'd been recently constructed. Constant fire from columns of armor were exchanging blows with their Kroerak equivalent. If not for the vast horde, the Kroerak wouldn't stand a chance. Their army stretched on for kilometers and where hundreds fell, thousands seemed to fill back in.

"I hope you have good news for us, Hoffen," Sergeant Casien said. "Bodies are piling up."

***

"Sam Murray." A reedy, unkempt scientist stepped forward from a group waiting for us at the elevators. "You say you have poison for the Kroerak? That's brilliant. How does it work?"

We'd been escorted to a laboratory deep below what had become the forward operating base, Stratcom. Originally, the purpose for the facility was intelligence and planning. In the months since the start of the Kroerak invasion, however, it had been fortified and represented one of the last fully-defended bases of the North American Alliance. Simply put, it was where the North Americans would make their last stand.

"Far as we know, it's a simple matter of eating these roots," I said, holding the remaining chunk out to him. "The Kroerak won't get near you if you have it in your system."

"Mandy Noster. You have more samples?" a woman introduced herself and asked.

"No," I said. "We didn't think we were going to make it, so we ate some."

"Why would you do that?" another asked, incredulous. "How are we going to work with such a small sample."

"Did it work?" Murray asked.

"It's not clear," I said.

"Easy enough to prove," Noster said. "We've more than a few guests."

"A demonstration then?" Murray asked. While asked as a question, it was obviously more of a demand. We'd been accompanied by armed Marines and so far, they'd been cordial, but I had no doubt we'd be agreeing one way or another. The group, consisting of lab-coats, Marines, Marny, Tabby and me, walked hastily over to a wide-open laboratory. Along the edges, penned Kroerak were on display, some obviously dead, others not much further from a similar fate, while others were quite healthy.

"Mildred here should do nicely," Noster said. "How quickly does it work?"

"She'll smell it right away," I said. "The poison takes twenty minutes or so if ingested."

I boldly walked up to the Kroerak they called Mildred. Initially, the bug charged at the cage. However, when I got within a meter, she backed away from the bars. The knot of scientists erupted in conversation. Some actually called for me to be thrown in the cage, while others requested I stick my hand through the bars.

"No need for that," Murray said, approaching me with a large needled syringe. I knew what he was after and held my arm out.

"Twenty milliliters should do it," I said.

After drawing the blood, Murray palmed a panel next to Mildred's cage. The Kroerak dropped to the floor, struggling against what I suspected was a heavy gravity field.

"I'll do it," I said, holding my hand out.

Murray nodded and swung the cage door open. "Just above the thorax beneath the skull cap," he directed.

Mildred attempted to move away from me as I approached. A flicker of pity was quickly quashed by the memory of the dead Marines being carried off by their squad mates in Morris. Remorselessly, I jammed the needle in as Murray directed, using my one good hand.

"What now?" Noster asked.

"Release her," I said, pulling the door closed, locking me into the cell.

"Liam, no!" Tabby said.

"We're wasting time," I said. "You've got my back, don't you boys?" I looked at the Marines who stood uncomfortably with their blaster rifles.

Murray locked the cell and released the gravity. For a moment, I thought Mildred was about to attack. It crossed my mind that perhaps I hadn't had enough exposure. In the end, however, she paced over to the opposite corner of the cell.

"Something's happening," a scientist who hadn't introduced herself said. "Mildred's internal pressure is diminishing. She's arresting." A moment later, the Kroerak collapsed on the floor of the cell and died.

"During the war, the Abasi inoculated their entire population," I said. "That war was a hundred fifty stans ago and they still inoculate their military."

"I'd like to draw more blood. It'll take us a couple of days to break it down, but we'll find what's killing them," Murray said. "We'll need you to stand by, just in case we need more samples."

"Would a shower be out of the question?" I asked.

Murray smiled. "I think that can be arranged."

***

Tabby held her arms out. "I feel like I've been attacked by a porcupine."

My AI projected a display of a small, trundling rodent with a back full of quills. The picture seemed about right. Dr. Sam Murray's estimation of a few more samples turned out to be a full-on bloodletting. For three long days, we'd been locked in the basement of Fort Stratcom. I couldn't imagine how any selich in my system remained, having been drawn out by vampires in the name of saving humanity.

"We've got it," Murray announced, finding Marny, Tabby and I seated in a darkened corner of the mess hall. He laid a stack of meal bars on the table. "We've begun distributing these by way of humanitarian drops over the contested areas."

"Is it working? Are the Kroerak pulling back? I know the Abasi had trouble replicating the chemistry without the actual tuber."

"We've had good luck with your blood samples," he said. "The human body is a masterpiece of engineering that we've mostly unlocked. With Marny's records from her time in the Marines, we distilled the changes in her blood samples and narrowed the changes to the selich root. With this information, we've begun replication on a mass scale. Eighty-two percent of North American ground forces have received or will receive a mega dose of this in their next meal."

"Everybody's getting chili?" Marny asked.

Murray smiled. The man seemed younger than when we'd first met him. "Capsaicin is a fabulous natural transmitter. Alas, not everyone enjoys it. We've bonded the requisite instructions to sugar molecules that are to be included in everything from coffee creamer to yeast breads."

"When will this make it to the general population?" I asked.

"We're working on a delivery mechanism that will utilize waterways and aerial drops," he said. "Within a week we'll inoculate as much as thirty-five percent of the non-captive human population. Within two months, that number should rise to forty-five percent and include those who are captive. Our research has been transmitted broadly to all human settlements in each of the four settled systems."

"You mean five. Right?" I asked.

He paused and then understanding lit up his face. "Ophir. Of course. For a moment, I'd forgotten you were part of that," he replied. "Believe it or not, an update is not the reason for my visit."

"Oh?"

"General Walkden has requested our presence space-side," he said.

ACE IN THE HOLE

"I thought we were cut off from the fleet," I said to Sergeant Patty Casien.

"And yet we're Oscar Mike in five," she said. Her chiseled face bore scars I had no doubt were well earned. "How's the hand?"

"Nothing a year in a med tank won't fix," I said. My exaggeration earned a chuckle from the serious woman.

"I hope you haven't eaten recently," she said, pushing open a door into a room where four Popeyes hung on the rack.

"I don't see a suit for me," Murray said.

"Dr. Murray, I'm afraid you'll be traveling with the cargo."

"Cargo?" Murray squeaked. "Is that safe?"

"You'll be out for the ride," she said, placing her hand on his shoulder. I glanced at Tabby who returned my look with a raised eyebrow as Casien helped him to the floor. The sergeant had delivered some sort of incapacitating drug in the med-patch she'd surreptitiously applied.

"Frak, Sergeant Casien," I said.

"Call me Patty Cake," she said. "You all earned that back in the meat grinder. Now, let's get loaded."

Without the use of my right hand, it was difficult to don the mech suit and, in the end, I needed Tabby's help. While some of the bones had been set, I'd pulverized enough of the hand that it would require a full replacement. There'd been a time when the loss of my foot had been a major event in my life. Since then, I'd seen enough death, dismemberment and other horrible things that it didn't bother me that much. If we were successful at pushing back the Kroerak, it wouldn't be hard to get it repaired. If we weren't successful, it wouldn't matter.

We joined Sergeant Patty Cake, who carried the unconscious

Dr. Murray onto an elevator. We stopped at level basement-eight a full eighteen levels above where we'd spent the last three days. "Your jacket says you're experienced with halo drops. The VC maneuver we're about to execute is like that, but in reverse."

The room she led us into contained a single object - a twelve-meter-tall, four meter in diameter missile. Six man-shaped cutouts were visible around the exterior on two levels, making its purpose obvious.

"We're getting on that?" I asked.

"I prefer to be on top," she said, not batting an eye. "Our load master, Mr. Solomon, will make sure each of you are secure on the drop rails."

"I've heard of these," Marny said. "Cap, this is still pretty damn experimental."

"Maybe when you were in the service, squishy," Patty Cake replied. "I've been making orbital exfil for most of my career."

"What's VC?" I asked.

"Informal term," Cake replied. "Stands for Vomit Comet. Unless you're doped up like the mad scientist there, whatever you had for breakfast is going to adorn the interior of your suit. Small price to pay for the rush."

"Feet on the platform. Let the lift do the work for you," a Marine wearing fatigues directed, uninterested in our chat. The clunk of my suit locking into the shoulder-width drop rail was followed by a green indicator on my HUD. "Just like you were born to it." He patted my shoulder armor reassuringly and moved on to Marny.

"See you on the other side," Patty Cake said once we were all locked in. "Only a one in fifteen chance we'll get pasted by space debris or an enemy ship."

If I'd expected ceremony, I'd have been mistaken. A moment later someone hit the launch button and the interior of the chamber filled with fire and smoke. Before I could think to object, we'd shot from the base and accelerated madly into the sky, a giant trail of burning fuel following us. My eyes started to black out as the incessant thrust tried to liquefy my body and push the slushy bits into my boots. A moment later, I was hurled back to consciousness as we literally rocketed out of the upper atmosphere and into space. The smell of ejected breakfast greeted me.

"That's it, Hoffen. Better out than in," Cake said. A moment later, I heard retching noises from multiple sources. "Now, if you thought that was fun, you're going to love this next bit."

We'd left Earth's atmosphere behind and were no longer accelerating. I had no idea how fast we were moving – *understandable*, since I'd never been strapped to a rocket and flung into space before. I was about to check my displays when I caught sight of what looked like a large ship looming above us. That's the last thing I remembered before I blacked out.

"Captain Hoffen. Welcome back to *Bakunawa*." The smell of conditioned atmosphere and barf filled my nose as I awoke. I attempted to track the voice and assumed it was coming from the face of the sailor who had just removed a med scanner from my forehead. "Eggs and toast this morning?"

"Coffee," I croaked.

"There's definitely coffee in there," he agreed, with an annoying grin on his face.

"No, can I get something to drink?"

He smiled and held a tube up to my mouth. I sucked down water and tried to clear the rancid taste from my mouth. "Congratulations on your first orbital exfiltration. Puts you in elite company, Captain Hoffen. Only a very few ever get to experience the joys. When I release your suit from the bar, I need you to step off. Can you do that?"

I nodded. The drop rail released and I fell about five centimeters, catching myself before stumbling forward.

"I understand you have an injured hand," he said. "I'm going to help you out of your suit. Copy?"

"Copy," I agreed.

"Time for a shower," Patty Cake said. "Best not to keep the General waiting."

We followed her into an open shower bay where she peeled

364

her suit-liner off and stepped beneath the steaming water. Her lithe body was somewhere between Tabby and Marny in musculature and didn't fit any classical definition of beauty, given the scars over her body. That said, she was amazing and I realized I needed to focus on other things.

"Eyes forward, soldier," Tabby said, catching that I wasn't prepared for the sudden nudity.

"Help me with the liner," I said, turning away from Cake and Marny, who'd started peeling off her own clothing.

No more than five minutes later, we'd all showered and were back into suit liners and vac-suits. It felt good to be in a military grade suit instead of the crap we'd manufactured on Zuri.

"Best not to keep the General waiting," Sergeant Cake said again, leading us from the shower down a long hallway.

"Our heroes have arrived." General Brownie Walkden greeted us as we entered an observation room where she and Alderson stood.

"You're just in time," Alderson said. "We've been coordinating with the Abasi fleet on their arrival. I may have misjudged you, Hoffen. Your actions truly appear selfless and humanity owes you a debt of gratitude. Of course, there are those who would argue it was because of your actions we're in this mess to begin with. But I don't subscribe to that."

I felt relieved. For a moment, I thought Alderson had lost his mind and was saying something nice about me.

"Captain Hoffen, Sergeant Casien, Marny, and Tabitha," Walkden interrupted. "House Mshindi, Perasti and Gundi will arrive in force within the hour. We felt it appropriate you have a front row seat, but the Admiral and I have duties to attend to."

Without further discussion, the bombastic Mars Admiral and reserved North American General disappeared through a hatch that opened upon their approach into a noisy room, full of military personnel.

"Liam, Tabby, Marny." Ada burst into the observation room trailed by Roby, Semper, and Jonathan. She hugged us each in turn.

"Where's *Fleet Afoot*?" I asked, after we'd greeted each other.

"General Walkden seized it," Ada replied.

"I knew I shouldn't have told them about the Strix and *Intrepid*," I said, with an ironic grin.

"Cap, I think any competent leader would have done the same," Marny replied. "Even with the Abasi, we're going to need every ship we can get."

***

"Look. There." Ada pointed out the observation window. We'd been chatting nervously for what seemed like hours, but was closer to forty-five minutes.

"They're here." My HUD outlined *Thunder Awakes* and *Cold Mountain Stream* as they arrived together, positioned between humanity's beleaguered fleet and the boiling mass of Kroerak. For a few moments, everything seemed to stand still as more and more Abasi ships appeared, ending their journeys through fold space.

A vibration in the deck of *Bakunawa* shook us and a low hum started and quickly escalated into a loud whine.

"Sergeant, what's that?" I had to shout to be heard over the noise.

"That's our ace in the hole," Cake said.

The sound reached a crescendo and quiet was restored, if only momentarily, as the vibration started over.

"What is that?" I asked.

"Railgun. Only way to bust through that Kroerak armor," Cake answered.

"Did they miss?" I asked. "Nothing happened."

The combined Earth fleet moved to join with the Abasi.

"It's not going to be that kind of fight," Cake said. "War's over, except for the shouting."

"You're nuts," I said as a stream of blaster fire, missiles and all manner of hell erupted from every ship in visual range, Abasi, Kroerak and human alike.

"Aren't railguns slow?" Marny asked. "We're looking at a deficit of a hundred ships. We'll never last."

"You're asking the wrong question," Cake yelled above the climax of the second round.

"What are they firing?" I asked. "I can't even see the impact. Shouldn't a railgun rip apart anything it hits?"

"That's the theory," Cake said. "Doesn't work on Kroerak for some reason. But you're headed in the right direction."

We stopped talking for a moment as a third round cycled through.

"Wait, what happened to Murray and his payload from Earth?" I asked.

"Now you're on to something," she replied. "Doctor and his team built pyrophoric tipped rounds that'll bust through Kroerak armor and deliver a very specific payload."

"What kind of payload?"

"A payload of specialized nanites that spread and replicate a very special formula. As we speak, three," the railgun completed another cycle, "make that four of the largest ships in the Kroerak fleet have been infected with the poison brought back by your crew from the Dwingeloo galaxy. It is a matter of hours before those ships become completely inhospitable to Kroerak life."

"We don't have hours," Marny said.

"Between General Walkden and Admiral Alderson, we've held the Kroerak off for months," she said. "Have faith."

"We're not going to need it," Ada said. "The Kroerak are pulling out."

We all turned back to the fight that had escalated from nothing to the most intense firefight I'd ever seen. Ada was right. The Kroerak were indeed fleeing from the field of battle and headed out in every conceivable direction. The Abasi and Earth ships showed no mercy and tore into the fleeing enemies, as all the while *Bakunawa* continued launching its deadly rounds.

EPILOGUE

I slowed *Fleet Afoot's* approach to the planet Zuri. We were all looking forward to the end of a long journey.

Indeed, the final battle over Earth had ended almost before it began. The fleet's capacity to deliver a devastating biological weapon directly into each ship had shaken the Kroerak's resolve. Within a month, Sol and Tipperary had been declared completely free of the uninvited guests, except for stray warriors abandoned planet side.

It wasn't lost on me that we'd withheld from the remaining Kroerak the very same mercy they'd withheld from mankind and the Felio - all Kroerak were rounded up and dispatched with no compassion. I understood. It was a matter of survival. We'd won this fight and humanity would recover.

It wasn't as if people hadn't been grateful for our efforts. We'd shaken the hands of more world leaders than I could possibly remember. To say there had been parties doesn't even begin to describe the bliss of an entire world that had regained the freedom it had so arrogantly believed was impossible to lose.

It was strange how much everything had changed - and yet, hadn't changed at all. *Fleet Afoot* had been all but shredded in the fight. You'd think we wouldn't have had difficulty getting repaired, but that just wasn't the case. Every part of humanity was racing to rebuild and we weren't high on anyone's priority list. We ended up limping back to Ophir to take advantage of the portable repair stations we'd procured from Freedom Station in our last adventure. It was great to see Mom and the progress she'd made on Petersburg. Before the war had started, over two million settlers had arrived from Mars. The Ophir cities were thriving, including a thousand who now called Petersburg Station home.

I tried to convince Mom to come back with us to Zuri. That is, until she let slip the relationship she and Commander Greg Munay had - something they hadn't been overly successful in hiding. The commander was due back with a small patrol. It would be his job to work with the new provisional government on Ophir which was now an independent state of Mars Protectorate.

It had been upsetting to learn that Munay had seized *Hotspur* and turned her over to a valiant crew. She'd been in the wave of ships sent to Earth to defeat the Kroerak. In the end, it was a just and poetic end for the stately old ship. She had run missions up to the point of her discovery and destruction at the hands of humanity's greatest enemy.

The real shakeup for us had come when we'd run into Thomas Phillipe Anino - or at least the body his consciousness was now occupying. The decision had been made to destroy the Anino trans location technology. Instead, in exchange for other significant technologies, the Abasi were going to help humanity develop the same wormhole technology used by the Confederation of Planets. Apparently, the wormholes were there, we'd just been ignoring them. If anyone had asked me, I would have said straight up that such an agreement wouldn't work. Technological advancement was the proverbial cat that could never be put back into the bag. Sure, they could destroy what Anino had built, but the idea was out there. Someone would eventually come along and make the same discoveries.

"Captain, I'm picking up a ship in the field adjacent to your accommodations," Jonathan said. "There also appears to be a significant gathering of humans contained within the workshop."

"What kind of ship?" I asked.

"It is *Intrepid*, Captain."

"*Intrepid*?" Ada asked, her fingers immediately flying over a virtual keyboard as she zoomed in on the ship.

"Our arrival appears to have triggered a message from the Abasi High Command," Jonathan said. "Would you have us forward it to your queue?"

"To whom is it addressed?" I asked.

"Loose Nuts Corporation."

"Play it over the public address," I said.

"Greetings heroic crew, ambassadors of Earth and friend of the Abasi." The speaker was Mshindi First. "The Abasi Government has seized and is returning the ship Intrepid to the rightful owners, Loose Nuts. Unfortunately, it has sustained significant damage at the hands of Strix. We have been assured by our Earth counterparts that you have sufficient technology to effect repairs. Please accept this as a symbolic gesture of our friendship. Mshindi First desists."

"Not really one for long speeches," Tabby said. "I like her style."

"*Intrepid* is not responding to my request for access," Ada said. "What did you do to my ship, Liam?" Apparently, Ada wasn't buying Mshindi's explanation that the Strix had caused all the damage.

"Nothing our new industrial replicator can't fix," I said.

"We'll see about that," she growled as I landed *Fleet Afoot* on the road between the bungalows and the field where *Intrepid* sat.

I was fortunate that Nick stood outside his workshop and waved to us, distracting Ada from diving further into the conversation.

We all followed Marny off the ship and I smiled as she lifted my friend and partner from the ground and swallowed him in a bear hug.

"How was your trip?" Nick asked, once Marny released him.

"New hand." I wiggled my fingers.

"Ada?" He asked, pushing past me and grabbing Ada by the shoulders. She'd successfully received synth-skin replacement for the burns, but there were no medical facilities available to repair her eye and she now wore a triangular patch.

She smiled and embraced him warmly. "Long story and well worth it. I would have traded an eye for my family and Marny's to have a chance at survival. It was an honor to have played a small part in humanity's victory."

"We brought presents." I knew Marny had been communicating with Nick ever since we'd re-entered the Tamu system and he was already up on all that had transpired.

"I hope you brought back trade goods," he said, holding Marny's hand. "Goboble is pissed we dumped his load. He's demanding interest payments."

"Interest payments on what?" Ada asked as Filbert leapt into her arms, apparently pleased she had returned.

"He bought our bond for the cargo Liam dumped. We owe Goboble four hundred thousand," he replied. "He says he's going to take *Fleet Afoot* back if we don't come up with payment."

"You'd think saving the world would pay more," Tabby said.

"Think you can do something with an industrial replicator? I talked Anino out of one." I said.

Nick just gave me a knowing smile. Not much for words, that one.

"Just so you know, Earth's transitionary government decided to leave TransLoc operational for another month before it's shut down for good. If we plan to go home, we'll need to figure that out before then," I said. "So what's been going on around here?"

"Glad you asked," he said, leading us over to the workshop and opening the newly enlarged doors. Hog and Patty walked out with big smiles as a large group of York residents poured out from the packed space. A banner hung above the workshop declaring 'Welcome Home.'

I caught a streak as Roby bolted into his father's arms, dragging Semper along behind him.

"What are we going to do now?" Tabby asked, wrapping an arm around my waist and leaning her head on my shoulder.

Ada joined us, hugging us from behind. "Be a shame to leave an entire galaxy unexplored."

But of course, that's another story entirely.

ABOUT THE AUTHOR

Jamie McFarlane is happily married, the father of three and lives in Lincoln, Nebraska. He spends his days engaged in a hi-tech career and his nights and weekends writing works of fiction. He's also the author of:

Privateer Tales Series
1. Rookie Privateer
2. Fool Me Once
3. Parley
4. Big Pete
5. Smuggler's Dilemma
6. Cutpurse
7. Out of the Tank
8. Buccaneers
9. A Matter of Honor
10. Give No Quarter
11. Blockade Runner

Guardians of Gaeland
1. Lesser Prince

Witchy World
1. Wizard in a Witchy World
2. Wicked Folk

Word-of-mouth is crucial for any author to succeed. If you enjoyed this book, please consider leaving a review at Amazon, even if it's only a line or two; it would make all the difference and would be very much appreciated.

If you want to get an automatic email when Jamie's next book is available, sign up on his website at fickledragon.com. Your email address will never be shared and you can unsubscribe at any time.

CONTACT JAMIE

Blog and Website: fickledragon.com
Facebook: facebook.com/jamiemcfarlaneauthor
Twitter: twitter.com/mcfarlaneauthor

65223645R00213

Made in the USA
San Bernardino, CA
29 December 2017